M000048465

Eternally Artemisia

Some loves, like some women, are timeless.

By

Melissa Muldoon

Matta Press • San Francisco

MelissaMuldoon.com

*Cover Illustration, Cover Design,
Interior Design, Interior Illustrations,
Typography & Layout
by
Melissa Muldoon*

MATTA
PRESS

Matta Press
46509 Mission Blvd, #162
Fremont, California 94539

Copyright © 2019 by Melissa Muldoon

All rights reserved, including the right to reproduce this book
or portions thereof in any form.
For information, contact Matta Press
46509 Mission Blvd, #162, Fremont, California 94539
MelissaMuldoon.com

Cover Design by Melissa Muldoon
Interior Book Design by Melissa Muldoon

Manufactured in the United States of America

1st Edition
Muldoon, Melissa.
Eternally Artemisia

ISBN: 978-0-9976348-7-7

ISBN: 978-0-9976348-8-4 (E-Book)

To all who have the courage
to take control of their destinies—
you are worthy of anything you want to accomplish.
Remember, that is your superpower.

To Edith Pray
for her love and support, and for encouraging
her daughter to reach for the stars and touch the moon.

Biblical Days

Modern Times

A Seventeenth-Century Season

1930s Epoch

Eternally Yours

My illustrious lordship, I'll show you what a woman can do.
– Artemisia Gentileschi

Each time a woman stands up for herself,
without knowing it possibly, without claiming it,
she stands up for all women.
– Maya Angelou

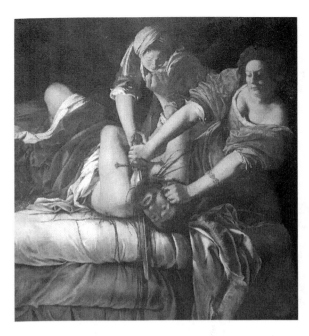

Judith Beheading Holofernes by Artemisia Gentileschi (circa 1620)

(photo credit: taken by the author while visiting the Uffizi Gallery in Florence)

Cast of Historical Players

Artemisia Gentileschi—Painter (1593 -1652)

Judith—Old Testament heroine, daughter of Merari, Simeonite, widow of Manasses

Holofernes—Old Testament Assyrian General

Orazio Gentileschi—Painter, father of Artemisia (1563 -1639)

Agostino Tassi—Painter, raped Artemisia in 1612 (1578 -1644)

Tuzia—Artemisia's Roman neighbor in 1609

Pierantonio Stiattesi—Painter, married Artemisia 1612

Palmira Gentileschi—Daughter of Artemisia 1618

Francesco Maria di Niccolò Maringhi—Artemisia's client and lover 1618

Michelangelo Buonarroti the Younger—Michelangelo's nephew, Artemisia's patron (1568 -1646)

Galileo Galilei—Scientist, friend to Artemisia, convicted of heresy by Pope 1615 (1564 -1642)

Cosimo II de' Medici Grand Duke of Tuscany—Patron of Galileo and Artemisia (1590 -1621)

Anna Banti (born Lucia Lopresti) published 1st fictionalized account of Artemisia's life (1947)

The first time I saw you,
I recognized your smile and I knew.
In your eyes, I saw the stars,
and in your laughter, I heard the rain.
Caressed by the sun, the journey began
to touch the Galilean moons.

Time is an illusion
but dreams are real.
In the dark and infinite skies,
never stop searching for me.

In every design, every word, every song,
you will find me at your side in another season.
It takes but a single thought to bridge the gap,
to melt the barriers that separate us.
Open your heart and let the river in,
and together we will be again.

We are traveling at the speed of light,
looking for the road signs to guide us home.
In the dark and infinite skies,
never stop searching for me.

Eternally yours, Artemisia

— M. Muldoon

Biblical Days

*Lord God, to whom all strength belongs, prosper
what my hands are now to do for the greater glory of
Jerusalem; for now is the time to recover your heritage and
to further my plans to crush the enemies arrayed against us.*

– Judith Chapter 13, The Bible

Chapter 1

Slaying the General

She was surprised how effortlessly the sword slid into his neck, slicing his vocal chords and just as astonished by the amount of brute force required to finish beheading him. Days before, the plan to kill the Assyrian general who was about to lay siege to her people seemed simple enough. Using her feminine wiles and beauty to ingratiate herself with the self-infatuated man had been child's play. That had been the painless part. Now, standing in a dark tent, outside of Bethulia surrounded by hundreds of sleeping soldiers, finishing the task of cutting off his head was proving more difficult than she imagined.

Judith peered over at Abra, her friend and confidant, who undeterred by his flailing limbs, was forcefully and determinedly pinning the drunken man's torso to the bed. The young widow hesitated ever so slightly, but when Abra glanced up, and she saw the same look of determination mirrored on the maid's face, despite her aching arms, ravaged body, and bruised thighs, she found the strength to continue.

Raising the blade high over her head, with the moral certitude of a warrior, Judith drove it back into the man's neck until his body went limp and she knew he was finally dead. As Holofernes shuddered and the life left his body, Judith observed in horrified fascination how his thickly muscled arms lay heavily upon the bed like the thick cuts of meat she had seen hanging in the butcher's shop.

She also noted how the general's head lolled back upon the soft cushion in a distorted way, still half attached to his body. With the attentiveness of the village's horse doctor, she watched as blood spurted from the punctured veins and how it ran in rivulets across his upper torso. In another life, if she had the finesse of an artist, she would have painted this macabre scene. The man's body, half cast in semi-gloom and his distorted face illuminated by candlelight, would have made a magnificent portrait to be captured for eternity; a masterpiece to commemorate this moment—a trophy, almost as precious as his sawed-off head.

"Judith, get on with it!"

Hearing Abra's urgent whisper, she let out a steady stream of air. The monster was finally defeated. The thug who raped her sisters and friends— who threatened to subjugate her entire tribe—was finally dead. Suddenly the thought made her giddy with relief. Her eyes darted back to Abra's face that was now entirely concealed by shadow. Her friend too had suffered terribly at the hands of these cruel and sinful men.

"Yes, you are right. There will be plenty of time in the coming days to mend our hearts, heal wounds, and relish this victory. We have killed the snake, but we need proof he is dead!" With a harsh laugh she added, "Once the Assyrian army sees what remains of their leader's brains on a stick, it will slither back where it came from. Only then will we be free of the tyrants who invaded our land and tried to enslave us."

Steadying the heavy blade over the man again, Judith sawed into the coarse tendons of his throat and worked relentlessly until she heard the soft neighing of a horse and the idle chatter of two men approaching. On the other side of the flimsy canvas, the women could hear their off-color jokes as they sniggered amongst themselves about the trollop that Holofernes was entertaining that night. They remained quiet, knowing for the moment they were safe. Unless the guards' suspicions were aroused, they would never dare to enter the general's tent while he was entertaining a female guest.

It was precisely this knowledge the widow had used to her advantage. Earlier that evening when she crossed the threshold of Holofernes' field command post, responding to his licentious invitation, Judith knew she was the one in control of the situation. It was she who plied the general with copious amounts of wine and sugared dates and beguiled him with stories designed to flatter his ego. When Holofernes patted the bed, nodding his head suggestively and letting her know he hoped to sully it with the sticky residue of their lovemaking, she was already one step ahead, intending to soil it with his viscid blood instead.

Distancing herself from the act, Judith had slowly undressed—sacrificing her body—letting him violate and brutalize her. Finally satiated and drunk on the obscene quantities of wine he had consumed, and with the aid of a sleeping potion she slipped into his drink, the general fell into a comatose stupor. Easing from the bed and dressing in the murky light, Judith had called softly to Abra who was patiently keeping watch outside.

Now, as the sweat dripped from her brow, the young widow listened tensely, waiting for the soldiers' voices to trail away into the inky black night. When silence descended on the camp again, Judith resumed carving through the thick sinewy muscles of his esophagus, undeterred by the river of red that splattered her arms and flowed onto the sheets.

Every so often the sword, catching a gleam of candlelight, flashed a silver shard across the canvas walls and over Judith's refined features. In the flickering gloom, as she worked, she scrutinized the silent scream frozen on his face, creating a grotesque death mask. Ready to be done with the grisly task, she bore down and, with one last decisive slice, Holofernes' massive head finally broke free of his torso and slipped from her grasp, falling to the ground with a pathetic thud.

Abra shuddered as if she could barely believe they had succeeded, then quickly sprang into action. Balancing a basket on her hip, she skirted the bed and reached down and collected the gruesome prize by the strands of the general's long black hair. As she worked, Judith rested her trembling arms, observing the dramatic shadow her maidservant cast on the wall of the tent. She inhaled deeply and her nostrils constricted at the smell of sweet wine mixed with the stench of fresh blood.

With one final act of defiance, she wiped the sword clean on the silken sheets of the bed. Then straightening her shoulders, she triumphantly proclaimed, "Abra, as long as I live, I will have control over my being!"

Modern Times

*I found I could say things with color and
shapes that I couldn't say any other way—
things I had no words for.*

– Georgia O'Keeffe

Chapter 2

A River of Time

*I*n a tiny apartment in an Upper Manhattan loft, the honking of impatient cab horns floated up to Maddie's third-floor window. She could hear the riot of rush-hour traffic despite the sluggish whirring of the spinning dryer. Her apartment was almost as chaotic as the pandemonium in the street below. Boxes and trash bags littered the floor and suitcases were strewn about, some fuller than others; two large ones held most of the contents of her closet—sweaters and work skirts—destined for Rome; another, still only half full, contained most of the summer clothes she would need right away. Into this bag, she placed her favorite T-shirts, leggings, and colorful skirts—all comfortable outfits—perfect for the relaxed atmosphere of the art retreat she would be conducting in Tuscany before her arrival in the Eternal City.

Standing in the midst of the confusion, Maddie assessed the room, thinking she really wouldn't miss the place all that much. Despite her best decorating efforts, the apartment was sterile, lacking charm and character. It had never really felt like home.

Maddie squinted at the clock hanging over the stove in her small galley kitchen, and seeing how late it was, she sighed tiredly. The movers were coming in the morning and she had hoped to be further along with her packing. Initially, it was easy work to dump the contents of the kitchen cabinets into boxes and fill others with memorabilia and pictures. But when Maddie pulled books off shelves, the task became overwhelming. It didn't help that she had a gnawing pit in her stomach.

"When was the last time I ate?" she wondered out loud as she walked to the nearly-empty refrigerator and took out a box of day-old pizza, sighing again at the unappealing sight. Deciding she needed further fortification and help washing it down, she poured herself a glass of wine left over from one of the many recent goodbye parties. Unstopping the cork with her thumb, she sloshed the bottle around a couple of times and said to no one in particular, "Might as well drink it now. Why waste a perfectly good bottle of Crociani wine?"

With a piece of cheese pizza in one hand, she sat cross-legged in the middle of the floor and dumped out a basket filled with old correspondence and museum postcards. All around her was the floating debris of her life; there were diaries, pencil drawings, old Christmas cards, and snapshots, as well as many paperback novels and dozens of art and psych textbooks—some she hadn't opened since her grad school days. Nudging a couple of them with her barefoot, to better read their titles, Maddie then kicked them aside and wondered what she was going to do with them all.

Knowing time was growing short, resolutely she popped the last bite of pizza into her mouth, wiped her hands on her jeans, and began making tough decisions. Some books she tossed into containers to hibernate in her sister's basement in Brooklyn and others into boxes to donate to the lender's library. Satisfied to see the pile diminishing, and congratulating herself on the progress she was making, she stood up to refill her wine glass. As she did, she nearly stumbled over one lone tome that remained on the floor.

Maddie looked down at her feet and saw it was one of her favorite art books. What to do with this one? she thought as she picked it up and tested its weight. With some reluctance, she decided it was much too bulky to take with her.

Her wine glass temporarily forgotten, she sank down on the floor, opened it, and read the inscription her father had penned on the interior page: To Maddalena, my dearest daughter—Always remember: Art is Eternal, but Life is Short.

Maddie remembered the book had been a housewarming present from her dad to celebrate her move to New York and starting her therapy practice years ago. Smiling at the memory, she flipped through the colorful plates that featured Bernini fountains, Baroque churches, and elaborate monumental religious paintings.

She hated to leave the book behind, but then again, she thought to herself, *Where you're going, you'll soon be admiring all these things in person. In fact, the first thing you should do is go see...*

Before she could finish the thought, as if the hand of the seventeenth-century artist directed her, Maddie turned to a page right in the middle of the book and found herself face to face with a very graphic painting of Judith beheading Holofernes. It was a horrific image, yet despite its brutality, it was exquisite in every detail and Maddie had always been strangely compelled by the subject matter.

It had intrigued her, even more, to discover it was a woman who had dared paint it. In a darkened lecture hall, after being introduced to the painting in college, upon learning the artist had been named after Artemis, the Greek goddess of the hunt and the protector of the moon, Maddie had whispered admiringly, "Pleased to make your acquaintance, Artemisia."

From that moment onward, Maddie developed an inexplicable female crush on Ms. Gentileschi, hailed by her hippy art professor as the first feminist. Like her instructor, she applauded Artemisia's recognition as one of the great painters of all time, eclipsing her contemporaries—male and female—mastering light and shadow and theatrical tension, rivaling Caravaggio.

But what Maddie felt for the artist went beyond pure academic interest. It was based on a more intimate and personal nature. And being someone who had a particular affinity for the moon, Maddie also believed it was a cosmic sign they both identified with a common astrological body.

Similar to the lunar orb and its changeable phases, Artemisia had also been a mercurial and complex being, not one thing but many. She had been fragile and strong; gentle and demanding. Illiterate and unable to compose a letter with a pen, she had been gifted with a visual imagination she illustrated with unparalleled dexterity using a brush. Artemisia painted heroines from the *Bible,* yet she used her own naked body as a model. She was toasted and praised by dukes and learned scientists; she was also tortured and abused by baser and ignoble men.

After Maddie learned that Artemisia had been raped by her painting instructor, her interest in the artist only increased. It seemed strange to say it out loud, but it was as if she and Artemisia shared a bond, having lived through similar experiences, and as a result, she could sense the artist's thoughts when she viewed Artemisia's pictures.

Like now, Maddie thought as she tilted the page of her book to deflect the shimmer of light from above as she considered the protagonists in Artemisia's painting—Judith and her maidservant Abra. She noted once again the steadfast determination etched on each of their faces as they worked together to subdue the thrashing man on the bed. She saw with new eyes the way the blood spurted from the general's neck, and vividly remembered the first time she witnessed the scene.

Intentions of packing dissolved, and instead of inhaling cheese pizza and wine made from Sangiovese grapes, Maddie caught the aroma of linseed oil and fresh paint and smiled. The old feeling was back, and once again she was gazing into a river of time that flowed right up to her doorstep. As it had happened to her many times in the past, hearing the voices of those who called out to her from beyond the fringe, she let herself be taken away by the current.

While the dryer continued its mesmerizing beat, time fused and became insignificant, equally the same for a flower to turn to the sun as it was for a man to fly to the moon. Maddie's current reality faded away, and she found herself in a room with rough plank floors and rustic shutters. Blowing in from the open window, she detected the fragrance of lush green vegetation and the aroma of fish-tainted river water, as well as the sounds of carts rumbling over a bridge, the chanting of washerwomen, and the call of boatmen.

Soon, church bells in the distance rang—*dong, dong, dong.* As the chimes faded, the door to the modestly decorated apartment opened, and a dark-haired woman dressed in a green gown cinched snuggly at the waist entered the room. Hidden in a far corner, behind a brocade curtain, Maddie followed the woman with her eyes as she took off her hat and hastened to pour herself water from a pitcher on the table. As the woman in emerald green wiped her lips with the back of her hand, she turned to a half-finished painting set on an easel by the window next to a table filled with paints.

Briskly, the woman walked across the room and stood before the canvas, regarding it keenly. As she did, she rolled her head slowly from side to side and stretched her hands in front of her, massaging them gently as if they ached. Then, scrutinizing her brushes, she picked one up and mixed pigments into ruby reds, deep maroons, and rich russets. Maddie watched, enthralled, unaware if fifteen minutes or an hour had passed as the artist applied colors to her canvas until it seemed to drip with blood.

Pleased with her progress, the artist cleaned her brush on a cloth and then, changing hues, defined the features of the women she was painting who, like performers on a stage, dominated the scene. Pushing back her thick mane, the artist -studied the line of her jaw or the shape of her brow quizzically, then turned back to her canvas making further refinements.

Maddie believed herself to be invisible, hidden in the shadows, until she peered into the mirror and caught the woman's eye. Like a startled doe, she hesitated and waited breathlessly for the woman to react. But, instead of showing signs of dismay or surprise to have found an intruder in her studio, the artist's eyes lit up, and a warm expression spread over her face. With her brush poised in mid-air, the artist greeted her like a friend.

"Ah, there you are, Maddalena! Come closer. I want you to see what I've been working on. I've been longing to share this with you."

Unable to contain herself any longer, Maddie approached the woman, ready to take an active role in a scene she had for years been wondering about and up until then had thought to be only a silent observer.

"So, what do you make of this, *mia cara*?"

Maddie contemplated the scene, noting first the face of the man and how his cruel features reminded her of things she'd rather forget. Averting her gaze from his, she let her eyes travel upwards to those of the females grappling with their aggressor and was reminded that heroes came in the most unlikely forms—even in the figures of two seemingly insignificant and vulnerable women.

Artemisia watched her closely and nodded her head in approval as if she could read her thoughts. "I see you are more interested in my women than the man on the bed. So, tell me, what do you think of my Judith?"

Maddie concentrated her attention on the woman holding the sword, then finally said, "I think your heroine is beautiful. She is strong and courageous—she looks just like you."

In astonishment, she turned to the artist. "It *is* you! You are Judith."

Artemisia appeared satisfied with her response. *"Brava!"* she said, then lightly tapped the canvas with her brush. "And what about the third person in this trio—my Abra. Who do you think she resembles?"

The light in the room had grown quite dark, and Maddie did her best to focus her attention on the maidservant.

When she didn't respond, the artist urged, "Do you not recognize yourself, Maddalena? It is you!"

"Me?"

Maddie peered back at the mirror, and this time, instead of seeing her own reflection, she saw the face of Abra.

"Don't you remember?" the woman said. "You were there with me that day. *You* were the one by my side, my friend and confidant, the one who gave me the courage to continue."

"In Bethulia? But, how is that possible? It was so many years ago. I wasn't even..."

Ignoring her, Artemisia said, "We have a connection, you and I. I've always felt it... certainly, you have too."

"A connection, yes, of course, but..."

"Trust the connection, Maddalena. You must believe. There is something bigger at work here, larger and grander than you can ever begin to imagine. The path of deep and profound love is a circuitous one. Sometimes we move forward, sometimes we move back, and other times we are on a parallel road. No matter what, you must always trust in the connection and never stop walking with me."

Artemisia stood up and kissed her on the cheek then took a step back. Maddie regarded curiously, wanting to know more. So many questions cluttered her mind and confusion clouded her eyes. She reached out her hand, but the woman continued moving away from her into a void of swirling memories and half-forgotten dreams.

The harder she tried to bring her back into focus, the farther away the woman drifted. As Maddie forced herself to make sense of the situation, her temples throbbed from an emphatic buzzing sound. She placed her hands over her ears to make it stop, but the sound only became more insistent. When it became too much, she reluctantly let go of the past and found herself once again in her Manhattan apartment.

Laying on the carpet, staring up at the ceiling, she identified the noise as the timer on her dryer. She had been on the brink of remembering a beautiful dream, and something as mundane as the mechanical clock on a household appliance had brought her back to her senses. Slowly she closed the book and stood up, and as she did, a postcard tucked deep inside fluttered to the ground.

Maddie bent down and picked it up, and when she turned it over she saw it was a lovely self-portrait of Artemisia, she had purchased in the museum shop of the National Gallery of London years ago. Studying the image, she thought there was something inspiring about the artist's expression—something rare and timeless.

Pensively, Maddie tapped the postcard against her cheek, once again feeling frustrated to have come so close and then drawn back again. When the annoying buzz of the dryer sounded once more, she was reminded again of the packing yet to be done. Gently she set the book aside to go into the box destined for her sister. The card, however, she chose to bring with her. It seemed appropriate Artemisia should travel to Italy with her. It never hurt to have a friend close by to keep her company.

Before tucking it into her purse for safekeeping, she looked at Artemisia and smiled, remembering how the artist had kissed her during her sleep. For a brief instant, the remnants of their encounter returned. But, like most dreams, the memory was fleeting, and the details quickly melted away.

Still, the pleasant possibility of having lived previous lives lingered. It would certainly explain many things and finally make sense of her world, as well as the unpredictable universe filled with things yet to be discovered. As she continued about her chores, folding and sorting clothes, Maddie wondered how many lives she might have already lived.

Wouldn't it be extraordinary, if indeed it were true? That through some cosmic twist of fate she was caught up in a never-ending story—where past lives converged and new ones started? The how and the why were not clear to her but, given time and many more lives, if she were patient, the mysteries of the universe would one day be revealed.

Chapter 3

That Peculiar Feeling

*M*addie rolled over in bed and, opening one eye, noted the watery light that crept into the room despite the closed shutters. Underneath the cotton sheet, she wore only a pair of underwear and a white t-shirt printed with the clever expression: I'LL BE THERE IN A PROSECCO. When she'd seen it in the Florence airport shopping galleria as she was passing through, she couldn't resist the impulse purchase.

She rubbed her face that felt gritty after suffering eight long hours in the stale, dry air of a United airplane. The flight had been bumpy, but still, she marveled at the miracles of modern transatlantic travel; despite a bit of turbulence, the cramped seat, and a lousy airline meal, she could be in New York one minute and standing in Tuscany the next. How had people put up with the slower-moving steamships which had taken days and days to make the transit from Pier 88 on the Hudson River to the Ponte dei Mille in the Port of Genoa?

Then again, perhaps there had been advantages to slow passage on an ocean liner. Sure, now she could zip like a rocket from one side of the globe to the other, but she had to admit, there was some appeal to slipping seamlessly into a new time zone while sipping cocktails and dancing the foxtrot under the stars as Ella Fitzgerald crooned a romantic song about love, loss, and longing.

Checking the bedside clock, Maddie saw it was very early in the morning. Inhaling the scent of wet grass, she could tell it rained sometime in the night. There was a clean aroma as if the countryside had been cleaned and the dust of previous generations had been tamped down. From across the field, she heard the trill of a lark announcing the start of a new day. It was hard to reconcile herself to this new reality because she knew in the States it was the middle of the night, and the streets were inky dark. She tried to calculate the time difference, but her brain stalled out, so instead, she picked up her phone and said, "Siri, tell me the time in New York."

Instantly, a friendly voice answered her prompt. "The time in New York City is 12:05 a.m."

A ghosting memory eclipsed her. She narrowed her eyes and tried to remember where she had heard those very words before. Odd how moments crept up on you like that, when the slant of light or the sound of a voice made you think you were re-experiencing something all over again. She forced herself to concentrate, but her thoughts were scattered by the sound of animated voices from the courtyard beneath her window.

"*Ma che stai dicendo?*" an indignant female voice said. "*Hai prosciutto sugli occhi!*"

"*Ascolta Rossella,*" a male voice responded. "*Conosco i miei polli!*"

Maddie smiled at the colorful expressions that involved ham covering one's eyes and knowing one's chickens. She could fully imagine the animated hand gestures that accompanied them.

Now fully awake, anxious to have her first glimpse of the countryside in the light of day, Maddie walked across the cool *terracotta* floor to the window. She unlatched a massive hook that stuck just a bit and released the wooden panels. With the shutters wide open, she turned her face toward the sky and basked in the warm morning rays.

Hearing the voices again, she looked down at the couple, and she saw it was Rossella and her husband Roberto, the villa's caretakers. Carrying out morning chores, on their way to the barn, they had stopped in the courtyard below her window to hammer out what seemed to be a life-or-death issue. From Maddie's bird's eye vantage point, she could see Roberto's wheelbarrow was filled with compost. Next to them, a giant golden Labrador, another of the villa's custodians who had greeted her the evening before, had plunked itself in the shadow of the building as it waited patiently for its owners to finish their heated debate.

When the trio heard the noise above them, they all glanced up. The Labrador, Maddie noted, seemed a little weathered and weary, but still quite noble. Seeing her, the dog let out an excited bark and cocked its head to one side, in that appealing way that melted human hearts.

Roberto, dressed in slim jeans, leaned over and scratched the Lab behind its ears, then called up to her, "*Buongiorno, signora! Come sta?*"

"*Bene grazie!*" she replied. The man like the dog displayed a bit of silver in his hair, yet it only added to his charm. Maddie was always trying to put her finger on what it was about Italian men, young or old, that set them apart from others. They possessed that quintessential quality—a fluid, confident stance—and only they could wear red or orange pants and get away with it.

Shading her eyes, Rossella asked, "*Ha dormito bene?*"

"*Sì*, I always sleep well in Italy. I really didn't mean to stay in bed for so long. Did I miss breakfast?"

"*Figurati!*" said Rossella. "*Non preoccuparti! La colazione è pronta,* and coffee is waiting for you on the little patio off the dining room."

"*Grazie.* I could use a cup."

Pointing to her shirt, Maddie added, "I'll be there in a prosecco!" Roberto laughed and Maddie was pleased he understood the joke in English. Rossella smiled too but didn't offer a comment, preoccupied with pulling a weed that was growing on the side of the path. Giving it a good, firm yank, she tossed it roots and all into the wheelbarrow.

Brushing off her hands, she looked up again and said, "Take your time. There's no rush. You can always find me in the kitchen."

Roberto grabbed the wooden handles of the cart and Maddie, seeing they were about to go, called out, "Wait, I forgot to ask you last night. Has anything arrived for me? I'm expecting a couple of deliveries."

"*Sì.* The big crates with the easels came last week," Roberto said. "I opened them and started to put them together."

"Nothing else has come?"

"Not yet," he said. Seeing the frustration clouding Maddie's face, he hastened to add, "But, they should be here soon. I just got a call from the

FedEx guy. He tried to deliver some packages yesterday, but he got lost. So, he gave up."

"*Cavolo!*" interjected Rossella. "It happens all the time. You think they'd know how to get here by now! Seems they always take a wrong turn somewhere between Montepulciano and Monteriggioni."

"Those boxes contain *all* my supplies!" Maddie said a little desperately. "It's important to have everything by tomorrow—I'll be in quite a bind without them. Last year, my stuff never did show up, and I had to buy new materials at the last minute. Eventually, everything I sent over in the first place got returned to New York six months later. It was such a pain."

"Don't worry, *signora*, I gave the man better directions. He said he'd send his brother out with them later today."

"What a relief to know they are at least here somewhere, even if they are taking a joy ride through the back roads of Tuscany."

"After he gets here, I'll help you unpack the boxes," said Roberto. "Then we can get everything set up in the *conservatorio* just the way you want it."

"It's a good place to paint," agreed Rossella. "In the afternoons there is good light and a nice breeze that blows through the room. For years it was used as a greenhouse, and my grandmother used to grow lemons there. During the war, it was also used to house orphans as well as a few refugee families who fled from Rome to find safety here in Tuscany."

"I saw the pictures Gaetano emailed and by your description, it sounds so lovely and peaceful. It will be a perfect haven for my group this week. And what about the easels? Are they set up and ready to go?"

Rossella gave her husband an aggrieved looked. "Most of them are *still* sitting in the crate in the shed. I asked Roberto days ago to assemble them, but you know how men are! I think everything around here would get done quicker if I did things myself!"

She narrowed her eyes at her husband, but unfazed, he just shrugged and uttered the typical single-syllable Italian non-committal-I-don't-know response, "*Boh!*"

When his wife launched into rapid Italian again, Roberto rolled his eyes heavenward and gave Maddie a long, suffering look. Not dignifying his Rossella's comments with a response, he said to Maddie, "Don't worry, I'll get to it later this morning, *non si preoccupa, signora.*"

Whistling to the dog, he said, "Okay. *Ce ne andiamo*—I'll let you know when the delivery man gets here."

As the two moved on, the Labrador reluctantly lumbered to its feet and padded after them. And even though the three rounded the corner, Maddie knew full well the couple had resumed their spat. She found the two quite *simpatici* and appreciated their warm reception. It only served to confirm her first impressions of the place she had the evening before, after arriving at the villa long after the sun had gone down.

Driving down the rutted gravel lane with only the moon to guide her, she had been a little awed by the giant cypress trees that looked like elongated hands reaching up to the sky in prayer. Now at mid-day, gazing out over the lawn and the massive urns of bright red geraniums placed strategically along the front path, Maddie's initial positive feelings were again confirmed.

She had been particularly delighted by Rossella, who had greeted her at the door, followed closely by the Golden Lab and a passel of Jack Russell Terrier puppies. In a flurry of yapping and barking on the part of the dogs, and excited exclamations and rapid Italian by Rossella, Maddie was given a tour of the large rustic farmhouse.

As the *padrona* of the house escorted her from room to room, the puppies accompanied them, tumbling and somersaulting over the slick-tiled floor and Maddie became privy to many things. She learned the big dog's name was Luna and all the complications Briciola, the younger dog, had endured during her recent labor. Rossella happily rambled on, giving her the scoop on local politics, even sharing with her the state of the tomatoes growing in the garden.

When they entered the kitchen, Maddie picked up one of the puppies and, cuddling it under her chin, admired the large open space with its hand-painted tiles and the gleaming copper pots that hung from the ceiling. Again, although she had seen the pictures of the kitchen her colleague had sent her, in person, it was even better than advertised.

Gaetano, having grown up in the area, knew Roberto and Rossella personally, and it had been his idea to select this villa as the venue for her women's retreat. Maddie made a mental note to call him to let him know she loved the place and to thank him for his help. She also wanted to give him the exact date she'd be arriving in Rome later that summer. She pinched herself again, realizing she was actually doing this—she was finally moving to Italy.

In the past, Maddie had made many excursions to Italy. It became a necessary tonic to soothe her aching spirit. While she had a successful New York practice and enjoyed her life in the city, it hadn't always been easy delving into the problems of others day in and day out. Often, her clients' pain became her own, and over the years, while some had progressed, there had been others who had not.

So, whenever she felt stressed and overwhelmed, and even thought about quitting, Maddie would pack her bags and traveled to Italy—a place that reminded her there was still something beautiful and worthwhile in the world. But those trips had been temporary fixes and only confirmed her urges and longings. It became a habitual pattern— going, but not staying. She never allowed herself to remain and put down roots, always making excuses, trapped by her self-imposed commitments and restrictions. The timing had never been quite right.

But when she met Gaetano at a psychiatric conference in Rome the previous March, he had been greatly interested in the art therapy programs she developed in Tuscany. Talking over spritzes, they discovered they were not only on the same professional page but in sync on a personal level as well. During the week, he introduced her to his associates, even his wife. With their encouragement after the conference ended, he suggested they join forces, inviting Maddie to work with him in his offices in Trastevere, near the banks of the Tiber River.

Her new partner could be quite persuasive and this proposition had been entirely appealing, both for her career and her private life. Her days were far too routine, and she needed a change. With no permanent ties to New York, the idea of making a home in Italy suddenly seemed plausible. And now, with someone offering her a well-paying job, the old excuse—that work restraints called her home—evaporated. It seemed Italy had finally grabbed her by the shoulders and shaken her, telling her this was where she needed to be.

And now here she was. Looking down at the lawn, seeing the terrier puppies trotting across the lawn following their mother, Maddie smiled and thought, Yes, this is the right thing to do.

Content, she rested her elbows on the rough stone ledge deciding her morning espresso could wait a few more minutes. She drank the view in instead, listening to the drone of honey bees in the garden below and tasted Tuscany on her tongue, detecting hints of lavender and sage. Italy was indeed a magical place. It had the power to nourish the spirit and heal even the most sorrowful hurt.

Perhaps it was the remnants of jet lag, but she was struck again by the sensation she had stood in a similar place before. And like the rolling fields of grain just beyond her window, she was experiencing the heights and depths of past lives. In an instant, she assimilated all the joys and sorrows as if they had left footprints on her soul. The fleeting impressions made her restless, and a bit sentimental.

Even as a child, she had felt these emotions, and early on had been intrigued by the possible implications. As she got older, these nostalgic shadows of things vaguely familiar only seemed to grow stronger.

"In the French language," her graduate school roommate Claire reminded her, "we have an expression for this. It is called *déjà vu.*"

Claire hadn't thought it odd at all. "Perhaps you've lived another life? What is the big deal?" she said, shrugging her shoulders.

And then, when Maddie had mentioned it to Gaetano, he said matter-of-factly, "*Boh! Ma sì certo.* What you are experiencing is what I call *l'arte di già visto*—the art of already being seen."

To both Claire and Gaetano, whether it was because they were romantics at heart or because they had been brought up in Europe where time and history blended so thoroughly together, this feeling was quite familiar and natural.

But Maddie, growing up in Chicago, never shared this kismet-wavelength with her siblings. She was the youngest and, given the disparity of ages, had always felt like the odd man out. Left to her own devices, she retreated into a fantasy world, caught in the pages of a book or in conversation with imaginary friends.

She often wondered why she felt so different from her siblings and why they didn't share her fascination for stories about phantom ships that would carry them to other worlds or tales about time travel. After a while, she came to think perhaps the stork had indeed dropped her on the wrong doorstep, and that she landed on her head, confusing her temporal clock.

Curious to know what made her this way, Maddie probed her parents about her background. Her mother, whose brisk temperament differed significantly from hers, gave her only a few perfunctory facts. Her father proved more helpful, coloring in the lines of their family tree, adding more branches and leaves. He told her colorful stories about a distant relative who had been a suffragette, a great-uncle who had been a mechanic for Charles Lindbergh, even an entertaining anecdote about an Italian countess who ran away with a French painter.

Tucking a silky lock behind her right ear, he said tenderly, "Most likely *that* is just a bunch of nonsense, passed down through the generations, but it would explain your dark hair, green eyes, and olive complexion, and account for your sentimental temperament."

Maddie mulled all this over but wasn't entirely satisfied with her mother's thrifty tidbits or the fanciful tales her father told her, believing—like him—dotty old relatives invented the stories. They hadn't explained why she often felt she was wearing her shoes on the wrong feet, stumbling through incorrect time zones, prone to fantasies about distant and unobtainable worlds. It was an odd way to go through life.

And then when she was about eight, the answer finally came to her. Of course! She was a time traveler! If Harry Potter could escape to

Hogwarts merely by running into a wall on Platform 9 ¾, she too could disappear into a world meant just for her, filled with fantastic friends who were anxiously waiting for her. As this idea took root, Maddie convinced herself she could hear the voices of the others who traveled with her in a parallel universe.

Desperate to break through and make a connection, her first plan involved stealing her father's prized possession—a telescope that had belonged to his grandfather, that he kept in a box in his study. Thinking her dad would never miss the old thing, she nabbed it when he wasn't looking. Then climbing to the top of her tree fort, she held the scope up to her eye and, like a pirate, scanned the skyline for stranded sailors. When she saw blurry images on the horizon, she waved excitedly and called out, "I'm over here! Wait for me!"

But it was useless. The little specks never responded or called back. Lowering the telescope, Maddie realized they were just the stupid old trees in her neighbor's apple orchard. Selecting a new direction, she tried again, but it was futile. As hard as she tried, Maddie could never dial in the right setting to bring her people into focus. In the end, the antique-spyglass was a very poor teletransporter.

Undaunted, like children often are, she turned to her next idea. After reading a story about a woman who parachuted out of an airplane, Maddie decided it would be a surefire way to time travel. So, on a windy day, she climbed to the top of Summit Peak, the steepest hill she could find. Opening a large umbrella, she flung herself into space, hoping to land in a new fantastic place. Instead, she plummeted to the ground and rolled into a patch of brambles. Disentangling herself from the stinging nettles and examining the umbrella that had turned itself inside out, she was mad that her brilliant scheme, once again, hadn't worked.

Of course, when she reached her adult years, Maddie liked to tell herself she had outgrown these childish notions and, entering graduate school, believed herself to be more world-wise and savvier. With a cooler head and more realistic expectations, she came down to Earth and made friends on this planet—even started dating. And when she and Claire became roommates, Maddie relished their strong bond, thinking she couldn't want for anything more.

In a sober state of mind, she might deny her time-traveling yearnings, but, then again, sometimes in the middle of the night, when she gazed up at the moon, her heart pined for something unseen and unknown. Listening carefully it almost seemed she could still discern the voice that called out to her just beyond the Milky Way, beckoning her to follow.

"Wouldn't it be an amazing thing, Claire," she once confided to her friend, feeling a little tipsy after having drunk a little too much wine, "to have an emotional bond with another human being so true that it survived many lives? And what if on this wonderful journey we never stopped learning from one another so that each meeting was even more passionate and intense than the last."

She sighed and added, "Maybe all I need is a stronger umbrella and a steeper mountain. Or perhaps a more powerful telescope."

And then one crazy night, about the time she enrolled in her first Baroque art history class, and had first been introduced to the artists Caravaggio, Bernini, Carracci, and Gentileschi, the strangest thing happened that reaffirmed her suspicions, making her believe all over again there were others out there who traveled through time with her.

She and Claire had gone to a carnival, and although they intended on getting tattoos at the last minute, they chickened out and opted instead to go to a séance reader. As they paid their fee and sat down in the dimly-lit room, they attempted to be good and smothered their giggles. But when a woman appeared, dressed in a garish costume wearing dime store beads and fake eyelashes, Claire looked at Maddie and rolled her eyes.

After lighting a candle and placing it in the middle of the table, the woman invited them to free their minds and leave their doubts behind. Then the mystic spoke to them in somber tones. "With the help of regression to past lives, we can recognize and find our soulmates. By reaching deep inside ourselves, we can know who they are. Whether in Heaven or on Earth, a special vibration or energy is perceived. A connection occurs, and our destiny becomes clear."

Maddie, thinking she had committed herself to a bit of trumped-up malarkey, tuned out, more interested in the bizarre tent filled with colorful scarves and tinkling wind chimes. To distract herself, she began to count backward, hoping it would all be over quickly. But, as the candle wavered back and forth and the mystic's voice droned on and on, a peculiar warmth enveloped her. From deep within, she felt a humming pulse that made her eyelids feel heavy, causing them to flutter shut. As they did, her mind unhinged and, free of temporal thoughts, it floated out and over a misty horizon.

Drifting into another land, the woman's words eased away and were replaced by another's. Although Maddie couldn't explicitly see a face, she knew she was finally encountering one of the companions she had been feeling beside here all these years. It was completely befuddling because the man—for he was a man, she realized after hearing his voice—spoke phrases to her in Italian and she responded in kind.

And that was the oddest thing of all because she knew no Italian whatsoever.

As the soothing, low voice continued to penetrate her mind, she was filled with heady excitement, and her lips turned upwards in contentment. At that moment she recognized him, and she believed him when he whispered into her ear, "When I saw you, I fell in love, and you smiled because you knew."

His warm words made her believe in the power of eternal and transcending connections, and every everything she ever thought or believed as a child was true—there really was someone out there, waiting on the other side, somewhere just beyond the fringe, who cared for her dearly.

That evening, Maddie left the gypsy queen's tent far more contrite than when she entered it, and shortly after the auspicious encounter, her full-on obsession with Italy began. As the months and years passed, she moved on with her life but never forgot the voice that spoke to her. And with each step forward and each plan she made, she surrendered just a little more to the gentle tug drawing her to Italy.

Now, once again in the warm Tuscan valley, she could feel it caressing her and whispering into her ear as it welcomed her home. Last night, as she lay in bed, she felt the familiar warmth and a force pulsating through her. Contented, she relaxed into the luxurious sensation of feeling loved and desired, despite the fact she slept alone. Into the darkness she smiled once again, knowing she was being drawn ever closer to something meaningful and profound—a discovery, a person perhaps. She wasn't quite sure.

It was a most peculiar feeling indeed.

Chapter 4

Vision Boards

Taking her time, as Rossella had encouraged her to do, Maddie brushed back her dark hair and dressed, then made her way down the stairs to the main room. As she trailed her hand along the smooth wooden banister to the large main room, she observed with pleasure the rustic beams, the stone fireplace, and the comfortable leather couches, as well as dozens of quaint little details she had missed the evening before.

Following the scent of strong coffee, she crossed into the dining room and out onto a small patio. There she saw a table for two, set with glistening silver and creamy white porcelain plates. Maddie looked around for the missing guest but, realizing she was the only one there, sat down and made herself comfortable. Flicking open her napkin, she smiled across at an imaginary partner and picked up a basket of mouthwatering pastries. After perusing the selection, she was just as glad she had them all to herself.

In a leisurely manner, she sipped her deep, dark espresso and ate a flaky brioche filled with cream, and another doused in powdered sugar. To walk off the calories from her first Italian breakfast in a long time, she strolled about the garden, gradually making her way to a picturesque stone terrace at the back of the house. Peering through a large pair of doors, she saw it was the lemon tree solarium. Intrigued, she turned the handle and found herself in an open, airy room. Rossella had been right; it was a perfect place to make art.

Hearing male voices, Maddie pivoted around to see a young man wheeling in a big stack of boxes and behind him Roberto lugging in the wooden crates filled with her easels. Pleased to see her things had finally arrived, she opened the oversized packages that held poster boards, canvases, several bags of clay, and more. As she worked, with the help of the delivery man, Roberto assembled the easels. Tipping him a little extra, he escorted the driver back to his van and went back to the garden, leaving Maddie to her own devices.

She checked over the charcoals and brushes and counted out tubes of paint, making sure there were enough for each art station. The rest of the supplies she stashed into an oversized armoire for safekeeping. Moving aside a few things to make room for hers, she discovered an old radio at the bottom of the cabinet. Italian music, especially schmaltzy love ballads, were a weakness of hers and eagerly she pulled it out, switched it on and spun through the stations. When she heard the refrain of a particular favorite, she began singing along to the refrain: *In every design, every word every song, you will find me at your side in another season. I will find you, then lose you, then we will meet again.*

As the song ended, she slid out a piece of poster board, arranged it on her easel and tuned out the sound of the rapid-fire announcer selling tires. But when she heard the voice of Paolo Fox—Italy's resident radio astrologer dishing out his daily dose of horoscopes, her ears perked up.

Prophecies based on the stars and the planets were never her thing, but still, when his melodic voice eulogized her sign, telling her Mars and Jupiter were soon to be aligned, which boded well for her love life, she couldn't help but pay attention. Peeking over at one of the terriers who had just trailed into the room, she said, *"Ciao cucciolo!* What do you think? Is romance in the air?"

When the puffball thumped his tail, she picked it up, and he licked her face. "For now, that will do. I'll settle for a bit of puppy love any day."

Maddie stroked his head as she took stock of the pile of the Italian magazines she had asked Rossella to collect for her. Inspired by the glossy covers, feeling the familiar urge to create, she set the dog down and reached for a pair of scissors and began cutting out images. After collecting an odd assortment, she set about arranging the photos into a colorful mosaic on a piece of poster board.

So absorbed in her work, she almost didn't notice when Rossella came into the room an hour later bearing a small tray with a cup and a *Bialetti* coffee pot. Close on her heels was the rest of the puppies. "*Ti va un espresso?* I thought you could use a break."

Seeing the stray little wanderer asleep next to Maddie, she laughed and said, "*Hai fatto amicizie!* I see you've made a new friend," said Rossella. Narrowing her eyes, she looked around and rapidly assessed the room. "*Managgia!* My husband didn't do what I asked. He never listens! Stubborn as an ox."

Before Maddie could say anything, Rossella, with the energy of someone who had just downed at least ten potent espressos, dragged the work stations and tables into a new arrangement. In a flurry of commotion, with dogs underfoot, Maddie followed her lead and helped the master and commander.

When the last easel was placed nearer the window, Rossella stepped back and declared, "Much better, no?"

Maddie agreed appreciatively. "*Sì! Direi di sì.*"

"*Beh*, as I said, *conosco i miei polli!* I always know where my chickens are and what I'm talking about." Looking over at what Maddie was working on, she said, "I was wondering why you asked me to gather up all those magazines. *Che strano!* I thought. I wasn't sure what you needed, exactly, but I got some friends to contribute, so I was able to collect quite a wide variety—*Donna Moderna, Panorama, Vogue Italia...* even some movie magazines. Roberto is a fan of old films."

"I know it's an unusual request, but these are perfect for what I have in mind. It's for one of the activities I'm planning for my group this week." Indicating a big box of postcards she had sent over from New York, she added, "I have these, but needed more images to add to my collection."

Rossella peered into the box then, reached in and withdraw a postcard of the Eiffel Tower. Running a finger over the glossy surface she said a bit wistfully, "I always wanted to go there."

"It is such a marvelous city," agreed Maddie. "My friend Claire sent me that. She was from France and my roommate at NYU. I visited her once in Paris during spring break, and together we visited the museums, and she showed me all the local hot spots."

"Your roommate was an exchange student from Paris?"

"Well, near to the city. She was actually from a smaller town closer to Chartres. Like me, she was an art student, but she painted ultra-modern scenes, while I was into making collages using paint, computer images, and found objects—and postcards and images like these. My pieces were hung from wires suspended from the ceiling, and you could walk in and amongst them. It was an 'art happening'. I wanted everyone to feel like they were interacting with the images personally. There was even mood lighting and music."

"It sounds quite impressive, I would have liked to have seen it," commented Rossella. "Why did you stop being an artist? Now you are a therapist—what do you Americans call it? *Una strizzacervelli?*"

"You mean shrink?" Maddie said, loving the Italian word that literally meant to squeeze the head. "I am. But, I've never stopped making art. Once an artist always an artist. In grad school, I decided to combine my passion for painting and collage-making with my interest in behavioral science. So, that's what I do now."

"Hmm, *interessante*," said Rossella. Indicating the collage Maddie was working on, she asked, "Can I take a closer look?"

"Of course," Maddie said, picking up her collage and placing it on an easel. "It's called a vision board."

"Vision board? *Che cosa? Per vedere il futuro?*"

"I guess you could say it helps you see into the future, but it also helps you to look back at where you've been—kind of like a glimpse into the past. But most importantly it gives you the motivation to obtain a goal you might have. It's very therapeutic."

"So, what do you do exactly?"

"It's a simple exercise, really. You just relax, and without thinking too hard, you sort through the magazines and postcards and find the images you are particularly drawn to—like the card you are holding in your hand of the Eiffel Tower."

"And then you put them all together like that?" she said.

"That's about it," agreed Maddie. "You'd be surprised. Often without realizing it, the images you select offer a snapshot of your personality. Sometimes it even uncovers a few secret desires previously unknown even to the person who created it."

Rossella referred back at the card she held and raised an eyebrow. "*Hai ragione.* I've never really had much chance to travel... I would have liked to have been an exchange student, too."

"It's never too late to make a change, I always say," said Maddie. "Look at me! I thought I wanted to be just an artist and now I'm also a therapist, moving from New York to Rome.

"You give me things to think about. Maybe, I take that husband of mine to Paris with me next fall."

Hearing a whimpering puppy, she said, "Okay, I better take this one outside." Scooting it in the direction of the door, she added, "I've got some shopping to do in town. Do you need anything from the market?"

"No, no. I believe I'm all set."

"Can I get you anything before I go? More coffee, some *biscotti*...?"

"I'm fine, really. The dogs will keep me company."

Rossella picked up the tray and returned to the kitchen. After she left, a calm settled back over the room, and it wasn't long before all the terriers were sacked out asleep on the warm floor. Turning her attention back to the easel, Maddie assessed her work with fresh eyes and was pleased by the bubbling cocktail of images that revealed her varied interests.

By the paradoxical mix of pictures, ranging from Salvador Dalí sketches, 1930s Hollywood movie stills, and Vera Wang dresses, one could readily discern her interests in art, movies, and fashion. But her Vision Board was also a kind of modern-day manifesto, celebrating the empowerment of women. For not only did Maddie include photos of melting clocks and high-heeled shoes with red soles, but there were also many inspirational faces ranging from Amelia Earhart to Ellen DeGeneres and Maya Angelou.

To Maddie, they embodied what every woman should strive for. Each of them used their wit to guide them, and they followed their inner compasses. It didn't matter what their age was, or their sexual orientation. To her, they demonstrated that intelligence was the new sexy, clearly discrediting the idea that pouty lips and perfect breasts were the things that made a woman attractive.

Seeing some open spots on her board, Maddie picked up a movie tabloid and flipped through the pages until she came to a vintage photo of Bogie and Bacall. *This will do nicely,* she thought. For not only did she believe in women role models she also believed in inspirational couples. And weren't these two classic actors the poster children for timeless true love, a reminder some men respected and admired strong-minded women?

Sometimes Maddie needed reminding of this, because, in her line of work, she often faced a grimmer reality, dealing with couples who weren't so glamorous or so progressive. Over the years, she had counseled many women who thought marriage was the ultimate goal and who looked for a man to solve all their problems, only to wake up one day disillusioned with their Prince Charming. She had also dealt with the repercussions of men who became angry, scared, and abusive if their wives dared to become autonomous.

How many times had Maddie reminded her clients they didn't need a man to fix, validate, or complete them? She continuously advocated that to be happy, a woman ultimately needed to make her own repairs as well as her own choices. No one could do it for her. And if a woman genuinely liked herself, she would never be lonely or bored.

As Maddie approached her fortieth year, she was well beyond fairy tales and white weddings. Still, she wasn't opposed to the idea of finding a suitable life partner. She knew a committed relationship required hard work and endless compromises. But that didn't mean she had to completely give up her self-sufficient lifestyle. As she told her friends, to their great amusement, she wasn't about to relinquish her dreams or enslave herself to someone else's—even if he was Manolo Blahnik holding a satin cushion upon which rested a sensational pair of glass pumps.

Despite being born with a fiercely independent streak, she also had a romantic heart, and when asked she readily accepted an invitation to dinner or the cinema. She liked a man who could make interesting conversation, but most importantly she loved a man with a great sense of humor. She thought if he could make her laugh, well that was the sexiest thing on Earth.

And if someone came along who made her heart beat faster and whispered Shakespeare's words into her ear, she definitely wouldn't kick him out of bed. It was precisely because of the "peculiar feeling" that she had never entirely shaken—she knew just the relationship she wanted and deserved. And in this life, or any other, she certainly wasn't about to settle for something mediocre.

Perhaps it had been too tall an order because, up to now, no man had captured Maddie's attention completely, and it hadn't been for lack of trying. In college, she dated, and after moving to New York, one love affair lasted a couple of years. But just at the point when there was talk of rings, commitment, and mortgages, she felt an inexplicable hand pulling her back from the edge. Perhaps she was overly critical, but in the final analysis, something hadn't felt right, and the relationship fizzled.

Picking up the movie magazine again, Maddie continued turning pages until she came to an article about Katharine Hepburn. Taking a moment, she admired the proud tilt of the young actress' chin, her steely eyes and prominent cheekbones as well as her firmly set lips. And when she opened that mouth, Maddie thought, Hepburn's authoritative, velvety voice ran circles around whoever stood in front of her.

Maddie paused a moment, remembering that voice.

Before tearing out the photo, she scanned the magazine article that referred to the starlet as a trailblazer, having shocked Tinsel Town by merely wearing a pair of pants. In an era before World War II, when women could be arrested if they wore them in public or detained for masquerading as a man—Hepburn paved the way for her fellow female thespians, daring them to pull on their trousers too, one leg at a time, and stake a claim in a man's domain. She was one of the first to battle her way to the top in Hollywood using her wit and gumption, proving people would pay to see intelligent beauties.

Still, it hadn't been easy. Hollywood during the '30s had been an appalling scene—where men used the casting couch to bend women to their will. As Maddie pinned Hepburn's photo to her board, she thought a little bitterly, despite advances that had been made and living in a more enlightened age, the problem remained. Women were still trudging up a very steep hill, locked in a seemingly endless fight to advance their careers and protect their bodies—not just their reproductive capabilities, but also from violent attacks of rape.

It hadn't solved the problem to outlaw the act, and no matter how much yoga a woman did, or how much weight she lifted at the gym, physically men would always have the advantage. And judging by the numerous accounts of abuse that filled news feeds, it was apparent that harassment of females was just as prevalent and unconscionable today as it had been back then.

How well she knew, for she too had been a victim of sexual assault. Maddie's incident occurred when she was in grad school and she still vividly recalled how she had been objectified and the terrible fear she felt when her "no" had not been heeded.

She had been alone, late at night in the teaching assistant's office, located in the basement of the psychology building. She always considered the subterranean room a safe harbor. It was a place where she could escape the pesky undergrads who hounded her with their numerous questions and hang out, instead, with her peers and professors.

Maddie liked it best, however, when everyone cleared out and she could claim the space all to herself. After locking the door and switching on the hot plate to heat some soup or coffee, she would tune into a jazz station and work into the wee hours of the night. Never in a million years had she even considered she might be attacked in her sanctuary, surrounded by stacks of psych books and piles of Art History notes.

Nevertheless, late one spring evening, her naivete was shattered.

Around midnight on a Thursday night, she answered a knock at the door. When she heard the familiar voice of one of her professors asking to be let in, she hadn't given it a second thought. She knew the man personally. In fact, she had been finishing a paper he assigned on cognitive processes—a subject on which he was an authority.

Thinking he was there to collect his grade book, she smiled and sat back down at the desk. At first, they exchanged a few polite comments, even shared a couple of jokes only participants in his class would understand. She felt a little honored he actually remembered who she was, and was taking the time to make small talk with her.

When he stuffed papers into his briefcase, preparing to leave, Maddie turned back to her note cards. But after a few minutes, aware he was still lingering on the other side of the room watching her, she felt the first flicker of doubt. Self-consciously she shifted in her chair, quickly adjusting her sweater, fastening up a button that had come undone.

The air in the room suddenly seemed hotter, and her throat felt unusually dry. Subconsciously, she licked her lips and, with a nervous cough, she reached for her bottle of water.

"I love it when you do that."

Maddie stopped with the metal canteen raised in mid-air, not sure she heard him correctly.

"Do you know how hard it is for me to have such a beautiful *and* intelligent woman in my class...?"

Again, his words surprised her, but because of the great respect she had for him, she chalked it up to clumsy social skills. She knew the man had a wife, and that there was no way this could go beyond anything but casual banter. So, ignoring his last remark, she hoped he'd pick up his things and go home.

And yet he remained.

After a moment, he moved casually across the room and leaned over her shoulder. "What are you working on?"

At close proximity, Maddie could smell his breath, his cloying aftershave, even the odor of his sweat-stained shirt. The warning bell clanged in her head, this time louder, and finally her flight instinct kicked in and she knew without a doubt it was time for her to leave.

But before she could move, he placed both hands on the desk, physically caging her from behind. "I see you're working on the paper I assigned the other day. Perhaps I can help. You know you can ask me anything—I'm always available for you."

Maddie panicked. Was it her imagination or was the situation spiraling out of control? Sickened by the smells and frightened by his words, she grabbed her notebook and reached for her purse, and hastily said, "Hey, I just remembered I'm meeting a friend over..."

She tried to stand up, but he put a hand on her shoulder, forcing her back down. "You seem tense, Maddie. There's no need to be. Here, let me take care of that."

As he spoke, he massaged her neck and shoulders. Then he leaned down and murmured, "You are such a bright, bright girl. You know that, right? Your questions in class keep me on my toes and arouse... Sometimes I can barely focus on my lectures when you're in the room, I fixate on those grey-green eyes and how you fill out your clothes—like the sweater you are wearing now, how it hugs your curves and shows..."

"Enough!" Maddie commanded, finally giving voice to her rage.

Deaf to her voice, driven by his growing lust, he lifted a hand and fondled her breasts. "I can't help myself. Come on, this could be fun."

"No!" Maddie shouted, slapping his hand away.

"That's not what you mean—you know you want it too," he urged, rubbing himself against her. "Forget about that paper, no need to finish it. Don't worry, I'll give you an A."

Maddie tried to stand up again, but this time he pushed her onto the flat surface, knocking over her stack of books. Roughly, he hiked up her skirt, ripped at her undergarments, and pressed into her. She was caught in a crushing vice from behind, and panic overwhelmed her. She struggled futilely, trying to break free of his grasp. But the more she fought back, the more he seemed to like it.

Acting on instinct, she shifted her hips to one side and swung her fist back, hitting him in the groin. He grunted and careened away, and when he did, she swiftly stepped away.

"You bitch!" he yelled as he reached forward and viciously grabbed her arm and dragged her back against him.

She screamed out in panic. Hearing the commotion, a night janitor opened the door and quickly assessed the situation. Shaking uncontrollably, Maddie watched incredulously as the custodian took out her attacker with two forceful blows to the head. At that moment, she realized the extent of her vulnerability and just how close she had come to being completely mauled and raped.

The situation left her feeling tainted and soiled—and utterly powerless. During the aftermath, reliving the scene over and over again in her mind, she even wondered if she had been the one to bring about the attack. Had she encouraged him with her jokes and the way she dressed?

But, mostly, she felt anger and wanted retribution.

She spoke out immediately to the dean and the local authorities. Shortly after her story went public, it became evident hers was not an isolated case. Soon, other women on the campus, secretaries and grad students, followed her lead and denounced the man, too. With so much damning evidence of his criminal behavior and prior sexual assaults, the professor's prosecution and punishment were swift; he was dismissed from the university, sentenced, and sent to prison.

To most of the faculty and staff, as well as the police commissioner and the DA, it seemed justice had been served and that things could go back to normal. However, the hurt the man left behind for her and others to cope with remained, and perhaps it would be with them forever.

To get her through the dark moments, Maddie threw herself into her art, expressing herself in bold, demonstrative strokes, first in a series of dark abstracts and then in a variety of self-portraits. In one representation, she depicted herself as a willow tree set against a dark purple sky, her head hung low with arms outstretched blowing in the wind as if desperately trying to embrace someone.

Each painting, like a barometer, reflected her mood that day. Over time, the act of simply picking up a brush and applying paint to canvas provided her with the necessary tools to sort through the turmoil in her mind and gave her new purpose. Gradually, Maddie overcame the depression that overwhelmed her and was able to return to the graduate school office and focus on her classes.

Yet, after what she had suffered, Maddie promised herself she would be more careful the next time someone knocked on her door and called out to her. She would be very, very sure of the voice on the other side before she ever unlocked it and let them in again.

Just as the pieces of her life were falling back into place, a woman who had testified along with her and the others approached her in tears. Months after the incident, she was still devastated by the assault, suffering from nightmares and shortness of breath. Art had given Maddie the means to work through the levels of her darkness, empowering her and drawing her back into the light. But others didn't have such outlets. They remained stagnant and bogged down by raw emotions that continued to haunt them.

"It was then I decided something more had to be done," Maddie had confided in Gaetano back in March as they strolled along the Tiber River in Rome. "The resources on campus for women who had suffered date rape and sexual abuse were paltry at best. There needed to be more communication and counseling for victims."

Stopping on the bridge near Castel Sant'Angelo, she looked at the statues of angels that graced the marble parapets, and said, "So, I began to reach out to the others who testified with me. At first, we were a small group of women, coming from varying walks of life, but we all experienced the same thing. It was quite powerful, really—the bonds we formed. Something profound occurred when we talked and just listened, knowing the others understood. After a while, the rage and the frustrated feelings diminished and were replaced by those of safety and peace."

"And that's when you decided to go into art therapy?" asked Gaetano.

"Yeah, pretty much. After grad school, I moved to New York. I joined a small practice and eventually took it over. That was eighteen—no, wait—twenty years ago," said Maddie, a little incredulously.

"I'm glad you decided to come to Rome and that we are joining forces," Gaetano said. *"Violenza sulle donne*—violence against women— is a growing problem in Italy and with your language skills and your field knowledge, you will be very instrumental here."

Maddie put her hand up to her eyes to block the sun and studied the statues of the guardians that hovered above her. She agreed with Gaetano and hoped to make a difference as she had done in New York. *Era ora*, she thought. It was time for a change, and the idea of carrying on her work in a foreign city had a certain appeal. Standing on the bridge looking over the Tiber River with Bernini's legion of angels, full of lightness and grace smiling down upon her—symbolizing the Passion of Christ—it seemed they too were calling her home to Italy.

Enjoying the warm cast of afternoon light that now drenched the villa's solarium, Maddie almost didn't hear the crunch of gravel indicating a van was approaching. But, the puppies did, and soon her serenity was disrupted as they barked in excitement.

Now alerted to the arrival of her group from Florence, Maddie walked to the window and saw the billows of dust stirred up by the vehicle flowing in big clouds over the cusp of the hill. Looking down at the dogs, she said, *"Stanno arrivando! Siete pronti?* Are you guys ready?"

Brushing off her hands, she looked back at her vision board, letting her eyes travel from woman to woman, admiring the impressive group of individuals she had selected. But still, someone was missing. Reaching for her purse which she had slung on the back of a chair, she withdrew the postcard of Artemisia she had tucked deep into an interior pocket before leaving New York.

She held the image of the artist with chestnut hair up to the light, admiring the face of her long-lost friend, then pinned the card to the center of her vision board. All the women, it seemed, were rotating around her heroine. The circle was growing ever bigger, reaching back in time then moving forward, each life touching the other and extending farther than ever before.

Before turning to go, Maddie whispered, "I'm pleased you are here with me, and we are joining forces too, Ms. Gentileschi. Together, you and I have important work to do."

Chapter 5

A Circle of Women

*W*hen the minibus pulled up in front of Villa Bresciani, Maddie was front and center to greet it. From the front door, she waved to the eight women who spanned the ages of thirty-eight to sixty. It was an eclectic group representing diverse backgrounds and professions, among which was a lawyer and a food blogger. Each had a unique story, but all shared a common bond; each had suffered a physical or mental assault by the worst kind of man—a small, self-important, pejorative abuser. Over the last couple of weeks, Maddie had gotten to know them through emails and video calls and recognized their faces.

As they made their way across the lawn, she cried out, "I'm so glad you made it! It's wonderful to have you all here with me at last." She hugged each one and then continued, "I know it was a long flight and a bumpy ride through the back roads of Tuscany to get here. But now you can relax! I want you all to take a deep breath and forget about things for a while. You are in good hands. Tonight is all about settling in and getting acclimated. Tomorrow, we will begin our first art project."

Hearing a vigorous thumping sound on the *terracotta* tiles behind her, she indicated the Golden Lab laying on the terrace. "I'm not going to forget you, girl," she said to the dog.

"I'd like you all to meet Luna—she's the villa's mascot. She keeps an eye on things around here." Pointing to the white terrier who sat a short distance away, she added, "And that is Briciola. That means a little piece of bread—kind of like Tidbit or Crumbles—and she is the star of the moment."

Looking around for Briciola's entourage, she added, "She is a new mamma and has a little posse of puppies around here somewhere."

The little white dog, seeing Roberto approaching holding a large basket of vegetables with several large zucchini balanced precariously on the top, let out a little yip of happiness and ran to meet him. Maddie smiled, beckoned him closer, and introduced him to the others. "This is one of the villa's caretakers, Roberto. You will meet his wife Rossella later, after she gets back from town."

"*Benvenute*," said Roberto, shaking each of their hands.

"As I'm sure you guessed, that means welcome," said Maddie.

"*Sì*. Sorry, I don't speak English well," he added with a self-deprecating shrug.

"Don't let him fool you," added Maddie. "His English is quite good. If you need anything, just ask one of us. By the way, *benvenuto*—it's a good word to know. It's the Wi-Fi password too."

"Important to know," said a tall woman dressed in tailored slacks and a blazer, already punching it into her phone. "How do you spell that?"

Maddie shook her head in mock disbelief. "I should have known you'd be the first to ask. After a few days, trust me, you won't even care! I bet you will even forget to recharge that thing!"

Kindly, Roberto helped the woman insert the correct code, then, seeing the taxi driver in the parking lot smoking a cigarette and scuffing the gravel impatiently, he said, "I'll take care of him and get your bags."

As he moved off across the lawn, Maddie turned back to the women. "Before we go inside, does anyone have any questions? Anything anyone wants to share or say?"

A woman in a pair of yoga pants and a tight-fitting fuchsia jacket held up her hand and wiggled her fingers comically. "I'd like to fess up…"

"Yes?" said Maddie, already knowing what she was about to say.

"Just a little color on me, y'all," she said with feigned seriousness. "I know this is an art retreat and all, but for the record I want you to know I'm an accountant from Dallas, not an artist. I'm a wizard at numbers but, I swear to god, I cannot draw a stick figure to save my life and I'm probably the only one in the world who has flunked kindergarten finger paintin.'"

"I know, I know," Maddie said, taking her hand. "It took more than a little persuading to get this one to decide to come. But, as I've told you all, this retreat is about letting go of things we think we can't do. For the next twelve days, let's forget about the outside world for a bit and not worry about emails, texting, and social media. And, while we are on the subject of letting go of things, don't worry about stepping on any scales. Instead, I want you to untether yourselves and eat all the pasta you like. Believe me, you aren't going to want to miss Rossella's *tagliatelle*, as well as trying the delicious red wines that this area is known for."

Pointing to her face, that was ivory soap clean with just a trace of mascara, she added, "And if you want to go without makeup, that's fine by me! As for the art projects, don't worry, I think you are going to enjoy them."

She caught a couple of the hesitant looks that passed between them, and quickly reassured them, "You've all come a great distance, literally and figuratively, to take part in this retreat. This week, we will get to know one another better and learn to draw strength from one another. This is not about miraculous cures, and I have no magic band-aid to fix all your problems. The point is not to turn you into a bunch of mini-Picassos— the goal is to get you to let go of the analytical side of your brain and let the other part come out and play."

Maddalena tapped her forehead and added, "You know, the side that is all about creativity and imagination? When you do, you are going to discover some interesting things about yourselves."

When Roberto approached them again with several bags under his arms, she said, "Okay, let's get you settled into your rooms."

Indicating the way with a tilt of his head, he encouraged the others to follow him. Maddie held the door for them, but instead of following them inside, remained on the front porch a few more moments, scanning the road. Even from outside the house, she could hear the excited cries of the women as they got a glimpse of their new home for the week, and she knew the exact moment the little Jack Russell terriers made their grand entrance.

As the exclamations and the voices trailed off and up the stairs,

Maddie's attention was caught by a car driving slowly down the lane. She held her breath a moment as the Fiat came to a stop halfway down the drive. With the motor still idling, Maddie waited to see what the driver would do. When the car inched forward again, she let out a relieved sigh. *Bene.* Camilla decided to come after all.

After the vehicle stopped, Maddie watched as a young woman in her late twenties stepped out and stood for a moment beside her car. She was but a slip of a girl and was dwarfed by the cypress trees. Dressed in white pants, a button-down shirt, and fashionable red shoes, she seemed like the quintessential Italian woman—cool, calm, and collected. But Maddie knew better.

The new arrival didn't seem to be in a hurry, as she shielded her eyes against the late afternoon sun and took in the details of the villa's facade. When she noticed Maddie standing on the front steps, she nodded her head and waved. She withdrew a bag from the passenger seat and walked with careful steps in her pumps across the pebbled drive to the house.

Finally, standing directly in front of Maddie, the girl reached out her arm and said, "*Salve, sono Camilla.* I live nearby in Montepulciano. I'm Gaetano's friend."

Maddie clasped the girl's hand firmly. "*Ciao!* I'm Maddie. Gaetano speaks very highly of you. It's great to meet you."

"That's nice to hear—did he tell you about...?" Camilla's voice trailed off, and she shifted nervously in her high heels.

"Yes, after you gave him your permission," Maddie said, wanting the girl to know there were no secrets between the three of them, nor any hidden agenda.

"*Ah. Sì. Va bene.*" The girl averted her eyes and turned to enjoy the view. After a moment, she asked, "So, how do you like our Tuscany?"

"It's beautiful," Maddie said enthusiastically.

"*Sì,* it *can* be quiet pretty in the summer. We get lots of tourists from all over. But... *Oh mamma mia! Che caldo!* It can also very hot—*è l'umidità! È terribile! Pazzesca! Credimi!*"

"Oh, I don't mind the humidity," said Maddie. "I lived on the East Coast, so I'm used to that. *Sono una donna di acciao*—a woman of steel.

I'll even take Tuscany in the middle of December!"

"*Davvero?* Really? But the winters here can be extremely cold and harsh. The last couple of years it's rained a lot—we even get snow and ice sometimes..." She caught Maddie's eye then laughed apologetically. "Sorry, I'm starting to sound like *la ragazza del meteo*—the weather girl!"

Maddie gave her a smile. "Yes, we're working hard here, talking about the meteorology here in Tuscany."

Camilla nodded self-consciously, thinking about the real reason she had come which had nothing in the slightest to do with tourism in Tuscany or its climate. Still, it seemed by acknowledging the banality of their conversation and pointing out the elephant on the terrace, had eased things a little, and her posture relaxed slightly.

"*Mi dispiace. Non volevo arrivare così in ritardo.*" Camilla said apologetically. "I really tried to get here earlier and...."

"There's no need to be sorry," Maddie assured her.

"*Sì...* I know, but it is so late. *Non volevo fare una brutta figura.* I never want to make a bad impression, and we've never met before..."

"We are all pretty casual here," Maddie reassured her, "and time really has no meaning for any of us this week. I was just telling the others, the next couple of days are all about letting go and being ourselves. So, no pretenses or excuses are necessary. And, in fact, you aren't late at all. The others just arrived from Florence."

"*Bene*," Camilla said. "You see, the day got away from me and coming from Montepulciano the traffic was..." She cleared her throat self-consciously, then confessed, "*Mi dispiace*, that's not true. You said no excuses or lies. *La verità è questa mattina, dopo essermi svegliata*—this morning I changed my mind."

Maddie, who already knew Camilla had been on the fence all week about coming, just nodded and let her continue.

"When Gaetano suggested this, at first it seemed like a good idea..."

"But..."

"*Come faccio sempre.* As I always do," she said, "I think too much and start worrying. It's silly, really. Anyway, I called Gaetano back to tell him I'd changed my mind *again*."

"I know," Maddie said. "Gaetano phoned me after he spoke with you. I told him it was your decision and only you could make it."

"That's what he said too." Shaking her head tiredly, she added, "*Uffa!* It seems these days I can't make any decision—even a simple one."

"You are here now, and I'm glad."

Camilla gave Maddie an uncertain look then, noticing the dog lying on the floor at their feet, Camilla asked, "Who's this?"

"That's Luna. She's a really big love."

When the Golden Lab gave her the kryptonite head tilt and regarded Camilla with baleful eyes, she knelt to stroke her soft fluffy coat. As she withdrew her hand, Luna nudged her with her nose, begging for more, and Camilla let herself be persuaded.

Continuing to pet the dog, she said over her shoulder, "Gaetano told me things about you too," she said with a hint of a smile.

"Such as?" asked Maddie, pretending to be worried.

"*Oh, non preoccuparti!* He told me many good things," she responded. "He said you are a therapist from New York, that you are a very sympathetic person *and* a talented artist."

"He said I was talented? That's so lovely of him."

"What kind of things do you do?"

"These days, I paint mostly in acrylics—and put together small multi-media pieces—in addition to the pieces I organize for my groups."

"And now you and he will be working together?"

"Yes, it seems I was destined to meet him last spring. He and his wife made a compelling case for me to leave my own practice in New York and join him in Rome. As you know, he can be pretty persuasive."

She nodded. "*Sì, so benissimo!* He got me to come here, didn't he?"

"Yes, but I can top that! He got me to move from one continent to another! From what I gather, the work we do is needed everywhere. In New York, I also ran a hotline and a battered women's facility. It seems rape and abuse is..."

She stopped when she saw a shadow pass over Camilla's face. Changing gears, she added, "Right now, I'm in the middle of my great-big-fat-life-changing move."

"I can imagine the difficulties."

"There have been plenty of ups and downs—I can't even begin to tell you—but I won't bore you with the details! Gaetano has been a big help in so many ways."

"He's a really nice man. I've known him since I was a very young child. You can trust him." After a pause, she added, "When will you go to Rome? After this *seminario*?"

"I can't move into my place in Trastevere until the end of August, so after this, I'm staying around here for the rest of the summer."

"Perhaps I can help, that is, if you need a place to stay around here. I know several places in Montepulciano..."

Hearing animated voices from overhead, Camilla stopped and her eyes traveled up to a second-floor window. Maddie followed her gaze and saw two women had flung open their shutters and, enraptured by the view, were singing its praises.

"Thanks for the offer! I might take you up on it." Then indicating her bag, Maddie asked, "So, what do you think? Are you ready to come inside? I'd be happy to show you to your room."

Camilla looked over at her car, then checked her watch. *"Senti..."*

"What is it? Do you have more bags in the car? I can get Roberto to bring them up later."

"No, it's not that. I..."

Seeing Camilla's attention caught once again by the women in the window, Maddie waited and held her breath.

"Lo so che sono appena arrivata," Camilla said, blushing slightly. "But I don't think I can stay. *Ho fatto uno sbaglio terribile..."*

"You've made a mistake? How so?"

"Mi dispiace davvero... I'm really sorry." She glanced back up at the women above her. *"Sinceramente... Non ci riesco.* I can't. I just can't spend a week with *sconosciuti*—you know—talking with strangers about..."

She released her clenched hands and pressed them against her thighs. "I'm not ready yet. I barely allow myself to think about what happened, so how will I ever begin to talk about it with them? I hardly know what I'm feeling or doing anymore, and I really don't want to share such a terrible thing with... *Sì*, it's better I just go."

"Okay," said Maddie, understanding. "I get that, and I'll call Gaetano and let him know. But you know what you are going through right now—it's normal, *you* are normal. And for the record, most of us don't know what we are doing or feeling half the time. When things get like that, you just have to slow down, inhale and exhale, and take things one moment at a time. When you focus on a simple task, it gets easier."

Seeing the girl weighing her words, Maddie cautiously continued, "Gaetano told me you are an oil painter."

"That's right, I am—or I was at one time. I was studying at the *Academia* in Florence, but I dropped out after..." She tucked a strand of long hair behind her ear and added, "I just lost interest in painting and just about everything. I'm not sure what I want to do anymore. Sometimes I just want to disappear." She bit her bottom lip as if sensing she'd revealed too much.

"Hey, it's okay to take a break now and then," said Maddie.

Camilla looked back at her and shook her head tiredly. "But it seems that's *all* I've been doing lately. I've stopped doing things that used to make me happy. Instead, I go about with a brave face because I don't want to let people down, *mamma, babbo*, my friends... I keep busy doing stupid, mindless things... trying to forget. Sometimes it works. There are moments when I do feel like me again—it's been a year, after all. I go about my day and then..."

"And then?" encouraged Maddie.

"*E poi...* Then it hits me all over again. Sometimes, when I'm all by myself with nothing to distract me, I get this unsettling sensation. Like..."

Maddie waited, giving her a chance to collect her thoughts.

Slowly Camilla said, "I get apprehensive, you know? *Una sensazione terribile—orrende.* It's a horrible out-of-control feeling." In a barely audible voice, she said, "*Oh, mio Dio...* It scares the hell out of me."

Holding her gaze Maddie said, "I get that feeling too sometimes. You aren't alone." Her words hung in the air between them as Camilla digested their meaning.

After a moment, Maddie added, "I know it's hard. But I'd like you

54

to stay. You can leave whenever you want, but give it a chance. We are a small group, and like you, the others are dealing with things too, trying to untangle anxieties and put things into perspective. This week is about listening to one another. It's about taking a break to rewire our brains. It's about creating positive..."

When Camilla raised an eyebrow, Maddie laughed. "Okay, okay. But the point is to let go, get messy, mix colors, and enjoy the feeling of cool clay in your hands. When you get back to it again, you'll start to remember."

Maddie watched Camilla carefully, and it seemed the artist inside of the woman was indeed remembering. For the second time since her arrival, Camilla's rigid stance softened. To the untrained eye, it was barely perceptible, but Maddie saw it and was encouraged.

As the Tuscan sun shone down upon them, bathing the veranda and warming the stones under their feet, the two women studied one another. And then, there it was—a connection. In that instant, it felt as if they had traveled together down this road before.

Suddenly, no more words were necessary.

Above their heads, despite the daylight, the moon was visible. This time, when the stillness descended upon them, the mantle was easy and light without fear or judgment. Slowly, they smiled at one another.

"Funny," Camilla said finally, turning to admire the well-kept grounds. "It's very pretty here. Very tranquil and quiet. I've never been to Villa Bresciani even though I live just a few miles away."

"How's that funny?" asked Maddie.

"I guess because a person who has traveled from so far away—from New York—is showing me something new that's always been a few miles down the road. Perhaps Gaetano was right after all."

"I'm glad you decided to stay," said Maddie giving her a light embrace. "Welcome to my circle of women."

Chapter 6

Artemisia's Superpower

Maddie picked up Camilla's bag and showed her the way to the upper floor. After helping her settle into her room, giving her a few pointers about the villa's temperamental plumbing, she left the newest arrival alone to unpack. Before going, she added, "Kick off those shoes and put on something comfortable. We'll meet on the patio in about an hour for an *aperitivo,* and you can meet the others."

Satisfied all the women were now present and accounted for, she descended the stairs, filled with a sense of anticipation, ready to begin the retreat. Walking through the dining room, she noticed the table was set for their first meal together. Once again, *la padrona della casa* had done an impeccable job. With some time on her hands, wanting to be of assistance, Maddie followed the tantalizing aroma of roast chicken to the kitchen.

Standing on the threshold, she was about to open her mouth to call out to Rossella, but stopped, intrigued by the sight in front of her. At the far side of the room, she saw the big farm table covered with the last of the artichokes. By the looks of things, Rossella had successfully enlisted the help of her husband. Roberto stood next to her wearing a sturdy leather apron, cutting away the green spiny husks to reach the soft center of the choke.

Undetected, Maddie listened for a moment as the two grumbled good-naturedly about a neighbor who had the nerve to construct a shed partially on their property. They carried on, their voices animatedly rising and falling, but, when a sharp thorn pricked his wife's finger, Roberto put his knife down. Gently, he examined the injury and kissed it. Rossella simply scolded him, telling him she was fine, but Maddie could tell, despite her protests, she thoroughly enjoyed his attention.

Seeing things were well in hand with the dinner preparations, Maddie continued on to the art room. Beyond the large window, she noted the misty purple dusk was creeping over the fields, making the trees that sheltered the villa cast long shadows over the lawn. Moving through the easels Rossella had arranged earlier, she remembered the morning spat between the married couple, which, judging by their demeanor in the kitchen, was now temporarily forgotten.

Reaching her table, she saw the mess she hadn't cleaned up. Grabbing a wastebasket, with her bare hands she swept away a pile of scraps then replaced a cap on a glue stick that had rolled under a pile of magazines. As she picked up the remaining postcards scattered about the table, her eye caught sight of her vision board and the self-portrait of Artemisia pinned in the center.

In this painting, the artist depicted herself in the robes of Catherine of Alexandria—the saint who had been martyred on a wooden wheel studded with metal spikes. Artemisia gazed out at the viewer, as if to challenge him. In one hand, she held a palm frond between her thumb and index finger while her other hand rested prominently in the foreground on a shattered and broken wheel embedded with vicious barbs.

Despite the solemnity of the portrait, and scarcity of further ornamentation, a threat of violence permeated the picture.

Perhaps it was a trick of the light, but just for a moment, it seemed the palm frond Artemisia held in her hand trembled ever so slightly. Maddie stopped what she was doing, noting the woman's strong and muscular arms, as well as her flawless skin and dark hair that was caught up in a scarf adorned with a crown. As she stood transfixed, staring at the image, admiring the artist's russet gown that dipped modestly in the front displaying a hint of ample bosom, it seemed she could almost hear the sighing sound of silk as Artemisia inhaled and exhaled.

Drawn in by the magnetic pull of Artemisia's expressive eyes, absentmindedly Maddie placed the wooden box of postcards on top of a loosely stacked pile of magazines and took a step closer to her vision board.

The portrait, Maddie recalled, had been painted when the artist lived in Florence. With limited income and few resources to acquire models, Artemisia often used her own image. Such portraits also served another purpose; being a newcomer to the city, she may very well have used it as a calling card and a calculated means of self-promotion to encourage new business.

But the way Artemisia chose to represent herself was another thing entirely. The significance of the spiked wheel, the palm frond, and the saintly virginal appearance wasn't lost on Maddie, nor the fact she represented herself as a martyr.

From a very early age, painting had been Artemisia's greatest passion. It served her in her darkest moments to assuage her grief; she turned to it when her mother died when she was only twelve and later when she suffered from traumatic life-altering events. It was also the means she used to communicate a provocative personal message—most vividly seen in her interpretation of Judith brutally slaying Holofernes. In a similar, but more subtle way, the self-portrait of Artemisia dressed in the guise of Saint Catherine made just as strong a punitive statement.

At seventeen, still almost a child, after being molested by her painting instructor, Agostino Tassi, her father urged Artemisia to take her rapist to court. But she sued him—not just for the sin of raping her—but also because he ruined her reputation and then reneged on his marriage proposal. That, and the fact he had stolen a painting from her.

As humiliating as it was for Artemisia to go along with her father's charges, and admit publicly to having been molested, during the trial she suffered even greater indignities. To prove she had been compromised and her maidenhead was no longer intact, they laid her on a table in front of the judge to be examined and probed by the cold, indifferent fingers of midwives. If that weren't bad enough, in the end, they tortured her to find out if she was fabricating her story and that it was indeed Tassi who defiled her.

The men in court tried to break her, but she hadn't been defeated. Like so many female martyrs before her, she stood her ground and persevered, holding steadfastly to the truth.

Maddie, after suffering her own abuse in college, found in Artemisia a torch-bearing-me-too role model. Like the seventeenth-century woman, Maddie turned to art as a means to exorcise her demons. And, despite great emotional pain, she too found the courage to stand up to her abuser. For days she sat in a courtroom suffering untold humiliation and...

"Maddalena," a woman's voice whispered, interrupting her thoughts. She spun around, but no one was there.

"Maddalena, over here..." the voice softly commanded.

Maddie looked back at her vision board but found herself once again in an artist's studio. As before, the artist was standing in front of her easel with a brush in her hand. Against the wall rested a spiked wheel, and on the table lay the palm frond.

"Maddalena! It is I, Artemisia. I can't even begin to tell you how I've missed you." Indicating Maddie's collage, she said, "It pleases me very much to be included in this circle of women of yours."

Maddie ran her hand through her hair and said in a bemused voice, "Maddalena? No one calls me that anymore."

"But, to me, you will always be Maddalena. That was the name you used the day we first met."

"The day we first...? What do you mean? It's so hard to grasp how someone can be in one place in one moment and somewhere else another."

"Maddalena, I told you earlier you ponder things too much. Here, let me try to explain." Waving her brush in the air, she said, "In this universe—this vast, immense, unpredictable, expanding space—time has no meaning. Lives exist in parallel moments. The past is still happening and the future is already written."

"How is that possible...?"

With an exasperated sigh, Artemisia said, "Have you not yet understood? *Mamma mia!* Even my six-year-old daughter is capable of grasping this. Children are much more open-minded and ready to believe."

She set her palette down, picked up a rag, and began cleaning her brush. "You think you stand on solid ground, that the Earth moves in a constant direction, causing time to hurtle forward as it circles the sun?"

She appeared greatly amused. "Maddalena, my dear friend, in this place, time is an illusion, but dreams are real. It takes but a single thought to bridge the gap, to melt the barriers that separate us."

"And you and I?" Maddie asked. "We share a special bond..."

Artemisia interrupted her, "*Siamo uno, parte dello stesso universo.* We are all one, part of the same universe. Every one of us shares a bond and are connected in some way—there is a thread, like a gossamer strand, that wraps and entwines us all. Some ties break easily, and drift away, but others are much stronger. Those bonds are forged between people who have experienced things so intense and profound their connections are eternal."

The artist's words sounded vaguely familiar and were starting to make sense. Feeling she was on the brink of a profound discovery, Maddie urged, "Go on."

Seeing the light of recognition in her eyes, Artemisia smiled and continued. "Some unions are romantic loves and then there is another special kind of love. It is a love like ours. The enduring bond that only women can share. It is especially strong amongst those of us who have suffered greatly yet have learned how to go on despite it."

She pointed with her brush. "Just look at my painting and perhaps you will understand."

Maddie took a step closer to the easel and, as if it were a movie screen, the figures came to life. She watched a man kiss a young girl, forcing her back against the wall. Roughly, he hiked up her skirts and ground into her, despite the girl's desperate pleas for him to stop.

"That's you," murmured Maddie.

"Yes, and the man is Agostino Tassi, my painting instructor. He was the worst kind of man. A rapist, an assassin, a liar, a thief."

"But you accused him publicly. You stood up for yourself. I've seen your court testimony, and I've read the words you said in court."

The woman laughed bitterly. "Oh, yes, I took the wretched man to the tribunal and the clerks wrote down every blessed word I said. They even recorded my screams. In the end, after much deliberation, they decided Agostino was a lying bastard guilty of all the charges. But, although he was convicted, my rapist never served his sentence."

"Why wasn't he...?"

"Punished and left to rot in Castel Sant'Angelo to pay for his crime? Because Agostino struck a deal with the Pope, that's why! He was his protégé, after all. Agostino was a gifted painter who astonished all of Rome with his talent. In the beginning, even Father regarded him highly. He liked and respected him almost better than he did Caravaggio."

Shrugging her shoulders, she added, "I, too, admit to having been dazzled by Agostino. But, as it turned out, Tassi had an ego the size of the Vatican. He told his lies, spun his little intrigues, took advantage of women wherever he could."

She paused and studied her painting. "I felt defiled the first time he fumbled around with my bodice, inserting his hands and stroking my breasts with his rough fingers. His actions outraged me, and I was beside myself with fury. But..."

Maddie waited. The scene seemed all too familiar.

In a deeply saddened voice, Artemisia continued, "In the end I let him continue helping himself to my body."

"But why?"

"He promised to marry me."

"Marry you? He *raped* you!"

"I know it is hard to understand, but Agostino took from me the only thing a husband rightfully should have. I was damaged goods, and no respectable man would ever consider me a suitable bride, nor a proper wife to raise his children."

"But surely the law was on your side. You could have immediately accused him and—"

"Maddalena! What would be the point? Women are invisible, and men have the upper hand. To even think of taking a rapist to court is absurd. Once soiled, women, not men, are the outcasts to be banished, locked away in nunneries or scuttled into unfavorable marriages to anyone willing to be paid to take them off their family's hands."

Maddie shook her head, trying to accept this explanation.

"You have to understand things were different back then," said Artemisia. "Of course, I was outraged by what Agostino did to me. In one selfish, lustful act, he ruined my chances of ever marrying well or of having a career. Don't you see? All I ever wanted to do was paint. But, along with my virginity, Agostino robbed that from me too. You can't imagine how furious I was with him. I even tried to kill him!"

She smirked in disgust. "Oh, what honeyed words he used, telling me he would make things right. He promised to marry me and that he would give me a ring to prove his intentions. I had no choice but to believe him. If I didn't hold on to that, I knew I'd be sent away to live the rest of my days with the nuns of Sant'Ambrogio. The thought of never holding a brush again was too miserable to contemplate."

Artemisia hugged herself tightly. "Agostino said since we were intimate, practically man and wife already, that I had to submit to him whenever he desired. If I didn't, he threatened to break off the engagement. To protect myself and my future, I let him creep into my bed when my father wasn't home."

"He blackmailed you!"

She added defiantly, "Yes, I know. But I had no other choice. I made my bed with the devil to keep on painting. But, every time Agostino took me, I hoped he might be beginning to have genuine affection for me. And when he left my side, I begged him for the ring he promised and to meet me in the parish church so we could be united in the eyes of God."

Artemisia laughed bitterly, "But he always had some excuse, and I never did see a betrothal band. After a few months, I began to worry he wasn't being truthful. And then things came to a head when my father found us together. We had such a terrible row. But when I explained we had intentions of marrying—father was greatly relieved. Tassi was an important artist after all. But everything fell apart when Agostino..."

"What did Tassi do?" Maddie asked.

"He just pulled on his britches and grabbed his coat to leave. He said to my father he had never asked for my hand in marriage. He called me a lying slut and that I was the one seducing him. Tassi said *he* was the innocent party and that my father should have done a better job of raising me. And then he just left, banging the door behind him."

"And that was when your father decided to take him to court?"

"Not at first... not right away. After Tassi left, my father wanted to beat me. He said Tassi was right, I was no good. He berated me for letting the man slip away. Stomping about and shouting, he said I deserved to be sent to a convent, away from him for the rest of my miserable life."

"Wasn't he angered Agostino deceived and abused you?"

"He wasn't upset that his daughter's virtue had been stolen, but rather he, Orazio Gentileschi, a talented painter whose fortunes were declining, had been robbed of his daughter's lucrative painting career."

She added in a harsh tone, "It was only later when my father discovered Tassi had stolen one of our paintings, *my* painting actually, he decided to make Tassi suffer. He fussed and fumed for days and then declared he'd take Agostino to court and denounce him as a rapist. He wanted financial retribution, and perhaps it was also a publicity stunt, to point out to the Pope I was an ingénue and to showcase my talents as an artist."

"And you agreed."

"No! Of course not. I was barely sixteen at the time and immediately terrified. I wanted no part of it. But Orazio said I owed him. Since my career was over, and money was tight, he figured he might as well be compensated for something. He told me it would be a simple procedure, over quickly, and that I would never suffer."

She shook her head again. "But he lied. The trial lasted seven months and enthralled all of Rome, being a titillating sex crime involving defilement, slander, incest, and murder."

She pointed at the canvas again. "Do you want to see what happened?"

Maddie warily focused her attention on the painting again, and a new scene emerged. Before her sat a dark-haired child—barely a teenager—in a courtroom, surrounded by old men peering at her lasciviously. To avoid their stares, she sat with her head tilted down, wringing her hands in her lap. Across the room sat the man who raped her, Agostino Tassi.

As it had before, slowly the scene animated, and Maddie heard a male voice call the courtroom to order.

"Let the court record show that in the year of our Lord 1612, Orazio Gentileschi and his daughter brought suit against Agostino Tassi, the master painter, for misconduct of a sexual nature, rescinding a marriage proposal, *and* for having stolen a painting. The petition was first addressed to Pope Paul V and is now being aired in this court, presided over by the Illustrious and Excellent Lord Hieronimo Felicio."

The man adjusted his cravat and cleared his throat. "On the 26th day of March, after hearing the testimony of said Agostino, it now reconvenes to hear the sworn testament of the plaintiff, Artemisia Gentileschi."

With a steely eye, the judge with a large, bulbous nose peered at the girl. "Please state your age and where you were born."

"Yes, Your Honor. My birthdate is July 8, 1593. I was born here in Rome. I am the daughter of Orazio Gentileschi and Prudentia Montone. My mother died five years ago. I now live at home with my father and three younger brothers, Giovanni, Francesco, and Giulio."

"What's that? Speak up, girl! How old are you?" the judge said impatiently. "The court can barely hear you."

Startled, Artemisia directly faced the judge. More firmly, she said, "Excuse me, *signore*, I am now seventeen years old."

"Much better. According to this summons and denouncement filed by your father, he is claiming that you, Signorina Gentileschi, were violated by Agostino Tassi. Is that correct? And that he proposed to marry you but later withdrew his offer."

"Yes, sir, that is correct."

The judge shook his head and said testily, "Someone is lying! Signor Tassi has already told the court repeatedly, and in no uncertain terms, that he did no wrong and never once made such a promise. In fact, he claims *he* is the one being slandered."

Peering at Tassi, he added, "He also has gone so far as to parade before us an interesting group of witnesses to prove his point. To clear up this matter and determine who is telling the truth, we need you, *signorina*, to tell us your side of the story."

"*Sì, signore.* I was at home..." She stopped when she saw the dark-haired painter scowling darkly at her—the fascinating painter who had once looked at her with longing and lust. She had hoped and prayed that, after being defiled by him, those feelings would develop into real affection and that he would be a man who would honor his promises.

"Yes? You were at home? Go on. We are all ears. Appease this court's curiosity and tell us the events leading up to your so-called rape."

"It is not so-called," the girl said, this time not needing to be told to speak up. "Agostino Tassi snuck into my house when my father was out and raped me."

The judge scrutinized her skeptically. "What exactly do you mean by rape? How do you define this act?"

In an incredulous tone, thinking him dense, she replied, "Sir! The man ripped away my clothes and forced himself upon me and into me, without my consent. He defiled me."

"But you continued to lay with him? How do you explain that?"

"As he had dishonored me, Agostino promised to marry me, but only as long as I granted him access to my bed," she said evenly.

From across the room, Tassi cried out in an indignant tone, "It's a lie. I never touched the girl or asked her to be my wife. Never have I had carnal relations, nor tried to have them, with the said Artemisia. I was her painting instructor and a friend of the family. Clearly, the girl has been duped by her kin into taking action against me."

"It is you who are deceitful, Agostino!" cried Artemisia. "I am the one telling the truth. Even your so-called friend, Giovanni Battisti Quorli, contradicted your testimony. He said it was *you* who stole my painting of the virgin. The one in which the Madonna resembles my mother."

"That is preposterous! Quorli misled the court only because he is infatuated with you. On many occasions, he told me how you lusted after him, too. He even showed me the love letters you wrote him."

"Come now, Tassi," the judge said. "Over the past few days, this court has been entertained by your colorful stories. We have already established the girl can paint well enough, but she is illiterate. There is no possible way Artemisia could have penned those letters. It has also come to our attention that a bit of coercion and bribery may have occurred. Be careful, sir. The evidence is mounting against you."

Stubbornly, Tassi repeated, "I never touched the girl."

Shaking his head again, the judge continued, "We have heard from credible sources that corroborate the fact you indeed had sexual relations with said Artemisia. Furthermore, she has been examined in this very courtroom by midwives to prove to us that she is no longer a virgin."

"That is exactly my point, Your Honor. She is trying to cover up her whoring ways by dragging me into this mess. Can't you see? She is a harlot."

The judge swiveled his head to study the young woman.

"Surely a man so learned as yourself," Tassi continued, "can see the girl has low morals. Observe her sly grin and the way she dresses. I know for a fact Artemisia has been warming the bed of another painter, a certain Geronimo Modenese, as well as a cleric in a cassock. It is rumored she has also had intimate relations with her father! Really, how can the court overlook a claim of incest?"

"That is not true!" Artemisia burst out. "He only used me as a model."

"Did you not pose in the nude for him? Did he not adjust and caress you and..." said Agostino, raising a questioning eyebrow at the judge.

"Enough of these outbursts, Tassi!" demanded the disgruntled judge. "You've gone a step too far, and now you are really testing the patience of this court. Be careful, Signore, of bearing false witness."

Addressing Artemisia, he said, "It is growing late, and I'm getting hungry. Please go on, Signorina Gentileschi. What happened that day?"

"*Onorabile, signore,* that afternoon I was at home alone. My brothers were out buying the pigments we crush into paint in the artist's quarter near Castel Sant'Angelo. As he often did, my father left me alone, believing I would be safe in the company of our neighbor, Tuzia."

Artemisia shook her head in disbelief before continuing. "It was she, Tuzia, also my friend, who disobeyed my father's orders and let Agostino into our home. When I saw him, I told him to leave at once. I knew my father would be displeased to find us alone together. But Agostino wouldn't go. Instead, he stood behind me and watched me paint for a while. Then, stepping closer until I could feel the heat of his breath on the back of my neck, he grabbed my brush and threw it aside."

"Remember, my girl, you are under oath," cautioned the judge. "This court will not abide exaggerations."

"What I say is the truth, *signore*."

"Go on then. What happened next?"

"He pulled me into his arms and kissed me roughly, thrusting his tongue inside my mouth. I struggled, but when he reached for my bodice and undid the laces, I pushed him away and..."

"And then," the judge said, growing more interested by the moment.

"Angered and panting, full of lust, he grabbed me again and forced me to the bed. Overcome with fear, I called out to Tuzia for help. But she never came to my aid. He must have paid her well to cover her ears."

To the court recorder, the judge said, "Let the record show the girl put up a fight."

"Yes!" she cried out indignantly. "But, to hide my screams, he covered my mouth with a handkerchief so I could no longer be heard. In retaliation, I pulled his hair and scratched his face. But it didn't stop him. He undid his pants and exposed himself to me..."

Directing her anger at Agostino, she added, "Remember, Agostino? Remember I clutched it so tightly that I tore off your skin?"

Showing an unhealthy curiosity, the judge prompted, "And then...?"

"I couldn't hold him back. He lifted my skirts and ground into me. I felt a strong burning sensation, and it hurt very much." With tears brimming in her eyes, Artemisia said, "I was shocked and beside myself with rage. When he fell off me, and I was free of his bulk, I ran to the dresser and opened a drawer where I kept a knife. I spun around to face him and told him if he touched me again I'd kill him."

"And Tassi? What did he do?"

"He laughed at me. He just stood there and mocked me."

"Nothing more?"

"He opened his shirt and taunted me by saying, 'Here I am. Go ahead, Artemisia. Throw the damned dagger!'"

"And did you?"

"Yes, of course, I did!"

"But you missed, didn't you, Artemisia?" Tassi said, taunting her.

Artemisia implored the judge, "See! He admits to being there. I threw the blade, yes, but it only nicked him in the chest. After that, to keep me quiet, he made his promise and continued coming to my house."

"Oh, I admit I came to your house often, you miserable, misguided girl. That doesn't mean a thing."

In a confidential tone, Tassi said to the judge, "The girl has a fiery temperament. If I was in her house, it was to safeguard her honor from the men she lusts after. I was hired by her father to teach her how to paint. She needed lessons..."

Looking back at Artemisia, he said, "You still need lessons to draw correctly, Artemisia. Oh, you have some talent, but really, you are but an amateur and will never amount to anything."

"So, Agostino promised to marry you, Artemisia?" asked the judge. "And you believed him?"

"Yes, sir," the girl replied. "I had no other choice but to trust him."

"But, *signorina*, did you not know he is already married? And he has several children, some by his wife and some by others."

Artemisia's face went ashen. "No, I did not. He never said anything about having a wife."

"Why bring up these insignificant details? This is not pertinent to this case! More lies and gossip."

"We will talk about that in a moment, Tassi. The court has learned of the death of your wife by nefarious means, at the hands of paid assassins."

Casually examining his fingernails, Tassi said, "Again, I claim innocence. No one can prove that. It's all lies invented by my rivals."

The judge leveled his eyes at Tassi. "It would seem you have many adversaries, Maestro Tassi."

In an irritated voice, he continued, "Things aren't any clearer than when we began. The two of you tell completely different stories. To arrive at the truth, I must resort to extreme measures."

He scrutinized Artemisia a long moment, drumming his fingers upon his desk. Finally, he said, "To prove *you* aren't lying, Signorina Gentileschi, will you submit to the sibille?"

"The sibille?" she said in a shocked voice. "My father never told me there would be torture."

"It seems necessary to me in order to move things along."

"But your Esteemed Honor, I am not the one on trial here. I am an innocent victim. It is Agostino who should be subjected to torture. He is the one who committed the crime."

"If your accusations are indeed correct," concluded the judge, "you will not hesitate to submit to the sibille. It makes perfect sense."

Slowly, the girl responded, "If that is what the court requires, then yes, I accept the truth test."

"Very well," the judge said. "Borgianni, bring the ropes."

The man called Borgianni appeared at the girl's side and wrapped her fingers with a leather cord, binding them tightly. Artemisia watched his expressionless, pockmarked face as he pulled the rope taut. When he indicated he was ready to begin, the judge said in a monotone voice, "Did Agostino Tassi rape you, Artemisia?"

"Yes, Your Honor, Agostino Tassi raped me."

Giving a signal to pull the ropes tighter, observing the girl's hand starting to swell and turn purple, the judge repeated, "Once more, I ask you, Artemisia Gentileschi, did Agostino Tassi rape you?"

Artemisia bit her lip and repeated, "Yes, Agostino Tassi raped me."

Despite seeing the tears slipping down her face, the judge demanded again, "Are you telling the truth, Signorina Gentileschi?"

With the next tightening of the ropes, the girl screamed, "Agostino! My thumbscrews are the wedding ring you promised me!"

In disdain, Tassi replied, "You aren't worthy of a wedding band, or any man for that matter, Artemisia. As for your paintings, history will quickly forget you. Trust me, there's nothing special about you—no one will *ever* remember a girl named Artemisia Gentileschi."

Ignoring Tassi, the judge asked, "*Signorina,* are you telling the truth?"

"Yes! It is true. I am telling the truth! It is true, it is true, it is..."

"Enough!" said the judge as he pounded his gavel upon his desk.

Maddie jumped. Coming slowly back to the present, she realized the wooden bin of postcards had fallen off the table and onto the floor. Seeing the jumble of cards scattered around her feet, Maddie swore under her breath and reached down to scoop up the mess.

As she dumped the pictures back into the box and tidied up the table, the scene in the courtroom and its ignominious participants—the lecherous judge, Tassi the rapist, and Borgianni the torturer—faded away. The only image worthy of remembering remained—that of Artemisia and her swollen and bleeding hands, and the expression of fierce determination on her face. It was the look of a woman who suffered great abuse but who hadn't let it define or defeat her. It was the face of Judith.

How wrong Tassi had been; Artemisia hadn't disappeared quietly into the night. Her passion for painting was real. Despite her scarred and damaged fingers, she picked up her brushes and changed her fate; like a phoenix, she rose from the ashes of her incinerated life and went on to touch the moon.

Although it had happened hundreds of years before, Maddie believed Artemisia set an example. She was proof a woman, with her two competent hands, could mold her future. More importantly, Artemisia demonstrated a woman was worthy of anything she wanted to accomplish—and *that* was her superpower.

Chapter 7

The Art of Golden Repairs

*M*addie thought it an auspicious beginning for her group to have Artemisia amongst them—enveloping them with her courage and fierce perseverance. Knowing full well how powerful the restorative powers of art were the following day, Maddie adeptly began her first group session. It was a simple project, but one she thought particularly poignant and relevant.

Slipping on a pair of safety glasses, she picked up a hammer and a small blue ceramic bowl from a selection she had set on one of the tables. Then, placing it between sheets of newspaper, she gave it a couple of gentle taps, just enough to break it into several pieces. "In Japan, they call it *kintsugi*. Translated, that means the art of golden repairs."

She removed her goggles and said, "You know, sometimes people think that women fall apart easily—that we are weak because we show signs of fragility. But those moments don't have to define us forever. That which threatens to destroy us can make us stronger. More to the point, it is how we choose to deal with the fractures that matter."

Unwrapping the newspaper, she picked out the large, broken shards. Then she carefully poured a bit of gold powder into a small plastic cup of setting compound and mixed it with a small palette knife until it gave off a luminous shine.

"I don't think there is anything wrong with showing our emotions, our imperfections, or our age. Sometimes we do stumble and fall apart, and we cry."

She dipped her brush into the pasty solution and spread it onto the rough, jagged edges. As she pressed the shards back together and held

71

them firmly, she said, "There can be beauty in the breakdown and, with the right tools, we can put ourselves back together."

Holding up the bowl, she added, "See. Just like this piece. All the spidery fracture lines now glitter. They take on new meaning. Instead of hiding the broken bits, or seeing the whole thing as defective, we choose now to celebrate its uniqueness."

Handing the small mallet to Camilla, she said, "Now you try."

The girl took the hammer reluctantly, and Maddie continued distributing sheets of newspaper and safety glasses to the others. Soon the room was filled with the sounds of gentle pounding and shattering of bowls. Looking back at Camilla, however, she noted the girl had put down the tool and was instead thumbing through a magazine.

Of all the women, Maddie realized she was the youngest, and her traumatic experience was the most recent. She could tell Camilla was struggling to maintain a perfect and unbroken surface, exerting far more energy keeping her feelings reined in than trying to expel the negativity inside of her. From personal experience, and from years of being a therapist, Maddie knew it was just a matter of time before Camilla fractured and broke into pieces. And with the introduction of each new art project, what Maddie anticipated was starting to come true; like the cracks that appeared when they hit their bowls with hammers, Maddie soon saw fissures forming on the girl's brittle facade.

Hoping to delve a bit deeper and reveal what lay beneath the surface, the following day Maddie asked each woman to draw their self-portrait. Handing them each a little handheld mirror, she said, "Be creative and as original as you like—stick to reality or go a little crazy. The important thing is to communicate what you find most attractive about yourself. It could be a physical attribute or something you like to do—even a spiritual quality."

An hour later, Maddie passed through the room and was impressed by their imaginations. One woman depicted herself as a fierce lion, and another, with just a few simple pencil strokes, drew a woman gardening. Continuing around the room, she saw a woman from Iowa, in a primitive way, modeled herself as an island goddess surrounded by blue water.

When Maddie came to Camilla's easel, she stopped and admired her portrait. She already knew the girl was a gifted artist and had anticipated her self-portrait to be quite lovely. And, as expertly drawn as it was—exquisitely shaded and life-like, capturing the shape of her lips and jawline—it was equally terrifying. A raven sat on Camilla's shoulder, holding a lustrous black pearl in its beak, and where her expressive dark eyes should have been, empty sockets dripped with tears.

Later that afternoon, alone in the kitchen while brewing cups of espresso, the two of them talked privately about her drawing. And as they spooned sugar into their cups, Camilla in a barely audible voice, began to describe the series of events that happened the year before.

"*Sono andata a Roma*. My friend Francesca had just gotten engaged, and we had planned to celebrate her betrothal and share a girl's night out together. After classes ended at the university, I drove down to Rome on a Friday, and we met up in a bar in Trastevere later that night. We were joined by other girlfriends who lived in the city and we were having a pretty great time, enjoying a few spritzes and listening to a local band. We were all feeling carefree and happy."

With great deliberation, she swiveled her spoon around and around then gently set it aside on the tiny saucer. Still staring into the dark brew, she said, "When the waiter approached me with a glass of wine, saying the man at the bar had offered to buy me a drink, I looked over at him, and thought he seemed nice enough—rather average height and trim build, with a pleasant face. So, I thought, *perché no*? He was well dressed too, and had beautiful shoes—they were Ferragamos. It's funny the little things you remember."

Shaking her head, Camilla added, "At the time I felt flattered and special to have been singled out of all the women in the room by this handsome guy. I accepted the glass of wine from the waiter then looked over at the man who had bought it for me and gave him an air toast with my glass—I think I even winked at him."

She fell silent again, and Maddie softly said, "Hey, it's okay. Don't punish yourself for a little harmless flirting. What happened to you wasn't your fault. You didn't cause it just because you accepted a drink and gave a man a wink and a smile."

Camilla looked up, and saw something in Maddie's eyes, and instinctively felt she could tell her things she hadn't even confided to Gaetano. Taking a deep breath, she continued, "We were just there to have fun, so after finishing our drinks, we all started dancing. You know, how girls do. We were in a tight little circle, and the music was really good. When the man tapped me on the shoulder and asked me to share a dance with him, I didn't see the harm in it. I was in Rome with my best girlfriends—it wasn't like I was going to break up with Davide over someone I had just met in a bar."

"Davide was your boyfriend?"

"*Sì,*" said Camilla. "He was—he still is actually."

Choosing her words carefully, she continued. "*Comunque*, after one or two songs, I thanked the guy—his name was Paolo—and then went back to my friends, thinking I'd never see him again."

She took a sip of coffee. "So, I was kind of surprised and a little *scombussolata*—how do you say it, rattled?—when he came back about a quarter of an hour later and said into my ear that he really liked me and wanted to see me the next evening. He thought my boyfriend was a pretty lucky guy—*un ragazzo fortunato*—to have landed such a *bella ragazza.*"

"So, he knew you had a *fidanzato* already?" asked Maddie.

"*Ma certo*! I'd made it pretty clear before we even began dancing that I was already seeing someone. Still, unfazed Paolo hung around making small talk. He told a few jokes and flirted with the other girls. He even moved closer to me and teased me, pleading with me not to break his heart. Putting a hand to his chest, he looked at me and said: *Please, oh please, won't you give me a chance?* After a point, it wasn't so funny, and I firmly told him *basta*! Enough was enough!"

Camilla tilted her head and contemplated the ceiling a moment. "Finally, he seemed to get the message and drifted about the room and started talking to another girl. I almost forgot about him. But, in the early hours of the morning, after our group broke up and I headed to my car, out of the corner of my eye, I saw this guy leaning against the wall of the club, partially hidden in the shadows. It was Paolo. He was there waiting, just waiting. *Stava fumando una cigaretta,* and when I smelled the smoke I had this sickening feeling. I should have known right then to turn around and go back."

Maddie reached for Camilla's hand as tears seeped from beneath the girl's lashes. "I tried to pass by casually, but seeing me, he pushed off the wall and flicked his cigarette away. Before I could do anything, he grabbed my arm and dragged me against his chest. His breath reeked of alcohol and, as he held a knife to my throat, he hissed into my ear that he thought I was a *puttana*—a whore. He said I led him on all night long— not only had I tried to seduce him, but I had betrayed my boyfriend and that *ragazze come me devono essere punite...*"

Having heard similar stories so many times before, Maddie was silent, choosing not to offer a response just yet. She sat quietly next to Camilla, providing a comforting presence. Eventually the girl let out a tired sigh and continued. "I thought I was making progress. I told myself after the trial everything would be better. Right now, I should feel relieved. The man got what he deserved and is in prison. But the truth is, I don't feel better. At all."

She threw out her arms. "I'm sick and tired of dealing with all of this. My life is on hold, and for months now, all I've wanted was to be left alone. Everyone tries to say the right things. But how can they even begin to understand the horrible thoughts going on in my head? And now Davide..."

"What about him?"

"Oh, he's been so supportive, but... I've had zero interest in..."

She shook her head and demanded, "Is that normal? Am I normal? I don't know anymore. Sometimes I think..."

Maddie continued to act as a sounding board as Camilla poured out her deepest fears and darkest frustrations. Occasionally, she offered a small insight or a brief comment gained from her own experience and from what she had learned from others over the years. But mostly she just listened.

When Rossella bustled into the room to start the evening meal, Camilla looked at Maddie in wonderment. "I can't begin to tell you how good it feels to talk to someone who knows what I've gone through. Finally, finally, someone gets me."

They left the kitchen on a more positive note, but Maddie still sensed the girl's emotional turmoil and knew there was much work yet to be done. Wanting to keep the flow and momentum going, knowing that music was an exceptional way to relax and let feelings out, the following day she moved on to the next project she called Painting Sonatas.

Early in the morning, she enlisted Roberto's help, asking him to pick a big bouquet from the garden. He happily obliged and brought her a massive assortment of yellow hollyhocks, red roses, and purple hyacinth. Taking the colorful blooms, she placed them in a tall urn on a table in the middle of the room. Then, raising the volume on the music player, the bright melodies of Mozart washed over them.

"For me, painting is a way to process the emotions I can't resolve in any other way," Maddie told the group. "With colors, I can express fears, hopes, and dreams. Today, I want you to paint like the Fauves and..."

"Like the Fauves? What does that mean?" one of the women asked.

"Matisse and Van Gogh are great examples," Maddie said. "People called them Fauves—in French, it means wild beast—because they painted using unnaturally bright colors. They chose intense hot pinks, acid greens, and neon oranges that often aren't seen in nature—but it was their reality. So, today, like the impressionists Vincent, Henri, and Raoul, I want you all to go a little wild today. Paint what you see and what you don't. Let the music and your emotions guide you."

As the afternoon unfolded, Maddie strolled around the room offering a comment or two about perspective or advice on how to mix colors. When she approached Camilla's easel, she was impressed once again by her talent. Just as the Italian girl had a gift for capturing human form, with great precision she grasped the essence of each tiny bloom down to a few lonely petals that had fallen onto the table.

But instead of painting in lush colors, Camilla chose to convey the scene using inky blacks and misty grays. There had been a small break through the day before in the kitchen but still, the girl wasn't painting with colorful abandon, as Maddie had hoped. Camilla continued to tiptoe through the jungle of emotions she harbored inside of her, and the caged animal had yet to be unleashed.

Despite the extreme control she continued to exert, Maddie noted with interest, however, during the group feedback session, by the hour Camilla was letting herself be drawn into the circle of woman that surrounded her. And now that she knew them all by first name, Camilla no longer hung back with her hands crossed over her chest. Instead, she was actively offering suggestions and willingly interacting with others.

By Wednesday, Maddie was ready to open the big bags of moist wet clay and invited them all to take a big chunk. "I want you to warm it between your hands. Then smash it, pull it, flatten it, even cut it with a knife. Make whatever you want, a little vase or a figurine. But really, what's important is that you enjoy the malleable feeling of molding the clay into any shape you like."

Checking in with everyone a little bit later, again Maddie was pleased with their results. The tax accountant from Texas created a series of small bowls that resembled sunflowers.

"These are wonderful!" declared Maddie. "And you said you weren't an artist."

When she came to Camilla's station, she saw the girl had created a symmetrical bust of Medusa. Flowing from its head were ribbons of clay that slithered around its face.

Maddie put her hand on Camilla's arm. "Wow, this is really great!"

Seemingly unimpressed by her praise, the girl picked up a piece of clay and squeezed it between her fingers. "They say whoever gazes directly at the Gorgon monster will be changed to stone."

"They also say," countered Maddie, "that Athena, the warrior goddess, put the Medusa on her shield to avert all evil."

Camilla simply lifted one shoulder in a dismissive gesture. *"Non ha funzionato per me.* It seems Medusa's magic doesn't work for me."

Seeing Rossella gesturing to her from the door, Maddie said, "Hold on. I want to talk with you more about this. I'll be back in just a minute."

But, when she returned, she found Camilla gone and the mythical beast's head distorted and unrecognizable. When Maddie inquired if anyone knew where Camilla had gone, one of the women responded, "She left a while ago without saying anything. Like you told us to do, she balled up her clay and threw it down on the table. I figured she was really getting into things, but then, as I said, she took off."

As Maddie cleaned up the forgotten project, she wasn't discouraged. She saw it as a positive sign. The assignment hadn't been to create a lovely piece of art; it was a means of releasing pent-up emotions. In the end, perhaps the act of smashing what she created against her table granted the release she needed.

By the end of the week, the art room had a well-used and chaotic appearance and showed signs of disrepair. The air smelled like wet paint tinged with earthy mud, and there was sand on the floor and wax on the tables. From a clothesline hung an array of colorful shirts that still dripped dyes onto newspapers spread beneath them. Despite Rossella's best-laid plan, the easels were now scattered about and upon them rested all sorts of paintings. And in the far corner was their community project—a towering sculpture they created together using cardboard tubes, crushed paper, and found objects.

All in all, it was an incredibly messy sight, and an untrained eye might think the session had been a waste of time. But once again, looks could be deceiving. In Maddie's professional view, this had been a very successful retreat, and she was proud of the work they accomplished together.

She watched as the women drifted into the room from the patio where they just finished lunch and listened with pleasure as they chatted about the upcoming weekend and their plans to visit Florence on Saturday and Pienza on Sunday for some cheese and wine tasting. As they settled into place, some sitting on the tables and others leaning back in their chairs, Maddie said, "And now for my favorite project. I call it a vision board."

Gesturing to the poster she had put together earlier, she said, "I want you to reflect on this week, and on your life—past, present, and future."

Picking up a few glossy images from the wooden box, Maddie said, "Around the room, you will find lots of old magazines and pictures. Take some time to flip through the pages and sort through the postcards. Don't think too hard about it. Choose whatever you like."

She held up a couple of pictures; in one hand, a sandy beach in Rio and in the other a publicity shot of Sonny and Cher. With a laugh, she said, "As you can see, there are lots of things from which to choose. But I want you to use the images that resonate with you—places you want to go, or things you'd like to do."

Pointing to the funky sixties singers, she added, "Like recording a hit song. Then I want you to take all those images and pin them to your boards. When you are done, we will see what you've all come up with."

Leaving them to their own devices, giving them time to play, Maddie returned an hour later to see what they had come up with. Circling the room, as had become her habit, stopping at each of their art stations, she saw that just as her Vision board had been unique to her interests, so were those of her eclectic group of women. Each collage showcased their various interests in travel, cuisine, and sports and overall, the vision boards presented positive messages. And then there was Camilla's.

Maddie studied the young woman's collage for a moment, then said, "This says so much about you and the things you are working through right now. Do you think you are ready to share it with the group?"

Camilla wrapped her arms tightly around her body and looked around at the other women. "I guess. Go ahead."

When Maddie dragged her easel around, so that the others could see, there was an audible gasp from the room. Like them, the girl had sorted through the magazines and the boxes of postcards and torn out images, but what Camilla had found no one else had seen. It was as if the most horrific images—burning buildings, soulless china dolls, and war-torn cities—had been drawn to her like a magnet and were displayed in a jumble of obscene notes. It was disturbing, but like some great pieces of art that take your breath away, it was hauntingly beautiful as well.

Unlike the day before, when Camilla expressed herself in lifeless monochromatic washes, she expressed herself in vivid reds and bloody maroons. And in a macabre dance, like the letters of a disjointed ransom letter, little phrases and obscene words were stuck here and there. It was apparent that, finally, she had let out the wild beast inside of her.

But perhaps the most startling image of all was the one she had pasted dead center. It was a photo of a semi-naked cabaret singer with heavily made-up eyes and cheaply rouged cheeks, who sat straddling a chair with one high-heel planted on the chest of a man who lay bound and gagged on the floor. In one hand, she held a smoldering cigarette, and in the other, she held a gun.

"Oh my god!" exclaimed one of the women who quickly covered her mouth. "I mean… I'm sorry, I didn't…"

"No, it's okay. Art can have extreme reactions. And this is really powerful, isn't it?" said Maddie. To Camilla, she said, "There is something wild and raw about what you have created. I've sensed it in your work all week, but this piece… How do you feel about it?"

"*L'odio*. I hate it. I hate everything about it," Camilla responded with disgust. "Why is everyone else able to show such positive, inspirational images? But, this—this is what I see!"

The room grew quiet as the women contemplated Camilla's collage, not knowing exactly what to say. Finally, Maddie broke the silence. "You may not believe it, but I think you are making more progress than you give yourself credit. The colors, these images, and words—all put together like this—are expressive. You have created something compelling and thought-provoking."

Camilla appeared skeptical. "*Sì ma… le immagini sono sgradevoli.* These things are not pleasant at all. Am I supposed to celebrate the fact this reflects myself? *Questo! Questo è la mia visione del futuro?*"

Maddie was quiet for a moment as she studied what Camilla had created. "I see brutal and ugly things here, but when I read between the lines and look past the shocking, violent images, I see something much more. And, it isn't something to be ashamed or afraid of. In fact, I think you are now fully aware of what happened to you and are now accepting it and reacting to it finally. And that is something healthy."

Picking up her own vision board, Maddie pointed to the woman in the center and said, "What you have created in your collage reminds me of how Artemisia Gentileschi stunned the world with her painting of Judith beheading Holofernes. You, of all people, I'm sure are familiar with her paintings. There are two versions of her painting in Florence."

"*Sì certo.* I'm very familiar with her. My great aunt did some research on her back in the '30s, and after the war she translated Artemisia's trial testimony and published a book about her."

"Really? You are related to Luciana Mancini?" asked Maddie, visibly impressed. "Well, then wouldn't you agree a comparison could be drawn? And like Artemisia, aren't you painting your rage, trying to expel your anger? Aren't you, too, revisioning what happened to you—shocking the world, defiantly letting it know you are not going to slip away and be forgotten?"

Indicating Camilla's vision board again, she added, "If you identify with Artemisia and the woman in the picture, you are not a victim. You have turned the tables on your abuser, just as Artemisia did, and you are the one in control. Those are the sentiments of a survivor."

Maddie saw a new flicker of interest in Camilla's eyes and could tell the girl was more engaged, tuning into her words. Reaching for a large pad of paper and a marker, she flipped to a fresh page. "Here, let me show you something."

Quickly she drew a circle, tapped it with her pen and said, "I want you all to pretend this circle is you." Returning her attention to the page, Maddie filled the circle with scribbly lines all the way to the edges. As she worked, she said, "I want you to imagine these chaotic squiggles represent grief or the result of something traumatic that has happened to you. When rape or abuse occurs, there isn't an area of your life that isn't affected, right? It touches every part of you—from your core all the way to the very pores of your skin."

"Now," Maddie said, drawing a larger ring around the smaller one, "imagine this circle is your life today."

She stood back so they could see her drawing better. "As we move on with our lives, lots of new things happen to us. Our lives grow larger around the smaller one with all its tangly lines. We meet new people, we go to school, we start new jobs, we resume love relationships—our lives become filled with other things."

Adding a few more scribbles to the interior circle, she said, "No matter what we do, though, this knotty little circle resides deep within us. Oh, the lines may fade and become less distinct, but it is impossible to be rid of it for good. That is why, on the anniversary of an assault, or the trial in your case, Camilla, or a reminder of the event for whatever reason—we are dipped straight back into that dark part. We have to accept that it is always going to be a part of our lives."

Drawing an even larger circle around the other two, Maddie said, "But, we don't have to reside in the black pit forever. If we have worked to unblock ourselves and have allowed ourselves to evolve and flourish, once the moment passes, we can move back out into the larger circle."

She looked around the room and then back over at Camilla. The two locked eyes and Camilla slowly nodded. Once again, Maddie noted there was something subtly different about her. The young woman stood even taller, and there was a new, determined light in her eyes that hadn't been there at the start of the week.

Maddie was filled with hope, for what she saw before her now was the face of Artemisia.

Chapter 8

Lucid Dreams & Florentine Fantasies

*O*n Saturday, Maddie found herself with the rest of her group sitting in a little minivan bumping along the rutted back roads, making its way to the *autostrada* that would take them to Florence. She knew from previous experience that by day ten of the retreat, they could all use a little break and a bit of shopping therapy. For this reason, she always scheduled an escape to the city so they could wander the leather markets near San Lorenzo and visit the gold shops that flanked the Ponte Vecchio.

From her position toward the rear of the bus, Maddie could see Camilla seated amongst the others. Shifting her weight on the hard bench of the bus, Maddie thought it was uncomfortable now as it had been way back in the day when the only means of transportation had been horses and rickety wooden carriages.

Unbelievably tired from the week's events, as well as from closing her practice in New York and packing, Maddie placed her knees against the bench in front of her, and she let her body loll back against the seat. She turned her head slightly to look out the window. She noted the city in the distance, and the silhouette of the Duomo rising against the gray sky that threatened rain. She closed her eyes and listened to the muted conversations and the occasional burst of laughter. It pleased her immensely when she heard Camilla's voice animatedly telling the others about things they should do and see when they reached Florence.

When the bus rolled into town and came to a stop in front of the train station, she distributed walking maps and city passes. Then she shepherded the women in a single file line, down the narrow street passing by the church of Santa Maria Novella and down Via dei Pecori all the way to the Cathedral. After admiring the pink and green marble facade, they made their way through the mass of tourists that filled the piazza and headed towards the Palazzo Vecchio.

Standing in front of the statue of Michelangelo's *David*, Maddie beckoned the group closer. She pointed to her right, indicating the entrance to the Uffizi, and said, "Feel free to visit the museum, climb to the top of the Duomo, or wander around—shop or just eat gelato. We will meet here at the *David* at six to go back to the villa. Call me on my cell if you get lost or need anything."

The women broke off in pairs and Maddie and Camilla remained where they were, admiring the other statues that decorated the loggia on the other side of the piazza. When a single drop of rain fell onto her cheek, Maddie peered up at the watery sky and said, "Oh, drat. Did you feel that? It's not looking good—I hope the rain holds off at least..."

"*Boh*!" said Camilla, matter-of-factly. "*Non ti preoccupare.* If it starts to pour, I know lots of little *trattorie* on the other side of the river where we can take shelter and have lunch. There's also good shopping, especially if you are into vintage clothing."

"That sounds right up my alley. I've always been a big fan of Coco Chanel. Point me in the direction of little black cocktail dresses and evening gowns with Joan Crawford shoulder pads, and I'll follow you anywhere!"

Together they set off down the street in the direction of the Oltrarno, passing the grand carousel in Piazza della Repubblica. To avoid being hit by a rogue taxi cab winding its way through the streets, they returned to the narrow sidewalk and immediately their attention was captured by a flashy, futuristic window display.

They stopped to take in the bizarrely dressed mannequins, wearing metallic coats and skirts made of sequins. In front of the outlandish models were a series of video monitors that, in a Max Headroom kind of way, played a continuous staticky film loop of a man and a woman in elegant attire walking on the surface of the moon.

In unison, they turned to one another in disbelief. "Oh, that is *too* funny!" said Maddie, raising one eyebrow. "Can you imagine wearing anything like that in real life?"

"Who knows," said Camilla. "Maybe it is a sign of things to come."

Maddie linked her arm through Camilla's. "*That* future is looking a little too splashy and bright for me. Let's stick to the original plan. Let's go back to the past."

"*Va bene! Vieni con me!* I know this great little store that you are going to like."

They continued down the street paved in large, smooth stones until they came to the river. Before crossing, Maddie pointed to a narrow side street. "See down there? That's where the silk dyers used to live and work."

"Silk dyers?"

"*Sì. Tintori di seta,*" said Maddie. "Back in the seventeenth century, this was their neighborhood. The women set up their big wooden vats to dye materials all along here. Then they hung the wet fabrics to dry in colorful swathes across the entire length of the alleyway."

Hearing the clip-clopping of hooves, Maddie moved out of the way as an old-fashioned carriage carrying a family of Germans snapping pictures with their iPhones approached them. As the horses passed by, Maddie could smell the scent of leather, hay, and the slight odor of horse manure, and a memory invaded her consciousness.

"I remember..." She gazed about her, perplexed. She had stood on this very corner before, just like this with her arms linked with another woman—she was sure of it.

"What do you remember?"

"Um, I..." Maddie tried to recall, but her mind was now blank. "That's odd. For the life of me, I can't seem to recall what I was just about to say. The thought was there, and then it just flew away."

"*Se il pensiere è importante,*" said Camilla. "I'm sure you will remember whatever you were going to say. That's what *mia madre* always said to me. Come on, *andiamo!*"

When the traffic light flashed green, they crossed the street to the Ponte Vecchio, but their progress to the Oltrarno was hampered by all the people. At the top of the bridge, they were forced to stop completely to let a group of bicyclists pass. As they waited for the street to clear, they admired the array of pendants, earrings, and wedding bands displayed in one of the jewelry shops that lined the narrow street.

"Oh, Maddie!" Camilla exclaimed. "Isn't *that* one pretty?"

"Which one?"

"That one, there in the back resting on the cushion," said Camilla, pointing to a gold ring with a large yellow diamond. "It's an antique, and I'm guessing by the cut it has to be from the 1930s."

Maddie scanned the rings, and when her eyes settled on the one that caught Camilla's attention, her heart skipped a beat. The setting was strangely familiar. Focusing on the intricate detailing, and the braided pattern etched into the band, she swore she *had* seen it somewhere before. When she was little, she liked to sneak into her mother's bedroom and go through her jewelry box and try on her antique pins and necklaces. Had she seen it there? She focused her thoughts. Was she remembering something that had belonged to her grandmother?

Pensively, Maddie rubbed her thumb around her ring finger and willed herself to remember. As she did, her heart constricted suddenly, and an intense wave of sadness washed over her. Feeling confused and embarrassed she averted her head so Camilla wouldn't see her confusion.

"Did you know Davide gave me a ring last year?" Camilla said.

Maddie glanced down at Camilla's hand but didn't see a gold band.

Catching her eye, Camilla said evasively, "I keep it in a drawer, for now. You know, for safekeeping."

Maddie nodded, understanding, and they continued walking.

"Tell me about him," said Maddie after a bit. "From the little I know, Davide sounds like someone special—someone I'd like to know. Every couple has a story. What's yours?"

"*Non c'è molto da dire.* There's not much to tell." Seeing Maddie's unconvinced expression, she said, "Okay, I guess it *is* kind of funny. We met a few years ago on a blind date. We were set up by his *mother* of all people. I knew her from the university. She's an art restorer and is a guest lecturer at the *Academia*."

"That sounds like a match made in heaven," laughed Maddie. "Right from the start, even before you met him, you had the seal of approval *and* the ideal mother-in-law. What more could a girl ask for?"

"Patrizia is pretty special," admitted Camilla. "So, of course I was curious to meet her son."

"What about Davide? What does he do?"

"He's an architectural engineer in a small firm here in Florence. In fact, his offices are around here, near the Medici Palace. It's just a couple of streets over."

Maddie looked in the direction Camilla indicated and saw the Pitti Palace rising prominently in front of them. Now an art museum, it had once been the home of the Medici Dukes, built by Cosimo II in the seventeenth century. As they drew nearer, Maddie took in the details of the impressive, stoic facade. In the past, she visited the palace many times and was quite familiar with the large, expansive gardens in the back. Inside, the mansion was also quite elegant, and Maddie fondly recalled the marble staircases and frescoed salons that Cosimo had filled with Artemisia's art.

So vivid were her memories she could almost hear the string quartet, bright conversation, and the clinking of glasses. Other images were coming into focus, and another memory was forming, but once again, at the sound of Camilla's voice, her thoughts were scattered.

"He has a small apartment here in Florence."

"Who? Cosimo?"

Camilla shook her head and laughed. "No, Davide! I was telling you about him. He has a place here in town, but his family lives near me just outside of Montepulciano. The Crociani estate. You've probably heard of it. They make wine."

"Oh! Right," said Maddie quickly. "I thought the name sounded familiar. I've had their wine before. It's really good."

"They pride themselves on it, as they do their heritage. The Crociani descended from an ancient noble family going all the way back to Lorenzo de' Medici's time. They have been a part of Florentine politics and society for years. Davide's father loves to tell stories about his ancestors. He's quite a history buff. Once you get him started, there's no stopping him."

Putting her hands into the pockets of her jacket, Maddie said, "You know, Cosimo was Artemisia Gentileschi's biggest patron here. After the rape trial, her reputation was in tatters, so, her father married her off to a Florentine man to rid himself of his problematic daughter. When she got here, running in Cosimo's circles, she might have met someone from the Crociani family. By default, then, I am in a way connected to her—I know you, and you know Davide who is a part of the Crociani clan..."

With a laugh, Maddie added, "You know what they say. We are all connected by six degrees of separation. Or, I guess in this case, six generations."

"I think the Crociani family definitely must have known her," said Camilla. "In their family gallery, they have two paintings by her. There is one of Bathsheba and a portrait of an ancestor from that period."

"Really?"

"Yes. Davide's mom showed them to me once. She told me Artemisia did more portraiture commissions during the time she lived here in Florence. It was her *pane quotidiano*—you know, her bread and butter work—how she really made her living. Patrizia, also said it was Galileo who introduced Artemisia to the Grand Duke in the first place."

"Galileo! Imagine that!" Maddie said, a little in awe.

Looking back at the palace, she added, "Can you imagine attending a fancy-dress ball here and rubbing elbows with the likes of that star-gazing rabble-rouser! It kind of boggles the mind. I mean, just think of saying to your girlfriends, 'Sorry, I can't go out with you this evening, I'm meeting Galileo for drinks... Perhaps tonight he'll show me the moons of Jupiter?'"

Amused, Camilla said, "Seems to me Artemisia must have played her cards right to enter into such an illustrious circle. I wonder, too what they talked about. Oh, to be *un mosca sul muro*—a fly on the wall in *that* salon!"

Maddie let her mind drift. "I remember there was this one time when she waltzed with her lover Francesco, right under the nose of her husband in Cosimo's grand ballroom. Archduchess Maria was seated in this kind of throne, and she appeared to be very bored—you know, smothering yawns behind her fan. And then..."

She stopped mid-sentence. Ahead of her was Camilla who walked on up the street and hadn't heard anything she said.

Maddie stared about her, dumbfounded. Walking the streets of this city for anyone—on any given day—was like taking a stroll into the past. But, for her, Florence was stirring up unexpected emotions, and she was remembering things as if she had rebooted her internal computer and old data bits, and lost files had randomly and unexpectedly sprung open.

When Camilla turned and beckoned, Maddie hastened to catch up to her. Not wanting to divulge any of these peculiar feelings to Camilla, casually she picked up the thread of the conversation they started earlier. "So, you were telling me about the Crociani Estate and their wine. When did they go into the business?"

"Oh, back in the late fifties or maybe the early sixties. It was started by Davide's father."

"Last summer when I was here I had some, and they carry Crociani wines in some of the better wine stores in New York..." Maddie stopped in her tracks in front of a small shop. "Oh, look at that!" she said, indicating a flapper dress on the model in the window.

When the door opened, a shopper came out, and she could hear jazz music playing inside. Looking over her shoulder at Camilla, she asked, "Is this the shop you were talking about? Let's go inside!"

With her eyes still focused on the elegant display of dresses and hats, eagerly she made for the door. But in her haste, not watching her step, she accidentally brushed into a man passing by on the sidewalk.

To keep her from falling off the narrow curb, a dark-haired man reached out a hand to steady her. "*Mi scusi signorina! Tutto a posto?* I'm sorry. *Mi dispiace... Colpa mia.*"

"*Tutto bene,*" Maddie said apologetically. "I'm fine, really. It was totally my fault. I wasn't paying attention to where I was going..."

She peered up at him and her breath caught in her throat. Although the man seemed courteous and friendly, after he continued on his way, she looked after him warily. Another memory had just crossed her mind. This very place, this same corner... It seemed she had stood here before and...

"Come on, Maddie," said Camilla, grabbing her arm. "If you think this is fabulous, just wait until you see inside."

Letting Camilla draw her into the shop, her attention was quickly distracted by the movie posters of Gregory Peck and Audrey Hepburn. She took in her surroundings gleefully, admiring the racks of vintage gowns and glass cases filled with evening bags and accessories. And when she spied a particularly amusing felt hat that resembled an upside-down shoe, she reached over and placed it on her head.

Swiveling around so Camilla could see, she drawled in her best Katharine Hepburn imitation, "What do you think *daaarling*? How do I look? Think I can pull off this shoe-hat?"

Camilla's eyes lit up and she replied, "Not *every* girl can wear a hat like that and get away with it... But on you, Maddie, *é molto elegante!*"

The saleswoman intervened promptly. "It is a unique design *ragazze,* modeled after Elsa Schiaparelli's version. She got her ideas from Dalì and other surrealist artists..."

"The woman certainly had a unique vision," said Maddie, peeking in the mirror set on the counter. She tilted her head to the side and added, "She also had quite a sense of humor."

Spying a lovely dress in the reflection of the mirror, she put the hat down and turned around to the rack of dresses. With Camilla on one side of the store and she on the other, they sorted through the gowns, rhapsodizing over the satin and chiffon concoctions, causing the woman at the cash register to smile as she tabulated her receipts.

As Maddie slid the hangers together, occasionally, she pulled an especially interesting one out. With a critical eye, she held it up to the light, and inspected the seams and zipper down to the buttons and embroidery, almost as if she had created the dress herself. Some of them, she noted, were modern knockoffs, but fingering the labels of others, she could see they were the real McCoy.

"You know, in another life, I'd have been a dress designer. I've always been pretty good at sewing. I once made this really cool velveteen skirt..."

"*Ehi! Vieni qua!* Come here, you have to see this one!"

Maddie peeked up from the gown she was admiring and saw Camilla pointing to a gown displayed in an alcove near the cash register.

"What do you think?"

Maddie's eyes grew big, and she glanced from the dress to Camilla and back to the dress again. "Oh, wow!" she said. "That is stunning, what a statement piece." She walked over to the mannequin and reverently regarded it and extended her hand, but drew it back, almost too afraid to touch it.

Before her was the most stunning evening frock she had ever seen. It was a little black dress to end all little black dresses, devastating in its simplicity. It featured a sweetheart bustier that left a woman's arms and neck bare, and the rest of the gown caressed the curves of a woman's torso like a lover's hands. The long full skirt fell from the waist to the toe, with a sensational split up the front revealing a shapely leg. But what set the whole effect off were the black leather kid gloves that traveled up a woman's arms practically to the shoulders, creating the most exotic femme fatale look.

"You should try it on," Camilla urged.

"Oh, I don't know," said Maddie. "Where would I ever wear this?"

"Go on. Every girl needs a dress like this at least once in her life."

The shop owner, wearing cat-eye glasses, immediately replied, "Your friend is right. You would be *deliziosa in questo tubino nero!*"

Camilla added, "Maddie, *non ti preoccupi! Non si può mai sbagliare con un tubino nero! Caspita!* You can *never* go wrong with a little black dress. She's a good friend. You go to her when you don't know what else to wear!"

Without waiting for a response, sensing a sale, the woman removed

of the ribs broke. *"Managgia!"* she exclaimed, and before entering the security line she threw it into the trash.

Inside the crowded museum, the air was humid and the odor of vinyl raincoats and wet leather permeated the main lobby. They stood for a short time in line, waiting to check their bags, and when their turn came, Camilla requested permission to hold on to her sketch pad. Holding it up, she said to Maddie, "I'm going up to the Botticelli room to do some sketching."

"Yes, do!" Maddie encouraged. "I think I'll skip the upper floors and go right to the Baroque section. You can find me later in Artemisia's room. There are lots of handsome cavaliers in there."

"So, you have a fascination for sexy men in paintings, do you?" laughed Camilla. *"Va bene*! I'll catch you later."

As Camilla climbed the wide marble stairs to the upper galleries Maddie moved into the halls on the first floor. She paused now and then to admire her favorite paintings. To her, they were old friends. In front of one especially beguiling portrait, she imagined stepping over the border and back into time to share a glass of wine with the fascinating dark-eyed seventeenth-century charmer.

Continuing, she passed by a Bronzino portrait of Eleonora de' Medici and her daughter Isabella the gallery had recently acquired after it had been discovered hidden away in the little antique shop in Arezzo. The Medici family had an illustrious and complicated familial history, but nonetheless Cosimo, like his famous ancestor Lorenzo, had gone to great lengths to make Florence a mecca of architecture and art, taking under his wing artists like Artemisia who showed tremendous promise.

When Maddie finally came to the gallery where her favorite artist's paintings were located, she stood quietly in front of *Judith and Holofernes*. It never ceased to amaze her how Artemisia skillfully captured the play of light on the blood-spattered sheets as well as the silent scream on Holofernes' face. As if on cue, she felt a rush of wind with a familiar buzzing that filled her ears, and the magic of Florence once again filled her senses. Listening carefully, she thought she could hear urgently whispered words of two women who stealthily worked together.

"Abra, hold him steady so I can plunge the blade in farther."

Massaging her temples, she took a step backward to gain a better perspective. There was a hollowness in her stomach, and she felt light-headed and dizzy. Maddie sank onto a padded bench and, feeling the warmth of the room, she shrugged out of her sweater and relaxed against the wall.

Soon the gallery grew foggy, like the mists that had encircled the bridge earlier, and she crossed into a dreamy netherworld. As if she were watching a scene from the wrong end of a telescope, the picture gallery faded away and was replaced by a small sitting room draped in red velvet curtains. Drifting up from the ballroom below, she could hear the murmuring of voices, glasses tinkling, and the strains of music played on a lute as a woman's voice sang of love, loss, and betrayal.

Focusing her eyes, Maddie saw there were gilded sconces on the wall holding flickering candles and, in a far corner, a large armoire, a washstand, and an elegant gilded screen. Wrinkling her nose, she surmised it hid a commode. Looking over at a marble table, positioned under a mirror, seeing jugs of water and linen towels, it came to her suddenly—oddly, she found herself in a cloakroom where party guests could repair, leave their coats, and take care of nature's call.

She ran her hands over her midriff and realized in wonderment she was dressed in a long gown with a gold satin skirt that cascaded to the floor. She sucked in her breath, made more difficult by the tightly cinched bodice that made her bosom spill out over the low, lacy neckline. Touching a hand to her hair, she was amazed to discover it was intricately coiffed in a complicated twist of braids.

Maddie ceased wondering about her attire when a movement from a dark corner of the chamber caught her attention. Narrowing her eyes, she peered through the shadows, surprised to see a couple lying together on a small divan. Both were in a state of undress, the man's britches around his ankles and the women's skirts hiked up around her waist.

It was quite evident what the couple had been up to, but instead of basking in the afterglow and enjoying the man's kisses, the girl rose and stepped away from his warm body. Adjusting her garment to recover her naked breasts, she reached down and picked up his dagger that lay near his discarded belt. By the way the girl smirked at the man, testing the point with her finger, it appeared she had more cold-blooded things in mind.

The man grunted and flopped over onto his back. By the way his head rolled back on the pillow, Maddie could see he had passed out. Perhaps he imbibed too much wine, or maybe his recent exertions utterly exhausted him. Maddie waited tensely to see what the girl would do next. But instead of causing the man harm, she tiptoed to the door and unlocked it. Then, gesturing to someone waiting in the hallway, she invited them in and turned the key again.

Through the gloom, the scene played out as a woman with dark brown hair dressed in a green gown entered the room carrying an oversized package wrapped in linen and tied in twine. Instantly, Maddie recognized the woman in the emerald gown—it was Artemisia once again.

From her dark corner, she watched the artist lay the parcel on a table, and the girl cut the strings that bound it with the dagger. Maddie inhaled sharply when Artemisia pulled back the protective drape and she saw an all too familiar painting of a woman beheading a man. In feminine intimacy, the two bent their heads together and spoke words that Maddie couldn't fully decipher.

What could these women be up to, she wondered, *in this odd and secluded space, alone with the man and the painting?*

When another groan emanated from the couch, all three women looked over at the man. Silently they followed his movements as he lifted his head as if he intended to rise then, giving up, settled heavily back into the cushions.

"Quick," hissed the girl, handing the woman the dagger. "We must hurry. The draught is temporary. It will only last a quarter hour more."

"Hold the painting steady," the woman urged. Without another word, she plunged it into the canvas. From far away, the female voice continued singing and Artemisia, as if in tune with her, worked quickly to remove the painting from its wooden stretcher.

Finally freed, the young girl loosely rolled it up, as Artemisia held up the dagger and examined it closely. Even from a distance, Maddie could see a T etched on the handle as the blade spotted with red paint glinted in the candlelight.

A pleased smile spread across the artist's face, and she moved to stand over the sleeping man. She regarded him for a moment, then slowly pointed the blade at his throat and rested the tip gently on his Adam's apple. Again, Maddie waited in heightened suspense, but instead of an act of violence, she replaced the weapon into the man's holster, and from across the room her whispered words reached Maddie.

"Seems once again you underestimate the talents of a woman and have chosen the wrong one to ravish tonight. But this time I will make sure you get what you deserve, and you are removed from Florence forever. I believe there is finally enough damning evidence to dishonor your name for good, Agostino."

Not wasting any more time, Artemisia wrapped up the discarded wooden frame in the linen cloth and moved to the locked door. She glanced cautiously around and watched as the girl opened the armoire and slid the rolled-up canvas into the deep pocket of the man's cloak.

When she opened the door a crack, the singer's voice grew louder. With a final quick nod at the girl, Artemisia slipped away and was gone.

Maddie flinched when she heard the click of the door. The man must have heard the noise too, for as the young woman trailed her hand down the side of his jaw and over his neck, he grabbed it and held it tight. Groggily awakening from his slumber, he pulled her roughly down and rolled on top of her, ready to take her again.

As he did, the woman cried out, "Maddie, it's time to go back!"

With a start, she saw Camilla standing over her. Pushing the hair from her face, Maddie asked, "Go back?"

"Yes, they are waiting for us."

"Ah... of course. I'm ready. Just give me a sec."

Maddie picked up her purse and slung it over her shoulder, but as she stood up, she stumbled, her left leg numb from having fallen asleep. She had covered a lot of ground walking through the streets of Florence, and her legs felt tired and unsteady.

Shaking out the pins and needles, she followed Camilla slowly to the exit. But just before leaving the gallery, she hesitated. She pivoted slowly and faced Artemisia's Judith again, but all was quiet; this time, no hushed words were spoken. The woman holding the blade to Holofernes' neck didn't move; she remained for all eternity, frozen in time.

Still, the memory of the strange sequence of events she witnessed remained imprinted on her mind. Like a painting that shows signs of its underpainting seeping through to the surface, Maddie believed she was seeing her past life bleeding into her current reality. How else could she explain all the images that were recently bubbling to the forefront of her brain?

The deja vu and lucid dreams piled up into a confusing array of half-remembered moments in time. Was her subconscious telling her she witnessed Artemisia framing Agostino? In itself, the idea wasn't so far-fetched. Tassi, after escaping prison time in Rome, drifted around Tuscany and eventually took up residence in Florence. According to public record, Cosimo, the ruler of Florence—who greatly favored his protégé Artemisia and did everything in his power to protect her—also sentenced Tassi to two years of hard labor on one of his galley ships for an unspecified crime.

The more Maddie thought about it, the more the idea intrigued her. But, still, it was somewhat puzzling. Why would Artemisia—a trustworthy and honorable woman—decide to frame Tassi? By the time she relocated to Florence, she had married, made a name for herself, and moved in prominent circles. The rape and trial were in her past; she had a daughter she adored, and her future was looking bright.

If Artemisia had something to do with getting Agostino convicted, Maddie wondered what it was that finally pushed her over the edge.

Chapter 9

Uncanny Encounter

*A*fter returning from Florence, the final days of the retreat went smoothly, and all that remained was the "Dear Me" project. Maddie saved this exercise for the end, asking each woman to write a letter to her future self. She told them to communicate their thoughts in any way they liked. It could be a poem or short messages—but each one needed to contain something they learned during the week and something they would take home and continue to work on. She also asked if they'd share them with her before they left.

Happily, they obliged her, and with great interest, she picked up the first one and read: "I've found recovery means being honest. About what I want. What I need. What I feel. Who I am."

Reaching for the next envelope, she pulled out a thin sheet of vellum, and when she did, a small pressed flower fell into her lap. Picking it up, she examined the delicate blossom then scanned the letter that said: "I'm going to buy real flowers for my bedroom. Go for more walks and sing more karaoke."

She smiled and reached for another. In bold letters, she read:

FIVE THINGS TO QUIT

1) Trying to please everyone.

2) Fearing change.

3) Putting myself down.

4) Overthinking.

5) Weighing myself.

Maddie nodded her head after reading item five, thinking she too could benefit from that one.

After going through all the notes, she reached for a small, narrow tube made of Florentine paper, knowing it was Camilla's. Feeling its weight and hearing a rattling sound, she curiously took off the lid. Inside, she found a piece of paper wrapped around a small purse-sized spritz bottle of perfume. It was the fresh fragrance Camilla wore—the one Maddie had complimented her on.

She took a moment to spray some scent on her wrist, then shook out the piece of paper from the tube. When she pressed it out, she realized it wasn't a letter at all; instead, it was a beautiful drawing of Botticelli's *Venus*—the sketch Camilla had made the other day at the museum.

With her finger, Maddie traced the elongated face of the goddess who represented love and rebirth, once again admiring Camilla's talent and appreciating the symbolism. But what moved her, even more, were the words that Camilla had written in a flowing hand using her soft graphite pencil: "*Grazie, Maddie, sarà difficile, ma non impossibile.*"

She believed Camilla now saw a light at the end of the tunnel, having realized that real healing could only be achieved if generated from deep within herself.

On their last morning together, Maddie stood on the front porch of the villa and watched as Roberto loaded luggage into the back of the idling van that would take her group back to Florence to catch their flights home. She, on the other hand, with Camilla's help, had found a place to stay for the rest of the summer in the heart of Montepulciano.

"*È molto carino.* It's a cute little bed and breakfast just off the main piazza," Camilla had told her. "I know the woman—Maria Grazia—who runs the place. She's my mother's friend, really, and she used to babysit me. The town is nice, but there's not so much to do. On the whole, it's pretty quiet. Still, the wine is good and the views are beautiful."

Putting a hand on Maddie's arm, she added, "*Devo avvertirti però*! Just be warned, it *is* a hill town and the streets are quite steep. Great for going down—but going back up is not so easy!"

"Sounds like an ideal place to get away from it all for a while," said Maddie. "All I want to do for the rest of the summer is—well, nothing!

As for those hills—I haven't met a Tuscan town I haven't liked. And for the record, they will be welcomed to get me back into shape—better than any old StairMaster!"

After her arrival, though, Maddie thought she could have eaten her words. Camilla hadn't been joking. By the third day, her calves were seriously challenged from hiking up and down Montepulciano's sharp, vertical inclines. But what made up for the steepness was the town was charmingly quaint and medieval. She soon discovered, from its high perch overlooking the Val d'Orcia, it was an oasis of silence that amplified the sounds of nature, the wind, the birds, and the insects.

Left to her own devices, at first Maddie hibernated like a hermit, sleeping sometimes way past noon. Gradually, however, she acclimated to local rural rhythms and grew accustomed, not only to the sounds and aromas but also the late summer light. Each morning, she welcomed the sun as it rose over the bell tower in the center of town, creating bold shadows and blinding patches of light over the ancient stones. But what she found most satisfying was sitting on the steps of the cathedral every evening, where she could keep an eye on the little boys who played soccer in the cool blue light of the moon.

As the days blended into one another, feeling rejuvenated by the tranquility of the place, she reached out once again to Camilla. Soon they met for coffee in the Piazza Grande or for a glass of wine on the terrace of Lucevan Le Stella, where they watched the big puffy clouds scuttling over plains, extending as far as the eye could see.

During each new encounter, Maddie was pleased to discover her new friend was showing further signs of improvement. The reserved, despondent girl who arrived at her retreat a month and a half before seemed more relaxed and confident. And when Maddie received a message one morning from Camilla, asking if she'd finally like to meet Davide, Maddie felt another significant milestone had been reached.

Not wasting time with a text, Maddie called her back immediately to set a time and place.

"He's spent most of the summer in Florence working," said Camilla.

"But he's down for the weekend, and we will be in Montepulciano tomorrow. I thought it was time to introduce the two of you."

"Can't wait," said Maddie, thrilled to hear the enthusiasm in Camilla's voice.

The next day, Maddie arrived in the main square around the appointed hour, but when she didn't see Camilla, she didn't mind; happily, she settled onto the warm stone steps of the cathedral. She discovered the large open piazza was the town's salon, and she observed with pleasure the couples, young and old, who strolled by. A lot could be learned from discreet people watching, and she found it more engaging than Italian television dramas, often creating made-up scenarios in her head.

Observing with interest young women wearing flowing sundresses and sunglasses carrying shopping bags and hurrying across the square, she waited in anticipation to see how they would greet their partners. Would there be a long, drawn-out kiss, or would the girl give him a distracted frown and then continue to text a friend, indicating they were already past the honeymoon phase? Or would the woman scold the man, ready to carry on a fight?

As she looked around, however, there didn't seem to be much activity. She realized it was probably because of a decisive soccer game being broadcast. As the sun continued to beat down on her, growing uncomfortable, she moved from the portico of the church into the shade of a breezy passageway that flanked the square.

Checking her watch, thinking she might have gotten the time wrong, she fished her phone out of her purse to see if she had any messages. As she did, she became aware of a solitary man standing several yards away. Like her, he too had taken refuge from the heat in the shadows of the seventeenth-century portico.

Her phone now forgotten, Maddie lowered her sunglasses slightly, to get a better view, and noted with interest he was very tall and somewhere in his early thirties. Rapidly, she took in other details, noting his distinctive jawline, the sweep and texture of his hair, his trim physique—and his eyes! They were dark and expressive and immediately conjured up images of Caravaggio's cavaliers.

Nudging her glasses back into place, she continued to study him, admiring the way he casually leaned against the stonewall checking his phone. Even performing such a simple thing, his manner was easygoing and graceful. She knew, instinctively, he too was following the match on his device, by the emotions that played over his expressive face.

Usually, she didn't have such an immediate physical reaction to random men in the street, yet there was something so right about him. What it was exactly, she couldn't put her finger on, and it wasn't just his appearance. No, it went much deeper; it was that old familiarity again, coupled with the unnerving feeling she had met him before.

Nonchalantly, she gazed about to see if anyone else noticed this extraordinary man standing in the shadows next to her. The piazza was filling now, and there were a handful of people passing by, but, apparently, she was the only who had been caught by his charms.

Suddenly, it dawned on her. Of course, this must be Camilla's Davide!

And, as if on cue, Camilla entered the piazza. She wore a large, floppy hat and when he saw her, Davide briskly left the portico and rapidly closed the distance between them. Maddie hung back. She didn't want to intrude upon their meeting, and besides, she was interested in what she might learn by the way the two greeted one another.

Like a well-meaning voyeur, as had become her habit, Maddie watched as the couple met in the middle of the piazza and noted how Davide stood for a moment in front of Camilla as if waiting for her permission before slowly drawing her into his arms. At first hesitant, Camilla looked up into his eyes, then relaxed into his embrace and raised her lips to kiss him tenderly.

Letting the private moment unfold, Maddie stayed hidden inside the loggia, but when a street vendor approached her asking if she'd like to buy a flower, his raised voice caused Camilla and Davide to look in her direction. When they saw her, Camilla whispered something into his ear then motioned for Maddie to join them.

Pleased she had just witnessed yet another milestone in Camilla's recovery, a smile spread over her face as she approached them. Davide, seeing her for the first time, responded in a friendly way by kissing her on both cheeks. It only took a few moments, and a few simple gestures, before the handsome demigod dissolved into a very likable down-to-earth person. Like so many times before, her moonlight fantasies, when examined in the light of day, vanished into thin air.

Indicating an outdoor caffè, Davide invited the women to join him for a drink. Adjusting the chairs on the uneven stones, careful not to wobble the rickety little table, they picked up the drink menus and began a light-hearted conversation. After placing their orders, Maddie noted how Camilla relaxed into the conversation, and her initial opinion of Davide was further confirmed, discovering he had a great sense of humor.

Returning with a tray and three glasses, hearing cries of jubilation issuing from inside the bar, the waiter looked back over his shoulder and exclaimed, "Did you just hear that? Benassi just scored again!"

With a broad smile, Davide agreed. "Fiorentina holds the lead, and there's hardly any time left in the match. Looks like we won, *amico mio!*"

The young man uncorked a bottle of wine and filled their glasses, and the two men lapsed into talk of football stats and Italy's chances for the World Cup. Maddie caught bits and pieces of their animated conversation, but quickly losing interest turned back to Camilla, saying, "I like soccer, but they take it to a whole new level!"

Raising her glass, she said so only Camilla could hear, "It's good to finally meet Davide. I like him." As the two women toasted their glasses, Maddie noticed a glint of gold on her friend's finger. Leaning over, she whispered into Camilla's ear, "I see you are wearing his ring again."

Camilla held out her hand and admired the gold band set with an amethyst. "Yes, I got it out the other day. It's pretty, isn't it?" she said. "I realized I missed it. It's a little loose so I was going to have it..."

When the waiter departed, and Davide turned his full attention back to them, noticing the pause in their conversation and their innocent expressions, he narrowed his eyes and asked, "*Che succede? Mi fischiano le orecchie.* Why do I feel like I'm the topic of discussion here?"

Maddie patted his arm and said, "Don't worry. It's all good."

"*Meno male*! That's a relief," he said, then added, "Sorry about all the soccer talk. It's *la mia passione*." He took a drink of wine and continued. "Camilla tells me you are in the process of transferring to Rome."

"That's right. I'm joining Gaetano Contrada's practice in the fall. Do you know him?"

Davide nodded. "*Sì, certo*. He's an old friend." Looking over at Camilla, he added, "He's been a big help to both of us recently. This thing..."

Camilla picked up her glass and distractedly swirled the ruby red liquid around. Seeing her frown slightly, Davide reached for her hand. "*Ehi, amore, tutto bene*? It's okay."

She nodded and gave his hand a reciprocal light squeeze. The exchange did not go unnoticed by Maddie. If it were at all possible, she found she liked the man even more.

"So, Davide," Maddie said brightly, "Camilla says you are an architect."

"That's right," he replied. "I'm currently working on the Mandini restoration project stabilizing the..."

Maddie became more engaged in Davide's words as he described for her all the headaches he recently encountered while reinforcing colonnades and securing barrel vaults, as well as a few amusing stories about his colleagues—some including his boss. When she asked him about his family, he told her about the Crociani winery and how his father was improving negotiations with American wholesale buyers on the East Coast.

"And what about your mom?"

Before he could reply, Camilla piped in, "Remember, I told you Davide's mother is an art restorer?"

"*Certo*—of course, she was the one who set you both up on your first date?"

"*Sì, mia mamma l'adora!* My mother has always had a soft spot for Camilla," said Davide. "They both have a passion for Caravaggio—maybe more for him than me, as it turns out."

Camilla pushed his arm playfully and said, "Davide's family has some important paintings in their collection, thanks to Patrizia."

"Soccer may be my passion, but art is definitely my mom's first love. Always has been. In fact, that's how she met my dad. After the war, my family had quite a collection of Baroque paintings thanks to a great uncle—also an art collector in Rome. But the family needed money to invest in the winery, so they decided to sell most of them off, a couple to private collectors, others to museums."

"But you kept some of them. Camilla told me your family has some paintings by Artemisia Gentileschi."

"That's right. One is a portrait of a distant Crociani relative, and another is a painting of Bathsheba. *That* one was damaged—not sure how—but when my grandfather met my mom who was working in the Rome gallery at the time, and he discovered she did restoration work, he invited her to the villa to repair it. She ended up staying the rest of the summer to do a full inventory of the family's pictures to prepare them for sale. That's when she met my father."

With a grin, Davide added, "Sometimes we tease her she married him not for his handsome face but because of Artemisia's painting!"

His words made Maddie smile. "That," she said, "is certainly one way to turn a girl's head. Sure, a girl likes to be courted and kissed and promised the moon. But offer her the family's art collection—that's a surefire way to seal the deal!"

"*Boh!*" he said. "Apparently things worked out all right—they are about to celebrate their sixtieth wedding anniversary. In a way, it was Artemisia's painting that brought them together. After that, he didn't want to sell the painting."

"Sounds like he is a romantic through and through."

Davide picked up Camilla's hand and kissed it. "Well you know what they say, or at least what my dad says, 'The Crociani men are known for loving very deeply—until the end of time."

"You should meet his dad, Franco," Camilla said. "All the Crociani men are charmers like this one. I believe Davide learned some of his best lines from his father. You should have heard him on our first date..."

She stopped and placed her hand on his arm. "Hey, Davide, I have got a wonderful idea! I think we should ask Maddie to join us this weekend for your parents' anniversary party. Then she could see for herself what your dad is like and what a character he is."

Without hesitation, he agreed, "Yes, you should definitely come. We'd love to have you, Maddie! It's going to be quite a big affair. There will be a lot of wine and food dinner and dancing. My sister, Martina, is planning the whole thing, and everyone in the area is invited. People are coming from Florence and Venice, and my older brother is coming up from Rome."

"You have a brother, and he lives in Rome?" asked Maddie, thinking there might be hope for her after all.

Clinking her wine glass with Camilla's again, Maddie said, "And wouldn't you know it, thanks to you, I just happen to have the perfect thing to wear. My little black dress. I accept your invitation!"

Where in the Universe is Matteo?

*I*n anticipation of the anniversary party, Maddie carefully unpacked her *tubino nero*, removed it from the layers of protective tissue paper, and laid it out on the bed. She considered it for a moment and hoped the outfit wasn't too over the top and that she wouldn't be overdressed.

But on the night of the party, after having driven herself to the Crociani Estate, her fears quickly abated. For when she crossed the threshold making her grand entrance and heads swiveled in her direction, her worries, she realized had been unfounded. As she basked in all the appreciative glances, her keen eye took in the elegant foyer with its glistening chandeliers high overhead and the glossy marble floor below her. She stood for a moment, in her impossibly high heels, enjoying the sensation of empowerment a well-designed dress that molded to her slender curves gave her.

Circulating around her were women in multi-colored cocktail frocks and complimenting them were their partners dressed in black and white formal wear. The contrast between silk ties and glittery diamonds made Maddie think of a 1930s movie. At any moment, she half expected the likes of Greta Garbo to cross her path. The Hollywood diva, seeing Maddie's gown, would take a puff on her cigarette secured in a long elegant holder. Blowing a stream of blue smoke high into the air, she'd raise an eyebrow in envious approval.

Hearing her name, Maddie looked around and was happy to see Camilla and Davide approaching. The couple appeared splendid together and Camilla was especially lovely in the vintage blue dress she had selected in the shop in Florence.

"Maddie! *Caspita! Sei bellissima.* In that gown you are simply sensational! Aren't you glad I convinced you to buy it?"

"I have to admit, I *am* feeling pretty posh," said Maddie. "If this is what it's like to be a star of the silver screen in the 1930s, well, Katharine Hepburn, move over! I sure could get used to this."

"Come on, let's get you a glass of prosecco."

Maddie joined them, and as they made their way to a fountain from which cascaded champagne, they introduced her to several of their friends and neighbors. The mood in the room was light and jovial, and floating around her was the hum of chatter and the occasional trill of laughter. Still, there were always those who stood out in such a pleasant crowd. Out of the corner of her eye, Maddie couldn't help but notice a small group was caught up in a heated debate. Hearing the names Boldrini and Salvini, she knew they could only be discussing the vagaries of Italian politics.

When the threesome came to a table filled with silver trays full of antipasti, Davide introduced her to his cousin Vittorio and his wife, Lizabetta, who were helping themselves to olive pastry puffs. Learning Maddie was a newcomer from New York, they politely made conversation, inquiring about her work and how she knew the Crociani family.

"And why is it *all* you Americans want to move here to Italy?" asked Vittorio in a way that made her feel she was being dumped into the category of wide-eyed optimists who only ate McDonald's.

"Oh, come now, Vittorio," Davide said. "Isn't it the other way around? The Italians want to go to America—to California—to find better jobs."

With a tilt of her head, Maddie interjected, "I guess we are all searching for something that is missing in our lives. You know what they say, the grass is always greener on the other side."

"You speak Italian beautifully," said Vittorio's wife in a complimentary tone. "What makes you so interested in our language and our country?"

Maddie thought back to the moment in college when she had visited the carnival mystic. She was about to open her mouth and explain but then thought better of it. She didn't think it would go over well if she revealed her real reason for her obsession with Italy—that a voice she had heard during a séance had encouraged her to do so. Instead, Maddie told the woman a more believable truth—that she had taken up Italian after meeting a handsome stranger.

This Lizabetta readily accepted, of course, immediately wanting to know more about the man and the circumstances. To avoid further discussion, she took a sip of prosecco and obliquely said, "A lady never kisses and tells."

Feeling Camilla touch her elbow, indicating Davide's parents standing a short distance away, Maddie gracefully excused herself from the conversation and crossed the room with them to greet the anniversary couple. Leaning in, she let Signora Crociani kiss her on both of her cheeks and then accepted the light embrace of her husband. After the initial round of pleasantries concluded, Maddie found herself warming to the elder Crociani, noting the distinctive family features in Davide's father that still in a seventy-six-year-old man were quite debonair.

As the cocktail hour flowed on and the music from a jazz quartette drifted through the airy salon, she watched a woman in a frothy hot pink gown embroidered with black roses flit amongst the guests. While keeping an eye on the buffet table, like an efficient pixie, she effervescently chatted with a woman here, a man there, and gave instructions to the wait-staff.

Maddie thought she was probably somewhere in her late thirties, close to her own age. She had dark hair that was short in a bob, which dramatically framed her face and accentuated her almond-shaped eyes. And when she smiled, it lit up her face and Maddie sensed, even from across the room, she was a force of nature. The familial resemblance was far too apparent, and Maddie quickly surmised that this was Martina, Davide's older sister.

Her assumption was proven correct when the young woman breezed up to Davide, kissed him on both cheeks, and said, "*Tutto bene*? Everything okay, *fratellino*? What do you think?"

Towering above her, Davide put his arm around his sister and said,

"Martina, relax! Everything is going fine. Just like you manage things in the winery, you've done a great job here tonight. Look around you! Everyone is enjoying themselves." Waving his glass in the direction of their parents, who were talking to another couple, he added, "And see over there? Mamma and papa—they couldn't be happier."

"Well, I guess... The *maledetta* cake didn't show up when it was supposed to and this afternoon, I got a little panicky. But, after I called Antonella at the *panetteria*, she said she'd make sure it got here on time. Have you seen it in the kitchen?"

"*Sì*. I might have even tasted it," said Davide. He winced in mock pain when she pinched him on the arm.

"*Va bene! Hai ragione.* You are right. I'm ready for that drink now." As a waiter passed by, she plucked a glass off his silver tray and took a long sip. As she did, she craned her neck to get a better glimpse of the packed room. "It seems like almost all the guests are here except..."

She paused suddenly, noticing Maddie. "*Oh, Mio Dio! Mi scusi! Che figuraccia!* I didn't mean to be rude! I'm Martina Crociani, and you must be Maddie. Camilla and Davide were telling me about you earlier. I'm sorry I didn't introduce myself sooner." Raising her glass to her, she added, "But I did see you make an entrance earlier! I must say that dress you are wearing is a knock-out. It's from that vintage store in Florence, right?"

Martina held out her arms so they could get a better look at what she was wearing. "That's where I got mine too. I've always loved shocking pink." Skimming her eyes over Maddie's dress, she added, "But, if I'd seen what you have on first, I'd have snatched it up. Then again, you can pull the whole thing off much better than I because you are so much taller."

"It's mainly because of the shoes," Maddie said with a laugh.

Martina pulled up the hem of her long fuschia skirt, revealing her foot encased in a spiky heel and lamented, "I'm wearing the highest heels I could find, and I'm still short!"

Looking more closely at Maddie, she pondered, "Something about you seems so familiar. I just can't put my finger on..."

Franco, just a few steps away, leaned in and said, "It looks familiar because, in that dress, Maddie is the spitting image of the Duchess."

"Of course! It was going to drive me mad all night trying to remember where I'd seen such a dress before. My dad is right. In that gown, you could be her twin."

"The Duchess?" said Maddie. "Who was she?"

"She is a part of this family's lore," said Franco, stepping into their conversation. "This family is a little unusual. Let's just say we have a long history and many characters are hanging, some quite literally, from our family tree. But, in answer to your question, the Duchess was the fiancé of one of my great uncles. His name was Matteo Crociani. They were quite an item and were together for over five years..."

"Oh, come on, Dad, no need to go boring Maddie with unnecessary family trivia," said Martina with a pleading sigh.

"Wait, you said his name was Matteo Crociani?" Maddie asked. "I've heard that name before."

"He was an art dealer backing in the '30s. Famous, really," said Patrizia, coming to stand by her husband.

"So, this Italian Duchess, she was engaged to your great uncle? What happened to her? Did they ever marry?"

"Oh, she wasn't a duchess, really," said Franco. "She wasn't even Italian. She was French. Her aunt was the famous Parisian dress designer. They just called her that because she was so headstrong and..."

"That's my dad's nice way of saying she was kind of bossy!" Martina said in a stage whisper.

"Just like you, *figlia mia*!" said Franco, narrowing an eye at his daughter.

"Go on, Signor Crociani," encouraged Maddie.

Seeing her interest was genuine, he continued, "When she arrived in Rome and opened up her shops, she ruffled a lot of feathers and upended the fashion scene. Her designs were bold and modern, just like the dress you are wearing now. They say she could have been quite famous, rivaling Chanel. That's why they called her the Duchess of Design."

"Duchess of Design? I do like the sound of that. Perhaps I'll borrow the title for the night," said Maddie.

Franco appeared amused by her comment. "From what I know, she was a force to be contended with. Both she and Matteo ran in an artistic crowd. But I'm sorry to say their love affair did not end well. It was really quite sad."

"Why?" asked Maddie.

"There was a tragedy one spring night... The date sticks with me because it happened on May 2, 1939, the night of the Pact of Steel— *il patto d' Acciaio*—the day Germany and Italy cemented their military allegiance. A double tragedy, in my opinion."

"That sounds rather ominous. What happened?"

"That night, there was a botched burglary and Matteo was shot in the chest."

Maddie, having swallowed her wine a little too quickly, coughed. "Excuse me, did you say he was *shot* in the chest?"

"Yes, according to things I've heard over the years. But I of course, was much too young to remember him."

"And the Duchess? What happened to her?"

"After Matteo's death, she was heartbroken," said Franco. "With the start of the war, it wasn't safe for her to remain in Italy, so she went back to Paris. She left everything behind—her business, even her portrait..."

"Painted by Ettore Tito, I might add," said Patrizia. "It's stunning, actually. Some of his best work."

"Yes, we were just discussing that, *cara*, how Maddie's dress resembles the one the Duchess wears in her portrait."

No longer interested in the portrait, or the dress, only what happened to the Duchess, Maddie asked with concern, "If she went home to Paris during the war, what happened to her? Where is the Duchess now?"

"She died during the Nazi occupation of the city. Over the past couple of years, it's been my hobby to piece together our family history, and I've read the letters she sent to my grandmother. The Duchess had a particular fondness for the *la Signora* and kept in touch with the family through her. After returning to Paris, to overcome her grief, she threw herself into volunteering and worked with the Red Cross. She used it as a cover to hide children from the Nazis during the roundup in the Jewish quarter. Still, so many were captured and sent to the camps... After '42, unfortunately, there was no more word of her."

"Nothing at all?

Franco shook his head. "Communication just stopped. One can only assume the worse. My grandmother used to say the Duchess was quite outspoken in her criticism of the fascist government. She wasn't one to back down from a good fight."

Franco took a sip of his wine, then added, "There is a good story *nonna* used to tell, about the night she met Mussolini and tangoed with him at a high society ball."

"The Duchess actually danced with the dictator?"

"I bet she gave him a run for his money," said Martina. "She probably had to dodge his roving hands too."

"In those days, it certainly didn't bode well for anyone who angered Mussolini," said Franco. "Those were dark and dangerous times."

"*Ehi!* If he had tried something with me, I certainly wouldn't have kept quiet about it."

Maddie, liking Martina, more by the minute, added, "Perhaps she finally stepped over the line with Il Duce, and that's the reason she had to get out of Rome so fast, after Matteo's death."

Davide looked at his mother, Martina, Camilla, and Maddie, who stood shoulder to shoulder in their vintage designer dresses and grinned. "If Mussolini could see you all now, I think he'd turn on his heels and run for the door!"

"*Sì! Siete tutte belle donne indipendente,*" said Franco. "The Crociani men seem to be attracted to beautiful, independent women. Maddie, you fit right in."

Camilla leaned over to Maddie and said, "Didn't I tell you Signor Crociani was quite the flatterer?"

"My father tells these stories to anyone who will listen and needs a new ear to bend," added Davide a little apologetically. "Perhaps you would have rethought our invitation..."

Maddie laughed. "Oh, I don't mind. A girl could use a compliment now and then. Plus, I think your family's history is quite fascinating. But, really, I don't see how anything could top being shot in the chest during a robbery."

"How about an ancestor who was convicted of heresy?" said Franco.

"Heresy?" Maddie questioned.

"*Mamma mia!* Here we go again," wailed Martina. "This is his favorite story of all to tell."

Ignoring his daughter, Franco said, "Matteo Alessandro Crociani was one of Galileo's protégées."

"Another Crociani named Matteo?" Maddie asked.

"In almost every generation of the Crociani family, the oldest boy has been named Matteo," Martina replied.

"That's right," said Franco. "*This* particular Matteo—the one from the seventeenth century—was fascinated with astrology. He helped Galileo..."

"*Dai! Ti prego*! Enough!"

She checked her watch. "*Basta!* It's getting late and it's time to go into dinner. You can tell Maddie the story later..."

Franco, who was just warming to the subject, seemed a little put out. "But your brother isn't here yet. There is still time..."

"You are right—where in the world *is* Matteo?" Martina said. She looked around the room, then shook her head in disbelief. "We've been waiting hours for him to show up. He promised me he'd be here by now!"

"Wait a minute..." interrupted Maddie, putting two and two together. "Of course! Your older brother is also named Matteo, right?"

Martina nodded and, when she saw her mother give her the eye and nod in the direction of the dining room, she said, "*Boh!* I don't know where he is—but, we can't wait any longer. Even mamma thinks it's time to move the guests into the dining room, and the caterers are..."

"*Aspetta!* Hold on," said Davide, punching a speed dial button on his phone. Martina appeared hopeful at first, but her expression turned to impatient displeasure when he finally said, "Sorry, he's not picking up."

"*Uffa! Che noia!*" declared Martina, "There's not much more we can do. The man is a workaholic. His job always comes first—Matteo can barely keep his feet on the ground. He is always somewhere else, floating around in the universe."

"What does your Matteo do?" asked Maddie.

"He's one of the lead scientists for Project Juno," said Davide.

"Project Juno? You mean he works on the space probe that has been sent to Jupiter?"

"*Sì*, Matteo coordinates the communications systems," said Franco proudly. "From a very early age, he was interested in astronomy."

Less impressed, Martina added, "Yep! That's Matteo. Even when he was little, he always had his head in the clouds—or rather lost in the stars. He used to run around wearing this silly red cape and pretended he was a space invader. He was always trying to figure out a way to travel forward and backward in time, or reach another universe."

"He would babble on and on about entangled particle phones," agreed Davide, "and how he was inventing a device that operated without radio waves so that you could talk to people in the future and the past. Kind of like being in the two places at once. Too bad for him his tin-can theories never quite worked out."

"And too bad for him he can't be here tonight!" Martina added in annoyance. "Because there is going to be hell to pay when he sees me tomorrow. He's missing my..." She glanced quickly over at her father and said, "I mean your fantastic party."

"*Tin-can communicator*, eh?" Maddie said as memories of her child fantasies of breaking past Earth's temporal barriers came to mind. "I like the sound of that. I think I'm going to like this brother of yours. Who knows, if we compare notes, perhaps we can figure out this whole space-time continuum thing together."

Chapter 11

The Rogues' Gallery

*F*ollowing Camilla and Davide into the dining room, Maddie found herself seated at a table in the back of the room filled with other odd-man-out acquaintances and distant relations. Still, she enjoyed their conversation as well as the deliciously prepared anniversary dinner that consisted of four courses, a dessert buffet, and the large cream-filled cake that had caused Martina so much concern.

By the end of it all, Maddie's dress felt a little tight, and she was more than ready to get out of her chair, pull up her bustier, shake out her long skirts, and reunite with her friends. Yet, she knew she must remain politely seated throughout the long round of toasts as various guests stood up and saluted the couple of the hour with long-winded speeches and good-natured jokes.

During the last few courses of the meal, the jazz quartet relocated to the patio just off the main salon, and now strains of a romantic salsa drifted in through the open window. Franco thanked his guests one last time then, taking the hand of his wife, he drew her out of her seat and invited the guests to join them for dancing on the terrace.

Needing no further encouragement, Maddie, along with her dinner partners, wandered out onto the patio that was illuminated with small votive candles. When she felt a light tap on her shoulder, she accepted an invitation to dance with the man who had sat next to her at dinner. Held lightly in his arms, they circled the moonlit patio.

She danced on for another hour, smiling at her various suitors, but still found herself glancing over their shoulders hoping she might catch a glimpse of the missing Crociani sibling. But, sadly, she had yet to feel her heart flutter at the sight of a tall man with dark hair that resembled his father or his brother. It seemed he was a no-show.

Resigned to her lackluster love life, as the last of the candles sputtered out, Maddie checked her wristwatch and realized the hour was getting late. So, as not to get lost on the back roads between there and Montepulciano, or suffer an encounter with one of the many *cinghiali*— the roving forest pigs the Tuscan countryside was inundated with—she decided it was time for her to take her leave.

Maddie scanned the crowd and spied Davide and Camilla sitting on a stone ledge at the far side of the garden. In the shadows, undetected, she thought how comfortable Camilla appeared resting her head on his shoulder. When Davide caressed her cheek and tilted her face upward, she also noticed Camilla accepted his kiss without hesitation. Not wanting to spoil what was developing into an intimate moment, she left them alone.

After saying good night to a few guests still mingling in the garden, Maddie entered the house in search of Davide's sister wanting to thank her and exchange email addresses.

When Martina saw her approaching, her eyes lit up. "There you are! I was just coming to find you. My duties as party hostess are officially over. Come on! Let me introduce you to the *rest* of the family!"

Maddie looked around the room expectantly. "So, did Matteo arrive? Has he come back to Earth?"

"Sorry, I'm afraid he's still lost in space—still adrift somewhere around the moons of Jupiter."

Taking her arm, she added, "No, I'm talking about the rest of our illustrious clan. Remember earlier? You seemed so interested in my dad's stories about the Duchess, I'd like for you to meet her. We'll start by comparing dresses. Let's see who wore the gown best!"

"I'd love that. Looking forward to meeting her!" In a challenging tone, she added, "May the best woman win!"

Martina grinned and directed her toward the stairs that lead to the upper gallery. "After you two have become acquainted, then I will introduce you to the other rogues still hanging around on our walls! If you believe my dad's stories, this family is chock full of intrigue—filled with blackguards, heretics, rebels and *partigiani* that go all the way back to the 1500s. Seems it is in the Crociani blood to be a rule breaker."

"Sounds like quite an impressive lot. Please—lead on!"

Together they climbed the wide marble stairs to the second floor, and with each step, Maddie took special care not to trip on the full skirt of her evening gown. When they reached the second floor, she followed in the wake of her new friend down a long hallway lined with doors.

At the end, Martina paused for dramatic effect, and with a flourish of her hand said, "Here we are in front of the Crociani's original Facebook." Pushing open the door, she added, "Cross over this threshold if you dare! But beware! When you do, you take a step back in time. *Sei pronta?*"

Maddie tilted her head theatrically. "Well, I don't know? When you put it like that, it sounds a little daunting. Should I take the leap?"

"Of course, you should!" Martina said, grabbing her arm and pulling her into the room. "Don't be shy. Despite their colorful characters at heart they are all gentlemen and ladies."

Maddie laughed and let Martina guide her to a full-length portrait of a woman displayed in an elaborate gold frame wearing an all too familiar dress. Besides her attire, she could tell by the modernity of the brushwork the painting had been done in the early part of the twentieth century.

But, even for the 1930s, it was an unusual portrait—*probably much like the Duchess herself,* Maddie thought. For the woman stood tall and proud, her neck and the creamy breadth of her shoulders fully illuminated, but her face was turned slightly away from the viewer, revealing a striking profile, but the rest of her face was hidden in shadow. And, although you couldn't see her expression, the manner in which the Duchess angled her head and the elegant line of her profile implied volumes about her personality.

For Martina's benefit, Maddie stepped in front of the painting and, looking over her shoulder, attempted to mimic the Duchess' elegant pose. Martina scrutinized them both, then said, "*È vero! Babbo* was right! The gown you are wearing is almost identical."

More curious than ever about the Duchess, Maddie practically willed the woman in the painting to turn around so she could see her face better. Moving a bit closer, she said, "The artist did a lovely job of capturing her. I just wish I could see her eyes."

After a moment, she asked, "What else do you know about her? Where exactly did she meet Matteo Crociani?"

"Somewhere in Rome near the Spanish steps, I think... Or was it Castel Sant'Angelo? I don't really know. I should ask my father. Anyway, her shop was in Via del Corso, so somewhere around there, I suppose. Great uncle Matteo had a stylish apartment—in the Aventine Hills near the Tiber River. Apparently, they ran in a fast crowd and attended gala affairs. Even hung out with movie stars from Cinecittà and Hollywood."

"That's intriguing, very Great Gatsbyish," said Maddie. "Can you imagine what the city must have been like then? I mean, with all the streetcars, the roadsters, and Bugattis, as well as Mussolini's infamous rallies? The '30s was such a different era, right before the war broke out."

"It was a glittering, *bel epoch*, the last of real refinement and elegance. Those people knew how to throw a party. I'm pretty sure tonight's little soiree pales in comparison."

"Oh, I don't know. You did an amazing job! Everything was very classy—very tastefully put together."

"*Grazie*," said Martina. With an exaggerated groan of exhaustion, she flopped down into a nearby chair and, as she did, her hot-pink gown billowed up around her. She kicked off her shoes and said, "*Accidenti*! These heels really are to die for—and now they *are* actually killing me! Tomorrow I'll be back to jeans and a t-shirt working in the winery. I'd love to give you a tour if you..."

Before she could finish her sentence, Davide poked his head through the door. In one hand, he carried a bottle of prosecco and two narrow glass flutes and with the other he held Camilla's. "I brought reinforcements," he said with a devilish grin. "Dad saw you two come up here and we thought you might like another drink."

"Why thank you, kind sir," said Martina. "I guess little brothers are good for something after all."

"At least *little* brothers show up for your party!" Davide said. "Who's your favorite now?"

"*Hai ragione*," said Martina. "I'm going to have a long talk with Matteo tomorrow."

"Don't be too hard on him, Martina," said Camilla. "I'm sure he was trying his best to be here. Anyway, we wanted to say good night too. Davide is driving me home."

Leaning over to kiss Maddie on the cheek, she whispered, "I don't know if it is the wine, the moon, or the dress, but tonight I'm feeling in a good place. Who knows what will happen…"

"It's up to you, Camilla. You are the one who chose the dress. This is your night and your decision. Go. Have fun. You deserve it."

After the couple left, Maddie said to Martina, "Looks like it's just you and me, kid. I think this could be the beginning of a long and beautiful friendship."

Raising her glass, Martina agreed. She sat for a moment fully enjoying herself for the first time that evening, savoring the sparkling wine Davide had brought them. "You know, that little brother of mine is really very thoughtful. Camilla is lucky to have him."

"It's nice to be reminded there are some wonderful men out there. I knew it the moment I first met him," agreed Maddie. "And your father! He really is quite a charmer."

Martina laughed, "I agree. There are definitely good men out there. But, regardless, after all these years of dating, I've concluded a woman will always be my best friend. We need each other in ways that men don't, and women friends get things without much explanation."

She took another sip of wine. "And let's face it, a best friend is someone who goes to get their nails done with you."

"That or goes shopping with you for vintage dresses," Maddie said, showing off her fingers tipped in red. Martina held up her own exquisitely manicured nails painted black with little pink roses.

"Don't get me wrong," Martina said. "I adore men. But I don't want a man just to guarantee I have a roof over my head or to fix a washing machine—I'm perfectly capable of doing that on my own. But..."

"But..." Maddie prompted.

"*Boh!* I'm a romantic at heart," Martina said, as she sank deeper into the cushion, massaging her foot, "so that might all change *if* and *when* I meet someone who can convince me otherwise."

The bubbles were going to Maddie's head and, remembering the old days and her conversations with Claire, she said, "Do you want to hear something crazy? I used to think there was someone out there who loved me so much that we were traveling through time together, and that we were destined to meet over and over again. And then, when we met and our eyes connected, he would seem like an old friend, and we would remember."

Eyeing Martina she quickly added, "Yeah, I know. Pretty out there, right? Mission Control to Maddie. You've broken your tether—last seen drifting toward the moon."

Martina shook her head. "No, I wasn't thinking that at all. In fact, I think it is quite romantic to believe that love reincarnates. Wouldn't that be the most incredible thing if it were true?"

Maddie leaned her head back and studied the room's frescoed ceiling decorated with plump cherubs frolicking amongst the clouds. "I've always loved all the old romantic movies with Bogart, Bergman, Gable, and Bacall. Those couples were timeless."

Martina eyed her inquisitively as she poured them more wine. "Sounds like you haven't met the one to convince you either."

"Not yet, but I have a feeling that he's out there."

"It's hard to believe you haven't met him yet. With that gorgeous figure—I'd kill for by the way—I'd think you would have slain someone's heart by now, and don't think I didn't notice all the men lining up to tango with you tonight."

"Oh, there have been a few..." Maddie began. Then, with a dismissive wave of her hand, she added, "But, in the end, nothing really felt right. Anyway, who has time for all that? This past year has been a roller coaster ride. I've upended my life and moved to Rome. I need to stay focused on my career."

Absently, she rolled the champagne flute around in her hands. "But I'm here in Italy now. Who knows what will happen? Or, maybe I just need to wait and come back in another lifetime to find the right guy."

Putting her hand to her forehead for dramatic effect, she mockingly intoned, "Oh, cruel Fate, when wilt thou weary be? When satisfied with tormenting me?"

Martina rolled her eyes and gestured with her wine glass, indicating the far wall behind Maddie. "*Ehi!* If you want a cute guy right now, I've got just the one for you! He is a very mature man—nearly four hundred years older than you."

With a raised eyebrow, Maddie peeked over her shoulder. Behind her, she saw another life-sized painting. She got out of her chair and crossed the gallery to study the fine figure of a man, noting his proud stance and how he rested his hand on his hip in a confident contra-posto pose. His eyes and the shape of his mouth were so vivid and expressive, Maddie thought it could almost have been a portrait of a modern-day man.

Still seated on the divan with her feet propped up on some pillows, Martina said, "Next to him is the painting of Bathsheba. They were both painted by Artemisia Gentileschi—our family's claim to fame."

"Camilla told me your mother restored this one," Maddie said, pointing to the one on the left. Leaning in closer to see the brushwork better, she added, "Patrizia did a great job. I can't even see where she made her repairs."

"*Mia mamma*, she worked very hard to restore it."

"It shows," said Maddie, impressed. After a minute, she returned her attention to Artemisia's portrait of the man. "I definitely see the family resemblance in this one's face. Your ancestor reminds me a lot of Davide."

Maddie reached out with her finger, and without actually touching the canvas, traced his jawline. "See? Right there—and there, around the eyes and cheekbones."

She shook her head in amazement. "Art has such a timelessness about it, you know? People meet, marry, carry on their lives, repeating the pattern. They paint pictures and they make scientific discoveries and the years flow by. Yet, here is tangible proof that a life was lived, a man existed. Viewing old paintings like this one is like stepping into the past, kind of like receiving a message in a bottle."

Over her shoulder, she added, "It isn't fair these Crociani men have cornered the market on good looks. I think I've developed a new crush. Too bad for me. It seems I am destined to be attracted to unattainable men—like five-hundred year old men stuck in paintings."

She eyed the man again but stopped abruptly with her wine glass raised halfway to her lips. She hadn't noticed it before, but now it appeared a smile played over his lips—almost as if what she said amused him immensely.

Craning her neck to see better, Martina said, "You're right, he does look a little like David. But wait until you meet Matteo. Now he really is the spitting image of my handsome ancestor."

"Really?" said Maddie. "Hmm... I was hoping to meet him this evening. I find it fascinating that Matteo is working on Project Juno. I have so many questions for him about the shuttle launch. As much as I'm a sucker for the past, I also wonder what the future holds."

Taking a sip of her wine, she added, "I sometimes feel sad, you know, that I will never know what the world will be like in a hundred years. Just think, if we have iPhones today—how will we be communicating in the future? What new things will there be—new art, new books, new inventions...?"

She sighed. "I don't want to miss out on that. If only we could peek ahead to see all the new worlds that will someday be discovered."

"You sound just like Matteo," said Martina. "He says stuff like that too."

Using her best *Star Trek* imitation, she said, "He's always on a *continuing mission to explore strange new worlds, to seek out new life and new civilizations, to boldly go where no one has gone before.*"

Martina smiled at her. "You guys are two peas in a pod... *Ehi!*" Sitting upright, suddenly serious, she said, "I've got a great idea. You're moving to Rome, right?"

"Yes," Maddie said, already knowing where this was going. "Are you planning on setting us up?"

"If you'd be up for it, you'd certainly have a lot to talk about."

Unable to look away from the man in the painting, Maddie said after a moment, "Well, if your older brother is anything like *this* guy here, I wouldn't mind grabbing a drink with him. If he can tear himself away from the stars and *actually* show up."

Gesturing back to the painting in front of her, she said, "Seems at this moment this is the only dateable Crociani." Looking back at Martina, she said with a laugh, "So, tell me more about this charmer here. Is he available?"

"Let's see..." Martina said. "He's one of the original Matteos of the family. Remember my dad talking about Galileo? They were the mad-gazing heretical scientists, crazy about the moon and the stars. Oh, and telescopes. I think he had a hand in helping Galileo do something or other, to improve it."

With wicked grin, Maddie looked over at her and said, "Well, I'd certainly have no qualms checking out this man's telescope, if you know what I mean, even if he were a bit of a rogue and a heretic!"

Martina let out a shriek of laughter. "Why, Maddie! Behave yourself! I probably shouldn't have gotten your hopes up. Handsome as he is, sadly he is married and not available for dating. He fell head over heels in love with a woman he met in Venice. Her name was Maddalena-Raffaella, and get this—she was a courtesan."

"She was a prostitute?"

"No, courtesan, not prostitute. There's a big difference. If you really want to know, she was *cortigiana onesta*," said Martina.

"An honest prostitute? That's refreshing. Aren't they all?" said Maddie with a grin.

"In Venice, in those days, there were lots of categories of prostitutes, and the *cortigiana onesta* were the educated and worldly women—independently wealthy despite not having husbands—known for their wit and personality."

"An independent woman in Venice? With her own money?"

"Yes, the courtesans were able to live on their own because they were supported by the Doge. He called upon them to appear at court to entertain him and..."

Maddie raised her eyebrow and Martina said in amusement, "Get your mind out of the gutter. Sex was just a small part of their—*ahem*—services. Let's put it this way, women like Maddalena were more esteemed. As I was saying, they were called upon to play their lutes, sing songs, and recite..."

With a smirk, Maddie said, "I guarantee she didn't just strum her lute and recite poetry for this guy!"

A little reluctantly, she bid *arrivederci* to the man in the painting and continued around the room, admiring the other pictures in the family's rogue gallery. When she reached the opposite end, she stopped in front of the large bay window where an antique telescope was set up. Over her shoulder, she asked, "May I?"

"Go ahead. My father won't mind. Just be careful. The brass ring attached to the eyepiece is a little loose. It falls off sometimes."

Maddie stooped down and fiddled with the attachments, trying to focus the lens.

"In addition to his obsession with Crociani family history, my dad is quite the closet astronomer. I think Matteo is living his dream working at the *Osservatorio Astronomico* in Rome. Together they are always dabbling around up here with his charts and maps of the stars..."

She paused when Franco entered the room.

"There you girls are! Your mother is saying goodbye to the last of the guests. Martina, it was a wonderful party. Thank you *mia cara*. But now we are going to bed."

Leaning over, he kissed his daughter on the cheek and then turned to say good night to Maddie. When he saw her standing by the telescope, his face lit with delight. *"Ah! Bene! Ti piace astronomia, Maddie?"*

"Oh, a little I guess. I love to see the moon in all its various phases, but I'm not much of an expert. I used to play at it when I was a little girl. Martina was just telling me about the Crociani men and their telescopes..."

When Martina let out a snort of laughter, Maddie shot her a warning look. Then, with considerable effort, she said with a straight face, "But this telescope—this one is really quite beautiful. Does it still work? I was just trying to see..."

"It's a little tricky. Here, let me help you bring it into focus," he said as he bent over to peer through the eyepiece. After rotating a couple of the dials, he invited her to try again.

This time, when Maddie peered through the lens, it seemed a new world had opened to her. "Oh. Wow! Now that's a view! The planets are so clear and close! It seems like I can practically touch them."

"Beginning tonight—in just a couple of hours," he said, checking his watch, "we are in for a celestial treat. The planets and stars are aligning in new patterns. There is about to be a meeting between Mercury and Mars, and there will be an excellent view of Neptune. The distant ice giant reaches its opposition this month."

"Okay, I'm lost. What does that mean?"

"Due to an optical illusion, it will appear as if the planet is circling backward and, for a few nights, it will seem brighter and bigger to our eyes than at any other time of the year."

As Maddie looked back up into the heavens through the telescope, she felt a sudden sense of staggering awe. In the grander scheme of things, she was but a mere speck on a small dot of a tiny planet spinning through complex systems of the celestial nebula.

For the second time that evening, she was humbled by the sheer immensity of time—the past and the future. There were so many things she couldn't comprehend. But tonight, as the planets drew nearer, disrupting their regular patterns, appearing to move backward in time, the idea of past lives blurring and merging didn't seem incomprehensible or far-fetched. It even seemed there was science to support it.

"*Allora*, my dears, it is getting rather late," said Signor Crociani.

"Thank you again for inviting me tonight," Maddie said, giving him a warm hug. "I've enjoyed the evening immensely." She gestured to the portraits and added, "Your daughter has done you proud. She's been telling me more about your family's history."

"*Davvero*? My Martina? Are you sure we are talking about the same girl? My independent daughter who refuses to marry, settle down, and start a family of her own?"

Maddie smiled. "Oh, you'd be impressed with how much she remembers. And I wouldn't be surprised if one day she didn't present you with a new heir to the Crociani throne."

Martina rolled her eyes, deigning not to say anything more, and took a sip of her wine.

"So, she has been paying attention, after all," he said with a chuckle. To Maddie, he added, "It pleases me. After all, family is very important here in Italy. The past is always around us." Gesturing to the portraits that lined the wall, he added, "And here, in this room especially, it doesn't take much to slip back in time."

He kissed her lightly on the cheek and added, "There is no need to rush home, Maddie *mia cara*. Stay with us a while longer and enjoy your time with the Crociani family."

Chapter 12

Into the Brink

Maddie and Martina took turns peering through the telescope, observing the last of the party guests as they departed. They pointed it at the red taillights of the cars and watched them roll down the rocky lane like flickering fireflies. Not quite ready to part company themselves, they relaxed into the late-night cadence, enjoying the feeling of being the only ones still awake as the halls grew quiet and the house settled around them.

At one point, Martina, holding up the bottle of wine and shaking it, said in a conspiratorial tone, "Hold on, I'll be right back. It's time to raid the kitchen." She came back a few moments later with a plate of *crostini* and another bottle of the family's wine. "Care for a midnight snack?"

Readily she accepted Martina's pilfered offerings, and as the moon continued its ascent into the inky blue sky, they carried on their midnight conversation. Finally, Maddie sat up and stretched out her arms and yawned widely. Then, adjusting her bustier which had slipped slightly out of place, she said, "Really, this has been lovely, and while I could stay here all night, I don't want to wear out my welcome, so I think it is time for me to go home."

She looked reluctantly at the little wine that was still in her glass and then down at her watch. Shaking her head, in amazement, she cried out, "*Oh, Mio Dio*! It's 12:05 in the morning!"

Martina laughed at Maddie's comical expression.

"I had no idea it was so late!" exclaimed Maddie. "I completely lost track of time. Just give me a moment to clear my head and collect my things and then I'll be on my way."

Seeing Martina stand up, brush the crumbs from her skirt, and start to pick up the bottles, she quickly added, "Oh, here, let me help you."

Grabbing her glass, she rose up a little too quickly, and as the blood rushed to her head her legs buckled slightly under her. Valiantly she gained her balance, but she felt challenged by the fact that the portraits now seemed to be bobbing up and down.

"You should see yourself!" said Martina, with a little giggle. "You are swaying around like you are on the bow of a pitching ship."

"Oh, come on! I'm not that far gone," Maddie said defensively. "Here, let me show you."

Confidently, she took a step forward as if the local *carabinieri* had pulled her over and asked her to walk a straight line. But, as she placed one foot in front of the other, her high-heeled shoe caught the hem of her dress, and she was pitched forward. As she did, Maddie heard a small rip and the last dredges of wine in her glass sloshed over the rim.

Mortified, Maddie checked the floor to see if she had stained the carpet. "Noooo... I'm such a klutz! I'm so sorry."

"Non preoccuparti! It's just a small spot—I'll tend to it in the morning. If it doesn't come out, it will blend in. No one will even notice," Martina said reassuringly. "Anyway, you on the other hand, I'm more worried about. I don't think you are in any shape to drive home tonight—or should I say morning. You can stay here."

"I don't want to put you out or anything," said Maddie apologetically.

"Oh, don't be ridiculous," said Martina. "We've got plenty of space. You can sleep in one of the guest rooms just down the hall."

"But this is all I've got to wear," Maddie said as she flipped back the long panel of her skirt. Holding it up, trying to focus, she inspected the ripped hem. "Drat, it's torn completely."

She let the silky material slip through her fingers and pulled up her dress again, noticing for the first time her bustier had been doused with red wine. "Great! Just great," she muttered. "Now I've gone and stained this beautiful dress as well!"

Maddie reached for a white linen napkin that the wine bottle had been wrapped in and blotted at the spots on her gown. With a frown, she said, "I'm afraid the Duchess is going to be very angry with me. I've worn her beautiful creation only one night and, not only have I wrinkled and ripped it, but it's been christened with Crociani wine..."

As she flipped the napkin over, her face blanched white. The crisp white linen was now discolored by a blotch of blood red wine. She closed her eyes and, when she did, the shades of the past fell over her like the dark shadows the cypress cast. A wave of confusion and panic gripped her, penetrating all the way to her core. It lasted only a moment but left her feeling drained and out of breath.

Martina, seeing her horrified face, giggled again. "Oh, Maddie! Don't worry about the dress. It can be cleaned. Those spots aren't that bad. I've got a trick to get them out, and it works wonders."

"I guess you are right." Shaking her head to clear her thoughts, she reached for her bag and gloves that had gotten wedged between the cushions of the chair.

"*Bene!*" said Martina. "Come on, I'll help get you settled."

She paused at the door and, before opening it, she comically put her finger up to her lips, and in an exaggerated whisper said, "Shhhh!"

Close on her heels, Maddie followed her to the guest room at the top of the stairs. When Martina opened the door and flicked on the lights, she nearly swooned seeing a most inviting site—a large four-poster bed covered with a soft duvet and a pair of feather pillows. It seemed to call to her, and she had half a mind not to undress, just lay down on top of that lovely mattress, and close her eyes and drift off to sleep.

She walked over to it and pushed down on the mattress a couple of times to test its firmness, then pulled back the covers. As she did, she detected the light scent of lavender and, closing her eyes, she remembered another very similar bed carved out of mahogany with a canopy. Like this one, it had been covered by a simple white coverlet, hand embellished with a design of *fleur de lis*. Coming into focus, she saw the face of...

"I have just the thing for you to wear tonight. Give me a second, it's in here somewhere," said Martina.

Maddie opened her eyes and the trace of the misty memory receded into the back of her mind. She looked across the room to the massive fireplace and saw Martina kneeling next to it in front of a sturdy Italian *cassapanca*. It was the kind of hope chest, made of wood with brass enforcements, that new brides filled with linens and lace. Maddie watched Martina rummage around, draping towels and doilies over the edge and smiled. With her pink skirt ballooning around her, she seemed like a giant chiffon cream puff.

"This trunk has been in the family for years. I used to play in it when I was a little girl. I would pretend it was a boat and, in it, I could sail away to a magical land."

"How old is it?" asked Maddie as she took off her shoes with a sigh of relief.

"Oh, it goes all the way back to Maddalena-Raffaella." She pointed to the front and said, "See here. Her name is etched into the brass plate on the top."

Kneeling next to Martina, Maddie examined the brass plate and imagined for a moment what it must have been like for a single woman in Venice in the seventeenth century. It certainly couldn't have been an easy life, but she imagined she would have gratefully accepted the job of a *cortigiana onesta* in order to have independence.

"*Eccola!*" said Martina.

Maddie's thoughts were derailed when she looked over at Martina who had picked up a cotton nightgown edged in lace. "This should appeal to your sense of romance. It certainly will be more comfortable than that dress you have on now. As beautiful as your little black dress may be, isn't it a bit snug? I know mine is!"

"I have to admit," said Maddie, "it has become a bit restrictive. I better get out of it before I set fire to it or something..."

"Here you go, then," said Martina, tossing her the old-fashioned negligee. "This belonged to my grandmother, but I don't think she'd mind if you borrowed it tonight."

"This is beautiful," Maddie said as she fingered the fabric, inspecting the embroidery and tiny pearl closure. Shaking out the soft gown, perfumed with the scent of lemon verbena, she added, "It's a bit flimsy, though, don't you think? Good Lord! You can see right through it."

Holding it in front of her face, she looked through the sheer material at Martina and added, "This seems to me more like something Matteo Crociani's Venetian wife might wear, than your grandmother. What do you think?"

Martina said with a wicked smile, "*Senti*, if it's good enough for Maddalena-Raffaella, it is good enough for you. Anyway, I don't think you'd mind that much conjuring up Signor Crociani tonight."

"You are drunk, Martina, *mia cara*," Maddie said, patting her on the cheek. "So, you think your great-great-great-great-great, I'm losing count here... He'd like to share a spot in my bed along with his beloved wife?"

"You have a point there. He'd be tempted, but I'm afraid in the end he would let you down. He loved his wife far too much. Plus, I don't think the mattress is big enough for all three of you."

"No worries. I want this delicious bed all to myself, thank you very much. I don't need it crowded with four-hundred-year-old ghosts," said Maddie.

Moving tipsily to the window, Martina quoted, "It is a midsummer's night! If you offend the shadows while you are slumbering here, these visions soon will appear." She giggled as she closed the blinds, wrestling with the latch. When she stepped back, seeing a puddle of silvery light on the floor, she exclaimed, "*Managgia*! That's the best I can do."

She gave Maddie an apologetic look. "The moon is so big and bright tonight. Even with the windows covered, the room is completely illuminated."

"Oh, don't worry, I'll be out like a light and dreaming soon..."

"We are such stuff as dreams are made on, and our little life is rounded in sleep," Martina said, followed by a little hiccup.

"Seems wine and late hours bring out the Shakespeare in you. Now get thee to thine own bed!"

"As you wish m'lady!" Martina said with a giggle. "*Buona notte, cara.*

Dormi bene. See you in the morning."

After the door clicked shut, Maddie didn't waste any time. Wriggling out of her dress, she slipped the nightgown over her head, letting the soft fabric settle into place, caressing her skin like a goodnight kiss. Then switching off the light, she gave in to the luxury of the soft mattress and fell instantly into a deep sleep.

Who knows how long she drifted, but, sometime during the night, she came fully alert at the sound of someone tapping on her bedroom door. She pushed back the sheets and sat up, listening intently. A soft breeze blew in through the open window, rippling the curtains and encircling her in a warm embrace. But the only sound she heard was the gurgling of ancient plumbing and the soft sighs and creaks of wood doors and shutters.

A flash of heat lightning briefly illuminated the room, and she detected the scent of night jasmine tinged with the sweet zing of electrically-charged air. She knew before morning it would rain. She waited expectantly, but not even a peep came from the garden below. It seemed the *cinghiale*, the serial night invaders of the flower beds below, and even the swallows who swooped through the dark skies had turned in for the evening.

Maddie was about to dismiss the sound to an overactive imagination and the anticipation of a massive storm, but then she heard the knock again and heard someone whisper the words: "Maddalena, open the door."

Curious to know what Martina wanted, she slipped out of bed and moved toward the door. She hesitated mid-way, remembering the flimsy gown she was wearing. To cover her breasts, she picked up a long white scarf that lay at the edge of the bed and wrapped it around her shoulders.

In the semi-dark room, she stood for a moment with her ear on the panel, but she couldn't hear anything on the other side. Slowly, she opened the door, half-expecting to see her new friend standing there, holding a bottle of aspirin or a tube of toothpaste. But, to her surprise, no one was there.

Maddie peeked out into the murky hall that was illuminated only by the silvery light of the moon that poured in from the windows above. The shifting shadows from the trees outside cast elongated shadows on the wall, and she narrowed her eyes to see better. As her eyes grew accustomed to the dim light at the far end of the corridor, she could have sworn she saw an indistinct figure slip into the picture gallery. And then the voice called out to her again. "Maddalena, *vieni qua.*"

In a raspy voice, she responded, "Martina. Martina, is that you?"

She paused and waited, but there was nothing. The house and all its inhabitants seemed to be sound asleep. Wrapping the scarf tighter around her arms, she decided her mind was playing tricks. Too much rich food and too much cake. And definitely too much wine.

This is entirely absurd, she thought as she turned back to her bedroom. But just as she had convinced herself all her senses were operating on overdrive, she heard the voice again—and this time she recognized it.

Her senses on high alert, she moved with greater purpose to the door of the rogue's gallery. Giving it a gentle push, it slowly creaked open. Standing on the threshold, as the silvery light bathed the room, it seemed now the eyes of the entire Crociani clan regarded her inquisitively from their lofty positions on the wall.

But there was only one portrait that held her interest.

Taking a deliberate step into the room, she could feel its gravitational pull. Like a moon caught in the orbit of a planet, she moved closer until she finally stopped in front of the portrait of Matteo Crociani. Maddie looked into the man's dark eyes once again, and it seemed he was waiting for her to make the next move.

Slowly, she smiled at him, and for a moment it seemed he smiled back at her.

Silently, she implored, "What is this connection we have, you and me? How do we fit together?"

She waited for an answer, but there was no response. Again, she whispered, "They say if you can't sleep, you are awake in someone else's dreams. Is that true? Have we met before in a previous..."

Before she could finish the thought, Maddie felt a gush of air flow in from the open window, and the scarf around her shoulders fluttered to the floor. Although the evening was warm, she shivered slightly. Unaware of the garden below, the gallery, or the pictures that filled the room, spellbound, she only had eyes for Matteo.

And then it happened—drawn into his seductive gaze—the puzzle pieces of her previous existences assembled, forming a coherent picture. There in the night, suspended somewhere in time between Jupiter and Mars, Maddie stepped into the brink. But, unlike before, she wasn't dreaming.

Caught in a current of time that ebbed and flowed around her, she was swept away into a parallel existence, caught between the moon and the Medicean stars.

A Seventeenth-Century Season

We cannot teach people anything;
we can only help them discover it within themselves

– Galileo Galilei

Chapter 13
The Spyglass

Maddalena opened her eyes and saw him lying on his back next to her, his arms crossed under his head gazing at the ceiling. She hadn't moved, or even sighed, yet, instinctively, he seemed to know the exact moment she shook off her slumber. Turning his head he looked at her, and as the early morning sun bathed the room in mellow light, slow smiles broke across their faces.

"Matteo!" she said, delightedly reaching over and caressing his cheek with her slender fingers. They observed one another in pleasure for several heartbeats, hardly daring to believe they had awoken this morning to find one another once again, still side by side, sharing the same bed.

"Good morning, wife," he said softly. As he spoke, he brushed back a wayward lock that had fallen across her cheek. Tucking it behind her ear, he caressed her soft cheek gently before leaning over and languidly kissing her mouth.

Raising his head, he said, "I've been waiting ages to do that again."

"If by one night an age does make," she said with a throaty laugh, "perhaps you should do it again. We need to make up for all the time wasted in sleep."

Needing no further encouragement, he drew her into his arms. As she moved closer, her leg slid across the soft cotton sheets—embroidered with fleur de lis and washed in lavender—until it encountered his firm muscular thigh. Feeling his skin against her naked body, she felt their heat rising.

He reached for the hem of the cotton shift she had worn to bed, now entangled around her midriff, and drew it over her head. To help him remove the garment, she arched her back and flung it aside, letting it fall to the floor in a transparent puddle of linen and lace. When she felt a damp draft travel up her nude back, she drew up the sheet, enveloping them in a private world where only they existed and time ceased to have meaning. Despite the misty morning air, they lay in their warm cocoon intimately exploring the scent and feel of one another—soft skin, sinewy muscle, and a hint of musky perfume that smelled of spicy oranges and vanilla.

As they drifted back to Earth, the moment spent, they lay side by side and let the world settle back into place. Reaching out a hand, she touched his arm as if to assure herself he really existed and it all hadn't been a marvelous dream. As she did, her eyes were drawn to her bare ring finger. Their courtship and exchange of marriage vows had been spontaneous and brief. They had met barely a week before, and now here they were— sharing a bed as husband and wife.

Feeling her light caress, Matteo leaned over to kiss her again. "*Ehi, tutto bene, amore mio?*"

She nodded. "It is a welcome way to start a new day."

"I, for one, have no objections," he murmured seductively. "But I fear, with such a loving wife, I may never step foot outside of our bed."

"What! Spend all day here?" Maddalena said playfully. "We'd never get anything done! You *really* are the maddest man I've ever met!"

"Mad about you!" he quickly retorted. "But, if the lady prefers I leave her side..." he said, calling her bluff, pulling back the covers as if to rise.

She grabbed his hand and pleaded, "Oh, it's so cold! No! Don't go. Keep me warm just a while longer."

He let himself be drawn down, and she nestled comfortably against him, pulling his arm around her. They remained entwined, in contented silence, as he toyed again with her wayward lock of hair. After a moment, he whispered into her ear, "So, what shall I call you, my love—after moments like this, I mean? Signora Crociani sounds too much like my mother and Maddalena—although a beautiful name—seems just a little too formal."

She shifted around to face him again. "A pet name, you mean? Let's see—my *papà* called me Lena... He said I had a gift for words—and that I was always rambling on and on, telling stories. He used to say I could entertain him for hours."

"Lena, eh? Well, I most definitely am not your father so that won't do at all. I can't have you thinking of him at moments like this! To me, you are—let's see..." He traced a finger lightly down her cheek. "To me, you are my Maddie-girl." Pleased, he added, "What do you think?"

"I do rather like the sound of that. No one has ever called me Maddie before. It almost sounds like an English name. And what shall I call you? Teo, or—I know! *Matto-Matteo*—crazy Matteo—I think the name suits you perfectly."

He smirked. "My family would all agree with you on that point."

At the sound of his silly new pet name for her, Maddalena's lips tilted upward. She started to speak but stopped, caught by the light in his eyes. It was a spark of recognition and it reached deep inside and caressed her soul. The moment was perfect and she knew without a doubt there was something so right about this man—and she knew it the first time she saw his face.

"Oh, Maddie, my love, when your face softens like that, and looks at me that way, I feel like I am the most desired man in all of Venice, the world—the universe."

She caressed his face, then said, "When I saw you, I fell in love, and you smiled because you knew."

"Is that one of your poems, Maddie?" he asked.

"No, they are the words of an English poet, William Shakespeare."

With her head resting in the crook of his arm, she returned her gaze to the ceiling and quoted in a soft melodic voice, "If I could go back in time, to a place before we met, I'd find you again, and our paths into the future would be forever set."

"Did Shakespeare write that too?"

"No, *amore mio*, I did."

Marveling at her gift for verse, and finding her current disheveled and flushed appearance quite alluring, he said, "Although I don't express myself in such pretty words, just know I am as content to be your husband."

Taking her hand and sliding it back along his thigh, he whispered into her ear, "Very content, indeed."

"Ah," she murmured, "you have no need of flowery words or pretty phrases, my love. This morning, you are making your intentions very— how shall I put it—firm and straightforward."

Groaning in pleasure, he pulled her into his arms again.

It took them a moment to hear the gentle tap on the door. But when the rapping grew louder, Matteo finally grumbled, "Yes, what is it?"

"A meal, *signori*. I have a tray of good things to break the fast: rice with almond milk, creamed cod, hot bread, assorted sweet biscuits—as well as some pork sausage. Oh, there is also mulled wine."

Matteo raised himself on his elbow and peered longingly at the door. It was apparent his senses had once again been awakened, this time by thoughts of platters of food and a spiced drink. She pushed him back down to the pillow and said, "I can see, my dear sir, you are not just tempted by my loving charms, but are hungry for other things too!"

She raised her voice and called out, "Very well, Valentina. Bring in the plates. It seems we must satisfy *all* of the new master's appetites."

As the door opened, Maddalena rolled off the bed and pulled on her dressing gown that lay on the back of a chair. While tying the strings of her robe firmly around her waist, she instructed her maid to set up the table on the balcony overlooking the canal. Tossing Matteo a linen shirt, she encouraged him to pull on his britches and his boots and make himself decent while Valentina finished her task on the terrace.

When the maid bowed out of the chamber, Matteo poured his new bride a cup of sweet wine and walked to the railing where she leaned, admiring the scene. Sipping the tangy brew, they watched the activity below them, hearing the calls of the boatmen and observing the quicksilver reflections that rippled across the straight to the sea beyond.

Finally, he asked, "Are you ready to leave all this and come with me to Florence?"

As she continued to stare out over the water, he probed, "Does it distress you to say goodbye to this floating city and move inland and reside on solid Tuscan soil?"

Reluctantly, she turned her back on the magnificent view. "I confess I will miss this city. For several years, it has been my haven. I have made a life for myself, and I've been happy here living as I choose and..."

"Yes," he encouraged, "and..."

"If truth be told, to give up my independence, to leave what I know and plunge into a future that is full of uncertainties is a bit daunting."

"All new beginnings are difficult, but I give you my word, I will be with you every step of the way."

Maddalena studied her new husband and instinctively knew this. "I come from Naples and am but a guest of the Doge in this city. As you see, I have always had a fondness for travel—I *am* a bit of a wandering spirit. So, wherever this journey of our takes us—to Florence, even if we land amongst the stars—if you are there, it will be my home."

Holding her lightly in his arms, Matteo leaned down to kiss her. Then resting his forehead on hers, he began to say, "Although..." He caught her eye and raised an eyebrow. "When we actually do arrive back at home in Florence, I'm not sure what I will tell my family. How will I explain the fact that I return from Venice with a wife?"

She leaned back in his arms and gave him a quizzical look. "So, you think they won't accept me? And why is that? Because I am from Naples and not from Florence?"

He scanned the canal behind her. "There is that..."

She narrowed her eyes, gave him a push, and stepped out of his embrace. "Or is it because they call me *La Cortigiana*?"

"*La Cortigiana*!" he exclaimed. "Of course not! That doesn't bother me in the least. No, what I think may come as a surprise not only to my father and my brothers—but Duke Cosimo as well—is that at long last I have finally decided to marry."

"Ah, so you *are* a rogue after all! And here I had assumed I'd wed a gentleman."

"Let's just say, until I met you, I lived my life on my own terms, following my own path. They keep bothering me to take a wife, but until now, until I met you, there was never a convincing reason."

Eyeing the food set out invitingly on the table behind her, he said, "Come, let us eat before the food grows cold."

Pulling out a chair, he took her by the hand and guided her to the seat. "Your meal awaits you, my darling *Cortigiana*!" His eyes lit up at the way she pursed her lips, knowing full well his quip hadn't amused her.

"Laugh all you like," she said. "Just remember I am not a typical courtesan!"

"I should say not!" he said with a grin. "*Your* talents are quite unique."

Ignoring him, she continued, "I am but one of the many courtiers that decorate the Doge's court. If that causes talk—I pity those small-minded chatterboxes, so quick to assume the worst of a person."

"Anything that is new is always thought to be suspect," said Matteo. "And you, my love, are a novelty here in Venice, and thus you are a bit problematic. If a woman is beautiful, assertive, and intelligent, they assume she is..."

"A courtesan!" she said.

Seeing her indignation, he said, "People can be incredibly misguided. And anything new is to be feared, ridiculed, or disdained."

"Still, I don't like being called that."

"But you must admit the title rather suits you. You have excellent social and conversational skills." Then he added slyly, "In addition to your other charms..."

She whipped out her napkin and set it on her lap. Then, giving him a challenging look, she said, "Well, sir, I am no prostitute."

"And I, madame, am no rogue," he retorted.

They smiled at one another again.

As he unfolded his napkin, he added, "You, my dearest, are a rarity among women. When I first saw you in the Piazza San Marco, I was quite taken with your beauty. But later, when I heard you speak, I was captivated by..."

"What? When you first saw me in the piazza" Maddalena said, with a spoonful of sweetmeats halfway to her mouth. "As I recall, we first met at the ambassador's ball."

He considered her for a minute, then confessed, "Actually, the first time I caught sight of you was through my telescope, Maddie-girl. When I saw those grey-green eyes of yours, it was then that I knew..."

"You saw my eyes! Through a telescope, you say? *Santo Cielo!* What, pray tell, is that?"

He stopped cutting the food on his plate. "Have you never heard of a telescope? It's a kind of spyglass—but much stronger and powerful."

When she shook her head, he said, "*Oh mio dio*! Maddie, my love, it's a wonderful invention. It is the way of the future! With it, you can see past the horizon and into the heavens. With it, even the tiniest of stars can be viewed."

She eyed him curiously. "Is this an invention of yours?"

He shook his head. "No, the idea was first conceived by a German and improved upon by my colleague Galileo. But now I have a hand in it."

"And with it you can actually see the stars?"

"As if they were right in front of your face," he said, taking another bite of food. As he chewed, seeing she was clearly interested, he set down his fork and asked, "Would you like to see it?"

Seeing her nod, he quickly rose out of his chair, his breakfast sausages now completely forgotten. Disappearing into the bedroom, he returned a moment later holding a long wooden box. When he opened the lid, Maddalena peered inside and could see, resting against a cushion of velvet, several metal tubes and brass rings. Intrigued, she watched Matteo assemble the pieces and attach the brass device to a tripod that stabilized it. Then leaning over, he twisted the metal rings back and forth.

When he was satisfied, he invited her to look. "Just see what a little imagination can achieve. The miracles of modern science! This little device will carry us to worlds that we never knew existed. And without it, we go nowhere."

She regarded him in puzzlement. "What am I supposed to do?"

"Pick a spot on the horizon," he said.

Shielding her eyes, Maddalena could just barely make out the silhouette of San Marco that now glistened white, bathed by the light of a new day. "Okay, the Doge's palace," she said.

"Perfect. Now, put it up to your eye—wait, here let me help you."

He steadied the telescope and slowly rotated the dials and stopped when she burst out, "I see it! It's incredible." Maddalena lifted her beaming face and said. "You are right! It's so close. It seems I can almost touch it!"

Leaning over again to peer through the scope, Matteo slowly moved to focus far out over the grand canal and then aimed it back at the piazza.

"This is fantastic. I can see everything so clearly. From here I can see the boats—and now the people in the piazza. Why, I can even see their faces—their expressions are so clear!"

With her hand, she adjusted the telescope a little higher and added, "Even the little fat friar in the bell tower is visible!"

"Isn't it wonderful!"

"Extraordinary."

"Galileo and I just presented this new high-powered design to the Venetian Senate, and they were quite impressed. We are already at work on an even more precise instrument."

She stood up and he eyed her thoughtfully. "I will be forever grateful to this spyglass, for, without it, we would never have come together or have been united."

"What do you mean?"

"I was demonstrating the device to the Doge and his most trusted signori, and as I pointed it at San Marco's square, I made the most astounding discovery."

"And what was that?"

"You, Maddalena. As I adjusted the lenses and things came into focus, I suddenly saw you. You turned in my direction and raised your hand to wave, almost like you recognized me, and it was as if the sun illuminated my horizon," said Matteo.

She stared at him in astonishment. "I actually waved?"

"You did. It seemed you were greeting me, beckoning me closer."

Bending down to look through the lens, he added, "After that I knew I had to speak with you. So, when the meeting with the Doge concluded, I made great haste to the piazza hoping you would still be there. But, to my utter dismay, you were gone. I searched all over Venice that day but couldn't find a trace of you. I thought you had vanished into thin air."

He disassembled the device, laying each of its parts carefully back into the velvet-lined case. "Imagine my surprise when I walked into the Doge's reception later that evening, only to find you the center of attention, strumming your lute and entertaining the crowd."

"And when I saw you there observing me so attentively, for a moment I quite forgot the words to my song." She hesitated, then added, "This may sound silly, but it gave me quite a shock—I was completely taken in by the sight of you. It was as if..."

"As if..."

"I can't quite explain it but..." she faltered to a stop. When he picked up her hand and entwined their fingers, she continued softly, "That night, it was as if I could see into the future and instinctively knew we were meant to be together."

"I know. I felt it too. There are no words to explain this attraction— it just is. I think we are both unconventional people, you and I, just beginning this unpredictable journey together. It will take a long lifetime to learn all there is to know."

Wiggling her ring finger at him, she responded, "It appears you are indeed an unconventional man. Seems you don't even honor the tradition of placing a wedding band on your new wife's finger to show the world she is married to you."

"Ah! So, Signora Crociani would like a sign of fidelity? That I can easily amend."

He turned back to the wooden box which contained the parts of his telescope. Carefully, he sorted through the pieces and selected the smallest brass coupling he could find. Then, taking her hand, he held it up to her and said, "With this token of affection, as humble as it is, I vow I will always be a faithful and loving husband, for now and forever."

Maddalena studied her hand, admiring her impromptu wedding band. Even though it was far too big for her finger, and it wobbled around a bit, she was deeply touched.

Seeing her bemused expression, he quickly added, "For the moment, this will have to suffice. But I promise you, Maddie, when we return home to Florence, I will have a more suitable ring made, and have it inscribed."

"And what will it say?"

"You are my sun and I am your moon—eternally yours, Matteo." He touched the band encircling her finger and added, "You know, Maddie-girl, I'd follow you anywhere—to the end of time."

For a moment, she had no words. Then, finding her voice, she said, "My husband is becoming a poet, after all."

Maddalena wrapped her arms around him and kissed him. Then, leaving his warm embrace, she walked slowly back into the bedroom. As she did, she pulled off her silky robe, peering seductively over her shoulder.

"Are you sure you are willing to follow me anywhere?"

His eyes grew smoky, and he took a step in her direction, objecting not in the least when she held out her hand and drew him to their bed. She pushed him down into the soft and fragrant sheets and undid the buttons of his shirt, trailing kisses up his chest and the smooth column of his neck until she reached his mouth. Then, leaning down, she drew off his boots one at a time.

Mesmerized and utterly beguiled by her touch, he followed her seductive movements, readily consenting to the plan she had in mind for them. Finally, he reached for her and pulled her down on top of him.

Looking into her grey-green eyes, he said, "You, madam, are very good at this. And you say you aren't a typical courtesan..."

She murmured huskily back, "And you, sir, are very eager to bed this woman. And you say you aren't a rogue!"

Chapter 14

Traveling Companions

*N*ot in a hurry to leave Venice, the enchanted city filled with bridges and watery passageways, they whiled away the morning in the haven of each other's arms. *La Serenissima* was a magical floating place—a place of dreams and illusions, yet it had endured over time, constructed on a solid foundation of wooden pilings. And, similarly, despite the romantic trappings, meeting by chance and quickly marrying, they were ready to believe their union too would endure the test of time.

After leisurely concluding their breakfast, by mid-day the servants were finally allowed back into the room. As Valentina bustled about the room, she finished adding things to the already quite full trunk that contained all of Maddalena's dresses and toiletries. As a wedding present, Matteo had given her the new chest made of polished wood accentuated with brass couplings. He even had her name engraved upon the faceplate: Maddalena-Raffaella Crociani, along with the family's crest of arms—a golden griffin holding up a half-moon.

When the maid saw Matteo hovering about, taking up too much male space in the room, Valentina shooed him away, telling him he was more of a hindrance than a help. She closed and locked the door and set about her work. From the armoire, Valentina took out a chemise, embroidered and trimmed with narrow lace. She briskly pulled from a drawer a pair of white stockings woven from finely spun wool.

"Here, put these on," she instructed her mistress, handing them to Maddalena along with two ribbon garters to secure them in place.

Next, she motioned for her lady to stand in front of her and, around her already slim waist, the young servant fastened a corset stiffened with reeds. Cinching it firmly, she asked, "Is that too tight?" Without waiting for an answer, the maid snugged it again.

As Maddalena sucked in her breath, Valentina eased over her arms a sapphire-hued partlet with a plunging neckline and skin-tight sleeves. Humming to herself, the girl's nimble fingers fastened the dozen tiny hooks that fastened the back of Maddalena's bodice.

Feeling a little light-headed, and with perspiration forming on her brow, Maddalena fanned herself with her hands, waiting for Valentina to place and secure the bell-shaped farthingale which held out her voluminous matching silk skirt. To finish the ensemble and to protect it from the dusty roads, the maid added a heavy overskirt made of gold brocade embroidered in blue thread, to cover the delicate silk material beneath it.

Last, but not least, Valentina reached into the cabinet and pulled out a narrow-brimmed hat. She placed it on Maddalena's head and tied the satin ribbons under her chin. Then handing her mistress an umbrella to protect her powdered, pale face from the sun's rays, she cautioned her mistress to remember to use it.

"Valentina, where is the case that contains my cure-alls?"

"This one, m'lady?" the servant said, holding up a small wooden case.

"Yes, that's it. I wouldn't want to leave that..."

She paused when she heard a rapping on the door followed by, "Maddalena, open the door!"

With her hands full, she instructed her maid to unlock the door, and when it swung open, she saw Matteo standing in the hallway looking at his gold watch.

"Sorry to hurry you my love," he said, "but it's already 12:05 and time to be gone from this establishment—that is if we are to arrive at a decent hour in Florence tomorrow morning."

Placing his timepiece back into his pocket, he finally glanced up at her. "Ah! Signora Crociani! I see the wait was worth it. Such a transformation from the last time I saw you!" In a teasing tone, he added, "But I must say, however you are dressed—in any guise you take—you make the most desirable traveling companion."

Then holding out his hand to her to cross the threshold and join him, he asked, "So, are you ready to begin this journey together?"

"I am indeed, *signore*. Here you can help me with this," she said, handing him her case.

He looked at her questioningly. "And what's in this?"

Valentina piped in, "It contains her special remedies. The mistress is quite talented."

"Remedies?" he asked feeling the weight of the case.

"Oh, it's filled with things with which to mix my special tisanes and draughts," said Maddalena. "Common things like chamomile, wormwood and coltsfoot, and trickier plants like henbane and hemlock..."

"Hemlock? Isn't that...?"

"Oh, yes, it can be quite dangerous, but mixed properly it is most effective for whooping cough and joint pain."

"Have no fear, *signore*," said Valentina proudly, "m'lady knows how to prepare a soothing drink to cure a sore throat, induce a sound night's sleep, as well as soothe a woman's monthly pains. Her skills are put to good use amongst the household staff."

"Ah, so you are a healer?" said Matteo, eyeing his wife appreciatively.

"I learned from my mother," Maddalena replied. "She knew a great deal about flowers and plants and how to distinguish between the good and the bad. She taught me about their properties and showed me how to dry and preserve them to make cures for almost every ache and ailment. It's become quite a hobby and I'm always improving my recipes. I try one thing and then another—finding things that work better all the time."

"It seems I have found myself a most accomplished partner. Not only can she sing and write verse, she possesses knowledge of medicine."

Taking the case from her hands, he directed her to the courtyard, where he helped her into the waiting carriage. After the morning's ordeal, now seated in the tiny compartment with Matteo opposite her, Maddalena felt quite exhausted. She watched as the stable boys loaded the last of their trunks on top of their cabin. As they worked, she listened to their jokes and blasphemies, as well as the sounds of whickering and the clicking of hooves as they fastened the horses' harnesses.

When the driver climbed on board, he hooted then whistled, and the impatient stallions ready to be away lurched forward. At first, the carriage lumbered awkwardly over the uneven cobblestones until it turned onto the open highway. With Venice falling behind them, Maddalena rested her forehead on the cool glass and watched in interest as the scenery changed from undulating seascapes to oscillating fields of grain.

At first, she was excited to have started the journey, but after a while, the jolting of the carriage hitting the potholes in the road, began to irritate her. Her shoulders ached from the constant motion, and her backside throbbed, despite being padded by mounds of crinolines, linen, and lace.

Maddalena looked over at her husband sitting across from her who was deeply engrossed by a small book. She watched him turn the pages one after another and it appeared he was completely oblivious to her discomfort. As the carriage wheels picked up a little more speed, she wished a little desperately to be free of the weight of her dress. From under the brim of her hat, she scowled at Matteo, miffed that he appeared far more at ease in his leather britches and black boots that reached up to his knees. Ah, to be a man and be able to wear a pair of pants.

Settling back against the hard seat, she tried to catch his eye, but, his attention wholly captured by what he was reading. She studied him for a moment, realizing this was a side of him she hadn't seen until now. *Well,* she thought, resigning herself to the silence, *I have things just as compelling to occupy my time.*

Untying her hat, she placed it on the seat beside her. Taking out a tablet and lead pencil from her bag, she jotted down thoughts and composed verses to soothe and distract herself. As the sun started to set and darkness descended, lulled by the rocking of the carriage, Maddalena let her eyes drift to a close. She leaned into the corner of the carriage, and after a bit, because of the swaying motion, her book tumbled from her lap to the floor, and she fell into a deep sleep.

She slept for several hours, far into the night, but becoming aware of warm rays filtering across her closed lids, her eyes fluttered open. Looking out the window, Maddalena noticed the sun was just rising, still a golden hue on the horizon but enough to illuminate the interior of the carriage. Letting her gaze drift back to Matteo who sat across from her, she saw he was still asleep.

As the light grew brighter, Maddalena observed her husband, noting the way his head rested against the cushions, admiring the cut of his embroidered coat that now lay open, revealing a bit of the dark blue vest and knotted cravat. His arms were crossed over his chest, and just a touch of white linen was visible around the sleeves of his jacket.

Her eyes trailed down his slim torso past his muscular thighs to his long legs, one of which was extended so that it brushed her own as if even in sleep he needed to touch her. Amused by the thought, she reached for her book, and when she lifted her head again, she saw Matteo was awake and watching her.

He said nothing at first, as he gently massaged his temple, grimacing slightly from the pressure he applied. Under his intense gaze, she grew self-conscious and wiped a hand over her grimy cheeks and rubbed at her swollen eyes to erase the traces of the previous night. She thought a little wistfully of their cozy chamber on Giudecca Island, their warm bed, and the private safe harbor they had created in Venice. She also missed the enticing breakfasts her maid always prepared. As the dawn broke and reality set in, she speculated he was thinking the same thing.

Maddalena turned her head to study the landscape and saw a heavy dew hung over the land. It bathed the trees and fields in an eerie light. She wondered what awaited her in Florence and thought how easy it would have been to carry on their love affair without the trappings of wedded-life; he could have gone back to Florence, maintaining his bachelor status, while she kept her independent state as a well-paid courtesan living in her Venetian villa. Yes, they were in love and shared great passion, but for two fiercely independent people, would they be able to blend their lives successfully together? Marriage, she realized, would take a lot of compromises and much compassion.

As the sun rose higher, and the landscape came into focus, Maddalena saw two peasants standing in the field beyond. The man dug in the dirt with a hoe, and next to him was a woman heavy with child, holding a large wicker basket. By the way the two worked together, it seemed to Maddalena they had endured many springs and harvests together.

She looked back at Matteo and saw he too was gazing out the window. Just the sight of him filled her with tenderness and, like the morning mist that was quickly evaporating, so did Maddalena's doubts. She wanted to grow old with this man and would do everything in her power to stay by his side forever.

Heartened by the idea, when their eyes met, as if they could read each other's thoughts, they smiled at one another again.

Rising into an upright position, he finally broke the silence and said, "Did you sleep well, Maddie-girl?"

"Passably," she responded lightly, warming once again to the pet name he reserved for her.

"And you?"

"I have a bit of a headache," he admitted.

"Will we be stopping shortly?"

"Soon," he said encouragingly as he opened a basket on the seat next to him. He reached inside and pulled out pieces of bread and some cheese wrapped in a linen napkin, and he offered it to her. "Here, eat this. It will tide you over for the next hour. When we get to the resting stop, to water the horses, we will have a bigger meal."

Gratefully, she accepted the food and took a bite, chewing the hard, dry morsels. Noticing he was still rubbing his forehead, she said with concern, *"Ehi, amore,* when we stop, I'll mix you an herbal tisane that will fix you right up."

She took another bite of bread and pulled back on the curtain to see out the window. "Where are we, exactly?"

"Oh, I'd say we are somewhere near Roncobilaccio. I was awake when we passed by Ferrara an hour or so ago."

"How much longer until we arrive in Florence?" she inquired, hoping for a favorable answer.

"The driver is making good time, and the weather has been decent. I predict we will reach the city by mid-afternoon."

She took another bit of bread then said, "The other evening, you started to tell me about your family. Will they be there to greet us when we arrive? And what about your father? What do you think he will say? Will he...?"

"There's no need to worry about my father just yet," Matteo assured her. "He isn't in the city at the moment. Since my mother died, he's lived on the family's estate south of Florence, where he can oversee the property. We will visit him next month at our leisure. I'm not quite ready to end this honeymoon of ours."

"But surely I will meet the rest of the Crociani clan soon. What can you tell me of them, so as to make a good impression?"

"Again, you mustn't worry. You will charm them all, I dare say."

"Come on now, be serious. You must prepare me a little. I fear I've already confused all their names."

"No wonder, we are a large bunch that seems to keep expanding. Even I can barely keep them all straight," he added, jokingly.

"How many of you are there, again?"

"Let's see... I have three brothers and two sisters, and upon last accounting, eight nephews and four nieces."

"And what is it that all you Crociani do?"

"One brother is a diplomat at the French court in Paris, another is a cardinal in Rome, and my younger brother is an emissary for Duke Cosimo. He travels back and forth between Florence and Naples, Mantova and Milan. He lives with his wife and daughters on the other side of town. My sisters all have families of their own. As you can see, we are quite a prolific family. The Crociani are not about to go out of stock."

He gave her a teasing grin and added, "And I'm willing to do my best to ensure the family line continues."

Maddalena ignored his comment. After traveling for hours in such a tight compartment, she wasn't feeling particularly amorous. Still, it pleased her to see the affectionate husband of the night before had returned.

She adjusted herself, on the leather seat, but as the carriage swerved slightly, she lost her balance again and was knocked back into the corner of the carriage. Righting herself again, she said with a sigh, "It seems we have been trapped in this carriage forever. I could use a break to stretch my legs."

"It is rather tedious, I agree."

He peered out the window and watched a flock of geese flying low over the rose-tinted horizon. "Just think, Maddie-girl, sometime in the future we will travel by other means than a horse. Like those birds, someday we will all soar through the air."

"Through the air?" Maddalena said skeptically.

"Yes. By air. I, for one, am convinced it will happen. There will be flight not just in the blue skies above our heads, but also into the dark heavens beyond." He leaned over and rested his elbows on his knees. "It is just a matter of time, Maddie, before intelligent men figure out a solution. Men like Galileo."

"And yourself, too, I'd imagine?"

When he shrugged and directed his attention back out the window, she added, "You, sir, are being far too modest. Being a part of the court in Venice, I've heard talk of Galileo before. By the way Doge goes on and on about him—it is far too apparent the all-powerful ruler of the Venetian kingdom believes Galileo to be the finest mathematician of our day and praises him to the highest heavens."

"The man *is* a genius."

"That is precisely my point. That you should collaborate with him—well then! It speaks volumes of your own reasoning and clarity of thought."

He was quiet a moment before he finally said, "I consider it a great privilege and honor to call Galileo my friend, colleague, and mentor."

"Where did you meet him? I thought he came from Pisa."

"He did indeed come from that port town. We were colleagues at the university—that is where we first met—and now together we serve Cosimo, the Grand Duke of Tuscany."

"Such illustrious circles you run in. Am I to be included?"

"Naturally. With your wit and intellect, I will present my wife to them with the greatest of pleasure. These men are extraordinary and recognize talents whether they be those of a man or a woman. In their eyes, art, science, poetry, and math are viable pursuits for either sex."

"And how do you and Galileo serve the Duke of Tuscany, exactly?" Maddalena asked.

"Cosimo, like Galileo, has an insatiable thirst for knowledge about the physical world—its mysteries and how it operates. He keeps the both of us very busy, investing in natural phenomenon, fine-tuning the magnets used in compasses, and..."

When they hit a deep, teeth-jarring hole in the road, Matteo beat his hand on the side of the carriage and cried out to the driver, "Federico! *Stai attento*! Watch the road!"

Maddalena seeing his annoyance, smiled and said, "Perhaps you had better work a little faster on this whole flying thing! I'm curious, have you made any progress?"

"Let's see..." He stopped then prefaced, "Just keep in mind, we've only just begun, and the path to the future isn't always a straight line. But we must follow the scientific process..."

"Meaning?" she asked, never having heard the term before.

"The scientific process? It involves experimentation and the testing of theories. You use it when you mix your herbs in new ways to improve your recipes. That is the way of a scientist too. We keep building upon our knowledge of our current reality to improve our understanding of how the universe operates."

Caught up in his words, Maddalena sensed the passion that boiled just beneath the surface. Not only was he a man of keen intellect, he had a remarkable vision of the world, one she had never considered.

She leaned forward. "What have you tried so far?"

"Don't laugh," he said. "We started with an umbrella."

"What? An umbrella!"

"See, I told you it sounded ridiculous. But, when Marco Polo returned from Orient with tales of seeing Chinese sailors hoisted into the air on large kites, we began to explore the idea that a gust of air might hold the clue to launching someone into the sky."

"Flying Chinese sailors!" Maddalena said in wonder, trying to imagine the scene. But, the more she thought about it, the idea didn't seem crazy or so foreign. "So what kind of experiment did you two devise based on that?"

Pointing to her parasol that rested in the corner of the carriage, he said, "We took that design, more or less, and built a much larger one, then waited for a blustery day."

"And did it work?"

"About as effective as flapping my arms like a goose," he said wryly. "The thing literally folded, collapsed, and turned inside out. But that didn't stop us. More recently, we've been experimenting with paper balloons heated by a small flame. Once again, an ingenious idea taken from the Chinese who used such sky lanterns for military signaling. So far, we've managed to get one to lift about four meters into the air."

"That sounds promising!" she said, intrigued by the idea.

"It is, actually. I'm quite inspired. Unfortunately, the lantern is only airborne for as long as the flame stays alight, after which it sinks back to the ground. But I've got other ideas—and if we keep at it, one can only imagine what the world will be like in one hundred years, or even five hundred. Perhaps my small air balloon will eventually take us to the moon."

"Fly into space and touch the stars! Just imagine!" exclaimed Maddalena. "That would be a wondrous thing! *Magari!*"

He regarded her intently. "Would you do it, Maddalena? Given the chance, would you walk on the moon with me?"

"Walk on the moon?" She sat back on her bench and viewed her husband in amazement.

Would she ever dare to take a step on the moon? The way he described things, air travel was entirely plausible and obtainable. His enthusiasm was contagious, and his faith in progress and the scientific process was unshakable. With each turn of the carriage wheel, she felt herself falling in love with him just a little more. Trusting him completely, she believed she just might take that step.

She was about to respond, but seeing a shadow fall suddenly over his face, she asked, "*Ehi,* what is it, *amore?*"

Matteo shook his head slightly, then looked back up at the sky. "One day it will happen—it just won't happen in my lifetime. I will be ashes, a mere memory when that day arrives. It will take many more years and many more lifetimes to see a man walk on the moon."

They grew quiet and Maddalena reached for his hand and squeezed it gently until he turned back at her. "They say the one who plants the seed of a sturdy vine, knowing he will never taste its sweet fruit, has at least started to understand the meaning of life. We have just begun our journey together, but I believe your legacy will live on through you. How can it not? You must trust in the connection of all things that bind us."

Seeing the light in his eye return, she teased, "If moon walking is in our future, tell me the steps we must take to get there, my love."

Matteo raised an eyebrow. "Are you sure I'm not boring you with this scientific talk? Wouldn't you prefer to speak of poems and verses of love?"

"Poetry and art feed the soul, but science will lead us to the stars," she responded lightly. "Go on! Tell me. I want to know more!"

"All right. But I want you to keep an open mind. What Galileo and I have discovered may be a little harder to comprehend..."

"What concept could be more difficult to grasp than flying to the moon? I've studied languages and dabbled in alchemy, but *Santo Cielo!* Ever since I met you, my mind is expanding by the moment." Putting her hands to her head, she added, "At this point, it's practically exploding. So, go ahead—I'm open to new possibilities."

"You recall the spyglass I showed you earlier? With it, I've made a fascinating discovery."

"Other than me?" she teased.

He raised her hand to his lips and kissed it but quickly grew serious, too focused on what he was saying to be distracted by further jokes. "The telescope is a powerful tool, and with it I can see far into the night sky. When I focused it on Jupiter—the brightest and largest body at the far end of our solar system—I discovered something miraculous. For the first time, I could distinguish the colors that paint the planet."

Matteo looked at her in awe. "Through the telescope, Jupiter resembles a precious Venetian glass bead patterned in hazy blue and amber tones that swirl together. The effect is quite hypnotizing. I also saw for the first time the four stars that surround the planet."

"Go on," she encouraged, caught up in his enthusiasm.

"As I began charting their trajectories and then after sharing my findings with Galileo, we realized they aren't stars at all. They are moons!"

"Moons? What does that mean? What is the difference between a star and a moon?"

"A moon is a small celestial body made of rock. A star is made of gases. Unlike stars, moons orbit planets and..."

Seeing her confusion, he said, "Here, let me show you."

With a gentle tug on her hand he still held, he drew her over to sit beside him then pulled out a parchment from his leather satchel. Carefully, he unrolled it and smoothed it out on the opposite bench in front of them.

"There, what do you think?"

She pondered the parchment filled with mathematical equations and trajectory of spheres, but could make no sense of it. Finally giving up, she asked, "What are all these strange markings?" Pointing with a finger, she added, "And what exactly is the meaning of all these little circles?"

"It is proof, Maddie!" he said excitedly.

"Proof? Proof of what?"

"Documented evidence that the Earth is not the center of the universe! The sun is!"

"The sun!" Maddalena questioned, her eyes widening. "We are not the center of everything? Everything I've studied, the scriptures in both Latin and Greek and the *Bible*, tells us..."

"I know, I know. But, hear me out. I've been observing the movements of the moons of Jupiter orbiting around the planet, but they never seemed to stay put or remain in a logical pattern. When compared to other planets like Mars, they appeared to move backward, but other times they traveled forward. This retrograde motion was particularly puzzling."

"Time traveling moons and planets?"

"Yes, it appeared so," he said, enjoying her poetic flight of fantasy. "When I showed this to Galileo, we began to theorize. Over and over, we pondered these drawings and nothing made sense. That is, until Galileo suggested we use the sun as a fixed point. It is then he made the discovery that the sun is indeed the center of our universe."

"The center... But...?" Maddalena stuttered. The concept so new and foreign, her brain could barely absorb the astounding information.

Seeing her confusion, he encouraged, "Yes! You can say it! It is the sun—not the Earth—that is the center of the universe. There can be no other explanation. It is the Earth that revolves on an axis and rotates around the sun, and not the other way around!"

"But that is heresy," said Maddalena in a shocked whisper.

"It is modern science!" he replied.

"Your theory contradicts common knowledge."

"Perhaps, but common knowledge is wrong. It's based on misguided information and partial facts. If you recall, when Columbus discovered the world wasn't flat it was an extremely difficult concept for people to comprehend. *Ed Allora!* And now it's common knowledge."

"Yes, but..." In a hushed tone, Maddalena continued, "What you say contradicts what the Pope and the *Bible* tell us! To go against the Pope is a sin—punishable by death!"

Matteo was quiet, then continued, "I have seen with my own eyes how the universe works. I have studied the natural order of things and documented it. My mind has been opened, and I now embrace what I now know to be true—and it changes everything!"

This time, it was he who took her hand. "Listen, my love, I am still a man of God. Don't misunderstand me," he said. "I give infinite thanks to Him, who has made me who I am. He has made me an observer of marvelous things. It makes no sense to me that the same God who endowed me with sense, reason, and intellect has intended me to forgo their use."

"But the *Bible* clearly states..."

"I believe the *Bible* shows the way to go to Heaven," he said. "Not the way the heavens go. Of that, I am convinced."

"To anger the Pope is suicide! You are kicking a hornet's nest," warned Maddalena. "No good can come of this! I know what happens to men who oppose the Church. When Giordano Bruno announced to the King of Naples that the universe was infinite..."

She paused, suddenly terrified. "The news traveled quickly and reached the Pope's ear. Bruno, upon the Pope's orders, was dragged off to Rome to face the Inquisition where he was swiftly denounced as a heretic—an enemy of God and the state. His punishment was obscene. They cut out his tongue, hung him upside down, and burned him alive in the Campo dei Fiori for all of Rome to see."

"It was a horrible thing to see," said Matteo.

"You were there that day?" she whispered.

Matteo let his eyes slide away from hers to stare out the window. Drumming his fingers on his knee, he finally said between clenched teeth, "I contend the authority of a thousand is not worth the humble reasoning of a single individual. It is arrogance to assert that we know all there is to be known. But even so, when presented with scientific facts and evidence to the contrary, people still stubbornly hold on to false truths. The Pope is a narrow-minded man who wants to maintain total control of his sheep—and they willingly believe him."

Maddalena's eyes widened in alarm. "But you must be careful, *amore mio.* I've only just found you. I don't want to lose you!"

Drawing her into his arms, he said, "Maddie, don't worry. We are not going to Rome, or Naples, for that matter. We are going to a much more civilized and enlightened place—a place that supports men like myself and Galileo. Florence, unlike Rome, has a warm and generous heart and a thirst for knowledge and innovation. Its energy is indescribable—it is teeming with life and new ideas. And reigning over it all is Cosimo de' Medici—a man of science and lover of art. Not only does he encourage our discoveries, he demands it!"

Keeping her safe in his warm embrace, he added, "Just you wait and see, Maddie-girl. There is no reason to worry. I'm firmly convinced that once our ideas have been explained, they will soon be accepted even by those who govern the Church. Eventually, intelligent men of science and cooler heads will prevail. Wisdom will trump ignorance, of that I am convinced."

He settled himself back in his seat and rested his head against the cushion. "Yes, of all the places on this Earth, we will be safe in Florence. Besides, the Pope will never touch us there."

"And why is that?" Maddalena asked, ready to be convinced.

"Why? Because, my dear lady, the Pope is a coward. He fears Cosimo almost as much as he fears God!"

Chapter 15

Return to Florence

*A*s the carriage ground to a halt, Maddalena drew back the curtain and saw they had stopped near the stables of a small roadside tavern. Realizing she was quite parched she gave Matteo a bright smile. "Finally, we can get out of this blasted contraption."

She soon found herself inside a small, dark building in the company of other travelers, mostly men. In the corner of the establishment, a small fireplace gave out an inviting glow and, seeking its warmth, she moved closer to the hearth and held out her hands. As she did, she admired the brass ring that now encircled her finger, gleam the light of the fire.

After a few minutes, the dampness and the aches she felt from spending the long night in the carriage subsided. Her face became flushed from the radiating heat of the fire and, feeling the weight of so many layers, she removed her hat and undid the strings of her cloak. Hearing Matteo approach behind her, she felt him lift the garment from her shoulders and then watched as he hung it on a peg by the side of the mantel to keep it warm.

Indicating a small table in the corner, she observed in pleasure the meal that had been prepared for them, and her mouth watered at the aroma of chicken broth and *lardo*, the thick salty spread made from the fat of a pig. Eyeing the brown jug in the center of the array of plates, which she assumed contained the proprietor's homemade wine, she thought the simple spread was as inviting as a fine supper laid out for a duke.

Maddalena nodded her head in approval and accepted the hand of her husband, who, like the day before, helped settle her into her chair. She discovered she was becoming used to not only his stimulating conversation but also his kind attentiveness.

As he made himself comfortable across from her, she removed a vial of powder and unfolded a small parchment envelope containing dried herbs from her small case. She poured them into a cup of boiling water then handed it to Matteo. He took a few sips and continued to eat, but when the meal concluded, he told her his symptoms were already subsiding.

Refreshed by the meal, and Maddalena's remedy, he directed her to an upper room, leaving her alone to make repairs, while he attended to the horses and the groomsmen. Maddalena took a moment to splash her face with water and slick back her hair with her fingers. There was no mirror, so she had no way of knowing if the signs of traveling were showing on her face. She wasn't a vain woman, but still, she took pride in her appearance. In the reflection of the glass window, she pinched her cheeks and bit her lips to restore a little color.

Feeling infinitely better, she buttoned up her bodice and adjusted her skirts, shaking them out and refastening the hooks. Without her maid, it took all her effort to reach the tiny closures in the back and put herself together again. At one point, she became so frustrated she impatiently stamped her foot on the floor and called out, *"Madonna! Che fastidio!"*

When the task was finally accomplished, she sighed in relief and retied the silk ribbons of her hat. Picking up her small vanity case, she made her way back to the courtyard and discovered Matteo standing in front of it holding a small puppy. When he held it out to her and placed it in her arms her heart instantly melted.

"And who's this?" she asked, eyeing her husband curiously.

Matteo grinned sheepishly. "A new friend. The man in the tavern said we could keep it. His bitch just had a new litter. I thought this little one would provide you a little more company in your new home."

Pleased her husband was so generous and in tune with her moods, she cuddled the dog under her chin. "And what shall we call him, or her...?" she said, lifting the small ball of fur high into the air to check.

"I'll leave the name to you," said Matteo.

Hmm, let me think of an appropriate name for a *maschio*. Well, let's see..." Then, with an inspired expression, she said, "In light of our conversation earlier, and in honor of your newest discovery, let's call him Jupiter."

Maddalena followed Matteo back to the carriage and only winced slightly when she heard the driver whistle and the jiggling contraption set off again for Florence. As the little dog slept in her lap, to pass the time, Matteo and Maddalena played word games and spoke as lovers often do about their future, as well as their past lives.

She watched with interest the array of emotions that crossed his face as he told her his favorite boyhood stories about growing up on the estate near Montepulciano and the winters the family had spent in Florence. She had already learned he was an innately inquisitive person, but the childhood anecdotes he painted for her further revealed more about his character. Especially an incident involving a stolen book.

"It belonged to my father," Matteo told her. "It was fascinating, really, filled with detailed drawings of the oceans and the continents. We all thought it was marvelous. I used to sneak into his study and hide away and pour over it for hours. Despite the fact my father was adamant that we should never touch it, fearing we'd smudge the pages with our dirty hands."

Maddalena smiled at the thought of a little boy enchanted at an early age with faraway places, hiding under his father's desk and dreaming about the future.

Shaking his head at the memory, Matteo continued. "So, when the book went missing, my father immediately decided I was the culprit, as I was the last one he had seen holding at it. Although I denied it, right then and there, he confined me to my room for over a day without any food."

"That seems a little cruel."

"That's how he was sometimes. He hoped to force a confession out of me and came to my bedroom door repeatedly demanding I tell the truth. But, over and over, I told him I had not been the one to take it. He even bribed me with a slice of sweet cake, but still I refused to give him the answer he wanted."

"What did he do then?"

"He became so enraged, he beat me with a birch twig."

"Did you take it?"

"Of course not! I knew I was right. I hadn't been the one to steal his precious book, and I wasn't about to be blamed for a crime I hadn't committed."

"What did he do then?"

"He beat me even harder."

"So, how did it end? Whatever happened to the book?"

"My father found it in my brother's room a few days later with a torn page. When finally confronted, filled with remorse, Marco confessed to having hidden the book because he had been the one to damage it."

"You were stubborn and defiant to the last, I see," Maddalena said, thinking to herself what a brave little boy he had been to take his punishment so stoically, never backing down or compromising himself with a bribe.

When he turned the tables, questioning her about her childhood, she told him she had been the youngest of three siblings and described for him the elegance and the beauty of the court in Naples.

"It is a fascinating city, but still, all my life I wanted to travel. I longed to see the world and discover what lay beyond the gates of the palace. When my father took the outpost in Venice, it seemed a most fortunate opportunity for our family. Finally, my dreams of seeing new places over the horizon, were coming true. But, by the time my family arrived in Venice, we were all very ill. And over the weeks, despite my mother's best remedies, I lost my family, even the man I was to marry, to ague— malaria."

She was quiet for a moment, patting the small sleeping dog in her lap. "For a long time, I was gravely ill too, but for some reason—God's will—I survived."

"And when you recovered, what did you do?"

"I chose to remain in Venice. I had trunks of clothing and enough money to establish my own household. My father had provided for me well. And then the Doge, after hearing me sing one evening, offered me protection in his court, providing a substantial income. I found I could live quite comfortably there, despite not having a husband."

"But, surely Maddie, it couldn't have been easy for you," he said.

"It wasn't. In Venice, because I was an educated foreigner, living on my own, I often felt as though I didn't belong or fit in. But, over time, I got used to it. I was never really lonely—I had my books to read and songs to write as well as herbal remedies to prepare. And, for what it's worth, the Doge was completely captivated by my stories."

"Tell me one now," Matteo encouraged her.

"Alright."

And, like she had diverted the ruler of Venice, she told a tale, amusing her new husband with her natural storytelling abilities. Seated next to one another, with his arm around her, the final hours of their journey melted away, and it wasn't long before the carriage rolled through the southern gates of Florence.

So eager to catch her first glimpse of the city, Maddalena opened the shutters, placed her elbows on the edge of the window, and leaned out. From under her, she could feel the carriage had ceased its constant wobbling, and the wheels were gliding smoothly over the gray stones that paved the narrow streets.

At first, still circumventing the town's periphery, all she could see was the skyline dominated by an austere tower and a magnificent rounded dome. From this vantage point, the city seemed awash in muted gray and purple hues that made the sharp outlines of the city scape dim and soft— as if it were floating on a cloud.

Matteo pointed to a crenulated tower in the distance and said, "Look over there. That is the Palazzo Vecchio, where Galileo and I have our offices. It is next to the Uffizi where Cosimo carries out the business of the city."

"And over there?" Maddalena asked, indicating the red dome, ribbed in white stone that rose up dramatically against a deep blue sapphire sky.

"That is the cathedral," he replied.

As they moved deeper into the town, she admired the warm, ocra buildings that radiated the late afternoon heat and watched in pleasure all the people milling about the markets where crates of green *zucchini* and barrels of grain were set out in grand displays. Alongside their carriage, men in fine coats rode on horseback, women carried baskets of fruit, and men pushed carts filled with stones bricks. At one point, she wrinkled her nose in distaste as they circumvented the areas where the butchers hacked and sawed at the carcasses of chickens, pigs, and goats.

Around every corner, she saw something new that delighted her. The energy of Florence and her citizens was palpable. It was much different from Venice, she noted. Here, the buildings built in local stone were more austere and formal, symmetrical without ornamentation. And yet, due to the muted colors and the glow of the light, there was a magnetic appeal about the city. It felt comfortable and homey, and she was easily beguiled by its subtle beauty.

Just before they crossed the river Arno, Matteo leaned over and pointed out the Pitti Palace, the home of Cosimo, the Grand Duke of Tuscany. "It will be just a matter of time before I take you there and introduce you to the Duke and Archduchess."

When they passed up and over the bridge, covered with the gabled shops of jewelers and goldsmiths, connecting the Oltrano to the opposite bank of the city, Matteo adjusted the make-shift wedding band on his wife's finger and said, "We will return here and you can pick out the finest gold ring for sale."

"Oh, I don't know," Maddalena replied. "I'm growing rather fond of this one."

On the other side of the bridge, they continued through shop-lined streets. Lifting the puppy, to see out the window also, she observed craftsmen making shoes of leather and others gilding chairs. The colors were marvelous, ranging from rich mahoganies to tarnished gold hues. When they rounded another corner and entered the silk dyer's street, Maddalena's attention was once again diverted by the jewel-toned hues of the fabrics that stretched high overhead on heavy cords, to dry in the hot summer air.

All around them women sang and chanted as they stirred the giant vats of dye, their hair wrapped up in turbans to protect themselves from the heat and humidity. With powerful arms, they lifted the paddles weighed down by the heavily soaked fabrics. Despite the sweat that slipped in rivulets down their cheeks, they were quite lovely.

As their vehicle turned down Via dei Calzaiuoli and entered the Piazza del Duomo in the heart of the city, Matteo called out to the groomsmen to stop in front of the baptistry. Ignoring the horses, that impatiently stamped their feet, sensing their home stable was near, Matteo told her a brief story about the doors that had been designed by Ghiberti, whom Michelangelo, Florence's most celebrated artist, had described as the Gates of Paradise.

Maddalena was much impressed, but as the horses moved again and the puppy yapped, she rested her hand on her husband's arm. "How much farther to Palazzo Crociani? I am so thirsty and have the urge to walk and feel the stones of Florence under my feet. Little Jupiter could use a break too."

Scratching the little dog behind the ears, and seeing her fatigue, he said, "We are very close, but, if you and my little friend here would like a rest, I propose we stop just up the street. My friend lives right here in via Ghibellina, who will gladly welcome us, and I'd like for you to meet him."

"Yes, I'd like that too," Maddalena readily agreed.

When the carriage finally rolled to a stop in front of a stately palazzo, Matteo opened the door and jumped to the street. Not waiting for the liveryman, he put his hands on his wife's waist and lifted her down to the ground. Maddalena handed the little dog to the stable boy, and together they approached the front door or the house. But before they could knock, it was yanked open by a servant.

"*Benvenuto, Signor Crociani!*" the man said. "Welcome back to Casa Buonarroti!" With a sweeping gesture, he invited them inside. The servant bowed and dismissed himself, saying he would inform the master of their arrival.

Inside, Maddalena found herself in an intimate space, decorated with sculptures and paintings. High overhead, light flooded into the courtyard and she could hear the gurgling of a fountain.

As moments ticked by, Maddalena asked, "Who is this friend of yours and how are you connected?"

"We studied together. His name is…"

"Matteo!" a voice from above interrupted. "You are a sight for sore eyes!"

The two gazed at the loggia above them and saw a short, rotund man leaning over the balcony. "We've been expecting you for days! But I heard you had been delayed in Venice due to the charms of a lovely young woman."

He beamed at Maddalena and said, "And you, m'lady, must be the one who captured this blackguard's affections! Come, let me greet you properly."

Rapidly, he descended the stairs, and with great enthusiasm embraced Matteo. "Ah, dear friend, it's been too long." The man patted him on the shoulder and said, "You appear sinfully radiant, my friend! It appears to me marriage agrees with you! Who would have ever thought *you*—of all people!"

Then, turning to Maddalena, he bestowed a kiss upon her cheeks, saying, "And you, Signora, are a vision. I am so happy you are here. You have arrived at a most opportune moment—your timing couldn't be more perfect! I have planned a little afternoon soiree that is about to begin. Galileo is already here, and the others will be arriving shortly."

Nodding in the direction of the upper floors, he added, "We are meeting in the library. I'm showing it off to my friends. Come! I want to see how things are progressing. My new artist friend is upstairs too and…"

"Oh, my!" He stopped in his tracks. "Excuse me, my dear, I do tend to twaddle on and on, and we still haven't been properly introduced!"

He looked askance at Matteo as if it had been his fault. "I believe Galileo told me your name was Maddalena."

Matteo just shook his head at his friend's capriciousness. "Yes, let me correct that blunder. Maddalena, this is my good friend Michelangelo."

"Michelangelo?" she asked in surprise. "Are you named after the great Florentine painter?"

"I am!" He placed a hand on his breast and made a slight bow. "I confess, I have the great fortune of being his nephew. And now they call me Michelangelo the younger, just to avoid any confusion."

"I am pleased to make your acquaintance, *signore*. I am familiar with your relative's work. I've been to Rome, and in the company of my father I have seen the great master's paintings in the Sistine Chapel. Do you paint as well?"

He shook his head wistfully from side to side. "No, I didn't acquire any of my uncle's sublime gifts. I have not his talent with a chisel and hammer, nor his agility with a brush. My talent lies in preserving and honoring his name for future generations."

He gestured broadly with his arms and said, "This was his home in Florence. It is mine now, and I'm the caretaker of my uncle's things, his papers and drawings."

"Please, please, let's go on up," he said, indicating they should they should proceed him. "I'm currently renovating the place and I want to show you what I have done so far."

As she climbed the smooth white marble steps, over her shoulder Maddalena said, "My husband was just beginning to tell me about you. He says you studied together."

"Yes, that's right. We met in Pisa, both students of Galileo. We've been friends for ages. If you have the time, I have lots of stories from our youth. As a young man, he—"

Matteo cleared his throat and said, "How about a drink? The journey has made us thirsty."

Michelangelo glanced over and, seeing the warning look on his friend's face, said, "Ah—yes, perhaps that would be best left for another time." With infectious good humor, he added, "As I said, I do tend to carry on... Come this way, my dear. Let's make a toast to the future!"

Taking Maddalena's arm, he escorted her past the long alabaster statues on pedestals and walls adorned with vibrant oversized paintings. At the end of the passage, he paused. "We are about to enter the library where my uncle's original sketches are kept."

For Maddalena's benefit, Matteo clarified, "To commemorate his uncle, my friend has hired the finest artists working in Florence to celebrate his uncle's life in a series of paintings."

"*Sì!* In the ceiling panels, there will be ten canvases in all that will depict the moments when my uncle met popes and sovereigns. I also want to honor his gifts—for painting, sculpture, architecture, and poetry—through the personification of these virtues."

"It sounds like quite an undertaking," marveled Maddalena.

"It has been. But I'm quite pleased with all the artists' contributions. There is one, however, whose work I find particularly pleasing."

"So, she finished her painting?" asked Matteo.

"*Sì!* That is what I am excited to show you."

"A female artist?" said Maddalena with growing interest.

"Yes, it is Cosimo's new protégé. Residing in Florence just a few years—but already making quite a name for herself. In my opinion, she deserves to be paid three times as much any other painter!"

Without another word, he opened the doors and invited her to enter. Curiously, Maddalena stepped into the spacious room. From two windows that faced the street, a soft light filtered into the room that illuminated the pictures of the Maestro, even the large statue of Michelangelo, the artist himself at the far end. And in the middle of it all, a man and woman stood near a massive table over which was scattered drawings, canvases, and several stacks of books. So absorbed in their work, their heads bent together, it appeared the couple wasn't aware of their arrival.

Maddalena watched in fascination as the woman rapidly sketched on a large tablet of paper. The man observed her progress closely and occasionally raised a finger and pointed to her drawing, murmuring inaudible instructions. Pausing to listen, the woman nodded in understanding and then rubbed away at the surface of the parchment with her charcoal-darkened fingers before continuing.

When Michelangelo called out, "Galileo, look who has arrived!" The gentleman dressed in a long, dark red cloak trimmed with fur glanced over his shoulder. A bright smile spread across his face, and he clapped his hands together and said, "Matteo! There you two are. We were just talking about you."

He stepped away from the table, walked in their direction, and with a great bear hug embraced Matteo. Over his friend's shoulder, he nodded at Maddalena. "Ah! Such a happy moment to have the couple of the hour here with us at last!"

Maddalena bowed her head and held out her hand to be kissed. "I am greatly pleased to see you again, *signore*. It seems we didn't get the chance to get better acquainted when we last met."

Comically raising an eyebrow, he said, "Quite understandable, my dear woman. I'm just an old man, and Matteo's charms are far more appealing."

She regarded him with pleasure, then surveyed the far side of the room again, more than a little curious to know the identity of the woman. But the artist, so absorbed in her drawing, seemed oblivious of the commotion behind her. Despite the raised voices, she continued to add more strokes to her paper.

Then, hearing her name called by Galileo, with great reluctance it seemed, she set down her chalk, placed the parchment on the table and slowly turned around. She blinked dazedly, as if coming back to the present from a faraway place. Then, dusting the chalk from her hands, she took a step in their direction.

As she did, Matteo took his wife's hand and drew her closer to the woman, and said, "Maddalena, I'd like to introduce you to Artemisia Gentileschi. Artemisia, I'd like you to meet my wife."

Chapter 16

Cosimo's Luminaries

*A*rtemisia and Maddalena observed one another without saying anything at first, seeking signs of compatibility that are often communicated when women first meet by a small gesture or expression.

In the time it takes for a bird to alight upon a branch, pause, and flit away, Maddalena rapidly took in the details of the other, estimating her to be in her mid-twenties. The artist's dark hair was caught up in a loose knot at the back of her head, and around her neck she wore a gold chain. There was a softness about her face that comes from childbirth, so Maddalena assumed she was a mother. The low-cut bodice of her emerald gown, revealing an ample and lush bosom, corroborated this fact. However, in sharp contrast to her pliant body were her firm, muscular arms.

Maddalena thought she was a pretty woman, but what made her especially attractive were her chocolate brown eyes. And then she smiled. It started out slow then illuminated her entire face, and at that moment Maddalena thought she was perhaps one of the loveliest women she had ever met. She felt a mystifying electric sensation and sensed the woman's confidence. Standing just a few feet from one another, still, without having spoken a single word, she felt an instant connection.

"*Buona sera Signora Crociani. Piacere conoscerLa*, it is an extreme pleasure to meet you." Regarding Maddalena thoughtfully, she added, "Have we been introduced before? You seem so familiar."

Reaching out her fingers, she touched Maddalena's cheek and tilted her head back just a touch to see the line of her jaw. "That face. It is a beautiful one—but there is something more that I see. It shows signs of character and intelligence, and it has seen sorrow but also much joy. I believe I'd like to paint it."

Maddalena was instantly flattered. "No, we've never met, for I am sure I'd recall meeting someone such as yourself. The way these men talk of you, it seems you are a most impressive and accomplished woman. But I do not believe our paths have ever crossed before. You are from Rome, and I come from Venice by way of Naples. My father was to be court ambassador to the Doge."

"Ah, yes, I do recall the story. Galileo was telling me about you earlier. He said you are a writer of verse and songs and that he heard you play at the Doge's court. I believe they call you La Cortigiana! *Beata te!*"

"Please don't praise me for that—and it is *not* what you think," said Maddalena quickly, glancing around the room to see if the others had heard her comment. "Like you, I am an artist. I paint with words and verse."

"Oh, I meant it as a compliment," Artemisia said. "To be a *cortigiana* means you are free to move at your own will and you are welcomed at court without the constraints of an unwanted husband."

She flashed a lopsided grin at Matteo. "Sorry, dear sir. I don't mean to offend or suggest that you are disagreeable!"

"No offense taken, my dear Artemisia," replied Matteo, laughing good-naturedly. "My wife has already set me straight on that account. She takes pride in her independence."

Artemisia nodded in pleasure. "By the besotted expressions on your faces, I can see it is to be a happy marriage. *Complimenti!* I extend warm wishes for a long and rewarding life together."

As a servant handed out glasses of wine to the guests, Michelangelo said, "Artemisia, I was just telling them about your painting. We must show Matteo and Maddalena the ceiling panel you designed for this room."

He took a sip from his glass and said to Matteo, "I just had it installed this morning. Come, my dear friends." Then, leading the way, Michelangelo walked to the middle of the library and pointed up at the ceiling. "*Eccolo!* Isn't it magnificent? I asked Artemisia to paint the virtue

Inclination—to pay tribute to my uncle's natural artistic ability."

Matteo bent his head back and studied the painting. "Artemisia! I see Michelangelo was right, your work does indeed stand out from the others—once again, I am slayed by your talent. The way you use light and shadow—it's absolutely genius!"

Maddalena looked up too and saw Artemisia had represented her virtue as a young woman with hair elaborately braided and massed around her face. The muse was seated on a billowing cloud, and in her hand she held a compass. And, although the face of the woman appeared quite virginal, she was depicted without a stitch of clothing.

"Your painting is quite beautiful," Maddalena said after a few moments. "It makes me think of the master Caravaggio. I saw his work once in the church of the Madonna of the Rosary in Naples. His colors are so vibrant, and the way he depicted the figures—it seemed they were actors on a stage—so lifelike and real, I swear I could see them move."

Moving a few steps away to view the ceiling from a different angle, she added, "I believe he's from Rome too. Did you know him, by chance?"

The artist viewed Maddalena with growing appreciation. "Yes. He and Orazio—my father—were excellent friends, and I met him several times when I was a child. I remember this one time he came to our home to borrow a Capuchin monk's habit and a pair of angel wings…"

"Angel wings?" Maddalena said, delighted by the idea. "Where did they come from?"

"Agata, one of the sisters in the convent of Santa Brigida sewed them together for my father using the feathers of geese she gathered down by the river. When no one was about, I used to put them on and pretend I was an elegant bird."

Artemisia added a bit wistfully, "How I wished I could fly away with those wings. Just to soar over the rooftops and be free… Such childish fantasies I had! Later, when I was older, I saw what Caravaggio did with those wings of Agata's. He attached them to some small urchin who modeled for him at the time and painted a picture of Cupid."

She stared off into space as she could see the picture hanging before her. "I was quite struck by the scene. In it, the little god of love is triumphant over everything. He is a handsome, happy boy who stands upon pieces of armor, a laurel wreath, and musical instruments that remind us *amor vincit omnia*—love conquers all. It prevails over science, art, fame, and power—it is the bond that intertwines and joins us all."

"I'm curious what was Caravaggio like? I've heard the rumors and stories, of course. Gossip always makes its way to the court in Venice."

The other woman thought for a moment. "I was quite small when I met him, but as I recall he was a mysterious man—very dark and serious. My father was greatly influenced by his style, and from Caravaggio he learned to paint directly from a posed nude model. Since my kin taught me, I too came to appreciate using a live model. Painting from life—it was the only way to really see. Only by studying nature does an artist know to capture the extreme highlights and murky shadows that fall across the human form, giving it bulk and substance."

As the men talked amongst themselves, Artemisia stepped closer and said in a low voice, "Do you recognize the woman in the painting?"

Maddalena looked back at the ceiling, noting the woman's expressive dark eyes, full mouth, and the way her thick dark hair framed her face. The image appeared so familiar—as if the muse were a real woman, someone Maddalena might pass by in the street.

"Well?" asked Artemisia.

And then it came to her. "Why, it's *you*!" Maddalena said in surprise.

"Yes," Artemisia responded with pride. "I used my face and my body to pay tribute to Michelangelo."

In the course of her short life, Maddalena had met many confident women—from savvy housewives to seasoned courtesans—but she thought Artemisia was one of the most self-possessed and assured of them all. To paint oneself naked—in honor of her mentor—she had bared not only her body, but also her soul.

"It is a lovely representation," said Maddalena, a little in awe.

"Yes, I'm rather pleased with how the painting turned out. As a woman, I have an advantage over my male counterparts. From the very beginning, when I first started to paint, I have been able to paint a woman's breast as it actually is, full of a mother's milk, heavy and sagging, or firm and supple like that of a young girl."

She directed her gaze back to the painting. "There are other symbols, too. For instance, the compass—and do you see the star I added?"

"Where?" Maddalena asked.

"There, in the upper right hand corner."

Maddalena followed the artist's outstretched arm. "Yes. I see it. What does it mean?"

"With them, I also pay tribute to Galileo. It is because of him I am doing so well in Florence. He is the reason I survive as a painter at all."

"I was wondering about that—your status, I mean. It is most unusual that a woman should earn a living as a painter and move in the circles of such prominent and learned men. My goodness! And this—you have been commissioned to paint a tribute to none other than the great Master Michelangelo!"

"It is rather extraordinary, is it not? Sometimes I can hardly believe it myself. But I was born to be a painter, and I have never let anyone, or anything dissuade me from my calling."

She turned her attention back to the ceiling panels. "My life hasn't always been so easy, but the day I arrived in Florence, my fortunes changed for the better. It was after I met Galileo at a party the Archduchess Maria had invited me to..."

Artemisia glanced over at Galileo and noticed he was listening in on their conversation. Raising her voice, she continued, "I was but a mere observer at the court dinner that night, a lone planet orbiting the outer perimeter of the cosmos. And then Galileo put in a good word with the Duke and that night he pulled me in closer so I too could feel the warmth of the Florentine sun."

Galileo appeared unperturbed to have been caught in the act of eavesdropping. On the contrary, he seemed quite pleased. "Such pretty words, Artemisia! You were but a shy young girl when I met you. Now you are a determined businesswoman. I believe you have learned a lot about court flattery in your years here in Florence."

"Artemisia, tell Maddalena the story of the day the Duke and Archduchess came to call upon you," said Matteo. Addressing his wife, he added, "Her fortunes in this city were sealed that day!"

Maddalena looked at Artemisia. "Yes, please do."

"*Dove cominciare?*" Artemisia began modestly. "When I first arrived, I was but a bride of eighteen or so, practically penniless with no connections and only a letter of introduction my father had given me. He told me to take myself and it to Cosimo's court and present myself. At first, I thought I'd find a patron with the Archduchess, but in the end, it was the Grand Duke Cosimo who took me under his wing."

"Yes, he took a particular shine to Artemisia that night," added Galileo. "The next day, he and his wife visited her apartments to see her work."

"How extraordinary," said Maddalena. "The Duke—*the* Grand Duke of Tuscany—came directly to *your* home?"

"Yes! It was a quite a thrill and a compliment," said Artemisia. "I showed the Grand Duke all my paintings, some that were done, others that I was working on. He lingered over my Judith for a long time, saying it pleased him greatly, and that he was drawn to the energy and passion he saw in my work."

"And his wife? What did she think?"

Artemisia raised an eyebrow and laughed. "She, on the other hand, found little merit in my work. The Archduchess stood before my Judith and wrinkled her nose in distaste, much offended by the blood and the violence of the scene. She hastily excused herself and told her husband she would wait for him in the courtyard below."

"What about Cosimo? Did he follow her?"

"Oh, no!" she said with a wave of her hand. "Quite the contrary. The Duke told his wife to go sit in the carriage, as he wanted to stay to commission a painting! It was the first of many requests."

"Upon Cosimo's recommendation, Artemisia has become the first woman admitted into Florence's esteemed *Academia del disegno*," said

Matteo. "It is quite an unprecedented accomplishment."

"When I received the news," Artemisia confided, "I was beside myself with pride, knowing the greatest man in all of Florence believed in me—a woman—to be equal to a man. With that invitation, he made it publicly apparent that I should be judged by my talents, not my sex. He opened a door for me and encouraged me to walk in. I was so overcome with emotion, I immediately had a letter penned to him in which I proudly declared: *My illustrious lordship, I'll show you what a woman can do!*"

Maddalena looked at Artemisia and they exchanged a glance. Only she—the only female in the room—could truly appreciate what an honor it really was. Raising her glass, Maddalena silently acknowledged Artemisia's triumph.

"And ever since that moment, she certainly has been showing us," added Galileo, with a chuckle. "Cosimo was right to let her admit Artemisia to the Academia. It's about time we had some female blood in that old man's club. I say we are all the better for letting a bit of fresh air into that crusty old society."

Maddalena viewed Galileo with a new appreciation, seeing why Matteo considered him such a good friend. Catching his eye, she said, "My husband has told me of your experiments and shown me the telescope you invented. He tells me both of you enjoy the patronage of Duke Cosimo as well."

Galileo smiled at her. "That's right, my dear. I have tutored Cosimo since he was a boy. I've always found him to be inclusive and open-minded. He grew from a curious boy into an intelligent man. Why—"

"You find him to be so intelligent," interrupted Matteo, "because he saved your hide, giving you asylum here in Florence when you ruffled the Pope's feathers with your theories about the stars."

"Yes, as I said," said Galileo, with a twinkle in his eye, "I did appreciate the gesture. So, when I discovered the satellites that rotate around Jupiter, the least I could do was name them the Medicean stars."

Galileo winked at Maddalena and said, "I can't tell you how much that delighted him!"

"It seems you too, Galileo, know the art of court flattery, and how to curry favors *and* indulge a few egos," said Matteo.

"Yes, quite! It is in our best interest to keep him on the side of science. It is a breath of fresh air that we have a ruler that can appreciate good reasoning and logic. He cares little for the rumblings that come from Rome and the small minds that want to hold the world back in the name of religion."

"Perhaps he should, perhaps you all should," interjected Michelangelo, his tone suddenly deadly serious, a drastic shift from the jovial demeanor Maddalena had observed earlier.

Galileo waved his hand dismissively in the air. "We will tread lightly, dear sir. But scientific facts must be acknowledged. We can't keep our heads in the sand forever. To move forward—to make any progress at all in this day and age—we can't back down or negate our findings."

"You may be the most famous scientist in the world, but you are also a troublemaker," said Michelangelo. "Just remember events of late— public hangings and people being burned alive in public squares."

"Such crude and utterly barbaric ways of terrifying and controlling the masses," said Galileo. "It is but the work of small-minded men."

"Precisely my point," said Michelangelo. "There are others all around us who aren't so enlightened as Cosimo. There are those who are out for personal gain and ready to throw good people to the lions. Just the other day, Tommaso Caccini was heard ranting and raving against you, Galileo."

"Oh, please! Caccini is a man of very great ignorance, no less a mind full of venom and devoid of charity," retorted Galileo. "He is an ambitious little fellow and uses his attacks on men of science to further his own gain within the ranks of the Dominican friars. The man is a pompous fool. A rooster crowing his own name."

"Even his own brother," added Matteo, "was so appalled by his sermon in Florence that he could scarcely control himself, saying he washed his hands of his kin forever."

"You see?" said Galileo, addressing the others. "No one takes Caccini seriously—and, never forget, we have the backing of the Medici court."

"For now, at least, as long as Cosimo is alive," said Michelangelo.

"Have you had news from him lately?" asked Matteo with a concerned frown. "Rumors abound that he suffers greatly."

"These past few weeks I have seen a great decline in him," said Michelangelo. "He puts on a brave face, hiding his illness from others."

"I pray for his recovery," said Artemisia. "He commissioned another painting of *Judith and Holofernes,* and I hope to finish soon before…"

A pall hung over the room, and no one spoke for a moment.

"A new painting of Judith, you say," interjected Michelangelo finally, trying to reanimate the conversation.

"Yes," said Artemisia. "In fact, I've enlisted Galileo's help."

"Galileo! Why ever for?" inquired Matteo.

Before she could respond, Galileo pointed to the drawings they had been working on earlier, and said, "Just look at this! I've been instructing Artemisia about the natural flow of blood through the body. It is especially helpful when you are painting an image of a woman decapitating a man! To depict it correctly, and really make it believable, she must get the science right."

Diverted from talk about Cosimo, the group continued to discuss less serious affairs. Soon the room was filled with more scholars, scientists, and mathematicians and as their numbers increased, they spoke of lunar orbits and the trajectory of planets. As Maddalena observed them, it seemed she could almost see the Milky Way and mathematical equations floating over the men's heads.

She tried to follow the discussion as best she could, but the cosine and empirical formulas seemed as confusing as listening to someone speaking a foreign language. After a while, she was relieved to hear Artemisia say, "*Scusi, Signor Crociani,* may I borrow your wife for an hour? I have errands in the city, and I'd like her company."

Matteo instantly viewed his wife with concern. Putting his hand on her arm, he said, "I'm sorry, *amore mio,* I didn't mean to exclude you."

He paused when Galileo called out, "Matteo! Show these gentlemen the new charts you have created."

His eyes traveled in the direction of his colleagues and Maddalena could see her husband was torn between his love for her and his passion for the stars. To help him make his decision, Maddalena encouraged, "Don't worry, about me. I'd like to go for a stroll."

"I'll take excellent care of your wife," Artemisia said, then added, "While you were away, I finished your portrait. Come by my apartments to view it later this evening. You will find us both there."

Maddalena looked from her husband to Artemisia in surprise. "You have painted a portrait of Matteo? He hadn't told me that."

"*Sì!* I hope it meets with your approval, Signora Crociani."

"You have nothing to fear, Signora Gentileschi," said Maddalena. "By the work I have seen here today, I'm sure I will find your painting of my husband equally as appealing."

"I found him to be a most agreeable subject," admitted Artemisia. "All the while, he entertained me with stories about flying... Can you imagine?"

Maddalena grinned at her husband. "Indeed, I can. It is a subject that consumes practically all his thoughts these days."

Raising an eyebrow, she gave him a playful look. "That and telescopes among other things..."

"Matteo!" Galileo urged again.

Maddalena smiled. "It seems you, *signore*, are much in demand. Go! They need you, and I'd like to see more of the city. I'll be fine. We will find each other again in just a bit."

"Alright," he said with reluctance. "We'll meet at..."

"We will see you later, *signore,* in my studio by the river," supplied Artemisia. "You know perfectly well where to find us."

Slipping her cloak over her shoulders, she reached out a hand and beckoned, "Come, Signora Crociani, let me show you Florence!"

Chapter 17

Agostino's Arrogance

*T*ogether, Artemisia and Maddalena stepped out of Casa Buonarotti and into the narrow dusky street, headed in the direction of the Arno. At the far end, Maddalena saw it gave way to a large sunny piazza. As they strolled side by side, they passed *palazzi* made of gray stones with enormous wooden doors and windows covered in iron grillwork. Farther down the block, as they neared a small leather shop, she spied a small stucco Madonna, praying over the entryway. Inhaling, she detected the scent of newly tanned hides and freshly cut lumber, combined with the pungent smell of cheeses and robust red wines.

She slowed her pace so Maddalena could peek inside at the man who was fashioning a fine leather satchel. She breathed in and said, "*That* Signora Crociani, is the aroma of Florence. It is the scent of creativity and passion, of a city and its people that celebrate the art of living well. This is a place where simply walking through the town transports you back into the past."

Tucking her arm with Maddalena's, she added, "I too am a relative newcomer to Florence, and I never chose to fall under her spell. Instead, she craftily invaded my senses and conquered me, and before I knew it, I was completely enamored." Smiling at Maddalena, she added, "You have just arrived, but give it time—you will come to love it as I do."

Waving to the man in the shop, the women continued walking. A bit farther down the street, she asked, "So, tell me, Signora Crociani—what are your first impressions thus far?"

"Please call me by my first name," Maddalena said, warming even more to her new companion. "As we entered the city, I was quite taken with the cathedral and its dome, and when we reached the city center, I was astounded by the baptistry doors."

"Ah, yes! Brunelleschi did a fine job with the *cupola*—and Ghiberti's golden portals—they are quite remarkable. What else have you noticed? You are a poet and an observer, are you not?"

Enjoying the game, Maddalena said, "Well, let's see... I was quite struck by the colors of the buildings in via Tournaboni, by the glint of gold jewelry I saw passing over the bridge, and by the rainbow hues of fabrics drying in the silk dyers' quarter."

"*Bene!* You haven't disappointed me. You notice beauty, not only the grandiose—you also notice it in the smallest details that, in their simplicity, are quite extraordinary. I like that!" Artemisia said with approval.

"I thought the silk dyers were especially impressive," said Maddalena. "There is beauty not only in their faces but in their very postures."

"Yes! Exactly," agreed Artemisia. "I take inspiration from those very women. You can see the hardships and struggles they must endure, as well as the joy of simply singing a song or finishing a good day's work brings them. When I pass by, I often pause and sketch them."

As they entered the open piazza, Artemisia gestured in the direction of the Palazzo Vecchio and said, "Speaking of noteworthy things— behold the pride of Florence!"

Maddalena placed a hand to her temple to block the sun and peered up at the crenulated building at the far end of the square and saw a tall, milky white statue of a naked man. They moved closer to stand in front of it, and turning to Artemisia she said, "Why, it's magnificent."

"That is Michelangelo's *David*. It was supposed to be placed on the top of the cathedral. But, when it was finished, the Florentines didn't want to place it so high up above the ground where no one could see its face."

Regarding her curiously, Artemisia continued, "There has been much talk and discussion about this work of art. But I'm interested in your opinions. When you look at *David*'s expression, what do *you* see?"

Maddalena considered the sculpture before replying. "I see determination. The boy has yet to throw the stone to kill the giant but by his confident demeanor, I already believe the monster who threatens him will be slain. There is no doubt in my mind."

"*Brava!* That expression of tenacity and perseverance against all the odds is what makes this city so special. The Florentines have always been considered the underdogs, at odds with the Pope and other city-states. But this young, innocent boy is a reminder that even the weakest warrior can defeat the mightiest of tormentors."

Artemisia added, "Perhaps it is what I find most attractive about this city, and why I flourish here. It is this sentiment Michelangelo achieved so well in his *David* that I also wish to accomplish in my work—especially with my Judith."

"I'd like to see your paintings."

"You will. When we return to my apartments. But first, I need to purchase a few things."

Indicating the way, they continued through the piazza in the direction of the Arno. As they drew nearer to the apartments over the stores that lined the Ponte Vecchio, she heard the clinking of plates of an evening meal being prepared.

At the top of the bridge, Artemisia paused in the open clearing between the buildings and placed her hands on the stone railing. Looking out over the river, she said, "This is one of my favorite spots. At any given time of day, the light changes here, and the colors of the sky and the city inspire my palette. When I run out of ideas or am feeling melancholy, just standing here soothes and inspires me."

"It's very serene," commented Maddalena.

Hearing a cart approaching, she turned to look behind her and saw two men hauling grain. As they passed by, both men tipped their hats, acknowledging them politely.

Maddalena smiled back at them then turned to her companion and commented, "Florence is smaller than I expected, and far more cordial."

"In comparison to Venice, or for that matter Rome, it is," said

Artemisia. "But don't underestimate Florence. She may be modest in size, yet she can be quite fierce when need be. She considers herself to be their equal—if not greater! Duke Cosimo has taken significant measures to ensure this. He rules the city with an iron fist, wrapped in a velvet glove."

"It is apparent people respect him, and they abide by his rules," said Maddalena. "I've only been here a few hours, but I feel quite comfortable walking with you, without the company of a man."

"One must always be cautious," Artemisia said. "But, yes, here, a woman has much more freedom. Nothing like the city where I was born."

"I'm a little familiar with Rome. I spent a summer there with my father when I was about sixteen. He thought it important to show me the city, and Saint Peters. Where exactly did you live?"

"We moved around a bit, but for the most part my family lived in the artist's quarters near Castel Sant'Angelo—close to the Pope's apartments."

"The city was so lively and immense, and full of beautiful works of art," said Maddalena appreciatively.

"Yes, but you only saw the part of Rome the Pope wanted you to see, *and* you were in the company of your father's military guards, I'm sure."

"Well, yes..." began Maddalena.

"Believe me, there is another side of Rome that isn't so pleasant. Apart from its alabaster marbles and amazing ceiling paintings, it is also a city filled with much crime, poverty, and brutality."

"But I thought the city of the Pope was a place of peace and..."

Artemisia shook her head. "It most definitely is not! Where I lived, every evening, roving bands of thieves came out and terrorized anyone who dared to walk the streets alone. I couldn't even open the window without someone making an obscene gesture or saying something foul. *That's* what Rome was like for me. It was not a place for an honest man— let alone a woman of virtue! The Pope tried his best to keep order, but in reality it was the thugs who terrorized and ruled the city."

Artemisia looked out at the river, remembering. After a moment, she said, "Do you see those people down there?"

Maddalena followed the direction in which she pointed and saw men rowing a barge piled high with crates. From the river bank walked a group of flirtatious young women who called out to them. As she watched their lighthearted exchange, Artemisia said, "Look how happy those girls are. In Rome, girls of a certain class can't walk about like that, so carefree and unprotected."

After a moment, she added, "Here the Arno flows serenely through Florence—there the Tiber ran red with Roman blood. And instead of shops that line this bridge, there were bodies of executed criminals that hung right in front of Castel Sant'Angelo."

Maddalena shuddered. "It seems, then, Rome is much like Naples. My city is also full of contradictions. Still, one day I hope to go back, if only for a visit. I'd like to show it to my husband."

"I don't share your sentiments. I have no desire to return to my home city and would do so only under great duress."

With a tilt of her head, she indicated they should continue walking. At the foot of the bridge, however, their path was obstructed by a caravan of carriages. As they waited for the way to clear, Maddalena asked, "What about your family? Are they still in Rome? Don't you miss them?"

"Not really," Artemisia said with a shrug. "My mother died when I was very young. I wasn't all that close to my younger brothers, and long ago I lost contact with my father. In the end, I became his biggest burden."

"Burden? But I thought you said your father was your teacher and that he taught you how to paint like Caravaggio."

When the street cleared, the women crossed into the Oltrarno and Artemisia continued, "Yes, in the beginning, he was. From him, I learned how to select the best stones to grind into paint, clean brushes, and stretch canvases. Usually, it was a task assigned to male apprentices—it was rarely something done by a girl. But difficult times required extreme measures."

"What do you mean?"

"My father didn't have a lot of money—or rather, he was just too stingy. He didn't want to hire an outsider to do such menial work when he could get by with having his daughter do it. And because he was tight with his purse strings, instead of hiring females from the local brothels as models, he used me—his daughter, and her nude body—instead."

"How old were you at the time?" Maddalena asked, thinking of the humiliation Artemisia must have suffered.

"About thirteen," she said. "But I didn't mind."

"You didn't mind?"

"I'm an artist, Maddalena. I didn't see the harm in modeling or baring my body—I understood it was all for the art. It was an important part of the process—to study a real woman's torso, breasts, and hips. Like studying how light and shadow define an apple or a pear."

She let Maddalena absorb this information, then added, "Don't you see? A fascinating new world was opening to me. I was completely entranced by the process. After a while, I wanted to make my *own* pictures. In the beginning, I was quite secretive about it. When my father wasn't looking, I started experimenting on my own—little things at first, you know—small paintings, drawings and such. Sometimes I used a mirror and used myself as a model. Other times, I set up a simple still life..."

Artemisia added with a wry smile, "But, of course, I couldn't keep what I was doing hidden forever. When Orazio discovered I was using his charcoals and drawing materials, he was angry. But it didn't dissuade me. Once I picked up a brush, it seemed I never put it down. It became a part of me—an extension of my hand."

Maddalena said in admiration, "Many people go a lifetime never knowing that kind of passion. To know right from the start that you are meant to do something..."

"But, *mia cara*, in all honesty, I didn't choose it—it chose me. It just overtook me, and I had no choice but to succumb. To me, it is like breathing or the necessity to drink water. Just like Florence invaded my senses, painting captivated my soul."

"And your father? What did he make of this?"

"After a while, he began to see the merit in what I was doing. It was then he decided to instruct me. Oh, how enjoyed working in the studio with him! When he was behind with his deadlines, he even allowed me to help him and sometimes passed my work off as his."

"So, in the end, he was happy with your efforts and talents."

"Yes, but there was always a great deal of friction between us. Orazio Gentileschi has always been an overbearing man, and he was torn between being proud of his daughter and being jealous of her. I could never really satisfy him, and we argued frequently. He criticized everything I drew or painted. When he was most frustrated, he called my drawing skills deplorable and said I had no concept of accurate perspective."

She laughed. "But I was just as stubborn and obstinate—I was a real thorn in that old man's side! I used to bait him to see how far I could push him until finally, one day in aggravation, he threw down his brush and said, 'Artemisia—you are impossible! There is nothing more I can teach you, you miserable girl.'"

"What happened then?" Maddalena asked, intrigued.

"At that point, my father, decided it was worth the money to pay someone else to instruct me. He saw it as an investment, and he hired his friend Agostino Tassi to finish the job he started. He was a master of perspective—very much in demand in Rome at the time—and had curried many favors with the Pope."

"That sounds like an agreeable compromise... And did you like Agostino? Was he a good teacher?"

"Oh, yes! I learned a lot from Agostino," she said, a bit heatedly. "I received *quite* an education from him. For almost a year, he came to the house to tutor me. He was such a fancy man, sometimes dressed as a Turk, other times a dandy, with gold chains dangling around his chest."

She closed her eyes remembering. "At first he took quite a shine to me. After he arrived, he'd caress my face, tell me a little joke, and settle his chair close to mine so I could smell his fancy cologne. But, catching sight of a drawing on my board, he would narrow his eyes and grab my pencil. Slashing it across the paper, he'd say: 'No, no, no! There, see what I've done, *mia piccola bambola?* If you are to dabble in design, at least pay attention to the foreground and how the lines merge in back to draw the eye in... Better, yes? Now pay more attention!'"

Artemisia was quiet a moment. "In the beginning, I didn't mind that his manner could be quite mercurial—overly attentive one moment and cruel and impatient the next—so anxious was I to learn from him. He was such an important man, so well thought of by my father and other painters in our quarter. I too was quite taken with him. Finally, I was able to associate with someone so important from beyond my little world and small house. It was like a breath of fresh air."

She looked over at Maddalena and gave a little shrug. "Even Tuzia, our neighbor, approved of Agostino. Though I was only fourteen, she'd say to me, '*Cara*, it isn't right that you are all alone in a house filled with men, and all the merchants and gentlemen who enter the studio ogle you. You should marry, Artemisia, to save your reputation.' And when Agostino showed up in our studio, when he wasn't looking, she'd wink at me and say, 'See that man there? He seems to fancy you. You should become his wife. You'll have a child of your own by the end of the year.'"

As they continued walking, she leaned over and whispered, "I must admit I started to consider Tuzia's words. After my mother died, you see, I had no one to turn to for advice—this silly woman, who really didn't know me well at all, was the only one who I could confide in."

"You had no sisters, no aunts—no one at all but this *neighbor*?"

"We moved around a bit and had no other friends and because I was the only female in the house, I had to take care of my little brothers Franco, ten, and Marco, not yet in trousers."

With a frustrated sigh, she added, "But, as they grew older, *they* were all free to come and go as they pleased, but *I*, on the other hand was practically a prisoner in my own home. How desperately I wanted to be free like those girls back there by the river! But my father feared I'd be molested by the vagrants and unsavory types who walked the streets."

She gave Maddalena a devious look. "Once, though, I tried to sneak out. I got it in my head to go to San Cecilia to see father's altarpiece which I'd never seen in position."

"Did you get away with it? Did your father ever find out?" Maddalena asked, admiring her spirit, thinking it was something she too would have done.

"Of course. And when he did, he slapped me across the face and locked me in the house, saying the neighbors would gossip about me—call me a slut and a loose woman if I ventured out again. Right then and there, he threatened to send me to the nuns, if I ever tried that again."

With a bitter laugh, she added, "But my father, who was so protective of me, saw no harm in the arrangement of having me tutored privately by Agostino Tassi—that's how much he trusted his friend. He had absolutely no qualms about leaving us together in the company of our neighbor, believing such a great painter would never trifle with a silly, illiterate girl. But, in the end, it was Agostino who..."

"What?" Maddalena prompted. "What did Agostino do?" When Artemisia didn't continue, Maddalena understood. "Ah!" she said, at last. "I see."

They walked for a moment in silence. "Forgive me. We've just met, and I didn't mean to intrude into your private affairs. You need not speak of it further if it pains you."

"No, on the contrary, it helps to confide my feelings. How I've missed female companionship and talking with someone who can sympathize and understand such things. And what happened to me—the rape and the subsequent trial—it's all now ten years past."

"A trial?!" exclaimed Maddalena. "You took the man who raped you to court?"

"There was a trial, yes," admitted Artemisia. "I was so young, and I trusted my father completely. He said Agostino Tassi had double-crossed the Gentileschi family and he wanted retribution. But sometimes I wonder now if Orazio was more worried about his financial loss and less about the abuse his daughter suffered at the hands of a trusted friend."

As they entered the piazza and passed by the church of Santo Spirito, Artemisia briefly described for Maddalena the events of her ordeal, the abuse, the lies, and the torture she had been submitted to. "When it was all over and the trial concluded, I parted ways with my father. He married me off to Pierantonio—actually paid him to take me off his hands. The last I heard, Orazio had moved with my brothers to Genoa. I tried to keep in contact, even sent word to him when my daughter was born, but he never replied. Since then I've lost touch with him."

"And Agostino? What happened to him?"

Artemisia replied harshly, "Ah! That miserable bastard. He always was a slippery fish. In the end, although convicted, he never served a day in prison for his crime. The Pope gave him a choice—spend time in prison or be exiled from Rome. He chose the latter and has recently taken up residence here in Florence."

"He's here in Florence!" said Maddalena in surprise.

"Yes, he…"

"Artemisia! Is that you?" a raspy voice cried out. "Come here, girl! I've been wondering when you would pass by my store."

The two women slowed their pace and directed their gazes towards a small shop on the corner. In the doorway, an old woman, missing her front teeth, stood staring them down.

"Signora Rossi, *come sta*?"

"I'd be much better if you paid me the balance of your bill! You owe a debt of ten florins."

Artemisia reached down for her bag and undid the drawstrings. She rummaged inside, then smiled apologetically. "I'm sorry, *signora*, today I have just enough to buy my pigments. I will have to come back tomorrow."

"You painters! It's the same story every time we meet," the old woman mumbled begrudgingly, rubbing her hands on her apron. "That miserable husband of yours never pays the bills, and you are always inventing excuses."

"If not tomorrow, then the next. I promise. I have just finished a painting for the Duke and…"

The woman waved her hands. "*Basta*! Stop with the excuses! I don't want to hear them anymore! I have a family too, you know! Come back when you can pay."

"*Grazie, signora*," Artemisia said as she cinched her purse.

Maddalena, noticing for the first time the scars that criss-crossed her fingers, whispered, "Oh my god! Are those the scars of the sibille?"

Instead of hiding her hands in shame, Artemisia held them up for Maddalena to see better. "They are! I was tortured to see if I was lying, yet Agostino, who glibly supplied one lie after another, watched as they bound my fingers so tightly, I feared they might be cut off. Despite the pain, I never backed down—instead, I pleaded over and over again that I was innocent. And that was the truth!"

When they came to an iron gate farther down the street, before she could ring the bell, Maddalena stopped, placing a hand on her arm. "You were very brave."

"Brave?"

"Yes, brave to stand up for yourself. I mean, not to be intimidated and coerced into saying what they wanted to hear."

Artemisia contemplated her earnestly. "Perhaps, you are right, but truth was on my side, I knew I was innocent. But, it wasn't just about me. I also did it for Beatrice Cenci."

"Beatrice Cenci? Was she a friend of yours?"

"No, I didn't know her," said Artemisia. "But I have never forgotten her."

"But what did she have to do with...?"

Artemisia looked up at the yellow stuccoed building, took a deep breath, and slowly let it out. "When I was ten years old, I witnessed the beheading of Beatrice Cenci. She was a girl not much older than myself who had been locked in her room and repeatedly raped by her father. The man was a monster. He abused and terrorized the entire family. Eventually, the family plotted together and killed him. When the Pope found out, to set an example to all of Rome that he would not abide murder in his city, he publicly executed the entire family."

"How horrible," said Maddalena sadly.

"One by one, the brothers and sisters of Beatrice and her mother were dragged upon the stage, and their heads were brutally cut off. I know. I was there that day in the piazza with my father. It was so awful. As they thrust Beatrice onto the stage, her hands bound behind her and her face dripping with tears, she screamed relentlessly, pleading she was innocent."

Artemisia closed her eyes. "But no one came to Beatrice's defense. The crowd cheered as the ax man swung his blade and chopped off her head. There was so much blood. That day, it seemed the river really did run red with the blood of Beatrice Cenci."

The women were silent for a moment. Artemisia raised her hand again to ring the bell. From the inner courtyard, they could hear a woman's voice call out to let them know she was coming. When Maddalena gave her a questioning look, Artemisia said, "This is where I buy my supplies. Now that I'm a member of the Academy, I can negotiate and sign my own contracts with patrons, *and* I can finally purchase my paint supplies myself."

"You couldn't before?"

"No, it usually isn't a woman's place to haggle with the merchants. Before, I had to rely on Pierantonio to buy them and it was a constant battle with him to get the right ones. He is so cheap and doesn't see the necessity. But I know. Those colors I need, the *lapis lazuli*, vermillion, and verdigris minerals. Those may cost several florins more, but they make all the difference in the world. Now, if I could just keep my husband from helping himself to our profits," Artemisia said grimly. "That man..."

"So, it isn't a happy marriage?"

"As happy as a marriage can be..." she said dismissively.

"What is it he does, this husband of yours?" asked Maddalena, resting her back against the warm building as they waited.

"He is a painter by profession. He might even be a decent one if he applied himself a bit more. But the poor man has no fantasia, no passion for his work. He paints to paint. Since arriving in Florence, I have far exceeded him."

"Does that bother him?"

"Yes, of course it does! He resents the fact that a woman, his wife no less, has usurped him. I am a member of the Academy, and he is not! It is a constant reminder that a woman is more accomplished than he—and it makes him extremely bitter."

She sighed. "But I don't mind, really. Pierantonio is barely around. He takes his pleasure elsewhere, gambles and drinks. *Boh!* Even when I hide our money, he seems to find it."

Growing impatient, Artemisia lightly rattled the gate and called out, "Paola! Are you coming, *cara*? I don't have much time to spare. I have to get back to Palmira!" Addressing Maddalena, she added, "I guess it could be a lot worse. We've had our ups and downs, and our fair share of grief—we lost two children—but in the end, he gave me a daughter. She is a beautiful little thing, and I love her dearly. And now, I, for the most part, can go about as I like. We coexist, and it suits us."

When they heard swishing skirts, they looked up to see a woman wearing a dirty smock and a scarf wrapped around her head. "Artemisia! I'm sorry to keep you waiting."

"*Buona sera*, Paola. How is the family?" To Maddalena, she added, "This is Signora Pampaloni. Her husband is a *vendecolori*. He specializes in selling coloring materials to artists and glass makers."

Paola politely nodded her head, then opened the gate. "It's about time you came to see us! Niccolaio has prepared the varnish you inquired about. He says it will help set your colors to help them dry faster. He has also set aside some orpriment, as well as some azurite, for you."

"Wonderful!" Artemisia beamed. "I will also require a new mortar and a bit of linseed oil."

As they entered the shop, Artemisia told Maddalena, "Signora Pampaloni's daughter is about the same age as mine. We take care of one another, don't we, *cara*?"

Paola gave her a wink and said, "Yes, yes we do, Artemisia, yes we do."

As the two women haggled over the price of the minerals, Maddalena poked around the shop, oblivious to their conversation, preoccupied with the sight of boxes filled with multi-colored stones and semi-precious gems that the artists ground to a fine silt to mix into paint. She walked to the far end of the room and ran her hand over the wood panels, used to build the frames upon which the artists stretched their linen tarps.

Hearing her name, she turned around to see Artemisia had concluded her business transactions with Signora Pampaloni and was beckoning her to join them again. Maddalena could tell by their expressions that both the artist and the merchant were satisfied with the deal they struck. As they left the shop, Maddalena seeing the bags filled with bundles wrapped in brown paper and said, "It appears you negotiated quite ably. I'm impressed. From the Duke all the way down to the *vendicolori*, you have made quite a few connections here."

"Yes, of course I must, if I am also to pay off my husband's debts, it is necessary to be a shrewd negotiator. I've learned how to take care of myself and my daughter."

With an oblique smile, she added, "It also doesn't hurt to have a few loyal friends—from the most prominent to the humble—to help with personal matters."

Holding out one of the linen bags, Artemisia asked, "Can you carry this? I'm almost done with my errands—I hope you don't mind, but there is one more quick stop I must make. It's very close, just a few blocks away."

Readily, Maddalena agreed, letting herself be led into the labyrinth of narrow side streets again. She stopped when Artemisia indicated a building with a sign that read: *Entrance by appointment only*. As Artemisia rapped loudly on the door, Maddalena couldn't help but notice lady's garments dangling from a couple of the upper windows and said, with a bit of amusement, "What are we doing *here*? It's a brothel!"

"How very astute you are," Artemisia said with a small laugh. "I am here to choose a model. Now that I am a member of the Academy, not only can I buy my own paint supplies, I also have access to its ledgers with all the names of the women who will pose nude for a painter. It is possible for me to hire my own models and not have to rely on my own body as..."

Before she could finish, a woman called out from an upper window, "*Aspetta Signora Gentileschi*! We've been expecting you."

Within a few moments, the door to the establishment was wrenched open, and a woman in a low-cut gown, practically revealing her nipples, appeared before them. "*Buona sera*, Signora Gentileschi. Come in!"

Maddalena followed Artemisia into a private courtyard where a small fig tree grew. Along the walls crept ivy, and in the corner a small fountain filled the patio with the with the bubbling sound of water. Pointing to a low bench next to it, Artemisia said, "Rest yourself there—I promise this won't take long. I want to speak with one of Signora Baldini's girls. Before I pay her good money to sit for me, I want to approve her."

Left to her own devices, as she waited, Maddalena wandered idly around the small patio. From the loggia above, she could hear a woman singing, and a bit of shrieking followed by some giggling. From the other alleyway, Maddalena detected the unpleasant odor of urine and rotting garbage. Feeling a little nauseous, she bent over to breathe in the scent of roses planted in sturdy stone vases.

As the minutes ticked by, Maddalena picked a fig from the tree and rolled it between her fingers. She was about to sit on the bench but stopped when she heard the tread of heavy booted steps and the sound of a key in the lock of the outer gate. She watched with a little trepidation as the exterior door swung open and a dark, swarthy man strode into the small, intimate courtyard.

At first, he didn't see her standing in the shade of the tree, but as his eyes adjusted to the waning light, he caught sight of her light-colored dress. When he did, a slow grin broke over his face. "Well, what have we here? It appears Signora Baldini has acquired some sweet young flesh."

A bit taken aback, Maddalena quickly responded, "Signore, I fear you have gotten the wrong impression."

As he sauntered a bit closer, his eyes traveled from her face, slowly down her body. Standing a few inches away, he said, "Ah, by the tone of your voice and use of language, I see you are an educated woman. And where might you come from, Signorina..."

"I come from Naples by way of Venice. I am newly mar..."

"So, a new courtesan from Venice?" he interrupted. "How entirely delightful."

Towering above her, obstructing her path to the door, Maddalena felt a sense of panic. She took a step backward, but he caught her arm and held it tightly. Attempting to yank her arm from his grasp, she implored, "Let me go, I'm not what you think…"

"On the contrary, you are a *very* sweet morsel."

When she tried to pull away again, he laughed and increased the pressure, pinning her to his side. In a cajoling tone, he said, "What is your hurry? Stay and talk to me. Let's get to know one another better."

Before she realized it, he pulled her to his chest and leaned down to kiss her, thrusting his tongue into her mouth. In a panic, she beat him back with her fists, but little good it did. Finally, she bit his lip, jerked her head away, and let out a piercing scream.

He raised his hand to slap her but froze when he heard a commanding voice say, "Leave her alone. She is with me."

The man's head swung up, and Maddalena could see the blood trickling down his chin. Still peering into her eyes, he said, "Such a pity, my love, it seems we have been interrupted. But we can go inside if you like and leave this nag out here. My name is Agostino Tassi and I…"

"*You* are Agostino Tassi?" Maddalena said in disbelief.

"Let her go," Artemisia firmly repeated, watching him warily.

Glancing over his shoulder, he said, "Ah, Artemisia! I thought I recognized your voice. I was just thinking about stopping by to pay you a call. Tell me, how is your little girl?"

When he saw the shadow of fear cross her face, he laughed out loud but was distracted from saying anything more when, with great force, Maddalena wrenched her arm free. Distancing herself, from him she crossed the courtyard to stand by her friend.

Peering at them with hooded eyes, he ran a hand suggestively down the front of his britches making an obscene gesture, and said, "So, this little whore is a friend of yours? It seems appropriate to find you both in front of a brothel doing what you all do best—teasing a man's cock."

"And this is where I should have expected to find you as well, Agostino. After all, isn't that what you do best—helping yourself to women? I see you even have your own key so you can come and go as you please."

They faced one another in a challenging standoff until he smoothly pulled back his coat, revealing the dagger that was attached to his belt. Lightly, he touched it. "There was a time when you tried to use this knife against me, Artemisia. Do you recall?"

She eyed him thoughtfully. "Perhaps I should use it against you again. I'm a little more experienced now, and I believe my aim will be more precise. This time, I won't miss my target."

"I'm sure you'd fail again, Artemisia. You are a mere silly woman. Oh, you may be an adequate painter who has a little skill, but you still need a master to guide your hand."

"You'd be surprised," she retorted. "I've learned a few things all on my own since Rome. I'm quite talented with a brush, as well as a blade."

"Be careful with your threats, Artemisia," he warned. "Just remember it is *I* who taught you how to draw. Never forget that, Artemisia. *I* am the one who changed your destiny."

"You are right on that account, Agostino. You may have been the reason for my first notoriety, as brutal and dismal as it was. But you have tempted fate once too often, and someday soon there will be a reckoning."

Agostino snorted. "Woman, your words don't scare me. They are as insignificant as you are! Don't you know by now I arrange things to my liking—I fend for myself and always land on my feet! You of all people should know that about me by now."

Artemisia said nothing, just watched him saunter leisurely into the brothel. As the door closed, a steely expression settled over her face. Under her breath so only Maddalena could hear, defiantly she said, "Beware, Agostino! In the end, I *will* have the last say. For, within the soul of this woman, you will find the spirit of a Caesar, and she too shall be avenged!"

Chapter 18

Judith and Holofernes

*A*rtemisia swung around angrily, but when she saw Maddalena's tense expression, her face immediately softened. Taking her arm, she asked, "Are you all right? Did he hurt you?"

"I'll be fine," said Maddalena. She brushed off her skirt and picked up her hat. "So that was Tassi?"

"Yes, that was him. A fine specimen of a man, no?" she said with a mirthless laugh. "Seven years ago, he was banished from Rome..."

"And now he shows up in Florence—is he stalking you? Does he seek revenge for being thrown out of the papal city because of you?"

"Oh, heavens no! He couldn't care less about me. Didn't you just hear him? He views me as an inconsequential fly on the wall. No, it is a mere coincidence we are once again thrown together. After being exiled from Rome, he drifted around from city to city finding new patrons. I heard rumors he first went to Pisa, then Livorno and after that Lucca. He had a wife there once—but now she is dead. Some say he hired assassins to murder her for running away with another man."

"After what just happened, and having listened to his insults, I certainly think he is capable of that. He is a despicable sort."

"I believe he would, too. The man is a braggart and most reprehensible—capable of the foulest things imaginable. If it served his purpose, and satisfied his ego..." She paused a moment, then added, "No, the reason Agostino is here now isn't because of me specifically. It has to do with money. With each passing year, his reputation and his fortunes decline a little more, and he becomes a little more desperate. When that happens, he moves on to a new place, hoping to milk it for all it's worth."

"So, now he resides in *this* city! How difficult it must be to see him here after the harm he caused you in the past."

"The first time I encountered him near the Medici Palace," admitted Artemisia, "it came as quite a shock."

"How long has he been here?"

"He showed up here late last spring, seeking work and new clients—especially the patronage of Duke Cosimo. Now I take great care not to cross his path. But Florence is a small town and, on occasion, we see each other. Each encounter, I have to say, is more distasteful than the last."

With a shake of her head, she reached down to retrieve Maddalena's purse. "*Basta*! Enough talk of Agostino. The subject wearies me, and I'd prefer to discuss more pleasant things."

Looking at the long shadows that now filled the street, Artemisia urged, "Come. The hour is getting late, and it is time to return home. There you can wash your face and rid yourself of the putrid stench that man has left behind."

Readily, Maddalena followed Artemisia and once again they crossed the bridge. At this hour, the crowds and the traffic had dispersed, and they moved with ease through the narrow streets until they came to a piazza dominated by a blue and white church. As they passed through the square, the vesper bells of Santa Croce rang: *dong, dong, dong.*

Around the corner in a smaller piazza, just as the chimes faded, Artemisia stopped in front of a tall stone palazzo and took a large key out of her pocket. After she unlocked the sturdy outer door, she ushered Maddalena into the building's cool, dim interior and up two flights of stairs. When they arrived on the third-floor landing, they were greeted by a small woman with a winsome smile.

"Signora Artemisia, where have you been? The child has been asking for you."

"I was delayed. How is she?'

"I gave her some broth and sat with her for a while. Now I must tend to my own family."

"Yes, of course, Mariuccia. I'll see you tomorrow."

The woman bobbed her head at Maddalena, then pulled a shawl around her shoulders and slipped on by them down the stairs. Artemisia motioned for her to enter. Once inside, she saw a little girl, about five or six, playing with a small rag doll near the window.

"Palmira, my love! Mamma has come home. Did you miss me?"

When she heard her mother's voice, the towheaded child stood up and ran across the room and into her mother's outstretched arms. Together, they swung around in a circle. Finally coming to a stop, Artemisia said, "Maddalena, this is my daughter, Palmira."

She set the little girl down but, too shy to say anything, Palmira clung to her mother's skirts.

"What do you have to say, *amore*? Has the cat got your tongue? Maddalena is a new friend. I think you are going to like her."

Wide-eyed, the little girl stared at Maddalena, then politely inquired, "Are you a painter like my mother?"

"No," responded Maddalena. "But I am an artist. Instead of using paint, I make pictures with my music. How about you? What do you want to be when you grow up?"

"I don't know yet. But I like to draw."

"Well, that's a start!"

"Would you like to see the monkey I drew?"

"A monkey?" Maddalena looked up at Artemisia. "I have only heard such an animal described to me. Wherever did your daughter see a monkey?"

"Why, Cosimo likes all sorts of exotic animals," said Artemisia. "Palmira and I saw it in the park behind his palace. The Medici are always throwing the most extravagant parties, and foreign dignitaries around the world are always sending him the strangest gifts, from exotic birds to dwarfs with which he entertains his guests."

"There's even a zebra and I got to sit on it once," chimed in Palmira.

"Okay, my little imp, show Signora Crociani your drawing, and then it is time for you and your dolly to go to bed."

After Maddalena paged through several pieces of parchment,

admiring a variety of animals the little girl had drawn with a piece of red chalk, Artemisia said, "Time to put your things away and follow me."

She took her child by the hand and said to Maddalena, "Make yourself comfortable while I tuck her in and tell her a bedtime story."

In the fading light, Maddalena took in the comfortable clutter of books and papers. Against one wall, a small table was positioned near an easel, and next to it a stack of finished canvases. Another table was filled with jars of oils, turpentine, and palettes. There were also several small mortars and pestles, and she could see several contained finely ground powders ready to be mixed into paint.

From a nearby open window Maddalena saw the sun, now a fiery ball of orange and red was dipping lower into the pale green waters of the Arno River. She imagined it would be just a short time before Matteo would arrive. But, she found she was quite content and comfortable, waiting for him in the home of her new friend.

When Artemisia entered the room again, Maddalena smiled in amusement as the businesswoman transformed into a domestic housewife and mother bustled about, picking up shoes and straightening books. Satisfied everything was in order, Artemisia then reached for a bottle of wine from a cabinet. From another, she removed two earthenware cups.

While she prepared their refreshment, Maddalena continued her walk about the room but paused when she came to a painting set on an easel that was partially covered with a cloth. She checked over her shoulder, asking silent permission, and when Artemisia nodded, Maddalena pulled away the covering.

As the drape fluttered to the ground, she stood back and gasped. The canvas, struck by the last ray of light from the setting sun, gleamed a vibrant red. So intense was the color she half-expected to reach out and touch the sticky residue of blood.

When she felt Artemisia's presence behind her, Maddalena whispered in awe, "So—this is your Judith!"

"Yes. That is my Judith."

Maddalena had been prepared for a vivid, dramatic representation of the biblical story, but what she saw went beyond her wildest imagination. The painting was powerful in its simplicity. The figures formed a solid triangle. The maid dressed in red at the top contrasted vibrantly with the vivid, blue silk gown worn by her mistress to the right. Judith's arms formed solid parallel lines that directed the viewer's attention to the man's death mask and the scream that was frozen on his face as the blade cut into his throat.

Immediately, she recognized the man's face. With a gasp, she said, "Why, it's Tassi!"

"Yes. It is Agostino."

"And what do you think of my Judith?"

Maddalena's gaze traveled up from the man to Judith's face and exclaimed once again. "It is you! You are Judith."

She realized the implications of what Artemisia had done and turned to face the artist. "You have had your revenge, after all. When the painting is presented to the Duke, all of Florence will see you as an avenging angel taking your pound of flesh."

"Yes, that is it to some degree."

Artemisia offered her one of the brown earthenware mugs and took a sip of wine. "To paint one's emotions is a cathartic experience. But there is something more important I wish to communicate in this painting. Look beyond the violent scene, see beyond the man's hideous face. Now tell me, Maddalena, what do you see? What do you hear?"

As Maddalena had done before, she rose to Artemisia's challenge. She studied the painting a moment more and, as she did, she heard the soft neighing of horses and the off-colored jokes of the soldiers who passed by on night guard just outside the tent. She listened as the camp settled into silence, knowing hundreds of soldiers lay just beyond waiting to attack her city of Bethulia.

Her arms felt weary from the pressure she exerted to hold the general's body in position so Judith could slice off his head. And when the final draw of the sword finished its gruesome task, she observed how the candlelight flickered over her friend's face, casting long shadows on the wall. She stood a bit taller, seeing the look of unflinching determination in Judith's eyes, and through the darkness and the mists of time, her words came echoing back to her: *"Abra, as long as I live, I will have control over my being."*

Maddalena blinked her eyes and wavered slightly. Standing in front of the canvas, she felt a tidal wave of emotions. She raised her eyes to Artemisia, who was quietly watching her, waiting for her to respond. "I see two women uniting and empowering one another, two women who know themselves to be inferior to no man, courageous and ready to map out their own destinies."

"Brava!" Artemisia said, raising her wine glass. "This painting is not about Agostino Tassi, or not just about taking my revenge out on him. My Judith is painted for Beatrice Cenci, for myself, for you—for my daughter—for all the women who are vulnerable and powerless. It is for those who haven't had their voices heard or have had punishment served upon them instead of upon those who harmed them. In my paintings, I tell a new story. I create an alternative and promising world in which women take control, turn the tables, and finally have the upper hand."

"It is a powerful message... rather ingenious, really."

"Yes, my patrons may supply the themes, the biblical stories they wish me to paint—most of the time I have no control over that. But," she added with a sly smile, "the manner in which I choose to depict them is entirely up to *me.*"

Picking up her paint brush, she ran the bristles over the palm of her hand. "Over the years, I have learned to transform my pain into my passion. Through my art, I have assuaged my grief and my rage—wanting to fight the abusers."

She smiled knowingly at Maddalena and said, "It is very ironic, wouldn't you say?"

"What is?" Maddalena asked.

"Men especially find my subjects and the way I choose to depict them extremely—how shall I put it—stimulating. The nude bodies, the blood, and the violence appeal to them and they seem to be quite willing to pay a good deal of money for my paintings. Right now, my real intent might be lost on them all, but given time, I believe, like Michelangelo's *David*, my message of empowerment will encourage future generations."

Referring back to the work at hand, she tapped her canvas lightly with her brush. "As you can see, the work here is unfinished. I still need to paint Abra's image."

The two women regarded each other for a moment, feeling a powerful connection. Finally, Artemisia said, "With your permission, I'd like to use your face for Abra."

Greatly overwhelmed, Maddalena simply nodded.

"Excellent!" Artemisia exclaimed.

Maddalena turned back to the painting and, as she did, her attention was caught by another. Gazing at her through the shadows were the dark expressive eyes of her husband—the very ones she had come to love.

"Oh, Artemisia," she said in a hushed tone. "I didn't think I could be any more impressed by your talents! You've caught the very essence of Matteo. It's almost as if he were here with us now, so lifelike is the rendering. You are quite adept at portraiture."

Artemisia indicated several paintings of Florence's prominent citizens that leaned against the wall in various states of completion. "As you can see, it's become quite a good source of income."

Setting aside her paint brush, she added, "Still, that's not why I do them. While I like the complexity of the larger paintings—those with lots of figures and historical drama—I much prefer these kinds of intimate paintings. I enjoy finding the essence of a person and capturing their soul and spirit on canvas."

Maddalena looked over her shoulder at her friend and said, "Knowing my husband, and how impatient and busy he is, it must have been a difficult thing for him to sit long enough for you to capture his!"

"*Mia cara*, you have no idea! He was the worst! The man is so full of energy and ideas. It is a good thing I saw that special quality in his eyes—the thing I knew I wanted to capture right away. He wears his convictions, and his heart, on his sleeve."

She took a sip of wine and said, "Just the other day I was commenting to Francesco about this very thing. Francesco knows Matteo well and said..."

"Francesco?"

"Yes, Francesco Maringhi," she said with a smile that made her eyes sparkle. "He is another patron of mine. He has exquisite taste and a discerning eye for art as well as artists. He has provided entry to Florence's wealthier families and has secured for me many portrait commissions. I will introduce you to him at the Grand Duke's reception and..."

When Maddalena raised her eyebrow at the warmth she heard in her friend's voice, Artemisia replied, "You have surmised correctly. Francesco is more than just a patron. He is a wonderful man who gives me a little hope I might too find the happiness you have found with your husband. He..."

Hearing a man's booted tread pounding rapidly up the stairs, she stopped speaking. Seeing Maddalena's startled expression, she said, "Oh, don't worry," said Artemisia dismissively. "I know that sound. It's only my husband."

Maddalena watched in trepidation as the door swung open and a slight man in an ill-fitting coat entered the room and heard Artemisia call out to him in a mocking tone. "So, you have finally decided to grace me with your presence, Pierantonio! It's only been three days."

"I won't be here long. I came for some food," the man said gruffly, barely raising his eyes to look across the room at his wife.

"What is there to eat?"

"There is a little broth left," Artemisia responded indifferently.

"Is there bread?"

"There is enough."

"How is the child?"

Maddalena listened as the tired couple dispassionately discussed their daughter and other domestic affairs. She could tell there was no joy in their conversation, and their eyes never connected. As their mundane conversation continued, it didn't take much to escalate their cool, brief exchange into a heated debate.

Pouring himself some wine out of the jug, Pierantonio muttered, "I'll pay the butcher tomorrow, Artemisia! Now, stop badgering me."

"You are wearing out our name with merchants all over town," she retorted angrily. "This very afternoon, the woman at the greengrocers admonished me for not paying our bill. What did you do with the money I gave you this morning?"

"*Basta!* Enough! Leave me alone, woman. I don't have to account for all my..."

Seeing Maddalena for the first time, sitting in the shadows next to Artemisia's easel, Pierantonio swiveled back to his wife and asked, "And who might that be? One of the models from the brothel?"

"*Stai attento, marito mio!* Show respect. This is Signora Crociani. She has just arrived from Venice with her husband, Matteo Crociani. The least you can do is..."

He jerked his head in Maddalena's direction. "*She* is Matteo Crociani's wife? I've heard talk of her. Isn't she a...?"

"Hush! No need to run on with your mouth. She is a guest in our home."

Pierantonio's interest in Maddalena increased as he let his eyes travel insolently over her slender form, then directed his attention back to his wife and asked, "Didn't you just finish his portrait?"

"Yes, it is just over there."

"I thought so," he said, taking another sip of wine and setting his cup down heavily. Sitting back in his chair, he broke off a bit more bread and chewed it carefully, the wheels turning in his head. After a moment, he stood up and reached for his hat. Narrowing his eyes at Maddalena, he said, "Tell your husband to pay the money due to us! We will take no credit."

"Pierantonio!" admonished Artemisia. "*Stai zitto!* Watch your tongue. Matteo Crociani will be here soon to collect his wife. Surely even you can't be so rude as to demand money from a patron's wife."

"What do I care if I offend her. She is only his wife. She isn't the

Archduchess, and he isn't the Duke."

"You are drunk, Pierantonio. Leave, us. I won't have you insulting my patrons. I don't want you here when he arrives."

At first, it seemed Pierantonio was ready to challenge her, but quickly losing interest, he shrugged tiredly and said, "As you wish, Artemisia." His eyes roamed from one woman to the other. "I'll take my leave. I've eaten the bread, and now there's nothing left here to tempt my appetite."

Without hesitation, he grabbed his wife's purse from the table and rummaged around inside. Expertly, he peeled back the silk lining and dug out a few concealed coins. With a satisfied expression, he pocketed the money then took one last swig of wine, this time directly from the bottle, and wiped his mouth with the back of his hand. Moving to the door, he called over his shoulder, "Don't bother waiting up for me..."

"As if I would," Artemisia retorted angrily.

"Tell Palmira her father loves her," he said, buttoning up his coat and yanking open the door. Without a backward glance, he took his leave, and the two women listened to the sound his heavy boots descending the stairs. With each step, it seemed the atmosphere in the room grew a little lighter.

When she heard the outer gate on the street level slam shut, Artemisia stood up to shut the apartment door her husband left open. She rolled her eyes and said, "I'm sorry you had to see that. He is boorish most of the time. But he knows there is a line he must not cross. I am the source of his income, and the man does love his daughter..."

"Does he know about Francesco?"

"How could he not! He may be the worst painter in Florence, but he isn't stupid. He's known for quite some time and I make no attempt to hide it from him. My husband even corresponds with Francesco from time to time writing messages about financial matters on the back of my love letters to him."

"What? Isn't he the least bit jealous?"

"Oh, *mia cara*... The man has no pride at all, and we are far beyond the rants of a lover's rage. No, the man couldn't care less as long as his bread is buttered. If he feels anything for me at all, it is envy. His heart is full of greed, so he tolerates my lover, only because Francesco is a powerful ally of the Duke and is the source of our income. Why would he want to jeopardize that?"

Artemisia sat down at the table and poured them both more wine. "Pierantonio is a small-minded, petty, egotistical man. My father, Orazio knew it too—right from the very beginning. And yet he settled, thinking an arranged marriage to such a man was the best solution to get me out of his house."

In disdain, she shook her head. "At first, I had hopes, as I once had for Agostino, that we could build a decent life once we married. We suffered many sorrows and many great delusions. For years we tried to have a child and lost many until Palmira finally came along. But still my husband, despite a few promising moments, remains a philandering, miserly man who doesn't wish to improve himself."

She was silent a moment, then added, "But, if you compare him to the spectrum of men, he looks like a prince compared to Tassi. *That* man is in a league of his own..."

Staring into her glass, Artemisia then added quietly, "Sometimes I'm not sure what he might do next. He raped the woman he took as his wife and then had her killed when she ran off with a man from Lucca. During that same time, he used and abused me and threatened me harm should I reveal he was sleeping with me."

Glancing up, she said, "Did you know I only learned he was married in the middle of my trial? And at the time he was promising to wed me, he also had an incestuous relationship with his sister-in-law, and by her fathered two children. The man's sins never stop. And now..."

"Yes..." encouraged Maddalena. "There's more?"

Artemisia was silent for a long moment, then looked over at the door behind which her sleeping child lay. "I fear for her."

"Palmira! But she is only a little girl of six."

"Yes," she finally said. "She is a little girl of only six. She is an innocent and must be protected."

"You can't mean to imply…"

Slowly nodding her head, Artemisia, continued, "Last month, I was in the market buying bread for our evening meal. When I turned around, Palmira had slipped away. I searched frantically through the stalls, calling out her name. I was terrified she had wandered down to the river. She likes to see the ducks. How many times has my heart stopped, finding her there, worried she might slip on the mud and into the Arno and drown."

"And was she down by the river?"

"Not this time. When I ran across the piazza in the direction of the Ponte Vecchio, I saw Agostino in the loggia and in his arms was my golden-haired child."

"*Oh, mio Dio!* What did you do?"

"I screamed at him to put her down."

"And did he?"

"He smirked at me and asked if this little angel was what I was searching for. I asked him again to let her go, but he just gave me a nasty grin and said the two of them were getting better acquainted and were just starting to have a little fun. And then Palmira called out to me, saying the nice man was teaching her a new game."

"A game," whispered Maddie, fear now filling her heart too. "What did you do?"

"I rushed right up to the portico and grabbed Palmira," said Artemisia. "It made me nauseous to imagine just what Agostino had in mind for my little girl. I slapped his face, but he caught my arm and hissed into mine, telling me to be very, very careful, that it was only a matter of time before he took my child as he had taken me."

"And then…"

"He said if I didn't put in a good word with Cosimo, Palmira would suffer my fate too. If, on the other hand, I helped him obtain a few prominent commissions, he would leave us alone."

The women were silent for a moment. Then Maddalena asked, "And have you spoken to Cosimo? Did you do as Tassi asked?"

Artemisia gave her a cryptic look, and instead of answering her question, she replied, "Wouldn't it be wonderful to be Judith and take matters into my own hands?"

Maddalena looked at her in astonishment, afraid of what her friend might do.

Artemisia threw up her hands and cried, "*Oh, Santo Cielo!* You should see the expression on your face! Put the thought out of your head! I'm not planning on beheading the man!"

She sat back in her chair and said, "Although it would serve him right. No, *mia cara*, I have other plans for Agostino."

"Other plans?" said Maddalena. "Such as?"

"There are those who would help me," she said at last. "Let's just say I have worked out a scheme to rid myself of the man for good. And yes, most definitely, Cosimo, my most loyal patron, plays a significant part."

When Maddalena shook her head, not understanding, Artemisia gave her a Cheshire smile and said, "Tassi might have gotten away with stealing from me what no man has a right to steal from a woman, but robbing a man's property! Now, that might finally count for something."

Raising her glass, Artemisia said, "I learned that lesson all too well. A woman's virginity is a commodity like any other. If she loses it, that is her problem. But stealing property that belongs to a man is a far greater crime—especially if it is a painting which belongs to the Grand Duke of Tuscany. Such an act of thievery might finally land Tassi in prison."

Chapter 19

The Sting

Maddalena leaned in closer and listened with interest as Artemisia outlined the plan she had devised to frame Agostino Tassi. She soon discovered the real reason they had visited the brothel that afternoon had not been to hire a model. Since the success of her plot lay in the hands of a woman skilled in the art of flattery and seduction, she had gone there to hire one of the madame's most desirable girls as an escort.

Knowing his insatiable sexual appetites, Artemisia planned to use this against him. In a fortnight, during the presentation of the *bozza*— the smaller version of the *Judith and Holofernes* painting Cosimo had commissioned—she planned to implicate Tassi in a robbery at the Duke's palace, before hundreds of guests. A titillating promiscuous interlude would be his downfall. Just as Tassi changed Artemisia's fate with a sexual act and the stealing of a painting—she intended to change the course of his destiny in the same way too.

It seemed to Maddalena that setting Agostino up for a crime he hadn't committed, although well-deserved and a touch Machiavellian, presented a myriad of problems. Hiring, organizing, and coaching all the players seemed a time consuming and dangerous responsibility. But, as it turned out, Maddalena discovered those involved—from servants and merchants to prostitutes—all participated willingly.

Wherever he landed, from Rome to Florence, Tassi had a particular knack for making enemies and burning bridges. It seemed the man was widely disliked, for his actions as well as his demeanor. To some, he owed debts, and others he had threatened and abused like he had Artemisia. So, in the end, the task of coordinating her sting operation against him hadn't been so difficult.

After Maddalena, and later Matteo, were been made privy to the details, they too had no qualms about aiding Artemisia. Matteo, hearing of Tassi's antics and the most recent attack on his wife, had been so outraged he wanted to kill the man with his bare hands. Maddalena, too, much disgusted by the assault on her person, as well as the threats against Palmira, agreed to concoct a drought of belladonna to render the man senseless temporarily. She knew just the right amount of the deadly nightshade plant to add to a bit of orchic—a powerful aphrodisiac-boosting substance to increase Tassi's already rampant libido—to make him unusually lustful then pass out.

It had also been Maddalena's idea to provide a diversion—singing a repertoire of her songs early in the evening—to distract the assembly so Artemisia could carry out her subterfuge undetected. Following the rhythm and beat of her songs, the half-hour would be marked when the substance wore off, and Artemisia would know precisely when Tassi would reawaken.

The night of the party, Maddalena and Matteo arrived at the Pitti Palace in the Crociani coach, emblazoned with the family's crest. As she stepped out of the carriage with the aid of Matteo's hand, Maddalena observed the scene unfolding around her in the interior courtyard that was ablaze with candles and liveried servants.

Before entering the palace, she fluffed out the skirts of her long golden gown and modestly adjusted the bodice that had slipped during the carriage ride, revealing a little too much of her cleavage. She touched a hand to her braids that her maid had spent several hours entwining beads into and securing them with velvet ribbons.

On Matteo's arm, the couple moved through the crowd that represented the city's glittering paparazzi. She held her head high and pretended not to notice when heads bent together and whispers were exchanged. Apparently, her reputation as a courtesan had proceeded her, and the news continued to circulate through Florence. But, undeterred, she stood her ground, confident in her new role as Signora Crociani. Her husband couldn't have cared less about the gossip, so proud he was to have her by his side.

They stood for a moment on the threshold of the grand salon, taking in the scene, and Matteo pointed out Grand Duke, Cosimo, and his wife, Archduchess Maria. Together, they reigned over their court from a raised dais, as courtiers attended their needs, bringing them plates of fruit and small date-filled pastries. Maddalena watched the Duke lean to his left to listen to a friend, then smiled at the way he rocked back in his seat in mirth.

His wife, however, didn't seem to share her husband's good humor. On the contrary, by the way she shifted uncomfortably in her seat and hid the occasional yawn behind her golden fan, to Maddalena it seemed Cosimo's consort found the entire affair rather dull.

Continuing to assess her surroundings, Maddalena saw Artemisia at the far end chatting with a cluster of patrons, and at the other, she noticed Agostino's familiar swarthy face. The man who had accosted her in front of the brothel was clothed in black and over his arm hung his long, distinctive maroon cloak edged in fur.

Close by his side was a woman in a provocative gown, and together they sipped on glasses of golden liqueur, laughing together at shared intimacies. Out of the corner of her eye, Maddalena noticed how the woman rested a hand on his arm and whispered something into his ear, and how Tassi ran his hand over her bosom, squeezing her breast and smiling at her suggestively.

After a servant passed by offering a glass of wine, Maddalena returned her attention to the magnificent scene unfolding around her in the mirrored ballroom. Casually, she took a sip of wine and admired the other ladies and men who mingled together like brightly-colored peacocks in their jewel-toned frocks and embroidered coats.

When she turned back in the direction of Agostino, the man whose dark colors should have stood out from all the rest by mere contrast was nowhere to be seen. Neither was his lady friend. Over the rim of her glass, Maddalena scanned the room once more, and as she did, a slow smile spread over her face. It was all too predictable. The bait had been taken and the prey had walked willingly into his trap.

As the evening progressed and more people filled the room, Matteo escorted Maddalena to a small alcove where a group of troubadours was playing music. When a man in a brilliant red coat stood up and extended his lute, she accepted it willingly. Holding the instrument, she strummed it softly a few times. When the melody caught the attention of a few guests closest to her, they looked up curiously. Maddalena, satisfied with the tone and feel of the instrument, raised her head and met their gaze directly and began to play more boldly.

Then in a clear, strong voice, she sang a ballad about love, loss, and longing. As her words encircled the room, reaching to the far corners, even drifting to the upper floor of the palace, conversation ceased, and the stunned guests listened in admiration. When the last chord died away, the usually aloof Florentine elite energetically clapped their hands, calling for another. Happily, Maddalena obliged them. She continued to sing, amusing them for nearly an hour, until seeing Matteo give her a signal, she strummed one last chord knowing she had carried out her part in Artemisia's plan perfectly.

Matteo reached for her hand and said, for her ears only, "Nicely done, Maddie-girl. Are you ready to meet the host?"

Taking the arm that he offered, together they walked toward the Duke and Archduchess. Seeing them approach, Cosimo stood up and cried, "*Complimenti Signora Crociani*! The court was quite entertained by your lovely voice and verse."

Stepping down to stand in front of them, he warmly embraced Matteo and exclaimed, "And you, sir! It delights me you are back in Florence! It has been a month, has it not? You left with only a telescope, and you came back with the praises of the Doge *and* a bride. It seems your mission to *La Serenissima* was doubly successful."

Maddalena curtsied, sinking low to the floor, and said, "It is an honor to meet you, signore. My husband speaks of you with the greatest of respect and affection. I'm pleased my songs have diverted you."

Cosimo eyed her with admiration. "I can see you have chosen well, Matteo. After what we just heard, your wife is as sympathetic and talented as she is attractive."

Looking over at his wife, he added, "May I present the Archduchess Maria? She is originally from Austria and, like you, a foreigner..." Before he could finish, he was racked by a violent cough. Holding a handkerchief to his mouth, he took a step away.

While Maddalena waited for him to regain his composure, she caught the eye of his wife who only acknowledged her with a slight nod of her proud head. Unlike her husband, who was warm and effusive, the Archduchess appeared cold and reserved, preferring to keep her compliments, if she had any to give, to herself.

After Cosimo's spasm passed, he folded the linen, but before he tucked it into his pocket, Maddalena could see the tale-tell signs of blood on the cloth. Being this close to him now, she was also struck by the paleness of his face and the gaunt hollows in his cheeks. The rumors of his illness seemed to be accurate, and despite the good wishes and prayers of his friends, it didn't appear his condition was improving.

Taking a glass that a servant offered him, he said, "Artemisia tells me you are friends and that she has used your likeness in the painting I commissioned."

"Yes, that is right," Maddalena said. "My husband introduced me to Artemisia shortly after my arrival in Florence. I am so honored to be included in her painting."

"I saw the *bozza* just a few hours ago as it was being delivered to my private gallery. It is a stunning piece that sends a strong message—the meek will overcome their tormentors—always a favorite theme among the Medici. I have given my permission to Artemisia to begin work on the final larger version that will hang in that will hang in the Grand Hall."

He glanced hesitantly at his wife. "But I fear I may have a harder time convincing the Archduchess. She finds Artemisia's paintings a bit—ahem—a bit unsettling. She prefers subjects of a more gentile nature—flowers and bows and whatnot. So, there is much discussion about where the final version of the painting will actually be displayed."

He looked over at his wife who was now chatting with his mother, Christina of Lorraine, and added, "Decorating aside, unfortunately, she also doesn't share my passion for stars or science. Neither of them do. My wife is a daughter of the Austrian court, and rather a traditionalist." With a wink, he added, "But you'd think a mother would indulge her son and keep a more open mind!"

They spoke a while longer, and after relaying their best wishes, Maddalena and Matteo, in a great show of respect, bowed deeply and took their leave. As they neared the dance floor, when she heard the music again and seeing her husband's silent invitation, Maddalena stepped lightly into his embrace. Whispering into his ear, she said, "Of course, *amore mio*, I will dance with you. It's been an age since you last held me in your arms."

They followed the steps of the dance for a quarter of an hour before Maddalena caught sight of Artemisia dressed in her lovely green gown dancing with a distinguished man with intelligent eyes. By the way the man held her friend tightly, in an intimate embrace, she could only surmise he was Artemisia's Francesco, the one who captured her heart.

Maddalena thought they made a stunning couple and, as they circled the room following the intricate steps of the *contredanses*, her emerald skirts flowed and swayed about her, practically brushing against Pierantonio who stood motionless on the sidelines. Every time they passed by him, Maddalena noted his sour expression and the way he glowered at Artemisia and her lover from under bushy eyebrows.

Then, finally tilting his glass, draining its contents completely, he left the party without saying a single word or making a scene. It was more than evident that Artemisia's claims were true. Pierantonio really couldn't care less who his wife danced with—or bedded. He was quite comfortable in his role of a cuckolded husband as long as his wife made a decent income and gave him the freedom to drink his share of wine in the local tavern, and taking his pleasure elsewhere.

When the music stopped, and the dancers dispersed, the two

couples came together. Embracing her friend, Artemisia exclaimed, "Matteo! Maddalena! It is so nice to see you here, in such an agreeable setting." With a knowing look, she added, "I heard you singing earlier, Signora Crociani, and it pleased me greatly. I believe it was the perfect entertainment to make the night complete."

Drawing Maddalena's attention to the man at her side, she said brightly, "May I present to you Francesco Solinas Maringhi."

"It is a pleasure, Signora Crociani," the man said.

To Matteo, he added, "It is good to see you again, as well, *Signore*! Artemisia has shown me the portrait she has done of you, and it captures your likeness quite remarkably."

Leaning closer to Maddalena, he asked, "And you, Signora Crociani, what do you think of the painting?"

"I may be a bit biased," she responded, "but I consider it to be quite possibly the most beautiful painting I have ever seen. We have decided to hang it in my husband's studio. I will draw inspiration from the portrait when I am composing my verses."

Francesco acknowledged her pretty words with a bow of his head. He was about to say something more, but when they heard the Duke's voice calling his guests to attention, they all pivoted around. As a respectful hush fell over the room, the assembly listened to what the Duke had to say. In a short speech that began by flattering his guests and paying tribute to his wife, he concluded his discourse by saying, "And now the moment we have been waiting for. Artemisia, where are you, *mia cara artista*? Come, take your place beside me."

Artemisia made her way through the crowd and, holding out her skirts, she curtsied proudly before the Grand Duke. When she rose, he took her hands between his and held them gently. "Artemisia! You are a gift to this court." He raised her fingers and kissed them gently. "With these remarkable hands of yours, you have created yet another masterpiece."

Addressing the Florentine nobility who crowded the room, he announced, "*Signori* I'm honored present you all with Artemisia's latest work." With a tilt of his head, he said, "Now, follow me to the petit salon where you can have a glimpse of what the final painting will look like.

Gesturing to a servant, Cosimo gave permission for the doors of the private picture gallery to be opened, and with Artemisia on one arm and his wife on his other, they proceeded their guests into the smaller salon lit by flickering candles in sconces. Close behind them were Maddalena and Matteo, and as she glanced around, she saw in the very center a small painting, covered by a shimmering gold cloth, had been prominently set upon an elaborate easel.

Taking their position beside the Duke, Maddalena watched the other guests flow into the gallery. In the crowd, once again she saw Agostino's familiar face. Unlike before, however, this time he walked a little unsteadily, as if slightly inebriated, elbowing his way to the front. Muttering into the ear of his companion, he dragged her by the arm until they too were situated advantageously in the front, standing just a few feet away from her.

At such close proximity, Maddalena couldn't help but observe the look of superiority Tassi flashed at Artemisia. She also saw him nod in the direction of the Duke, as if to remind Artemisia of the lingering threat that hung between them. But more importantly, when Agostino turned away, Maddalena also saw the complicit self-satisfied smiles that passed between Tassi's evening companion and Artemisia.

As the guests continued to accommodate themselves in the small salon, the anticipation in the room was palpable and the chatter increased. Cosimo waited a moment longer, then beaming at his guests like a giddy child, with a courtly flourish of his hand he pulled off the cloth covering Artemisia canvas to reveal the painting. As he did, the noise level spiked again, and an audible gasp echoed through the room, like a rolling roar of a tidal wave.

But the dramatic reaction wasn't in response to the powerful and disturbing sight of a woman bloodily decapitating a man—instead, it was to the sight of an empty canvas frame, where only ragged bits of a red canvas dangled forlornly.

Hysterically, a woman cried out, "The painting is gone!"

"*Capo delle guardie!* Shut and lock the doors. No one leaves," demanded the angry Duke.

"Stand back!" a guard roared at the crowd. Signaling his men, he dispatched some to the salons on the first and upper floors, others he sent out to patrol the expansive gardens behind the Duke's palace.

To contain the pandemonium and send a strong message, Cosimo stepped forward and addressed his astonished guests. In a low husky voice filled with rage, he said, "Let us be very clear. This act of vandalism and insult against the Duke's house will not go unpunished. If anyone has information pertaining to the crime, I bid you to speak out now."

In shock, the guests snuck furtive glances at each other, and a pensive hush fell over the room. After a few minutes when no one stepped forward, as the heat began to rise, indignant rumblings started to be heard. But, before tempers flared completely, the doors to the salon burst open and in strode one of Cosimo's soldiers holding in his hands a familiar maroon cloak edged in fur. He stopped in front of the Duke and reached into the deep inner lining, pulling out a rolled canvas wrapped in a protective linen cloth.

"M'lord, we found this cloak hidden in the armoire in the guest chamber, secreted inside was the canvas. We have made inquiries, and the servants say they saw Agostino Tassi wearing the cloak earlier this evening."

"What!" cried Agostino in disbelief.

"Is this your cloak, *signore*?" questioned Cosimo.

"Yes, but... I don't know what the canvas is doing inside it. I'm not the one who put it there. Why would I do such a thing? Your Lordship... Please, you must believe me."

"Come, man! Did you not put the cloak in the armoire?"

"It wasn't me. It must have been the woman! Yes! The woman placed my cloak in there earlier."

"What woman?" asked Cosimo.

Glancing around, Tassi saw his companion of the evening was

nowhere to be seen. Appealing to those standing next him, he added, "Surely, you all saw her too."

Confronted by their blank faces and heads that shook in denial, Tassi turned back to the Duke and said in growing alarm, "*Onorevole Signore*, I can say with great conviction I did not take the painting. I am a man of honor. I've been set up!"

"Set up? By whom?"

"*That* woman! It must have been her, not me. She seduced me earlier and took advantage of me. She must need the money..."

Wiping a hand across his face, he said, "There was something in my drink. She must have drugged me. It has to be her—you must find the whore!"

"Drugged?" challenged a woman incredulously. "A woman seduced you? How could you let that happen?"

The noise in the room grew louder, and holding up his arm, Cosimo ordered, "Quiet!" Instantly a hush fell back over the room. "If indeed you are a man of honor, as you say, why would that woman—any woman for that matter—want to implicate you in a crime?"

"I... we..." He looked over at Cosimo and then at Artemisia, who stood next to the destroyed painting. When Maddalena came forward to stand beside her friend, suddenly he understood.

Agostino took a step backward. Shaking his head, he stuttered, "No, no, no. If you think..." Narrowing his eyes the at two women, he raised his arm and pointed at them. "Those two there. They are trying to disgrace and defame me I'm quite innocent! It must have been Artemisia and Crociani's wife."

"You think the artist destroyed her own painting? Whatever for? What could possibly be her motive? This is a party celebrating her, held in her honor. Why would she ruin it all by implicating you in a crime?"

"She is jealous of me and wants to ruin me. Just the other day, she made threats against me."

"Just so we are clear," Francesco said, moving closer to Tassi, "Artemisia has been dancing with me throughout the evening."

Raising his voice, Matteo added, "And my wife has been in plain sight the entire evening, entertaining the assembly with her songs. That you should even think of blaming her is absurd! And you say you are a man to be trusted."

"I too am a guest here," cried Tassi. "I would not steal from the Grand Duke! And besides, it's been cut from its frame for Christ's sake. Clearly, it was premeditated. Look! They've used a sharp blade to…"

"I see you have a knife hanging right there on your belt," said Matteo interrupting him. "Perhaps that is the weapon that was used."

"Yes, Tassi, show us your blade," cried a shrill voice from the back.

"I haven't committed a crime here tonight," repeated Tassi. "I deny being involved in any of this."

"If you've done nothing wrong, then you have nothing to hide."

"This is ridiculous," said Tassi. "I do not need to prove I am blameless—I am Agostino Tassi—my word speaks for itself."

"Be done with it, man. Give up the knife," demanded Cosimo, finally tiring of the whole affair. Holding a handkerchief up to his face, he breathed in heavily. "You test my patience. It is a simple matter to prove you are telling the truth."

"Yes, of course," Agostino said, pulling his dagger from its sheath. "Here. See for yourself. There will be no telltale signs that there has been wrongdoing on my part here tonight."

Holding up the blade, he waved it triumphantly in the air. In the light of the candles, the blade glinted cold and hard. "No one has touched this knife but me. It has been attached to my belt all night."

With a nod, Cosimo indicated to one of his guards to take the knife from Tassi and bring it to him. Then, running his finger along the flat side of the dagger, he lifted his hand into the air, displaying the red streak that now smeared it.

The Archduchess' face blanched pale. "Is that blood? Has that man murdered someone too?"

Cosimo rubbed his fingers together and said, "No, it is paint. The blade is covered with it."

"What? You lie," said Agostino, swiveling around. "Give me back my dagger. You have no right..."

"How dare you insult the intelligence of the Duke of Tuscany," Cosimo said through gritted teeth. "Even if I thought you were innocent, I don't like your tone. I am far too aware of your unscrupulous ways since the first day you came to Florence. It is my goal to protect her citizens, men, women, *and* children." Glancing over at Artemisia, he added, "Perhaps it is about time you paid for past crimes as well."

He raised a hand and signaled the guard. "I believe a more thorough interrogation is in order. Sit for a few days in prison, and we'll see what you have to say then."

At the snap of his fingers, Cosimo's men closed in around Tassi. The painter tried to struggle from their grasp, but they were too strong. Containing him easily, they bound Tassi's hands tightly behind his back with a rope, as he repeated, "I'm innocent. I tell the truth!"

As he was pushed toward the door, the crowd cleared a broad swath and watched in disgust as Tassi passed by. To avoid the jeers and the astonished faces, he kept his head high, but with eyes focused on the ground. Haughtily he strode through the room but struggled to a stop just before the door when he saw the hem of Artemisia's emerald green skirts.

Still pinned by the guard, he looked at her, and in a voice full suppressed rage, he said, "I know you had a hand in what happened here tonight. But, rest assured, I will be released shortly. This will all pass quietly, just as it did before."

"That may be so, Agostino," Artemisia said into his ear. "Duke Cosimo is my very good friend, and I *do* have his ear. As you asked, I spoke to him about you. Believe me, he was quite an attentive listener."

With a small smile, she added, "Cosimo is an excellent judge of character, and after tonight I'd be surprised if you are ever allowed to set foot again in the Medici court—let alone Florence."

Chapter 20
Falling Stars

Cosimo's retribution followed and, after rigorous questioning, a trial concluded Agostino Tassi was guilty of thievery, misrepresentation, and falsification of facts. His reputation was further blackened when the duke declared, as Artemisia had predicted, the exiled Roman artist was also banished from Florence due to his crimes against the Medici.

To punish him, and to provide example to all Florentine citizens that he was a benevolent ruler as well as an enforcer of peace, the duke sentenced Tassi to serve as a galley slave in the Grand Duke's Fleet. There he would work as human chattel, rowing the boat that would defend Cosimo's empire from the Ottoman Turks, the pirates that sailed the Mediterranean Sea. To Artemisia, it seemed the perfect punishment. Because of Tassi, her hands had been forever marked by the sibille, and now his would be blistered and bloodied from the hard labor of handling an oar.

As days passed into weeks and weeks turned into months, a new season began and Maddalena became accustomed to her new life in Florence. She was accepted into Matteo's wider circle of friends as well as his family and she could barely remember any other existence. Matteo proved to be an excellent partner and together they grew into their marriage. They moved gradually through the first blush of new romance, learning to accept their peculiarities and sometimes annoying little habits, letting their relationship mature and deepen with each passing hour.

While Matteo spent his mornings in the company of Galileo, theorizing and entertaining Cosimo with diverting mathematical equations, Maddalena adeptly assumed control of her new home, directing the servants and delegating responsibilities. As in Venice, she soon came to be relied upon by the household staff, as well as friends and neighbors, for medical treatments, more reliable than their own physicians. Making her daily house calls, she was often followed by Jupiter, now a fully-grown puppy with a golden coat.

The afternoons she passed in the company of Artemisia. She was such a frequent guest that eventually Palmira overcame her shyness, and when she heard Maddalena climbing the stairs to their apartment, she welcomed her at the door of her mother's studio with warm hugs and sticky kisses. Sometimes they strolled through the city together, their arms entwined. Other times they worked together in her studio. Maddalena wrote verses or practiced her lute while keeping Artemisia company.

Despite being cast back into the public eye, the incident hadn't harmed or tarnished Artemisia's reputation in the slightest. Rather, the incident served to catapult her even higher. Proudly, she told Maddalena she was now receiving requests from the far-off courts in Naples, as well as England and France.

Maddalena was quite content with her days, but the nights when she was alone with her husband were by far her favorite moments. Often, they wandered the gardens behind their palazzo dressed only in their nighttime attire. Free of heavy robes and embroidered corsets, they walked through the cool damp grass in their bare feet. And when Matteo set up his spyglass on the stone terrace, Maddalena peered into the midnight blue sky and with his guidance followed the planets orbiting the heavens over Florence.

When she leaned back into his warm embrace, and his voice grew husky, she he often told her, "Just as the planets revolve around the sun, you, Maddie my love, are my center."

"Ah, *sì*," she said playfully. "Even if I should disappear over the horizon, you will know where to find me?"

"*Mia cara*, wherever you wander, even if you disappear beyond the moons of Jupiter, you will never be lost to me."

Their idyllic days slipped together as if they were pearls on a silk thread. But later that fall, the harmony of their existence was broken, and the translucent beads spilled to the floor when they learned of the death of the Duke. Since the grand soiree honoring Artemisia, Cosimo's condition continued to disintegrate and the doctors, despite their potions and cures, were not able to revive him. He slipped further into decline and was confined to his bed, attended only by his wife and visits from his most trusted advisor and scholar, Galileo.

By the time the rains fell, and the city prepared for the yuletide, the Duke was practically comatose. Still, he clung to life, buoyed by the talk of stars and planets. But, eventually, the most powerful man in all of Tuscany succumbed to death. Barely making it past the new year, the Grand Duke of Tuscany died in February at the age of thirty-one.

Black banners hung from the *palazzi* in Florence, covering the distance from the Pitti Palace all the way to Fiesole. A solemn despondency fell over the town, and people bent their heads and prayed. The city had lost its brightest star, a man of letters and science. Artists put down their brushes and wept, and scholars laid down their telescopes. Everyone wondered what would become of Cosimo's vision and the projects he championed now that he was gone.

No one wondered this more than Artemisia and Galileo.

For, with the passing of the Grand Duke, Artemisia no longer had a patron who would protect and provide for her. The Grand Duchess had made no claim to support her, never really warming to her style or manner in which she depicted her themes. With Cosimo dead and the Grand Duchess in charge, Artemisia knew her days of finding patronage in Florence were numbered.

There was no way for her to survive in this city without a steady income. Heaven only knew her husband couldn't provide for her. Gazing out her window, observing the setting sun over the Arno, Artemisia thought about her future, wondering, if it wasn't time for her to move on.

Galileo, instead, hunkered down in his apartments, knowing for the moment Florence was the one place he could remain. The world was an unstable place and the only men he dared let into his sanctum were his closest companions and associates, among them Matteo and Benedetto Castelli. Together they mourned the loss of their leader; they also feared for the death of logic and reasoning. With Cosimo gone, they had no one to pave their way to the stars. Instead, daily they were pulled back to Earth to wallow in the mud surrounded by ignorant swine.

And so, they waited, their fortunes hanging in a precarious balance. Cautiously, they continued their activities; the men quietly charted the planets and the women resumed their pursuit of the arts.

To assist in the completion of an allegorical painting of Diana, the Roman goddess of the moon, Artemisia asked Maddalena again to be her model. Because Diana was also an indigenous woodland queen, she gave Maddalena a bow and an arrow to hold and placed a crown set with a crescent moon on her head. Around her body, she draped a soft blue cloth that clung to her curves and positioned in a way so that one of her long slender legs was revealed as well as a naked breast.

According to their established routine, Maddalena arrived at Artemisia's studio, quickly disrobed, and took her spot in a chair. Her state of undress didn't bother her, despite the small bulge of her midriff that indicated a child was on the way. Usually, they were left to their own devices; Palmira was in the company of Mariuccia and Pierantonio never returned home before eight.

So, it was to some surprise and a bit of fear when the door suddenly banged open early one afternoon and Pierantonio barged into the room. Maddalena reacted quickly, pulling the sapphire blue drapery closer around her, covering her nakedness.

Barely noticing her state of undress, Pierantonio announced roughly, "Artemisia! Get your things together. It is time to pack. We must leave this city at once!"

Artemisia gaped at her husband. "What do you mean, Pierantonio? What has happened?"

"The city has gone mad. There is a mob massing in the central piazza. Men are being arrested all over town."

She paused, her brush hovering over her canvas. "*Santo Cielo!* Why ever for?"

"Tommaso Caccini is at it again. Last night he preached a sermon in the Santa Maria Novella, and practically half of Florence must have been in attendance. Throughout a two-hour tirade, he attacked Galileo and his conspirators as heretics. He called them demons and the anti-christ. He said Galileo's teachings countermand the *Bible*. He concluded his blathering with a verse from the Acts of the Apostles: *Ye men of Galilee, why stand ye gazing up into heaven?*"

"Can't you see?" he said to the women. "It was an obvious reference to Galileo and his followers. They are now under attack."

"Caccini has ranted and raved before," said Artemisia. "This is nothing new."

"What is new is that there isn't a calm head to be found in the piazza. People are rising and Cosimo isn't here to settle things down and keep order. Now that the cauldron is boiling and about to overflow, someone is soon to be scalded. Caccini's followers—among them Lodovico delle Colombe—are calling for arrests."

"And what of Matteo?" Maddalena was suddenly fearful for her husband.

"I haven't a clue," said Pierantonio. He gestured impatiently to his wife. "Come, Artemisia. We must leave the city at once."

"I think you are overreacting. Those men aren't coming after me. I'm an artist, not a scientist. Where would we go anyway?"

"We will go to Genoa and stay with your father."

"No! I won't go to him," said Artemisia heatedly. "He has little regard for me. Orazio abandoned me a long time ago. Never once has he traveled to see me or inquired about his grandchild."

"Very well," Pierantonio grumbled. "We will go to Naples."

"Naples, but..."

With a dismissive wave of his hand, he said, "There is no time to argue, woman. Bring your lover with you, if you like, if that is what concerns you. We could still use his income."

"Sometimes I think you are no better than Tassi," she hissed. "At least he had some talent."

Maddalena barely heard their argument as it escalated, thinking only of Matteo. Interrupting them, she asked, "Where was the mob going? Have they started making arrests?"

Swiveling in her direction, Pierantonio spat out, "*Basta!* Enough! I have no time to worry about you or your husband."

As the weight of his words took their toll on the women, Artemisia slumped tiredly against the table and Maddalena clutched the drape tighter around her breast, feeling her heart constricting. They looked at one another and exchanged sad smiles, their eyes expressing volumes of unsaid words.

The artist took a step closer to her friend and embraced her. Whispering into her ear, she said, "I have grown to love Florence, she has been good to me. It will be painful to leave her behind. But, you! How will I endure parting with you?"

"Don't worry," Maddalena told her firmly. "I won't lose you. We have come too far and have shared so many things. But now you must go. You have greater things ahead of you. I'm sure of it. You will travel the world and hold kings and princesses in your palm, all clamoring for your paintings."

Artemisia reached up and caressed her cheek, and once again Maddalena could feel the scars that marked her friend's hand. "You will always live inside my heart," she said. "We might not see each other for a long, long while, but let us promise to always stay in touch—wherever we find ourselves in the days to come."

With a final hug, Maddalena moved behind the screen at the far side of the room, pulled on her simple morning frock, and buttoned the bodice. She fumbled with the closures, her hands shaking uncontrollably. Losing patience, she left the top ones undone. Despite her disheveled appearance, she picked up her bag and her hat and brushed past Pierantonio, who was shoving things into a leather bag.

On the other side of the room, she saw Artemisia already packing things into large wooden trunks. Their promises to remain close were sincere, but she knew in this lifetime they would likely never see each other again. Silently she blew her most treasured confidant one last kiss.

Then, without saying another word, she lifted her skirts, descended the stairs quickly and, in her haste, stumbled on the last one. Putting a hand on the wall to keep herself from falling, she righted herself and moved unsteadily to the front gate.

By the time she reached the street, she was aware of a peculiar energy that circulated through the air. From a short distance away, she could hear the calls of men and the chanting of the crowd. Someone tossed a bottle, and she heard it crash against the stone pavement.

To avoid being seen, she dodged into a side street and hastened down the narrow alley until she came to her home. When she arrived at the door, she threw herself upon it, beating on it with her fists to be let in. But as she pressed her weight against the panel, it slowly swung open. It was an ominous sign.

Maddalena hesitated a moment. Cautiously, she stepped into the courtyard. At this time of day, there were usually servants and tradesmen making deliveries. Today, the place was eerily deserted. In the corner, a barrel lay toppled over, and a chair was smashed in the corner.

Wildly, she called out, "Matteo!"

Maddalena paused to listen, but there was no answer. Panicked, she pushed through and into the main salon and looked around, but again was met by a deadly silence. She backed out of the room and climbed the stairs to their bedchamber, yanking the door open. Inside, she discovered a servant girl huddled in the corner with tears streaming uncontrollably down her cheeks. When she saw Maddalena, she cried, "They've taken him, mistress. They've taken the master."

"Taken him! Where? What happened?" Maddalena said, sinking to her knees in front of the girl.

"They came. A great number of them. They stormed into the house and dragged him away."

"What did they say? What did they do?"

"The man in charge said they were arresting him."

"Arresting him? For what? Did they say?"

"They said he was a heretic."

"Oh my god." The blood drained from Maddalena's face. Her worst fears had been realized. In a hushed tone, she demanded, "Where is he now? Where did they take him?"

When the girl didn't answer, Maddalena shook her forcefully and demanded, "Answer me! Come on, you useless girl! Surely, they said something! What did you overhear?"

Her lips trembling in fear, the girl said, "When they arrived, the master was in his study. He heard them coming. We tried to bolt the doors, but the men smashed through."

Maddalena whipped her head around in the direction of Matteo's room. In her heart, she felt a small shred of hope. Perhaps he left her a message.

She left the girl and hurried down the hall. As she approached his studio, she saw the door was flung wide open. Inside, the room was in shambles. Papers and books lay scattered about the floor, and near the window, his beloved telescope lay shattered and in pieces. Maddalena bent down and picked up a shard of glass and one of the brass rings and remembered the day he had placed one of those rings on her finger.

Moving quickly to the desk, she pushed aside a ledger and saw the letter he had been composing. Next to it was his gold watch whose hands had stopped working. She reached for it and shook it, but still the hour remained frozen at 12:05.

With great care, she slid the timepiece into her pocket then picked up the letter Matteo had started to compose. Seeing his familiar script, the tears fell as she read his words of love and encouragement:

Amore mio, do not worry. We will survive this misunderstanding. Surely, the Pope can be reasoned with. We will plead our case and make them see the light of logic. Keep a cool head. Pack up your things. Go to Rome, Maddie-girl. Never stop searching for me. I will be waiting for you and our child...

Maddalena swiped at her face with the back or her hand and then walked to the window and stood a moment gazing out vacantly at the courtyard below. *Go to Rome. Go to Rome. Keep a cool head. Do not worry.* His words reverberated in her head and reassured her. *Of course, this will all pass*, she thought. She believed in Matteo and knew truth and logic would win in the end. *Surely the Pope would see reason.*

Filled with new hope she swung around and started for the door, but her steps faltered. Suddenly fear gripped her heart again as she remembered the story of Beatrice Cenci and another vindictive Pope who executed a victimized family, beheading them on a public stage simply to set an example. As her stomach churned and a red-blaze of panic plunged into her heart like a steel dagger, she also recalled poor Giordano Bruno who had been burned alive by merely claiming the universe was infinite.

She grew faint and leaned against the desk for support. It seemed her world was spinning out of control and her heart beat even faster. *This couldn't be happening*, she thought wildly. Surely, the Pope wouldn't be so cruel as to exact a similar punishment in the case of Matteo and Galileo. But the thought did not console because these were not reasonable times.

Awkwardly she pushed away from the desk and forced herself to think clearly. Wrapping her arms around her middle, caressing her unborn child, she turned to face the portrait of her husband, encased in a golden frame. Seeing the reassuring look in Matteo's eyes, an expression of self-possessed courage and confidence that Artemisia had captured so well, Maddalena suddenly understood.

Matteo had always helped her see into the far away skies, and in that instant, she too saw clearly beyond the horizon. This time, no telescope was needed. In that instant, she knew, although their love story had been suspended for a moment, this was not the end. Their story would continue, of that she was sure. Come hell or high water, she would never stop searching for him. They would be together again.

With one hand on their child, she reached up to caress Matteo's face and closed her eyes and prayed.

1930s Epoch

*I never realized until lately that women
were supposed to be the inferior sex.*

– Katharine Hepburn

Chapter 21

We Meet Again

*S*tanding with one hand resting on an ornate, albeit dusty, gold frame that encased a life size portrait of a timeless man, Maddalena blinked her eyes in surprise, seeing a familiar face gazing back at her. She regarded him, caught for all eternity in a relaxed but confident pose as if he challenged her to contradict his opinions. Lifting a finger, she lightly caressed the line of his jaw and the shape of his mouth. Looking into his eyes, she was caught by a vivid gleam, unable to tear herself away from his mesmerizing stare.

As the seconds ticked by, she let herself be carried back to the Baroque and was barely aware of her surroundings—jazz playing over a staticky radio as she stood in the back room of an auction house cluttered with catalogs and packing crates. She forgot about the Olivetti typewriter on the desk sitting next to a stack of yellowed *Corriere della Sera* newspapers—especially the one left on top which proclaimed: *Mussolini Annexes Ethiopia*. Thoughts of the African invasion that had occurred two years before seemed unimportant—for one blessed moment, she cared not the slightest about current events, her backlog of work, or the clients she needed to please.

Instead, gazing at the painting, like a willing voyeur, she found herself wanting to know about *this* man's secrets. She felt a little disoriented and a small sadness welled up inside of her, causing her to wonder who he was and what had become of him, but most importantly what it was about his expression that made her think...

She started when she heard a familiar voice call out to her: "Maddalena, open the door!" On the brink of remembering, she closed her eyes, and fuzzy shadows took shape. She let herself drift, but when she heard a loud beating and was brought back to the present, the past slipped back into its place, and the universe continued to spin normally. Opening her eyes, she realized the pounding wasn't just her heart—someone was knocking on the office door.

This time when the voice called out summoning her, she swung around in pleasure and responded, "*Arrivo!* I'm coming."

Dusting off her hands, she turned the door handle and beamed at the man on the threshold who held in his arms several large packages on top of which rested a very wet newspaper.

"There you are, Matteo! I'm glad you're back. I've been waiting ages for you to return."

When he saw her, he smiled too, so happy to see her, despite the fact it had only been a few hours since they had woken up beside one another and shared a morning espresso in his apartment that faced the Tiber River.

Apologetically, she added, "Sorry, I didn't hear you at first. Here let me help you with those." Reaching out she relieved him of the packages and set them on a nearby table.

As he entered the room, his leather wing-tipped shoes squished just a bit. Putting her hands into the pockets of her wide pleated pants, she scrutinized his soggy appearance from the damp cuffed flannel trousers to his rain-splattered coat and an umbrella with broken ribs hooked over his arm. She gathered it was the reason his felt hat was dripping water from its brim.

Maddalena thought back to the night before when it had first started to rain. They had been strolling through Piazza Navona after dining in a little trattoria near the Pantheon and, feeling the first splash of water on her cheek, she exclaimed in dismay. But launching his umbrella, he had assured her if they hurried they would avoid the expected downpour by taking refuge in his apartment. To avoid the long walk back to her place in Trastevere, he had encouraged her to spend the night—something that was becoming a habit.

With his hands now free of packages, he took her into his arms, bending her back slightly and giving her an intimate kiss.

Smelling the scent of late fall in his damp jacket, she laughed delightedly and said, "Careful, *amore*, you are going to get me completely drenched! Good heavens, you are wetter than a duck on a pond! Whatever happened to you?"

"I was just a couple blocks away when a big gust of wind got a hold of me," he said, dumping his packages onto a nearby table. Gingerly, he unhooked the umbrella from his arm and shoved it forcefully into the trash bin. "This worthless thing gave out and turned it inside out. Little good it did me!"

Looking over at the antique pendulum clock on the wall, he said "It's just past noon. I wasn't expecting to see you until later this evening at the Astoria. When did you arrive and to what do I owe this surprise?"

"Oh, about a half-hour ago. The girl at the front desk let me in. I thought I'd treat you to lunch. I didn't realize you'd be out or gone so long. After a while, I got tired of waiting up front, so I came back here and started to dig around. I wanted to see if you had any hidden gems in this magnificent misfit collection of yours."

Matteo slid out of his wet coat and took off his silk scarf. "Anything, in particular, catch your eye?"

"Well, yes, as a matter of fact. You know how much I love this place of yours, it feels like home. I get lost in time sorting through all your boxes of tabloids and old newspapers."

Pointing to a stack of pictures leaning against the far wall, she said, "I was admiring the pictures of wistful Madonnas and scenes of Venice and the Grand Canal—and then I stumbled upon this. The man in the painting looks just like you! Why, he could be your brother!"

Seeing the painting she pointed to, he said, "Ah, you saw it then? It just arrived the other day." He pulled out a silver cigarette holder and offered one to her, then, pulling a lighter out of his pocket, he lit them. Together, as blue smoke circled and entwined them, they studied the canvas. After a moment, he scratched his head and asked, "Do you really think he resembles me? I don't see it."

"The spitting image! How can you *not* see it? Wherever did he come from?"

Cocking his head at an angle, he studied the painting. "Hmm. Well, he is a distant relative of mine."

"That explains the likeness," she said. "I see now where you get your good looks."

"That's Matteo Alessandro Crociani. He was a count, or maybe a marquis, I can't remember. Anyway, he was some big wig in Cosimo II de' Medici's court in the fifteenth—no, wait, it must have been the sixteenth-century. I just remember as a child being told that he had been hung by the neck and left to dangle in a piazza in Rome—so of course we children used to make up ghost stories about him."

"Ghost stories? How delightful! I absolutely adore a ghastly grisly tale!"

Matteo leaned against the desk and smiled at her. "I have to admit mine were the most gruesome. When I was a boy, we used to play in the attic. Grubbing around up there was great fun..."

"Up to no good, undoubtedly," she added. "Inventing all kinds of schoolboy pranks, I'd imagine. Spinning stories and scaring your younger cousins? Poor little Silvia, I bet she was the brunt of your jokes."

"You do know me well, don't you *cara*?" he said with a laugh. "Silvia was always so gullible. We used to go up to the attic on rainy days like this, even though we weren't supposed to. If mother found out, she'd scold us. But, still, when she wasn't around, we'd sneak back again and entertain ourselves for hours with games of hide-n-seek and I Spy."

"Why weren't you allowed up there?"

"It was a treasure trove, filled with breakable things my relatives didn't want any more in the main house—you know, curios, outdated tables, old chests. There were also all kinds of old pictures piled about, some of ancestors no one knew anything about. But still, they were valuable, and they didn't want us to go knocking into them."

Looking around, she said, "Sounds very much like where we find ourselves right now. It must have been a lovely place for a child to explore," she added, wishing she had known him back then.

"It was, actually," he said. "There were all kinds of things to discover and places to hide—inside old armoires, under rusty beds." Indicating the portrait before them, he added, "And behind paintings like this one."

"It's nice and big—that's for sure."

"Sometimes I'd wait and spring out from behind it..."

"And scare Silvia out of her senses. You mean little boy! I bet she thought the painting was coming to life and the phantom of poor noose-necked Matteo was coming to life ready to spirit her away with him into the afterlife!"

"Ever since then," he admitted, "I've had a fondness for this fellow, seems we've always been in cahoots together."

"I, for one, am convinced this Matteo was a very nice man, as well as a charming ghost. I'm certain Silvia had nothing to fear at all. Why, just look at his eyes, he seems a decent sort of man—full of courage and conviction.

She raised an eyebrow at the man beside her, and she teased, "But, aren't all you Crociani men that way? From my experience with the whole lot of you, he was probably just as stubborn!"

"Careful, Maddie-girl," he said with a grin. "You too can be pretty—how shall I put it..."

"Be nice," she said.

"I was going to say single-minded and..."

"Opinionated?"

"That too," he said, pulling her back into his arms. "But, Maddie-girl, I couldn't be with any other woman and I wouldn't want you any other way."

"The feeling is definitely mutual. You are my one in a million, Matteo. I dare say when they made you they broke the mold."

As she spoke, Maddie glanced over his shoulder at the portrait and completely lost her train of thought, caught unaware once again by the spark in his eye. She had the strangest sensation that he could read her thoughts and knew more about her than she did about him. Bemused by the silly notion, she asked, "What else can you tell me about this fine gentleman? Was he married?"

"I suppose so. If I'm descended from him, it would make sense, wouldn't it? Anyway, I just had the portrait shipped down from the villa in Tuscany. All these years it's been sitting up in the attic collecting cobwebs."

Maddalena held up her hand and wiggled her fingers covered with grime. "Yes, I noticed. The painting is rather dirty. Your ancestor needs a good cleaning behind the ears. Perhaps a hot bath is in order!" She leaned back against the desk, making herself comfortable, taking care not to disturb his typewriter or his papers. "So, what made you decide to go and unearth him just now? Surely not just for digging up an old ghost? Or do you have intentions of scaring Silvia again?"

Slicking a hand through his wet hair, he said, "Now there's an idea! No, actually I have an even better reason for bringing old Matteo back to life. A few months ago, some paintings came across the auction floor at Signoretto's. When I saw them, I sat up in my chair and was immediately interested. There was something so familiar about the brushwork, the use of light and shadow... Then it came to me. I remembered this portrait!"

"This one here? Really?"

"This very one."

"So, based on your ancestor's recommendation you decided to buy up the lot?"

"That's about it," he said. "But the best part... Because the artist was unknown, and because there was no clear provenance—no way of proving where or when they were painted, or who owned them before, I got an excellent price—five canvases for the price of one."

"Sounds like quite a find," she said. "You've always impressed me with your knack for discovering unusual things in the most unlikely places."

"Like the day we first met?"

"The day you nearly bumped into me with your roadster," she teased.

"Yes, that day," he said. "The day you wore that silly hat that looks like an upside-down shoe."

"I love that hat! Was that what first attracted you to me?" she said with a grin.

"Not the hat, Maddie-girl. It was your grey-green eyes that I fell in love with that day."

"That was two, wait three, years ago? It seems like yesterday."

Taking her hand, that still didn't have a ring, he said, "What do you think? Is it time to make things official?"

She appeared thoughtful. "Hmm. I *could* be persuaded by the right man. I am a modern woman, though. Do you think I'm cut out for domesticity?"

"You know we've kept all of Rome abuzz, wondering when we will tie the knot," he said, nuzzling her ear.

"I like to make people gossip. It gives them something to do," she said. "You and I are so good together—I really haven't missed making things official. In my heart, it feels like we are already husband and wife."

"Perhaps next spring," he suggested, "after fashion week and things settle down following your show we could..."

"It would definitely have to be after the show!" Maddalena interjected. "There is no possible way I could even start to plan a wedding until after that. I'm already working on the designs—but the ideas just aren't coming. I'm going completely mad, trying to come up with a sensational idea to top the last. And right now, Bettina and I are up to our ears in..."

When she saw a young woman pass by in the outer hall, Maddalena called out, "Luciana! Come see who's finally back!"

Hearing her name, an attractive woman with sleek dark hair stepped into the room and walked over and gave her a hug. "Maddalena! *Che piacere, vederti di nuovo! Come stai?*"

"*Bene! È tu?*" she replied, kissing Luciana on both her cheeks. Then with a nod of her head indicating the portrait, she added, "Matteo was just telling me about some new paintings you just acquired."

"*Sì, sì, sì!*" Luciana smiled over at Matteo. "We are quite excited about them—as we are with our dashing cavalier here. There is a riddle here to solve and now the puzzle pieces are fitting together and we are about to make an exciting discovery."

Maddalena looked from one to the other. "I love an intriguing mystery, almost as much as a good ghost story. What is it?"

"As you know, for quite some time, Matteo and I have been interested in a seventeenth-century artist named Caravaggio."

"Caravaggio? The one you featured a few months back in your gallery? The one who did those powerful, dramatic paintings?" asked Maddalena, recalling that the people the seventeenth-century painter had depicted looked like actors illuminated on a dark stage.

"Yes, that's the one" said Matteo. "After Longhi started singing his praises a few years ago, claiming La Tour, Velázquez, Rembrandt—even Manat—could never have existed without his influence, Caravaggio has become the man of the hour. Even in his own time, he turned the art world upside down with the emotional intensity and realism he captured in his paintings, imitating nature down to the dirt on the feet of the Madonna."

"Except for Michelangelo," agreed Luciana, "no other painter has had such an influence on Italian art."

"And now that his paintings are back in vogue," added Matteo, "they are bringing top dollar at auction. We just sold one to the Marquis Zarantonello last month for a very substantial amount."

"It was a painting of Bachus," confirmed Luciana, "and it seemed to please the Marquis immensely to add it to his collection."

Slipping off the desk to stand beside them, Maddalena indicated the portrait of Matteo's ancestor. "So, you think Caravaggio painted this portrait too? Is that what the fuss is all about? That would be rather exciting. I can see why..."

"Oh, no!" exclaimed Luciana. "This painting is similar in style, but more likely it's done by one of his followers."

"You of all people know how it goes," Matteo said. "As with all great ground breaking artists, when they become popular everyone jumps on the bandwagon and tries to copy their style."

"All the time!" agreed Maddalena. "But I take it as a compliment. Imitation is the highest form of praise." Indicating the painting, she asked, "So, if not Caravaggio, this was painted by someone who knew him?"

"Definitely. That's the conclusion we've made," said Luciana. "This has to have been done around the same time, and by someone who had firsthand knowledge of his work. But what is interesting is that the person who painted this portrait wasn't *just* a copycat artist."

Stepping forward, Matteo said, "Look here, for instance. See the detailing in the man's coat and the way his face is modeled and the line of his torso. There is something innovative and original—almost lyrical— about this artist's style. You get a sense of the man's character. There's an immortal quality that few artists can achieve."

Glancing back at Maddalena, he added, "This was done by a very talented person. After that day at Signoretto's, Luciana and I have been quietly scouting around Rome, searching for other paintings by the same hand, making discreet purchases."

"We've now accumulated a small collection," said Luciana. "In fact, one of the paintings is on its way here today. I was just on my way to the loading dock to let the delivery men in." Checking her watch, she said, "Oh, they must be here by now. Excuse me. I've got to unlock the door."

"Tell them to bring the canvas in here," said Matteo, "so we can have a good look at it."

When Luciana left, Matteo smiled broadly at Maddalena. "Now, this is the part that you are really going to enjoy."

"What's that, *amore*?"

"We have discovered the paintings were done by a woman."

"A *woman*? Off the top of my head, I can't think of *any* women painters—well, except for Mary Cassatt..."

Before she could continue, she was interrupted by the commotion of shuffling feet and the gruff voices of men. She looked over her shoulder and watched as two delivery men carried in a large crate. Behind them followed Luciana, who held in her hands a clipboard and a pen.

"Where do you want this, Signorina Mancini?" asked the tall, swarthy man.

"Against the far wall, Domenico."

Luciana caught Matteo's eye for confirmation. "*Che ne pensi? Va bene, cosi?*"

"*Sì, perfetto*," agreed Matteo, walking over to hand one of the men a crowbar to pry open the lightweight wooden crate that housed the large painting. When the top was opened, together the three men pulled the painting wrapped in a linen cloth out of the narrow box and leaned it against the wall. As the delivery men moved the discarded crate to the hall and picked up the bits of packing straw that lay scattered on the floor, Matteo addressed the women, and asked, "Are you ready?"

At the same time, they responded, "*Prontissima*! Ready," then looked at one another and smiled. The two delivery men, also curious to see the painting they had lugged all the way across town, took a step back into the room and joined the others.

Then Matteo, with the dramatic flair rivaling a showman, pulled back the linen protective covering. As he did, a hush fell over the room. For a moment, no one said a thing, and they could hear the patter of rain on the roof as they stared at the picture of a woman and her maid caught in the act of decapitating a man.

Matteo laughed delightedly at their reaction. "*È stupendo, no?* So, what do you think?"

Eventually, Maddie broke the spell. "Why, Matteo! This is indeed an astonishing find! I can now see what the fuss is all about! And the subject?"

"It's *Judith and Holofernes*," Luciana told her in admiration.

"Right, right... I recognize it now," said Maddalena. "I've seen other versions, but this! This representation of Judith is—it's simply spectacular." She took a step closer. "Just look at the blood flowing all over the place. It's all over the sheets—and look at the expression on Judith's face! It's got moxie and determination written all over it."

Luciana bent down and rubbed her hand gently over a grimy corner of the painting and read out loud: "Artemisia Gentileschi."

She smiled up at Matteo. "See that!"

"Artemisia," said Maddalena, saying her name for the first time. "That's very unusual."

"I believe she was named after the Roman god Artemis—the Goddess of the moon and the hunt and protector of women," said Luciana.

"When we have the portrait of my ancestor cleaned," Matteo said, "I think we will discover Artemisia's signature on it as well. Or at least that is what I'm hoping to find."

Maddalena nodded her head, deep in thought. "This painting is intriguing—mesmerizing, really. The colors are beautiful and will be even more so after you have it cleaned up. But those women—and their dresses! The artist caught the texture of the satin and the linens perfectly. The sheen of the light playing off the silky sheets is exquisite. And look at their arms—they are so powerful, as are their postures!"

Luciana stood up, brushed her hands together, and said in a reverent voice, "The women are united together, empowering one another. They aren't afraid."

Maddalena nodded in silent agreement. She opened her mouth to comment, but paused a moment, struck by a peculiar feeling. It seemed she had stood in this very spot before, having this conversation with someone else.

"That's quite good," Matteo said. "Luciana, I believe you've gotten right to the heart and soul of this piece." He took a linen handkerchief from his pocket and offered it to her to clean her hands. Addressing the delivery men who regarded the painting intently, he asked, "So, what do you think, Milluzzi? I hear you are a painter. Do you have an opinion?"

The man hesitated for a moment, then shrugged nonchalantly. "*Boh! Non lo so.* You say a woman did this? It seems too bold and sophisticated for a female to even contemplate painting."

"It is rather extraordinary, isn't it?" said Matteo. "To think a woman in that day and age was able to produce something of this magnitude."

"How much will something like this go for?"

"I think quite a lot. I mean, if a painting done by Giovanni Gambara, a minor follower of Caravaggio, sold for over ten million *lira*, imagine what a painting Gentileschi, who is a much more gifted artist, might bring?"

The man let out a whistle. "Ten million *lira* for an old, dusty painting of two women cutting off the head of a man? Not bad."

"Not only that, but when we find out more information about Artemisia, reanimate her spirit—so to speak—and find all her paintings, I believe they are going to start selling for even more."

Nodding at Luciana, he added, "We are just starting to piece together information, digging through the archives trying to find a trail of ownership. But, unfortunately, there isn't much to go on."

The workman continued regarding the painting, and a speculative light came into his eye. "Why is that?"

"In Artemisia's case, because she was a female, she was probably dismissed, considered not worthy of notice. You know what I mean. You could put Stravinsky on a street corner with a bucket to collect coins and people would pass by without paying him any notice. But put him on stage at Carnegie Hall, and they are willing to pay top dollar for a ticket."

Maddalena observed the two men as they spoke. She had a keen eye for dressing a person and silently took in his ill-fitting jacket and worn leather shoes. She waited for him to notice her, but instead, for whatever reason—shyness or embarrassment—he didn't acknowledge her.

Instead, he directed his attention only at Matteo. Reaching for his hat he had left on the table, he said, "*Senti capo,* I've got to go, but I was hoping to pick up some hours tomorrow. I can be here at nine if you still need me."

"Let's see," said Matteo, rummaging around on the desk for the delivery roster. As he checked the following day's schedule, the dark-haired man finally glimpsed in Maddalena's direction. But instead of treating her with a pleasant expression, he peered fixedly at her and only gave her a little nod of his head.

Again, she was made aware that the man lacked certain social graces, as unabashedly, his eyes traveled over the strand of pearls at her neck down to the gold bracelet on her wrist and back to the emeralds that dangled from her ears. After a few moments, his intense scrutiny made her uneasy, and she was about to address him directly when she felt the light touch of Luciana's hand on her shoulder.

"It was wonderful to see you cara, but I've got to get back to work."

"And just when the party was getting started," quipped Maddalena. Leaning over to give Luciana a kiss on her cheek, she added, "We'll see each other later for cocktails, right, Signorina Mancini?"

Luciana smiled over at Matteo. "Well, that depends."

"On what?"

"If my partner here will give me the time off. He's already got a list a mile long of things for me to start investigating about Artemisia."

"Don't worry," Maddalena laughed, "I'll put in a good word for you."

Without looking up, Matteo replied, "Not necessary!" Pulling back his jacket cuff to see his watch, he added, "I plan on giving her at least a half-hour break."

With a laugh, Luciana headed back to her office, calling over her shoulder, "We'll see about that, Signor Crociani. See you later, Maddalena."

When she was gone, Matteo directed his attention back to Milluzzi who had watched the scene patiently with hooded eyes. "Yes, I think I could use you again tomorrow, Domenico."

Gesturing to the other man standing next to him, Matteo added, "And you too, Rinaldo. Do you know the Villa Pampaloni? It's outside of town near..."

As the three men talked, clarifying delivery routes, Maddalena picked up a newspaper and scanned the articles. Now and then, she peeked over the top of the paper and discretely scrutinized the delivery man named Milluzzi. There was something about him, but she couldn't quite put her finger on it. Perhaps it was the overly keen way in which he assessed her— not as a person, but as an object—or the fact that simply his massive bulk made her uncomfortable.

After the men concluded their business, the man named Rinaldo shook Matteo's hand, nodded at Maddalena then departed. Milluzzi remained, coping down the address. When he finished, he picked up his hat and shook Matteo's hand too then turned briefly to Maddalena and said, "Signora."

Matteo realizing the two had never met before, quickly said, "I'm sorry, Milluzzi, I got so caught up with the painting and talking about other things I forgot to introduce you both. Reaching his arm out to Maddalena, inviting her to stand next to him, he said, "*Cara*, this is Domenico Milluzzi. I just hired him to help with deliveries and do some heavy lifting."

Maddalena stepped closer and said, "Pleased to meet you. I'm Maddalena Paquin."

Still holding his hat in his hand, the man said, "I've seen your pictures in the newspaper. You are some kind of seamstress? A foreigner, right?"

She dropped the hand she had extended and raised her elegantly-shaped brow. If he was attempting to make small talk, or even a joke, she certainly hadn't found it funny. Finally, she replied a little coolly, "Yes, that's right. I am the proprietor and fashion designer at the House of Paquin."

The two regarded one another and the sound of the rain could be heard again. Clearing his throat, Matteo rechecked his watch, and said, "Well, alright. It's getting a bit late. Was there anything else you needed— Domenico? If not, you are free to go home. I'll see you in the morning."

Domenico bowed his head politely at his boss then placed the hat on his head. Then, with a curt nod at Maddalena, he swiveled around and walked out the door. Alone once again, the two looked at one another, and Matteo let out a small laugh. "What the hell was that all about?"

"What?" asked Maddalena innocently as she walked casually back to stand in front of Artemisia's painting.

"It seemed the two of you took an instant disliking to one another."

"You noticed?"

"Noticed? Of course, I noticed. So did he. The air positively sizzled with hostility."

"I didn't mean to be rude. I can't explain it, but something about him put me on edge."

"Oh, come now, *cara*! You've only just met the man."

"Let's just call it women's intuition. There is something about him that I don't quite trust."

Maddalena picked up a small brass letter opener shaped like a dagger and tested its weight. "So, what's up with Signor Milluzzi anyway? Where did you find him? You said he was an artist, but he seems more like a day laborer."

"He is a painter, but the man has fallen on hard times. I've seen some of his paintings, he's rather good—has an eye for perspective and coloring. But really a bit average on the whole. These days, it's hard to make a name for yourself. If you aren't Picasso or Dalí, good luck!"

"So, he's given up?"

"Oh, I don't know. I think he earns a few commissions, copying the paintings of others for people who want cheaper versions. But, even that kind of work is hard to find. He's been out of luck and out of work for a while now."

"And he just showed up on your doorstep asking for work?"

"Actually, Signoretto called me the other day vouching for him. Said he had run out of things for him to do at his gallery and wondered if I needed any help. Lucky for him, I did, so I've hired him temporarily to do some odd jobs around here."

"For your sake," she said, looking at the open door, "let's hope he works out. But I have to tell you I have a bad feeling about this."

Chapter 22

Designing Women

Seated at her drafting table, Maddalena tapped her pencil impatiently on her sketch pad, contemplating her latest design. Something just wasn't quite right about it. She'd been working all morning trying to come up with the keystone design for next spring's collection, but the ideas weren't coming together and she was in a foul mood.

Maddalena pulled a cigarette out from the silver case that rested on the desk next to her charcoals and drawing pencils and lit it. Taking a puff, she relaxed back in her chair, crossing her leg over the other, enjoying the feel of the loose fitting culotte pants and the jewel-toned silk shirt. Her hair was caught up in a brightly colored scarf and around her neck was a strand of her signature pearls.

She picked up the pad of paper and scrutinized her design. Perhaps if she added a bit of tulle around the peplum, she thought optimistically, making a few quick strokes with the pencil. Then stubbing out her cigarette, she let out a steady stream of smoke along with a disgusted groan. "Oh, *merde*! What a bunch of rot—this won't do at all."

Massaging her throbbing temples, she raised her eyes to the window and saw it was raining. She flinched and swore again when she saw a flash of lightning, followed by a loud boom. It seemed even the weather gods were berating her, saying her designs were no good.

"Everybody is a critic," she muttered to herself.

Realizing there was nothing she could do to save her current idea, with a quick stroke of her pencil, she slashed a big X through the page, tore off the sheet, wadded it up, and tossed it in the direction of the wastebasket. With dismay, she looked at the balls of crumpled paper that already littered the floor and let out another string of expletives.

From the other room, a female voice called out, "Don't think I can't hear that! You've been cursing all morning. Good thing there are no sailors walking in the door. You'd have them all blushing."

Hearing Bettina, her assistant typing in the outer office, Maddalena glared at the door and raised her eyes heavenward.

"And stop rolling your eyes at me," the voice continued. "Go on, Duchess! Get on with it, times a wasting! Those dresses aren't going to design themselves."

The clattering of typewriter keys continued, and her last comment was punctuated with a little ding. As she heard the typewriter carriage slam back into the starting position, Maddalena raised an eyebrow and stuck out her tongue in the direction of her assistant.

"And don't think I didn't just see you stick your tongue out at me!"

This time, Maddalena couldn't help but laugh in spite of herself. She reached for a small rubber eraser and rolled it around in her hands as she absently listened to the patter of drops on the stones in the courtyard. Combined with the steady clicking of Bettina's typing, it helped to unwind and untangle thoughts.

She arched her back slightly, tight from sitting too long at her desk, and lit another cigarette. As her mind drifted, she stared blankly out the window that faced a small piazza beyond filled with stately Ionic columns. In the center was a cascading fountain that sprayed water up to mingle with the rain.

It was always a magical sight, and once again she was reminded beauty and inspiration could be found in the simplest details—the cornice of a building, the colors of the trees in the Borghese Gardens, as well as the colors of the Tiber River as it changed hues with each passing hour of the day. She liked Rome now, in late fall, but to her it was most magical in the spring when the multi-colored flowers the vendors sold in front of the Pantheon melted into the misty rain, making her think she had stepped into a *Mary Poppins* chalk drawing.

Given the many hats she wore—businesswoman, artist, and

socialite—sometimes Maddalena needed to remind herself to slow down and appreciate her surroundings. When she did, she always found all the inspiration she ever could need or hope for. After all, Rome was like an open-air museum, adorned by hundreds of artists since the time of Romulus and Remus.

She recalled the first time she had been introduced to the charms of the city. It had been in the company of her favorite aunt when she was just a slip of a girl. And over the years, despite growing up in Paris, every time she returned to Rome, something about the city welcomed her, and she felt like she belonged. It was here she discovered little pieces of herself she had never been able to find anywhere else.

What made it most special was that here—in this Eternal City—she had met Matteo Crociani.

In her mind's eye, she clearly saw him standing on the bridge near Castel Sant'Angelo. It had been a windy day, and the portfolio she was carrying blew out of her hands. As she stooped to retrieve her drawings in the middle of the road, a horn sounded, causing her to jump. Glancing around, she saw a man stop his car and jump out to help her.

So preoccupied with gathering her precious designs, it wasn't until she saw a pair of handsome leather shoes come into view that she finally glanced up. Following the crease of his elegantly pressed pants, all the way up his slim torso until she encountered his eyes, she stopped, arrested by the sight of him. Standing up, surrounded by Bernini's angels, there on the windy bridge, they smiled at one another and they instantly knew.

As she thought about the moment, still peering out at the rain-soaked piazza, Maddalena slowly doodled and remembered the other day in Matteo's back room when she had first been introduced to Artemisia. It had been a revelation and she had been a bit surprised by the instant connection to the woman from another era. It was a peculiar feeling. As if they shared a similar kismet.

It was natural, Maddalena thought, considering they were artists and shared a similar passion for creating. But it was more than that. From what she had seen in Artemisia's painting, it seemed they both had a clear vision of what women could do when they united together and inspired others through their art.

Letting the sounds and her Roman muses inspire her, Maddalena continued working. After finishing her sketch, and she saw what she had drawn a pleased expression spread over her face. Her headache completely forgotten, she grinned in satisfaction—this was what she had been missing.

Maddalena ripped out the page and tacked it to the wall in front of her. Riding the wave of inspiration, as if another hand guided hers, reaching for another pencil, she sketched with more intention. As she worked, the present blended into the past, and the past merged into the future, and elements of Rome—and specifically one female artist—guided her hand.

Deep in concentration, she lost track of the hour until, finally feeling emotionally drained, she leaned back in her chair, tapped out another cigarette, and lit it. This time, when she blew out the smoke, it was in a satisfied stream of contentment and relief.

Bouncing her pencil lightly on the desk, she complimented herself on her brilliance. Out loud, she said, "Ah! Goddess of design, you haven't forsaken me after all! Do I have you or Artemisia to thank for this?"

She ran a finger tipped in bright vermillion over the page, tracing the lines of a stunning cocktail dress with an asymmetrical hemline. The model's body was lithe and impossibly elongated, like the columns beyond her window. And the train that fell to the floor from the cinched bodice reflected the water that flowed from the fountain.

Checking her watch, she thought, if it wasn't too soon, she would put in a call to her New York vendor to order fabric samples. She knew exactly what she needed and where to get it. But seeing it had stopped, she shook her wrist in disgust, realizing she had forgotten to wind it—again.

Raising her voice, she demanded, "Bettina! What time is it in New York?"

After a moment, a voice called out, "It's 12:05 a.m."

When Bettina appeared at the door carrying a tray upon which rested two small cups, she said, "It's too early to make a transatlantic call. No one is awake at this hour in the States—it's still the middle of the night."

Moving across the room, she added, "It's been too quiet in here for too long. I take that as a good sign." Glancing around, she said, "Is it safe to come in? I thought you might need some fortification. Want some coffee?"

"Love some."

As she sipped the hot brew, Maddalena wondered for the umpteenth time what she would do without her Girl Friday. They met when she had been apprenticing at the House of Boutilier where Bettina worked as a seamstress with uncommon aspirations—much like herself. They had taken an instant liking to one another, despite coming from opposite sides of town—she growing up in a rich bourgeois family and Bettina in a working class neighborhood.

Bettina, on first impression, was a pretty girl with burnished chestnut hair that she wore in a short bob. But what had drawn Maddalena to her was her natural sparkle and sense of humor. She discovered this shortly after they had been teamed up to create a dress for Mademoiselle Blanchard. She had done the design and Bettina had prepared the patterns, and after sharing many late nights together, and several bottles of wine, they snuck into the back room. They had become fast friends.

Now smelling the scent of freshly brewed coffee, and hearing Bettina quietly humming, Maddalena said, "Seems somebody's in a good mood today. So, this weather hasn't gotten you down?"

"Oh, I like the rain! It makes me think of Paris. It's a good feeling—happy and sad at the same time. I think about the Seine and the Champs Elysés... and the croissants fresh out of the oven! Do you remember that little caffè just around the corner from the Boutilier Atelier?"

"Of course. That's where we used to go to get those pistachio macaroons."

"*Oui*! Those were the best," Bettina said. "On days like this, I remember that caffè and reading a French newspaper and sitting in the window. I never got tired of looking out on the boulevard, watching all the people pass by with their umbrellas..."

Bettina sighed then handed Maddalena a cup. Taking it from her Maddalena spooned sugar into her tiny cup. "So, do you miss it terribly?"

"What? The macaroons or the people with umbrellas?"

"Paris, silly! The place you grew up."

"Only now and then." With a wave or her hand, she added, "I love Rome equally as well. It's home now, and you and Matteo are like my family. Anyway, if I was there now—in gay Paris—who would take care of you here? Certainly not Signor Crociani! He wouldn't even know where to begin to shop for a pair of little black shoes or find your favorite Parisian éclairs in this city."

"You mean the ones filled with *ganache* in the little French restaurant just off Piazza Navona?"

"Precisely," Bettina said. "See, I know you have a sweet tooth—you need me to keep you stocked with coffee and chocolate too."

Maddalena nodded. "You do have a knack. So, you are glad you are here then, and I haven't driven you to distraction yet?"

"You've asked me that dozens of times before and the answer is always yes—you drive me completely nuts!"

Leaning against the desk, Bettina took a sip of her coffee and added, "All kidding aside, you know I'll always be thankful to you. You gave me a chance—an incredible opportunity. When we first met in the House of Boutilier, when I was just a pattern maker learning the trade, you believed in me and encouraged me—for that I would follow you anywhere."

"I just recognized your talents that were going unappreciated by Monsieur B! I did what any sane person would do—invited you to run away with me to Rome to discover fame and fortune—and love."

Finishing the last dregs of her cup, she added, "And you're right, Betti, no one gets me better than you. Half the time you know what I'm thinking before I even think it myself. By the way, did you check...?"

"On the zippers we ordered from Signor Bellini last week?" Bettina replied, pulling out a small tablet from her pocket.

"See? There you go again!" Maddalena said.

Bettina grinned and removed the pencil from behind her ear. Holding it poised over her notebook, she checked through several pages of notes. "Give me a sec. Hold on..."

Maddalena watched Bettina's efficient movements. When she planned out a new collection, they were constantly inundated with infinitesimal details. But, with her assistant, they approved everything from the last pleat and dart to each button and hook. It was, after all, her attention to detail that made her a star of the Roman fashion scene, rivaling her competitors and colleagues in Paris. Without Bettina to keep her organized, she would be a disorganized mess.

"Ah, here we go," said Bettina. "The delivery is scheduled to arrive later next week. Thursday around noon."

"That is a very good thing," said Maddalena, "because I have finally figured out what I am going to do with them all!"

Bettina looked at her questioningly.

"Don't tell me I've stumped even you! Okay, here is a clue—it's time to ring up Montanari and..."

"But you said you didn't want to talk to him until you had the first evening dress design done... Wait a minute." Peeking over Maddalena's shoulder at the design on the drafting table, she said, "Oh! Oh, that's good!" She contemplated her skeptically. "But..."

"But what?" Maddalena said, knowing exactly what her assistant was about to say.

"Zippers have never been used in high-end fashion gowns!"

"I know! Isn't it a fantastic idea? It's time to make zippers elegant and sexy, and this dress simply won't work without one."

Feeling quite elated, she added, "This coming year, I'm going to revolutionize the way women think about zippers. Not only this dress, but in countless others. It will be the keystone idea of my new spring collection. Just think of the convenience! This, my dear, is a step toward liberating women!"

"It is quite original, that's for sure," Bettina said with appreciation. "I, for one, like the idea of zipping myself up without the help of someone fastening hundreds of buttons up my back."

"Exactly. Getting dressed should be something a woman can do quickly and efficiently."

Slipping the pencil behind her ear, Bettina said, "I'll get Signor Montanari on the phone right away. But I predict he will be quite appalled. The man is a traditionalist. He comes from a long line of couture tailors and pattern makers."

"Oh, I don't give a fig if he throws a fit. It will do him good to embrace something a bit more modern. He will thank me later when the orders start pouring in. Remember last fall, how he carried on about the buttons I'd designed in shapes that resemble little cauliflowers?"

"Yes, he thought you were crazy designing the little scarabs, butterflies, and crickets, too. He said they'd never sell."

"Yet, despite his grumbling, we set a five-day sales record after the fall fashion show."

Maddalena added with a dismissive toss of her head, "What can I say, I love whimsical things. That is precisely the creative flare that people expect in my work! And no matter what Montanari thinks, we are going to produce them together."

Bettina smiled. "And that's why you are the Duchess of Design." Flipping over the drafts of a dozen others that were now scattered about the table, she added, "And these designs are gorgeous. You've combined modern lines with a touch of the past—there around the necklines, and the use of trains."

"Once I got started, it seemed they flowed right out of my fingertips. And this is just the beginning. I've got a lot more ideas ready to be set down on paper."

"You are positively *un vero volcano*! Just a few hours ago it seemed you were a simmering cauldron and the flame was about to burn out."

"I know! The funny thing is, I got my inspiration from a very unlikely source. As I was gazing out the window, listening to the rain—I wasn't consciously thinking about her—and yet, she was there in my head, and then everything started to come together."

"What do you mean? Who is 'her'?"

"Artemisia—she's an artist from the 1600s that Matteo has discovered. I must take you to his auction house to show you. The gowns the women wear in her paintings are fabulous. They are jewel-toned, made of exquisite silks and satins. When I started envisioning the dresses and bodices with low decolletages and cascading trains it started me thinking. Of course, my take on the Baroque will be much more modern! No corsets and hooks for me, only streamlined zippers will do."

"Now that we are off to a good start," said Bettina, "I think this is a cause for celebration."

"How about drinks and dinner later tonight?" Maddalena agreed. "I'm buying."

"You're on," Bettina said as she flipped to a new page in her notebook. "Let me just pencil that in... How about six? No, wait, let's make it a bit later. I almost forgot you have a four o'clock appointment with Katharine Hepburn."

"Katharine who?"

"Hepburn!" said Bettina.

"Who's she?" asked Maddalena.

"She's some fresh young starlet from Hollywood hoping for a little fashion advice. Elsa in Paris told her to look you up."

"Elsa referred her, what a love!"

"Yes, when Katharine rang us yesterday to set up the appointment, I penciled her in for this afternoon. I thought we could fit her in right before your five o'clock fittings with the models."

"Okay," Maddalena said distractedly. "What else do we know about Miss Hepburn?"

Bettina raised an eyebrow.

"Oh, dear! A complete disaster, am I right?"

"Elsa implied she needed a little sprucing up. Apparently, she's a little on the dowdy side."

"For what exactly do we need to dress her for? Anything special?"

"She said Miss Hepburn is in search of a new image—apparently she has an upcoming audition next week with some Tinsel Town bigwigs."

"Well," said Maddalena, "I'm always up for a challenge. I'll ring Elsa back later and thank her for the referral."

"Do you need anything else? More coffee, biscotti..."

"No, I'm fine." As Bettina moved toward the door, Maddalena picked up a piece of chalk and filled in her design with jewel-toned hues. Suddenly, she stopped and called out, "Wait, have you heard from Fabrizio? Has he finished up with the new color swatches I ordered?"

"I was on the phone with him earlier," said Bettina, "going over all your instructions."

"What did he say? Did he understand the color has to be much brighter? What he sent over last week wasn't bright pink. It was more along the lines of dull-dishwater rose!"

"I think you are going to be happy this time." Imitating Fabrizio's deep voice, she continued, "Tell the Duchess this is the very best I can do. The color is as shocking as shocking can be."

"It is about time! And I like that. I believe I will call my new color *shocking pink* after Fabrizio—it only seems fair."

"Shocking pink? It has a nice ring to it. He'll be glad to know he's satisfied you at last," said Bettina.

"Oh, that poor man!" said Maddalena, biting her pencil, feeling the smallest pang of guilt. "I'm always making him redo the dye formulas and changing my mind."

"Yes, well, he *was* the first to start calling you the Duchess," said Bettina.

"To this day, I can't tell if it is a compliment or not," said Maddalena.

"You're right, but in his defense, he really is a sweet and reasonable man, and you can be very demanding at times," said Bettina.

"If a man asked him to do the same thing, he would be admired and said to be strong and decisive. A woman, on the other hand, when she acts the same way, is considered a witch or a shrew."

Looking at her design, she added, "I only ask for what I know you all can give. And I have this vision, Bettina. Can't you see it too? A pink so bright it will blind you! It came to me the other day while drinking a slow gin fizz at the Astoria. Just think, this time next year all the women in Rome will be wearing it. It will be my new signature color."

"So many ideas Maddalena! Your enthusiasm is contagious. But, if you ask me, you will make more headlines and turn more heads with that little black dress you just designed."

"And this is just the beginning. Wait until..."

When the shop door jangled, and a sultry voice called out announcing her arrival, they looked at one another in surprise.

"That's some voice!" said Maddalena.

"Oh, yes, that's Miss Hepburn," Bettina said, glancing at her watch. "She's early."

"A woman ahead of her time, eh?" Maddalena joked. "That's a good sign. I like her already. Perhaps I can convince her to wear a pair of my flannel pants in one of her movies. Now, that is sure to set her apart from the rest of the young starlets, not to mention turn Hollywood upside down and on its ear."

"This town—this whole world—could use a fresh breath of air, *and* a little more innovation."

"You are right on that account, Betti. It's a start, but fashion is just a small part of a very big and complicated equation."

As Bettina moved towards the door to properly greet their new client, Maddalena called after her, "You know I couldn't do this without you."

"I know. Designing women and fashion divas need to stick together," said Bettina over her shoulder. "Together, there's nothing we can't do— we will change the world one pair of pants at a time."

Chapter 23

Ship of Fools

*A*s the chilly days of winter set in, Maddalena and Bettina continued mapping out plans for their spring show set for the end of May, designing dresses for hot Roman nights. And now that their plans for fashion week were underway, Maddalena breathed just a little easier.

With more time on her hands, she found herself dialing up Matteo's number more frequently, asking him to lunch in their favorite caffè near the Borghese Palace. Walking hand in hand, they strolled through the gardens, bundled in their overcoats. Blowing into the cold air, they laughed at the foggy clouds they made and even delighted in the light snow that flurried around them. At night, they took long walks along the Tiber and, stopping on the bridge where they met, they looked up at the stars in the clear winter sky that seemed to shine brighter than ever.

Despite the rumblings around them and talk of war and the glory of a fascist nation, they chose during the winter holidays, when things were icy and cold, to take refuge in one another's arms. As lovers do, they thought the world was a magical place, made just for the two of them.

As Christmas came and went, and after celebrating Epiphany, Bettina started the serious work of piecing together new patterns, and Maddalena ordered fabrics and had lengthy conversations with her various vendors she knew she could count on. Matteo and Luciana were keeping busy, digging deeper into the life of their mysterious protégé Artemisia.

"We don't have a lot to go on," Matteo said a little dispiritedly to Maddalena one night as he mixed cocktails in his apartment overlooking the Tiber. "There isn't much documentation or records of ownership, or at least we haven't found anything significant yet."

"Meaning...?" asked Maddalena, lounging back against the cushions of the couch in a pair of silk pajamas and her close cropped-hair slicked back, allowing just a few pin curls to frame her heart-shaped face.

"Meaning, identifying Gentileschi's paintings is going to be tough," he said, handing her a champagne flute rimmed with sugar.

"Because you can't determine the provenances?"

"Yes, to verify authenticity we really need a proper trail of dates of purchases as the paintings were passed from hand to hand. You know, bills of sale, that kind of thing."

Holding up her glass and admiring the presentation, she took a sip of her Bellini and savored the flavor of lush, ripe peaches. When Matteo indicated there was a bit of tell-tale sugar on her upper lip, she smiled at him and licked it off.

"So, where are all the records?"

Matteo poured himself a drink and set down the gin bottle. "They probably don't exist. Things were a little slack back then. Also, because she was a female artist, they didn't feel the need to keep them."

Settling comfortably next to her, he said in a more encouraging tone, "But Luciana is an excellent fact checker. Her research skills are impeccable, and absolutely nothing discourages her. She is pursuing other avenues and found letters pertaining to Artemisia's family and her father. Turns out he too was a painter of merit."

"Where did she find that?" Maddalena asked, snuggling comfortably into the crook of his arm.

"In one of the local churches near the old artist's quarters near Castel Sant'Angelo. The Gentileschi family lived there for a time. She found a death certificate for Artemisia's mother Prudentia. There was also a scribbled comment in those papers about Orazio—that was the father's name—who apparently trained his daughter when she was only fourteen or fifteen. It also briefly suggests she was later instructed by a somebody named Agostino Tassi."

"Agostino Tassi? Never heard of him."

"I hadn't either until I started investigating, sifting through some records in the Vatican archives. It didn't surprise me I was able to find more about him than Artemisia. Art connoisseurs in the past tended to write more about male artists, considering female artists minor players in the art world—hardly worthy of mentioning."

"Typical," she said with a snort.

"Apparently, this Tassi person was one of Pope Urban's favorite painters. He was a *trompe l'oeil* painter and worked in some churches in and around Rome. But here is another interesting fact," said Matteo. "Following the Gentileschi trail, Luciana went down to the National Archives to nose around a bit to see what she else she might find. There in a vault she discovered several dusty legal ledgers pertaining to a trial involving Orazio Gentileschi—Artemisia's father—and Agostino Tassi."

"There was a trial? Whatever for?"

"Something to do with a stolen painting. That's it, really," he said, swirling the ice around in his glass. "We won't really know what the cause of complaint or who the injured party really was until Luciana reads through all the documents."

"It's all very strange, isn't it? That Artemisia should suddenly be coming to light now, almost as if she was finally making herself visible after all these years. I mean, look at the coincidences—you have a painting of an ancestor done by her and then connecting it to her others, and me being influenced and inspired by the women in her canvases. It's like a timeless gift she has given us both, from one friend to another."

Maddalena took a sip of her cocktail and added, "I think she'd be pleased with our efforts to keep her paintings and her memory alive." When Matteo picked up the evening paper, she leaned her head against his shoulder. Seeing her half-finished drink, she added, "I think she would also like this too."

As Matteo read the evening paper, she dreamily stared at the fire he had built earlier, mesmerized by the flickering flames. After a moment, as if being quietly summoned, her eyes traveled slowly from the hearth to the mantel, to the face of the original Matteo Crociani that now hung over it. She observed his handsome features with fascination as well as the cut of his coat and the black boots he wore. Around his neck was a touch of lace and she thought about a new design she would create based on the style of that very jacket.

Once again, she marveled at the uncanny resemblance between the original Matteo and the man who now sat beside her. As the fire burned on, emanating warmth from the grate, Maddalena broke the peaceful silence and said, "We've talked a lot about Artemisia, but what about him?"

"Him who?" Matteo asked, glancing up.

"Our ghost," she said, gesturing with her glass to the portrait of Matteo the First. "Did you ever find out anything more about him after you and Luciana verified it really was painted by our girl? What did your mother say on the phone the other day?"

Matteo lowered his newspaper slowly and looked at his ancestor. "I was right. He was caught up in the same trial as Galileo. While Galileo was given a life's sentence, locked away in Castel Sant'Angelo, Matteo was sentenced to death."

"How old was he?" Maddalena asked, feeling a wave of grief pass over her turning her thoughts melancholy.

"Matteo? He was only thirty-six."

"So young," she whispered. "Did he have a wife or family?"

"According to my mother, from the letters kept in the family vault, he had a young wife and a child on the way. After his death, she returned to the villa and raised the boy all by herself. She called him Matteo, and that, according to my mother, is how the tradition of naming the first-born sons Matteo got started."

"What a lovely tribute. To think you are a continuation of a long line of Matteos—I think it really is quite beautiful."

"I told you I've always felt a kinship with this man, from the moment I first saw him up in the attic."

"But why was he executed and not imprisoned along with Galileo?"

"Unlike Galileo, who they forced into renouncing his beliefs..."

"Which beliefs? That Earth revolves around the sun?" she asked incredulously.

"Yes. Galileo backed down and was placed under house arrest for the rest of his life. But, Matteo—he steadfastly refused to recant his theories, and so they hung him for heresy."

"Couldn't the proceedings be stopped? They were from Florence. Surely the city would have protected them?"

"Cosimo, his patron in Florence had just died, so when the Pope started his witch hunt there was no one to protect him and in the end he was executed in broad daylight on the bridge near Castel Sant'Angelo."

In astonishment, she asked, "The very place where we met?"

"The very place. They used to hang the bodies of executed criminals there in front of the Pope's residence. It was a way of sending a strong message that the church would not tolerate heretical theories that went against church doctrine or who might think about contradicting the current regime in power."

"What? To hang a man simply for believing strongly in something—something that in fact over time has been proven true," said Maddalena.

In anger, she set down her cocktail glass down with a sharp click on the glass table, and added, "Thank god we live in a modern era, where such things don't..."

Her rant faltered to a stop when she saw Matteo holding up the newspaper. Across the top of the page, the headlines screamed: KRISTALLNACHT—NAZIS SMASH, LOOT, AND BURN JEWISH SHOPS AND TEMPLES.

"Oh, my God!" Maddalena whispered in shock.

"By today's headlines, it seems we aren't so far away from a seventeenth-century mentality," he said grimly.

"When did *that* happen?"

"Last night in Germany—and now it's happening here in Rome, according to this article."

He folded the paper and tossed it aside. "Now that Mussolini has withdrawn us from the League of Nations, things in Italy are starting to take a very strange turn."

"He's getting closer to Hitler and Franco too..."

"And now the government is imposing sanctions and anti-Semitic laws! We might as well be having a modern-day inquisition," finished Matteo grimly.

"You think we'd learn a few lessons from the history books—I shudder to think what we will wake up to read in the papers tomorrow. Will this ever end or only lead to further violence? My God! Could there be a pogrom against the Jewish people? It's insane even to think that. It will never come to that—right?"

Matteo shook his head. "God only knows. With Mussolini in control—spoon-feeding us propaganda—we are all in big trouble."

And true to his word, as the weeks of March and April slid together, headlines worsened. Mussolini's regime crowed daily about the benefits of a pure Italian nation, but instead of making things better, the economy continued to spiral downward. The foreign wars in Ethiopia and Spain were taxing the purses and the patience of the Italian people.

Each day, they read of new economic bans and trade embargoes on oil and coal. Poverty was at an all-time high and civil unrest was setting in. Resources were limited, and jobs were becoming scarce. Like Domenico Milluzzi, so many people in Rome were drifting about, finding work wherever they could to make ends meet.

A way of life was passing, and they were frustrated and desperate as they lost more autonomy and freedom. It had started small, but the slow, steady chipping away at personal hopes and aspirations was incrementally building, and people's spirits were crumbling. Merely surviving meant conforming to the party's doctrines and rigid ideologies. But most concerning were the penalties being heavily dealt out, not only for minorities and Jews. Italian women, too, were under scrutiny and oppressed.

Daily, the "gentler" sex was bombarded by Mussolini's propaganda machines that churned out messages encouraging Italy's wives and daughters to focus on family responsibilities and relinquish any frivolous notions of having a career or independent life. To live in Mussolini's world meant conforming to an idealized vision of what a woman should be. According to him, all a female was good for was sex, procreation, marriage, and being an exemplary housekeeper.

God forbid if women should want to have a career or go into politics. And if they didn't comply, they were imprisoned in asylums for not adhering to the morals held by the government. As each new act of aggression, and mysterious disappearance was reported, people grew more and more worried, and fear showed on their faces, especially Maddalena's.

She firmly contended a woman had the right to pursue a career compatible with her talents, and that they were on equal footing with men. So, when Maddalena felt the pressure of Mussolini's misogynist government that harkened back to medieval days—binding her hands in red tape so the circulation was starting to be cut off—it enraged her to no end. She wasn't about to take things lying down, be shipped off to a "nunnery," or thrown in an asylum, just to shut her up.

Barging into Matteo's office late one afternoon, Maddalena threw down her coat and paced the floor. "I'm so mad I could scream. Do you know what just happened? I swear..."

She turned to look at him holding the telephone to one ear, and seeing him motioning to hang on, she waited for him to finish his conversation. Leaning back against the desk next to him, she listened to a jazzy tune that was playing on the radio, trying to calm her racing mind.

When he finished and put the receiver back into the cradle, he leaned back in his chair and, seeing her anger, asked, "What's happened now? They didn't run your adverts again?" he asked, picking out a cigarette and lighting it for her.

"It's all so discouraging. This government! There is just one restriction after the other... one foul up following another. They are always mucking around in my business, but this time they have gone a step too far."

"What do you mean?"

Trying to keep her voice steady, she said, "Losing my ads, or not running them at all in the morning paper, is just a small annoyance.

Now they are tampering with my shipping orders! Can you believe that? Everything is tied up at the Port Authority. How am I supposed to get my fabrics from the warehouse to the manufacturer in time to start production? We are only weeks away from our spring show, and the timing is critical."

Matteo grew pensive as she continued to vent.

Pushing off from the desk, Maddalena paced the room again. "I am a businesswoman, and now everything I've worked for is slowly being taken away. We can own property and run businesses, but now the reality of the situation is we don't have the right to do what we want with them."

She spun around and faced Matteo. "It's outrageous! They are trying to control us all, pressuring the masses to tango to their tune. Well, I've got news for Mussolini. I won't ever be a willing dance partner."

Matteo nodded his head in agreement. Seeing his support, she calmed a bit, but then, remembering all her orders tangled up at the docks in red tape, she stubbed out her cigarette and said, "I am so fed up, I'm about ready to fumigate that den of rats."

Sighing heavily, Matteo agreed, "These little 'inconveniences' we've been faced with are mounting by the moment, transforming into something much deadlier and ominous. But we have to move cautiously. We are up against a clearly established government that has a stronghold on this country. If we..."

Hearing a light rap on the office door, they looked up as Luciana walked into the room carrying an armful of documents. Noticing Maddalena and the tense expression on her face, her welcoming smile faded and she immediately grew concerned. "Things not going so well?"

Maddalena shook her head and rolled her eyes, and Luciana nodded sympathetically. "You don't even have to say a thing, I can just imagine what the problem is."

Turning to Matteo, she said, "I wanted to give you these notes before I left. I need to get home before dark."

"Are these the transcripts from the Gentileschi trial?"

"Yes, I've just gotten started on them. I've also been reading some letters Artemisia exchanged later in life with Galileo. It is clear to me the woman was a force of nature. From what I've pieced together, she was a woman who upheld, in her speech and in her work, the equality of spirit between the sexes and the right to pursue the same line of work."

Luciana placed the paper file folder secured with a string onto his desk in front of him and looked steadily at Matteo. "Artemisia was a rare spirit. The world needs to know about her and it angers me that I have to stop my work. I'm not sure when I'll be able to get back to it..."

Matteo held her eye a moment, then sliding the file back in her direction, he said, "This is only temporary. I want you to take this with you and continue your research."

"But..."

Rising out of his chair, he picked up the file and handed it to her. "I'm putting Artemisia into your capable hands. That's how much I believe we will see this thing through together."

He gave her a brief hug and said, "For now, just be safe. Make sure to pass on to your father what I said earlier, but remember to be discreet. Stay low. Antonio will be driving the truck. He will have more instructions for you the day after tomorrow."

Luciana nodded and gave him a confident smile, but when she looked back, Maddalena saw a bit of moisture in the woman's eyes. "Good night, Maddalena. Between the three of us, Artemisia's star will not be forgotten." Holding the documents containing Artemisia's recorded words from her trial to her breast, Luciana leaned over and kissed her cheek and said, "And we will all meet again, of that I'm sure. *Statemi bene*—stay well, the two of you."

Then, without another word, Luciana quietly left the room. As her footsteps echoed down the long hallway, Matteo stood by the door for a moment, watching her go.

Walking to his side, Maddalena put a hand on his sleeve and asked, "Has something else happened?"

He hesitated, then shook his head. "A few days ago, coming out of the synagogue, she was accosted on the street by some brown-shirted thugs who wanted to see her papers..."

"Did they do anything to her?" Maddalena asked with concern.

"Not in so many words. Luciana brushed it off, you know how she is, but it gave her a fright. She knows it is a clear warning, too—time is running out for her and the rest of the Mancini family. Jews all over the city are being dismissed from professional jobs and children are now forbidden to attend public schools. Things are getting bad..."

"I know, I've seen the papers. Surely we can..."

Matteo motioned for her to keep her voice down. Looking out into the hallway again, he closed and locked the door. Stepping close to her side, he quietly said into her ear, "With the help of Don Gregorio and the partisans, we are using my delivery vans to help move Luciana and her family out of the city."

"But where will they go? What will her family do?"

"For now, they will stay with friends near the villa close to Montepulciano. They will be safe there, as long as we keep things quiet and don't arouse suspicion."

Maddalena nodded, understanding the gravity of the situation. She knew Matteo had been involved before, working with the anti-fascist movement, meeting behind closed doors and coordinating and organizing counterattacks on Mussolini's regime. But now that he was helping move people, instead of just distributing flyers and messages, he was involved on a whole new level, and the risks were much higher.

"How can I help? Surely, we can also use my business as a cover in some way. I've got contacts..."

Matteo shook his head. "I don't want to put you in that position. It's too dangerous. Mussolini's spies are everywhere. We must move cautiously. For now, you are somewhat safe, being a foreigner. But you haven't escaped their scrutiny—just look how they've been treating you. Up to now, you've been a minor annoyance. Your image upsets their propaganda machine, but once you become a real threat and join in the resistance, they *will* harm you."

"I'm not just going to turn a blind eye. Surely, there is something more I can do for the Mancinis."

Matteo's face softened. "I know how you are feeling. But, for now, we have to stay under the radar and not arouse suspicion. Can you work with me on that?"

She nodded. "Yes, of course."

"I don't want attention drawn to our operations," he paused. "But then again, you can help by dazzling and distracting them with your fashion designs and the fanfare of your upcoming show. You will be the perfect smokescreen to take some of the heat off us."

"I can certainly do that," she readily agreed. "If they won't run my ads, I'll have my delivery boys stand on corners handing out flyers. I'll do my own marketing. This will be..."

Her voice faltered to a stop as the radio broadcast changed from the normal music hour and they heard the voice of an agitated reporter crackling through the speaker: *"It's burst into flames! It's burning and the... Oh my God, it's falling on the mooring mast. This is the worst of the worst catastrophes in the world. Oh, it's... crashing, oh! Four... five hundred feet into the sky and it... it's a terrific crash, ladies and gentlemen. Oh, the humanity! And all the passengers are screaming..."*

"Oh mio Dio!" Maddalena said in a hushed tone.

When the radio broke up, Matteo dialed in the setting until the announcer's voice could be heard again. Tensely, they listened to the broadcast from America and learned the terrible news of the German airship, the Hindenburg—the ingenious aircraft loaded with hundreds of commercial passengers—had erupted into a fireball and then plummeted to the ground, incinerating many of its crew and passengers.

Heartsick, Maddalena leaned into Matteo's arms and cried. "The world is going mad. When will it end? How will things ever get better?"

Holding her tightly, he whispered into her ear, "Together, given time, be assured, we *will* open a door to a better future. *Fidati di me*—trust me—we *will* make a difference."

Chapter 24

Dancing with Mussolini

For a few days, Maddalena was genuinely encouraged by Matteo's words, believing they were destined for a better future if they just stayed the course and continued in the direction of the distant horizon. But later that week, dressed to the nines in a form-fitting gold dress that left her shoulders bare, she was once again filled with doubts as they entered the Marquessa dalla Ricca's foyer in via Giulia.

Stopping on the threshold of the ballroom together, they took in the elegant mirrors that decorated the room and the chandeliers with large crystal pendants. The setting was nearly perfect, except for the red and black fascist banner that hung against an entire wall. Maddalena shivered at the site of the ominous image.

Whispering into Matteo's ear, she said, "Just look around you, drinking, dancing, designer dresses as if we had no care in the world. Are we no better than them? This feels so wrong to me." Placing a hand on his sleeve, she implored, "I want to leave right now. Please, let's go."

"We can't just yet." Glancing cautiously around, Matteo added, "Remember what I said about not kicking the hornet's nest? They are watching us. If we leave now, it would just call attention and make matters worse and right now I must protect Luciana and her family."

Observing the firm set of his jaw, she said, "Yes, you are absolutely right. We can do this if only for an hour. Then promise me..."

Her words were interrupted by the blare of trumpets, and they and the dancers pivoted around to face the door. Soon, clapping broke out and cheers could be heard as Mussolini made a grand entrance.

And what an entrance! The dictator rode into the Marquessa's ballroom on a white stud. As he slid off his mount, he was immediately encircled by his sycophants, who led him to the front of the room, where he was greeted by Clara Petacci, his current paramour. He kissed the hostess on her cheek and the party formed a reception line to welcome the other guests.

"Why does he do that? It is obscene," hissed Maddalena into Matteo's ear. "Must we bow and scrape to such a pompous ass? It makes my stomach churn to see him."

Matteo placed a calming hand on her arm and said, "Put on your party face, *cara*, and dust off your good manners. Come on, it's show time. We'll do the meet and greet, dance a dance, and then be on our way. I too am quickly losing my appetite."

Letting him guide her, they moved to the far side of the ballroom where they joined the others. When their turn came, and Maddalena stood directly in front of the short, barrel-chested dictator flanked by henchmen dressed in black, she did her best to be vivacious and smile nonchalantly. Still, thoughts of Luciana occupied her, and it took all the nerve she could muster to raise her kid-gloved hand to be kissed.

"Ah, Mademoiselle Paquin," Mussolini purred. "It's a pleasure to finally meet you. I hope I'm not being too forward, but may I just say you are a vision. Why, all the others in the room pale in comparison."

Maddalena, bowed her head slightly, acknowledging his glib compliment. With a modicum of politeness and a hefty dose of tolerance, she responded, "Oh, I wouldn't say that, Il Duce. Half the women in this ballroom tonight are wearing my creations."

"*Giusto!*" said Mussolini with a glint in his eye. Slowly, he lowered his lips to kiss her hand. As he did, he applied steady pressure, rubbing his thumb suggestively over her palm. She attempted to pull her hand away, but he continued to hold on to it.

"You are as lovely as you are perceptive, Mademoiselle Paquin," he said, tracing his eyes over her bare shoulders, lingering over her bosom until finally he raised them to meet her gaze. "Please, save a dance for Il Duce, one of your most admiring fans."

Despite the fine, soft leather separating her skin from his, she felt the sudden need to wash her hands. With a tight smile, she tucked her arm into the crook of Matteo's and, feeling him give her a slight squeeze of caution, she replied, "I'd be charmed."

Smiling broadly, Mussolini gave her a little bow of his head, dismissing them. As they walked away, Matteo asked, "Are you alright?"

Repulsed, she said, "There is no doubt in my mind, the man is an absolute pig. He has no regard for women. Did you see the way he ogled me and how he held on to my hand?"

"It was all I could do not to intervene, but you were civil, very well-behaved. I knew you could handle the situation."

"Yes, but it took a lot of self-control." Swinging around to face Matteo, she added "I'll tell you one thing—I'm not about to dance with him! I can't stand the thought of being held in his arms. If he thinks I'm one of the dozens of women he has on call, to have a five-minute sexual encounter with, he's sadly mistaken."

"The man has a highly inflated ego..." agreed Matteo with an edge in his voice. "He considers himself the greatest man since Napoleon and equates sex with power. Narcissism at its best."

Maddalena turned her head and glanced over at a bevy of young women, with platinum, red, and dark hair who surrounded the dictator. At the sound of their giggling, Maddalena shook her head sadly. "They are *all* on some power trip. Do you see and hear those girls back there? They think by sleeping with him his aura will rub off on them and they will be treated to a night of fantastic sex."

She snorted in disgust. "He has that reputation, you know. That he is a fantastic lover and can skyrocket a woman into erotic pleasure. I think he propagates that rumor himself."

Matteo said nothing, just looked over her shoulder at the dictator. Leaning closer, she whispered into his ear, "The other day, some women from Palazzo Braschi, the fascist party headquarters, were in my showroom, and I overheard them talking. One of the women was a willing participant and said his valet Quinto Navarra brings him a woman every day and every afternoon like clockwork. They even recorded her name in a guest book called Fascist Visitors."

Matteo shook his head in disgust barely fathoming what she was telling him.

"This woman," Maddalena continued, "said Mussolini took her so violently she became terrified. He told her straight out he wanted to harm her and be brutal. But the woman just brushed it off with her friend. When I heard that, I wanted to shake her and tell her Mussolini didn't give a damn about her—not about what she was thinking or feeling—let alone her sexual pleasure. And the saddest thing, he will never remember her face, let alone her name, because he will just help himself to the next in line who is ready to answer his booty call. That woman in my salon—in his eyes, she's already yesterday's trash."

Hearing the music resume again and animated conversation fill the ballroom, she pleaded, "Oh, please. Let's just go home."

Instead, Matteo reached for her hand. "Come, *amore mio*, just a half hour longer—then I will take you anywhere you want to go. Remember why we are doing this. And, as I seem to recall, you never say no to me when I ask you to dance."

Seeing her acquiesce, he tugged her closer to him. "Maddie-girl, it's been over an hour since I held you in my arms. Let's dance and try to forget everything, if only for a little while."

Together they marked the time, waltzing about a quarter of an hour. With her humor restored, Maddalena suggested they stop and drink a glass of champagne and chat with their hostess, and her good friends Signor and Signora Marocchini. Feeling at ease, and much more social than when she had entered the ballroom, Maddalena entertained them with one of her witty stories.

But, as she paused to take a sip of prosecco, just as she was about to resume her anecdote, she felt a hand caress her bare shoulder, and a shiver ran down her spine. When she glanced around, she saw Mussolini had stepped behind her and was now looking at her with a feral grin.

"Mademoiselle Paquin, I'd be honored if I could now claim that dance I spoke of earlier."

Despite his honeyed words, the authoritative glint in his eye told her refusal wasn't an option. Instinctively, her eyes sought Matteo's to gauge his reaction and, as she had expected, his eyes darkened and he imperceptibly clenched his jaw. Mussolini, seeing the exchange between them, said in a jovial tone, "Surely, Crociani, you won't deny me the pleasure of this remarkable creature for just a few minutes."

Before Matteo could reply, despite what she had said earlier, Maddalena calmly put a hand on his arm. Without speaking a word, she communicated a private message as she handed him her champagne flute. With her head raised high, Maddalena looked Matteo squarely in the eye and, in that moment, he recognized the spirit of Artemisia's Judith.

Then, out loud, she said, "Just wait here, *amore mio*. I'll be back soon. You won't even know I'm gone."

"Have no fear, I will keep her warm for you, Crociani," the dictator replied, taking Maddalena's hand in his and leading her out to join the other couples on the ballroom floor. As a new waltz began, he drew her close, and they circled the room several times in silence, but the way his fingers intimately squeezed her small waist spoke volumes.

Then, leaning so that his breath warmed her neck, he murmured, "I've been watching you, Mademoiselle Paquin, over the past couple of months. But lately it seems I've been hearing more and more interesting things about you—and your business enterprises..."

She gave him an innocent look, wondering where this was leading. "Why, yes, I'm preparing my spring fashion show. It is coming up in just a few weeks, and I've been working night and day..."

"Night and day—my, you are quite a passionate woman," he said in a manner that twisted her innocent words.

Caressing her back, he added, "As I said, I'm quite impressed with your ardor and devotion." Indicating Matteo standing near the window, he added, "You two make a fine pair. Your ideas are quite modern— perhaps a little too—unconventional."

Laughing lightly, she said, "So you find me a little too foreign? Or is it because I am a fashion designer?"

They danced another turn around the room. In measured, deliberate words, he added, "In my Italy, a woman's place is in the home raising a large family..."

"I adore children," Maddalena said, keeping the conversation light.

"*Bene*," agreed the dictator. "To serve this country well, the future mothers of the new regime should be round and plump stirring the kettle over their hearths. At all times, they should be docile." He paused, then added, "And always submissive."

He chuckled when he saw a fleeting grimace of disdain cross her face she couldn't quite contain.

"You look particularly lovely tonight, Mademoiselle Paquin. The gown becomes. Clara was saying to me the other day she would like a dress designed by you." He eyed her intently and added, "I was even thinking about buying a new painting from your *fidanzato*. Perhaps Crociani would make a special delivery and bring it to me in one of his vans?"

His words hung between them and Maddalena raised a wary eyebrow.

"Oh, come now, Mademoiselle Paquin. You are an astute woman, and by now you know I have eyes and ears all over Rome." He paused, letting his words take effect. "For some, that could be a problem."

The man was mercurial, and his actions unpredictable, but to Maddalena his message was becoming clearer by the second.

Pulling her a little tighter and running his fingers over her arm and lightly caressing the side of her breast, he said, "You know, you move divinely, and we fit together so well—like two puzzle pieces meant to be joined. They say those who dance well together, make the best bed partners. I'm Il Duce, and you are the Duchess. It only seems appropriate we should be joined together in ecstasy and share a passionate night."

Her breath caught in her throat and she gaped at him in astonishment.

"Come now," he murmured. "Surely, you feel it too. Are you embarrassed, or perhaps a little in awe that I should find you such a suitable and highly desirable partner?"

Glancing in the direction of Matteo, he whispered, "I'll make all the arrangements. It will all be very discreet. Crociani never needs to know."

There was a ringing in her ears so intense she could barely hear the music, let alone the dictator's word. Not only was he trying to seduce her in front of Matteo—flaunting his power—he was also blackmailing her with his proposition. With every ounce of her being, she tried to remember Matteo's warnings. She too sought out his familiar face in the crowd, but her vision was clouded by the red fury that coursed through her veins.

Encouraged by her silence, Mussolini continued, "Surely, you feel it too—there is chemistry between us. From the moment I saw you at the opera several months ago, I was quite smitten. Although I'm not a big fan of that kind of entertainment—I prefer to take a nap in the back of the box—I must say your charms certainly caught my eye that night and kept me stimulated and on the edge of my seat. I knew then we would be lovers."

When the waltz concluded, instead of releasing her, Mussolini held her firmly in his grasp. "You know, *cara mia*," he said, "with this body of mine, I could make you tremble with pleasure like no one else."

Maddalena, disengaging her arm, took a step back. She noted, with distaste, he wore the entitled smile of a man who thought he could help himself to a woman as though she was a piece of chattel. Taking her silence for capitulation, Maddalena knew by the glint in his eyes Mussolini believed he had made a conquest. By backing her into a corner, he fully anticipated she would submissively and eagerly give herself over to him. It was just a matter of time before he would lay claim to her body.

But what Mussolini had failed to see in the look that passed between them, was that in Maddalena he had met a woman who knew she was inferior to no man and that *she* was in control of her own mind and body and would not be a pawn in anyone's game.

Blissfully ignorant, Mussolini kissed her hand and let go of her hand. With a slight bow, he dismissed her. "Until next time, Duchess." Then, raising an eyebrow suggestively, he backed away and focused his attention on his next partner.

When she reached Matteo, Maddalena didn't say a word. She took the arm he offered her and, without a backward glance, they exited the Marquessa's salon and left all the fools behind.

Later that night, as she lay next to Matteo, listening to the radio, she hummed along to a song in which a woman crooned of love, loss, and longing. When the refrain began again, she sang with the blues singer: *Time is an illusion, but dreams are real. In the dark and endless skies, never stop searching for me. Love erases the boundaries that separate us and together we will be again.*

Maddalena looked over at Matteo, and she knew what he was thinking as he smoked a cigarette in the dark. She saw his pensive expression and watched the embers arc through the dark room and disintegrate onto the marble floor like falling stars. She reached for his cigarette and took a long draw, letting out a stream of smoke. Handing it back to him, he tucked an arm under his head and continued staring up at the ceiling.

The unspoken words and the unasked questions hung over them like the smoke that filled the room: Should they stay in Rome or go somewhere far away?

Maddalena sighed and turned into the shelter of Matteo's strong arms and rested her head on his chest. And, regardless of their better intentions, and what they both knew was coming, Maddalena and Matteo decided to stay where they were. At least for a little while longer. They believed that time was on their side.

Chapter 25

Death Comes at Midnight

*A*s the weeks progressed and the days grew warmer, tensions stretched thinner by talk of war, military parades, and demonstrations. After Maddalena's disturbing encounter with Mussolini, she urged Matteo and the others to take greater precautions. Realizing the noose was tightening around their necks, they changed their strategies slightly but were still able to help get Luciana and her family to a more secure location, in the hills of Tuscany outside Montepulciano, near the Crociani Estate.

Undeterred by the dictator's veiled threats and insinuations, Matteo and the partisans continued their work in secret, delivering messages, distributing information, and helping others in peril avoid altercations with the growing demands of the rigid regime. Maddalena did what she could to create the allusion that she and the others were adhering to Mussolini's plan; she kept up appearances, focusing on her designs and orchestrating her upcoming fashion show.

But it wasn't easy keeping a calm exterior. The only thing that helped her get through each day was the one true constant in a universe spinning out of control—her love for Matteo. Given the fact everything else was disintegrating, like silver sand through an hourglass, she held on to him firmly, knowing their love was invincible and together they could weather any storm.

With Bettina by her side too, Maddalena worked feverishly through the final details of the 1939 House of Paquin Fashion Show. She wasn't at all sure what the future held or the likelihood there would be a fall show later that year, so she wanted to make this event exceptionally special.

Putting on a brave face, the Duchess of Design rolled up her sleeves, encouraged her staff, and led by example. She joined her seamstresses, fabric vendors, and delivery boys, doing whatever she could to facilitate matters, and continued according to plan.

She was quite content with her new line of ready-to-wear day dresses and pants. She catered not only to the fancy elite, but also to the working-class woman with more outfits affordable on a limited budget. Many of the designs included zippers—the hallmark of economy and ease of use.

Despite her intent to maintain a low profile, and not ruffle Mussolini's feathers, she couldn't help but include Freud's insightful words in the flyers she handed out the weeks before the show: *To dream of fastening one's clothes with a zipper is a sign you will preserve your dignity in the face of great provocation to do otherwise.* She had to be true to her vision of what a woman should be and thought now more than ever—regarding the times—there could be no statement more appropriate to promote her new dress line.

The extra effort she exerted did not go unnoticed by her adoring public, and during the final days before the launch of her spring collection, everyone waited with bated breath to see what Maddalena might dazzle them with next. Would she raise hemlines once again, or make a woman's shoulders even broader and more pronounced? Would she soften the look with casually cut blouses that draped elegantly around the neck?

Each collection, as was her tradition, had a specific theme and her shows had become a form of entertainment, known as much for their artistic flair as for their fashions. She hired dancers, carnival magicians, and actors to dress up, all set against a background of dramatic lighting, music, and elaborate sets. And because of the hype and her superb marketing skills, after each show sales skyrocketed.

The past fall, she had entertained Rome's elite with a circus motif. Her collection had been held together by striking red silk tops, navy blue skirts and trousers, and gold braided bolero jackets. And the year before that, she leaned heavily on pagan patterns. Her dresses were trimmed with leaves and delicate flowers embroidered on clingy slips. Her models had strolled down the runway with their hair entwined with wreaths, seeming like Botticelli nymphs.

This spring, in honor of Matteo's discovery of Artemisia and her *Judith and Holofernes*, Maddalena decided to dedicate her show to women warriors. She even asked Matteo if she could hold the event in his auction room, arranging Artemisia's paintings to act as a backdrop for the dresses.

"Because of you, I discovered a designer's muse in Artemisia," she told Matteo while dining one evening in a small trattoria, around the corner from his offices near Castel Sant'Angelo. "You brought her alive, as you will for the rest of the world, and for that I will be forever grateful."

Raising her glass, Maddalena added, "I know you have big plans for her later, but I'm thinking of this as a debutante party, and I am more than happy to share the stage with Artemisia."

Inspired by the woman who had been named after the Greek Goddess Artemis—Mistress of the Moon—Maddalena worked tirelessly to create beautiful gowns made from silks and brocades that featured nipped-in waists with necklines with cunning cutouts that would set off a woman's throat and bosom in a most provocative way. The fabrics themselves she had printed with the patterns of crescent moons and five-point stars, and buttons that resembled tiny bows and arrows—even some that resembled an artist's paintbrush.

Almost all the frocks had been produced and they, along with their accessories—shoes, gloves, stoles, and hats—were hanging in a delightful array of gem-like colors in the back offices of Matteo's auction house. All that remained was to coach the models, hang the paintings, and illuminate the stage.

To help with the latter, Matteo put Milluzzi in charge of the work crew to set up the lights. Despite the fact he knew Maddalena wouldn't approve, over the past few months he had grown to trust the man. Milluzzi was an artist, after all, and of all the day laborers who had drifted in and out of his showroom, Milluzzi had remained, and by now had the longest tenure. Because of this, Matteo had no qualms giving his new foreman keys to the warehouse and workrooms, necessary to let the others in and lock the back door to the alleyway at night.

When Matteo conveyed this to Maddalena, she looked at him askance. "Surely, you are joking? Milluzzi is to be the foreman of my stage operations? The man is an absolute pain—he doesn't even like me. How are we ever going to work together?"

"Oh, please, *cara*," Matteo had admonished her. "He is really a decent and likable fellow once you get to know him. He's fallen on hard times. You know how it is these days."

"Yes, you're right," she said slowly, "I do."

Caught up in a myriad of details, Maddalena didn't get the chance to visit Matteo's place for several days. When she finally did, she was half afraid she'd find things in shambles. But, walking into the large central hall, with a sigh of relief she realized things were shaping up nicely, and she conceded Milluzzi had done an excellent job.

All around the stage, Artemisia's paintings were hung, suspended from wires attached to the ceiling. It had been Maddalena's vision to have the models emerge from behind a dark curtain wearing the deep red and emerald green gowns, giving the illusion they had magically stepped out of the seventeenth-century artist's pictures. The key to the whole effect, of course, was the glow of radiant lamps that would create a rich contrast of darkness and light.

Hearing a muttered curse, she peered up and saw the foreman himself, standing on a ladder a short distance away. With pliers and cutters, he spliced an electrical cable. Moving to stand under him, she called up, "*Complimenti, Signor Milluzzi*. The stage looks wonderful."

Milluzzi nodded curtly, saying nothing as he concentrated on adjusting the light to focus on the portrait of Bathsheba. Maddalena pursed her lips and put her hands on her hips. She was about to open her mouth and say something impulsively rude but, remembering what Matteo had said earlier—to be more cordial—she attempted to draw him out with a bit of small talk.

"So, tell me, what do you think of all this, Milluzzi?"

With a shrug of his shoulders, he didn't say anything at first. But after a moment, when Maddalena didn't move, Milluzzi looked down at her and tiredly responded, "I'm not a fan of this particular artist."

Adjusting the light slightly to the left so that it fully illuminated Artemisia's painting, he added, "This one here is okay—I like the portrait of her—but that one next to it—I find that one disturbing."

Following his gaze, she saw he referred to a smaller version of Judith beheading Holofernes. Recently, Matteo and Luciana had discovered Artemisia had painted several versions of this subject and had acquired another one. Calling up to him, she asked, "Do you object to the subject matter—that a woman is cutting the head off a man—or by the fact a woman painted it?"

Continuing to splice together a cable, he said, "It's hideous, in my opinion. Obscene, in fact! If you want to know the truth, Mademoiselle Paquin, I find it irritating that a painting by a long-forgotten woman should now be more popular than my own—and her paintings are worth more than God's teeth."

Looking down at her, he added, "I can't sell my work for more than a handful of coins, enough to buy a loaf of bread to feed my family, but this painting alone is listed in the gallery catalog for more lire than I've ever seen in my life."

Maddalena hadn't expected that response and reacted in surprise. "But, as a painter, aren't you at all pleased to play a small role in bringing back Artemisia and showing respect for another talented artist? Surely, you have the humility to appreciate someone else's success."

He stepped down from the ladder slowly. "Humility? Perhaps *you* can take satisfaction in the resurrection of this artist. But I wasn't born a fancy foreigner with a silver spoon in my mouth." He looked pointedly at the lustrous strand of pearls she wore around her neck. "No, we Milluzzis have to fend for ourselves. We find our opportunities and take them."

At first, Maddalena was at a loss for words, understanding to some extent the cause of his bitterness. But still trying to reach the man, she said encouragingly, "But, if we can't appreciate and take pleasure in the beauty around us—and put others before ourselves—then there is little hope left in the world for any of us. You'll just find yourself alone very soon, Signor Milluzzi, drifting through time without a higher purpose in your own self-imposed purgatory."

He regarded her intently for a moment. Then, picking up his hat, he said, "Signora, I'm already in hell."

Without another word, he walked to the door, leaving Maddalena standing by herself surrounded by Artemisia's paintings, thinking once again what a horrible, unlikable man he was. When Bettina walked into the gallery and called out to her about some new problem that had arisen, she made a note to let Matteo know she had tried hard, but Milluzzi was as distasteful to her as the day they met. Moving on with her day, confronted with ten new complications, she let the incident slide away, and by evening it was completely forgotten.

As things continued to see-saw—and just when it seemed everything was falling apart—with Bettina's help, everything finally came together. They were used to the hectic sequence of events. It left them breathless up to the last minute, but they also enjoyed the adrenaline rush when everything finally fell into place. And now they stood side by side dressed and ready to face the crowd.

Peeking through the backstage curtain, Maddalena saw the showroom was abuzz and overflowing with the creme de la creme of high society. She recognized many new faces, as well as some loyal fans. Sitting in the front row was a special client, the Contessa Bassani, and her daughter, both outfitted in her designs from the previous fall.

Maddalena wore the stunning black evening gown she first designed, the one that inspired the rest of the spring collection. It fit her sleekly, fitting tightly over her hips and ending in two side panel trains. To complete the effect, she wore black high heels and a pair of kid gloves that skimmed up her arms and past her elbows.

At first, she thought to let one of her girls model it, but Matteo encouraged her to showcase the jewel of her latest collection instead. "It suits you," he said. "It is your signature piece. After all, you wore it for the portrait Ettore painted of you, right?"

Maddalena smiled when she thought about her recent portrait. It had almost been a total fiasco. Yes, it was a picture-perfect gown, but still, she hadn't been an easy subject to paint. Poor Ettore! His original idea had been to pose her facing front, but given her propensity to swivel her head to speak with Bettina over her shoulder about this detail or that, he gave up.

Instead, he concentrated on highlighting her figure in the incredible dress and settled on showing her profile, her head averted and turned slightly into the shadows. But, in the end, she admitted to Matteo she quite liked the effect. "Perhaps someday I'll end up hanging next to your great ancestor, and we will be together for all eternity," she quipped.

And now, moments before the show was to begin, Maddalena felt a new surge of confidence. Matteo had been right again; she should wear this dress—it was her destiny.

Embracing wholeheartedly her role as mistress of ceremonies, Maddalena stepped out from behind the curtain and addressed the crowd. She welcomed her guests and set everyone at ease with witty jokes, applauding them for their excellent taste in showing interest in her designs.

She only hesitated slightly when she noted, out of the corner of her eye, Clara Petacci—Mussolini's long-time mistress. Despite his long list of paramours, the twenty-seven-year-old groupie had risen among the ranks, having dug her claws into the dictator's side, adoring him relentlessly, refusing to be shaken.

Seated next to her, Maddalena recognized several of the men who surrounded Mussolini the night of the Marquessa dalla Ricca's ball, the evening the dictator had propositioned her. Seeing them now, Maddalena could only imagine, dressed in full military regalia, they had been sent to send a silent if not threatening message to the House of Paquin.

Catching Matteo's eye, seeing him smile at her, Maddalena came back to herself and regained her composure. Raising her hand, she signaled to Bettina they were ready to begin. When a string quartet started playing

Baroque chamber music, she took her position behind a small podium.

As Milluzzi dimmed the house lights and adjusted the spots, the stage was bathed in glowing ambient light, accentuated by dusky shadows. In the surreal light, Artemisia's paintings, stars in their own right, glimmered and vibrated, dancing on their wires, and a hush fell over the crowd.

Hearing the strains of the violins, the lithe young models emerged and struck poses next to Artemisia's portraits of women warriors. It was quite an impressive circle of women—Cleopatra, Susanna, Venus, Danae, Mary Magdalen, Jael, and Venus. Each female captured by Artemisia's hand evoked a sense of strength and beauty, united by a common bond— triumph over great suffering. In the center of them all was Artemisia's self-portrait, wearing her emerald green dress, captured in the act of painting.

After the models walked down the main aisle and into the crowd, previewing Maddalena's magnificent creations, they pivoted and returned to the shadows, as if melting back into the paintings. The show concluded when the last young woman impersonating Artemisia—dressed in a green gown and carrying a palette and paintbrush—disappeared behind the painting of *Judith and Holofernes*.

When the house lights went to black, a stunned silence fell over the room, but after a moment people rose to their feet and began to clap. Maddalena took to the stage, illuminated once again, inviting Bettina and the other models to join her. Holding hands in a bond of unity, they gracefully accepted the audience's adulation. Looking over at the portrait of the artist next to her, Maddalena felt a rush of pleasure, sensing Artemisia's presence too. Artemisia too had been an important part of the evening's success.

As people stood up and their animated voices filled the room, Maddalena circulated through them, ready to chat with clients and friends. She was deep in conversation with the Contessa Testi, priding herself on how well things were going when she heard a sharp crack that sounded like a gunshot. In a panic, she spun around but calmed instantly, realizing it was only Bettina popping a champagne cork.

She shook her head and laughed as she watched her assistant on the other side of the room attempting to stop the fizzy wine from spraying into the crowd. Despite Bettina's best efforts, though, a frothy stream spurted into the air and spluttered down the sides of the bottle.

The reception, as well as the prosecco, bubbled sweetly on for another hour, the only sour moment being when she came face to face with Clara and her bodyguards. Keeping a close eye on the men on either side of Il Duce's lover, Maddalena accepted the young woman's gushing praises.

Just as Maddalena was about to walk away and talk to another client, Clara placed a hand on her arm and said, "Mussolini wanted to be here with me this evening. He is sorry he missed another grand affair with the Duchess. He told me to tell you he hopes he will get another chance to see your designs in private." Clara then confided, "I think he intends to have you make a dress for me!"

Maddalena smiled politely at the woman, but as the threesome turned away, she narrowed her eyes and followed their movements carefully, making sure Mussolini's cronies left the gallery. For the life of her, Maddalena couldn't understand how a woman who seemed reasonably intelligent could be so fatally attracted to the dictator. Did she not understand the significance of the message she had just delivered? Either Clara knew and didn't care or she was indeed addled by love.

Maddalena was chilled by the notion but quickly warmed when she felt Matteo's constant presence beside her. Thoughts of Mussolini and his threats faded away into the night as she heard him say, "Everything all right, *amore*?"

With a relieved sigh, she said, "Now that you are here next to me, everything is better."

Together they mingled a while longer, but toward eleven the crowd dispersed. Some returned to their homes and a few select clients were invited to a celebratory mid-night dinner she was hosting in a restaurant across town. Still sipping on champagne, Maddalena observed a couple of workmen who remained and who were beginning to clean up and stack chairs. Waving them off, Matteo told them all to go home, that the work could wait until morning.

Leaning back contentedly into Matteo's arms, Maddalena raised her glass to Bettina, who sat a few feet away jotting down notes, and said, "A toast to you, Betti! Here's to another success. I trust you with my life, just not with bottles of prosecco."

"All in a day's work," Bettina said. "And it all starts again tomorrow. The orders are already coming in. I think we need to check on the manufacturer's deadlines and ask..."

"Relax, Betti! It's too late for that," said Maddalena.

"Alright," she said, snapping her notebook closed. But seeing Matteo slowly spin Maddalena around in his arms and begin to kiss her, she rolled her eyes. "Ehi! Stop that, you two! There will be plenty of time for that later."

"You go on to the restaurant, Bettina," encouraged Maddalena. "Make sure things are set up properly, and guests are taken care of. I need a moment to catch my breath."

"I see where this is going. I wasn't born yesterday," she said raising an eyebrow. "Just don't be too long. And remember, before you get to the restaurant, wipe the lipstick off your face, Matteo!"

Maddalena smiled and checked her watch. "When you get there, make sure Signora Balestrini is seated at our table. I noticed she took a particular liking to several of the gowns."

"Now who is the one who can't stop thinking about work?" she said with a raised eyebrow.

"*Touché, mon amie!*"

"Okay, I'm walking out the door now. You two kids better be right behind me." Reaching for her bag and evening wrap, she added, "I'll leave from the back... My car is parked in the alley."

"Betti, don't forget to..."

"I know, I know. Don't worry. I'll make sure to shoo all the models out and lock up behind me." She gave Maddalena one last warning look. "See you in just a bit. *D'accordo?*"

"Yes, mademoiselle!" said Maddalena, saluting her back like an obedient foot soldier. "We won't be that far behind you."

Eyeing Matteo, she added, "I'm counting on you, *signore*, to bring her over in one piece, with that dress still zipped in the back."

Maddalena's eyes sparkled as she watched Bettina go, then turned back to Matteo and, seeing the smudge of lipstick on his face, gently caressed it away. "Are you ready to go, *cara*? The public awaits us. We don't want to keep them..."

She stopped in surprise, seeing that in his hand he held a small box wrapped in silver paper.

"What's this?"

"Oh, just a little something I thought you might like."

"Really? And what might that be?" she asked, reaching for the box.

"Wait a minute," he said, raising the present over his head.

A smile spread across her face. "What? Don't I get to open it now? You know I can't wait until later."

"*Cara*, believe me, I know you are not a patient person," he said with amusement. "But first, I wanted to ask you something."

"Ask me something?" Maddalena said, a teasing expression illuminating her face. "Ask away! I'm all ears."

"Okay. Here goes. Maddie, my dear, you are the only woman for me. I want you to know how proud I am of you and that I love you and..."

Before he could finish, she plucked the box out of his hands and, holding it up to her ear, rattled it.

"And?" Maddalena encouraged.

Before he could say anything more, she undid the silver bow and opened the box. Inside, she discovered a smaller one inscribed with the Tiffany logo. She stared at it for a moment then cried out, "I knew it! Oh, Matteo, yes!"

"I thought it was about time."

She opened the box and nestled inside was a platinum band with a large yellow diamond. She held it up and tilted it so that it caught the reflection of the overhead lights. "It's beautiful," she murmured. "A ring to cherish a lifetime."

"And this is just the beginning, Maddie," he said. "We have years and years ahead of us." He took the ring and slid it onto her slim finger, then gave her a long, drawn-out kiss. Leaning back, he teased, "Are you prepared to spend eternity with me?"

Maddalena entwined her arms around his neck. "Yes! Yes! Yes! *Amore mio*, I've never been so happy in all my life. First, the success of the show, and now this! You clever, clever man! How I adore you."

She kissed him again and then, extending her hand, she wiggled her fingers, admiring the cut of the ring. "Your taste in diamonds is exquisite."

"Just like my taste in women."

"Now, to add to our marital bliss," she said, "we just need to find a house suitable to our needs and a faithful old dog—I think a Labrador will do just fine—and we'll call him..."

"Putting a ring on your finger has turned you positively domestic!"

"*Caro!* You should know by now there are many sides to me. A woman is many things, not just one. I can run my fashion house and..."

"And?"

"Perhaps we should also acquire a baby carriage."

He raised an eyebrow, clearly pleased by the notion. "I wouldn't mind all the practicing." He leaned back and eyed her seductively. "In fact, I'm not averse to trying right..."

He stopped when he heard the phone in the other room ring. Together, they glanced over at the door, reluctant to answer the summons. Matteo held out his arm and looked at his wristwatch. He sighed and rested his forehead against hers, and said, "It's 12:05. We are late for your mid-night supper. We should get going..."

In contentment, they walked down the hall, but when they pushed through the doorway into the main reception area, they saw the front glass was streaked with rivulets of rain.

"Oh, no! It's a deluge out there!" said Maddalena.

Matteo set his hat on his head, wrapped his silk scarf around his neck, and said, "Signora Crociani—we don't want to ruin that pretty dress of yours. Wait for me here. I'll be back with the car."

Then, swinging her around, he bent her back and gave her one final kiss. Opening the door, he called over his shoulder, "Wait for the sound of the horn. I'll honk when I pull up."

"I'll be right here, but be quick!" Maddalena said as she watched him disappear into the rainy night.

Humming softly to herself, she reached for her evening wrap and gazed out the window into the foggy night. In the distance, she could see the golden dome of Castel Sant'Angelo glowing in the distance. For one of his manifestations, Mussolini had ordered red lights installed around the Pope's ancient domain. In the misty night, the ruby reflections splashed over the street and onto the river coloring the Tiber blood red.

When a flash of lightning illuminated the room, followed by the crash of thunder, she flinched uncontrollably. As the noise subsided, she heard the steady beat of rain on the pavement and the splash of water thrown upon the curb by the occasional passing car. She was about to draw on her gloves but stopped and held out her hand admiring her new ring.

"Signora Crociani. Maddalena Crociani," she said out loud. "I think I'll like being called that almost as much as I love being called the Duchess."

As the seconds drew into minutes, Maddalena shook her head, wondering what was taking him so long. She picked up a magazine, lying on the front table, and paged through a couple of articles. Seeing headlights approach, she looked up hoping to see Matteo's roadster. When the car passed, she tossed the magazine aside impatiently.

She jumped again as another clap of thunder rattled the building. This time, as the noise subsided, it seemed the tremor had masked a sound that came from inside the gallery. Perking up her ears, she listened, her senses on high alert. Once more came a flash of lightning, followed by a low rumble of thunder, only this time a bit softer. All was quiet again, and hearing the pattering rain, it seemed the storm was abating.

Maddalena visibly relaxed, reminding herself she was the only one left in the building. Everyone had gone half an hour before, and Bettina promised she would securely lock the back door. She shook her head, thinking the acoustics in the building must be playing tricks on her.

Still... she thought. *What if...*

Glancing behind her, she saw a light shone into the hallway from the main gallery. She thought Matteo had shut off the lights when they left, but in her bliss, perhaps she hadn't remembered correctly. Checking the window, seeing Matteo still hadn't arrived, she retraced her steps back to the gallery, her high-heeled footsteps echoing on the marble floor. At the door of the gallery, she paused a moment but heard nothing.

She shook herself firmly. *Silly woman, get a grip*, she thought. *Turn the lights out and go to your party! Matteo will be here any moment.*

Unnerved by the deserted building and the eerie silence that pervaded it, she peeked her head inside the door. As her eyes adjusted to the dim light, she saw everything was cast in murky shadows and only a small spotlight illuminated the front of the room where Artemisia's painting of Judith and Holofernes hung, twisting oddly on its cord.

In the gloom, Maddalena's eyes traveled from the face of Holofernes and his silent scream to the expression of sheer determination on Judith's face. She observed how the beam of light now focused on the painting made the colors of the women's dresses shine brighter than usual, and the blood of the decapitated man was redder than ever.

All else was still, and the room was silent like a tomb. From the roof overhead, she could tell the rain was slowing. She was about to walk away but glanced back at all the women in the room, including Artemisia.

And then she saw him.

At first, she thought it was a trick of her imagination, just a shadow that had crept across the stage. But when he stepped into the light, she recognized his face. "Signor Milluzzi? Is that you?" Relief flooded her voice. "Good heavens! What are you doing here? It's just a little after midnight."

When at first the man didn't respond, she took a step farther into the room to see what he was up to. When he saw her approaching, he quickly said, "Signora, there is no need to worry. I'm just cleaning up."

"What? It's the middle of the night. Oh, please! I'm sure Matteo will appreciate the gesture, but really, go on home, there is no need..."

Maddalena reached out and flicked on the main gallery light and walked into the room to join him. Matteo had been right to hire the man. He was a hardworking, faithful employee and her opinion of him had changed. She thought to shake his hand, but when she drew nearer, she saw he was holding a knife. Looking at the painting of Judith, she now realized why it had been twisting so oddly. Milluzzi was using it to pry the canvas from the back of its frame, and she'd just caught him in the act of stealing.

"What the hell do you think you are doing?" Maddalena demanded angrily. "For Christ's sake! Are you insane?"

"Get out of here," he said through gritted teeth. "I don't want to hurt you—I found my opportunity, and I'm taking it."

A fury overcame her, and she knew she had to stop him. Seeing the stack of chairs the men had left at the front of the room, she picked one up and swung it at him.

"Don't," Milluzzi warned. She paused as he held his knife up to the painting, pointing it directly at Judith's throat.

Not believing he would harm the valuable painting, Maddalena called his bluff and took another step forward. But she had underestimated the man, as in horror she saw him plunge the blade into the painting of Bathsheba hanging next to Judith.

"Stop!" she cried out in a panic, putting down the chair.

Milluzzi shook his head grimly at her. "I thought you'd come to your senses."

Turning back to Judith, with a few more flicks of his wrist, he removed the last pins from the back of the painting, and the canvas fell free of its gold frame. Sorrowfully, Maddalena watched as the oversized canvas fell to the floor. Dropping the knife, Milluzzi kneeled beside it and rolled up the canvas, binding it quickly with string. As he did, Maddalena cautioned, "You can't possibly think you will get away with this. They'll find you, they'll..."

"Where I'm going, no one will find me," he muttered bitterly as he cinched the last cord. Standing up, he added, "Just stay where you are and I won't hurt you. I'll be gone in just of a moment and…"

"Maddalena, where the devil have you gone? What's taking you so long? I've been waiting outside. Didn't you hear me honking?"

"Matteo!" Maddalena screamed.

He looked from her to Milluzzi to the empty frame, and then down at the canvas rolled up on the floor. "What the hell is this? What's going on in here?" he said, striding into the room.

"Stop!" she screamed. "Oh, my god, he's got a gun."

Matteo swiveled his head in confusion back toward Milluzzi who had pulled back his coat, revealing the silver-barreled weapon tucked in his belt.

Undaunted, Matteo advanced but halted when Milluzzi swiftly pulled out the weapon and pointed it directly at Maddalena.

"Don't come any closer," Milluzzi warned as he cocked the gun.

Matteo hesitated. "Easy…"

The three were caught in a standoff. Slowly, Milluzzi turned the gun on Matteo and moved closer to stand next to Maddalena. "Stay where you are, Crociani, and she won't get hurt."

Pulling Maddalena with him, he inched his way to where the canvas lay rolled and bound on the floor. As they shuffled slowly backward together, Maddalena silently pleaded to Matteo not intervene. But not heeding her warning, when Milluzzi bent down to pick up and shoulder the heavy canvas, Matteo rushed toward them. Plowing into the man, he punched him violently in the face. Momentarily dazed, Milluzzi staggered a bit, blood gushing relentlessly from his nose.

Matteo pushed Maddalena out of the way and onto the ground but reeled around when Milluzzi came back at him, dealing him a blow to his skull. Entangled in a macabre dance, the men continued to fight, grappling for the gun. Hearing the thunk of heavily dealt blows, wanting to stop the man, Maddalena looked wildly around her. Seeing the knife Milluzzi had dropped a few feet away, she reached for it and wrapped her fingers around the hilt.

Standing up, she raised the blade into the air, and when she got the chance, she took her opportunity and plunged it into Milluzzi's back. The man grunted, and his eyes grew wide. And then there was the shot of a gun.

In horror, Maddalena stepped back as both men fell to the ground.

Time stopped and stood still, then began again.

Seeing Milluzzi's lifeless eyes, she cried out, "He's dead, Matteo. He's dead!" When he didn't respond, Maddalena screamed, fear now flooding her heart. "Matteo, Matteo... *Amore mio*! Are you okay?"

Seeing the sea of blood around him, she fell beside him. With the strength she didn't know she possessed, she pulled him into her arms. Cradling him, she crooned words of encouragement and hope as his blood seeped onto the bodice of her evening gown, staining it red.

"Matteo! Matteo! Don't leave me."

"*Non finisce mai*—this is not the end," Matteo rasped out breathily.

He closed his eyes briefly, then gazed foggily back into hers, and said, "*Amore mio*, you know I never will. But I want you to be safe. This is no place for you now. You must return to..."

Beside herself with grief, Maddalena leaned over and kissed his lips to quiet him. As she did, her tears ran down her cheeks and onto his. He was delirious and yet, in his final moments, he was trying to comfort and protect her. She closed her eyes and willed time to slip backward to just a few moments before when he had held her in his arms telling her he wanted to spend the rest of eternity with her.

He coughed and rolled his head a little to the side. Reaching up, he touched her face. "Ehi, Maddie. Don't be sad... I see it all so clearly now. We've been together before and will be together again. This is not the end. Trust me. I will always know where to find you, Maddie-girl. You are the sun, the moon, and the stars—the very center of my universe—and someday you and I will touch the moons of Jupiter."

And suddenly she could see it too, the brightly colored mosaic of their previous existences assembling. Leaning in closer, she heard him say, "You will always be my home—and we will meet again..."

She tried to respond, but the words simply wouldn't come. All she could do was nod. As the light left his eyes, and his breath faded away, she heard his last whispered words, "Maddalena, promise, me. *Non smettere mai di cercarmi*—never stop searching for me."

"I won't... I..."

And then there was nothing left to say.

Maddalena remained seated in the middle of the room, holding Matteo. She lost track of time, her body racked by sobs looking at the man she had loved through time and would love again. Finally, she kissed him one last time, letting him go.

Gently, she laid his head on the ground and slowly stood up in front of the portrait of Artemisia. In a trance, she watched as the painting trembled back and forth as if the artist was overcome with grief and weeping for the loss of Matteo. Strangely comforted, she caressed the artist's face with her finger, leaving a small trace of his blood on her ivory white cheek.

In a hushed whisper, Maddalena said, "He saved you too, you know." A soft sob caught in her throat.

Then turning around, not thinking clearly, not thinking at all, Maddalena walked in a daze down the center aisle to where Matteo's umbrella lay. Beside it was the scarf he had worn that had fallen to the ground. Reaching down, she picked it up, and she clutched it to her body and made her way to the street. She stood on the curb and glanced around blankly as a light misting rain continued to fall.

She buried her face in the soft silk, noticing how Matteo's scent mingled with the sweet smell of the wet spring evening that just an hour earlier had been so full of promises. She closed her eyes tightly, wishing she could disappear over the horizon too. But as hard as she tried, she remained where she was, and her tears continued to seep down her cheeks, mixing into the rain of the night.

Eternally Yours

In your eyes I saw the stars,
and in your laughter I heard the rain.
Caressed by the sun the journey began
to touch the Galilean moons.

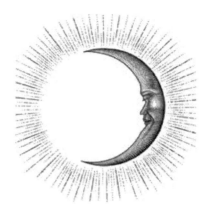

Chapter 26

The Moons of Jupiter

*S*ix seconds before take-off, the transit pod vibrated. A low base note was first heard, then felt, as it moved through the deck of the ship into the core of her being. She looked over at her co-pilot and smiled giddily while at the same time feeling a small tangle of fear churning through her. This was the most exhilarating moment, as well as the most terrifying. Furiously, the violent rumble grew to a roaring fevered pitch, and from her toes to her teeth, she shook. As the unrestrained ship shot out of the containment bay and rocketed forward, the high pitch wail of increased pressure on the outer metal walls was clearly audible—the sound of unleashed power.

Now the horrible bone-numbing rattle was gone, traded for a blast of force that thrust her back into her seat. The rush of adrenaline shooting through her veins was euphoric and replaced the pit of dread in her stomach. These were the moments she'd been dreaming of since she was a child of seven—to break free and fly through space toward a new and distant horizon.

Gradually, the thrust waned, and her sense of weight vanished. The ship floated effortlessly, and she experienced the full pleasure of zero-g. She turned to the view-screen to her left. Ceres, the small dwarf planet situated just off Mars, was falling away and soon it'd be a speck in the distance. Just another star, and then not even that. But for the moment, it filled her screen and looking away was impossible. The planet seemed to glisten and sparkle as the ice ringlets that surrounded it gyrated and swirled in a timeless motion. It could be a difficult place to inhabit; nonetheless, it had been a safe harbor and, for a while, she had called it her home.

She was used to living under domes on the outer planets or on the space station in the pockets of air and water that hovered above them. And now, after spending a year doing scientific research on an ice rock that spun tipsily in an ecliptic orbit, she was headed toward Jupiter, the giant gas planet where she and Marti planned to rendezvous and dock with the space station Artemisia. It had been a rather sudden and unexpected assignment for them—albeit well deserved, having come down from Rehbar Station on Mars after two other scientists had taken a pass on the four-year mission.

As the ship stabilized, and gravity was restored, the roaring burn gave way to a steady drone. As expected, the com lights flashed green and a smooth voice said, "This is Ceres Flight Control. Commander, please report your status."

She moved her hand in front of her face, and as she did a series of computer screens flashed open. Tapping on her mic, she responded, "This is Maddalena Ghezzi of the *Athena Scout 2*. All flight systems are normal. We cleared the ice rings, and the craft has engaged auto-trajectory. We are good to go."

"Copy that, *Athena*. It was a bumpy lift off Ghezzi, but your ship held steady. Those crystal fields can sure look pretty, but they can be a bitch to plow through. We have you on screen and will monitor things from here out. Have a safe flight out there, *Athena*."

"Will do, flight deck. Will do."

With a flick of her hand, she closed the com panel and brought up the mission's data log. Tapping the screen, she said, "Ceres to Jupiter flight mission 72690. Sun date stamp Jupiter year 209, Ceres year 629 and..." She did a rapid calculation in her head and added, "Earth year 2519. Launch successful. Orbit reached at 3:12 braxometers. Estimated docking time..."

Addressing her navigator, she said, "Marti, confirm the time we will make contact with Artemisia."

The woman seated next to her checked her monitor and punched in the new flight speed. After the series of numbers appeared, she ran the calculations then replied, "Docking time estimated at 12:05."

"Thanks. Got it." Entering the last bit of information into the computer, Lena waved her hand, the screen flashed away, and she breathed in deeply. Take-off was thrilling, but this was the moment she could finally relax and revel in the magnitude of how far she had come and where she was going.

Hearing the steady, contained roar of the engines pulsing on through the night, she gazed out of the wide front window before her, observing the shimmering stars that danced around her. Even at this far distance, she could already see the vibrant colors that painted Jupiter's surface. She knew what she was looking at was the strata of hydrogen and helium and other trace gases, and from this distance they were hypnotizing. The misty blues and amber tones swirling together in a varied array of marbled patterns seemed as precious as a rare painting, and she was filled with contentment knowing there was so much beauty around her.

Way out here, time ceased to have meaning, and she was humbled by the sheer immensity of it all—there were still so many things she couldn't comprehend. Although each new mission revealed a little more of the universe's secrets, she knew it would take many lifetimes to see and learn it all.

On Ceres, she had spent her time working on Superluminal Communications and Tachyonic Particle Theory and had made several exciting breakthroughs. People were always asking her to explain her work, even her father. When she launched into a lengthy explanation about space-time continuums, seeing his confusion, she gave him the simple version. She told him, simply, that she was working on a device that operated without radio waves. "It's kind of like talking to people in the future and the past. Like being in the same two places at once."

Her father, more interested in art than astrophysics, merely nodded and said, "Sorry, Lena, my dear. While you are dedicated to the stars, I'm more of an art connoisseur—love my ancient artists, always have. Art is the gift of time. It is like receiving a message in a bottle. Our lives may be short, but art is eternal." Smiling at her, he added, "Oh, I know your thoughts have always been millions of miles away, focused on moons that encircle Jupiter, always wanting to make contact with someone just over the brink of time, but remember it is not in the stars to hold our destiny but in ourselves."

And Lena had believed him. The stars were her dreams, and while she had always wanted to discover more and push herself further, deep down inside she knew if she put her mind to it there was nothing she couldn't accomplish.

As they drew closer to Jupiter, Lena saw with her naked eye its many moons starting to appear. There were seventy-nine all together, the four most massive ones having been discovered in 1610 by Galileo Galilei and his colleagues. It had been a magnificent discovery, the start of everything, even though many of those early astronomers had paid dearly for their efforts.

She thought about all the other scientists upon whose shoulders she now stood upon. There had been so many, from the first man to step foot and walk on the moon to those who had spearheaded and masterminded Project Juno. Back in 2019, they had sent an unmanned spacecraft into Jupiter's atmosphere and had accumulated data about the planet's magnetic and gravity fields, mapping and revealing the planet's deep and mysterious structure hidden underneath its dense cloud cover.

If not for them, she wouldn't be here today, winding her way through the dark and endless skies to land among the Medicean stars. As the twinkling lights of Io, Europa, Ganymede, and Callisto came into view, Lena thought about Cosimo, the Florentine Duke. These very moons had been named for him by Galileo, and she believed the Renaissance man would have treasured this moment to see his namesakes so miraculously close—the ones she would soon be walking on.

Lena waved her hand in front of the panel again, activating her computer. Logging in, she reviewed the specifics of the upcoming five-year mission, dubbed the Galileo Project, that would be undertaken on board the base station Artemisia. It seemed appropriate that both

Cosimo's proteges had been reunited, way out here in space. Their gifts were timeless—Galileo had paved the way to the stars with his telescope and Artemisia had empowered a generation of women with her paintbrush.

And now she and Martina were joining other mission specialists for this space-breaking collaboration between scientists from Mars, Ceres, and Earth. They had hoped to arrive sooner for orientation and debriefing by Artemisia's Project Director, who was also a new addition to the team, but due to the ice geysers on Ceres that blew huge plumes of water into space, there had been massive launch delays. As a result, Lena and Marti were the last to join the team that was now anxiously awaiting their arrival to proceed with the planned operations.

When the automated flight control flashed on, indicating it was time to take back manual control, Lena zipped up her vac-suit, cinched her harness, and took control of the ship guiding it toward the space station that loomed ahead of them. As they made their final approach, she looked over at Marti and said, "Okay, let's see if we can land this tin can."

Drifting closer to their destination, with the booster pack light intermittently guiding them in, they felt a gentle jolt when they finally made contact. From her window, Lena saw the circular, rotating space station and watched as two large robotic arms reached out and around their craft as if embracing them, helping them into their final docking position.

At this distance, Lena could also see the space station's insignia emblazoned on the side of the south bay pod doors. The logo featured an artist wearing a seventeenth-century emerald green gown and her muscular arm was raised, caught in the act of painting, as if she were putting the finishing touches on the large flowing letters that spelled out her name: *Artemisia*.

Into her com, she said, "Initiate rendezvous lockup." Then to her co-pilot, she added, "Systems are set. Begin shut down protocol."

Marti nodded and powered down the craft while Lena sent a message to the station: *This is Maddalena Ghezzi of the Olympus 72690. Docking successful. We are ready to board.*

Lena unlatched her harness, slid out of her seat, and made her way to the bay pod doors. She pushed the sequence of buttons on the auto-control pad and listened expectantly for the sound of the release mechanism unlocking. But oddly nothing happened.

From the other side, someone pounded on the door lightly. After a moment, a man called out impatiently, "Maddalena, open the door."

More eager than ever to reach the other side, she manually pushed down on the release lever until the portal finally swooshed open. When it did, a cloud of condensation billowed up and around her, obstructing her view. As the filmy mist cleared, she saw a tall man with dark hair standing in front of her.

They regarded one another for a moment as the light of the moons of Jupiter poured in from the high-domed ceiling of the space station, illuminating their faces.

Time stopped and stood still, then rewound and started again.

In a voice that sounded so familiar, he said, "It's about time you got here—I've been waiting ages for you to arrive. I'm First Science Officer of the Artemisia, Matt Crociani. Welcome to your new home."

Indicating the stars above their heads, he asked, "So, tell me, Maddalena—are you ready to walk on Cosimo's moons with me?"

Caught by the look in his eye, she nodded and smiled.

And once again they knew.

Time is an illusion—but dreams are real.
The sequence of events in the novel take place at 12:05.

Eternally Artemisia is the imaginative telling of the life of Artemisia Gentileschi—the first prominent female artist who lived in the seventeenth-century. All references to incidents in the artist's life are based on documented historical details, including the transcripts of her rape trial, which still exist today and can be found in the *Archivio di Stato*, Rome. After her trial, a marriage of convenience was arranged and Artemisia went to Florence with her husband Pierantonio. In Florence, Artemisia flourished under the patronage of Cosimo II. It was the Grand Duke of Tuscany, who invited Artemisia to join the *Accademia di Arte del Disegno* in Florence and she was the first woman to become a member. In Florence, she also met Galileo Galilee, and he was a friend as attested to by letters she wrote to him after he was imprisoned.

Artemisia painted several versions of Judith and Holofernes, and they now hang in the Uffizi, and the Pitti Palace in Florence, Naples, Detroit, and Cannes. The nude self-portrait she painted to the honor Michelangelo—*the Allegory of Inclination*—proved so embarrassing to later generations, in 1684 drapery was added to cover Artemisia's nudity.

It is a documented fact that Duke Cosimo II sentenced Agostino Tassi to serve time on one of the Medici Galley prison ships for an undisclosed crime. It is also a fact that Artemisia had a long, passionate affair with Francesco Maria Maringhi. Her husband knew of the relationship and accepted the situation as an economic advantage, as attested to letters he wrote to Maringhi.

Galileo was convicted of heresy and spent the rest of his life under house arrest. The trial could have been stopped, but after Cosimo's death, the Archduchess aligned with Pope Urban II and allowed the proceedings to go forward.

Beatrice Cenci was beheaded with her family in front of the Sant'Angelo Bridge and Tommaso Caccini was burned alive in Rome for heresy.

Creative license was evoked regarding the Hindenburg. It crashed in 1936, not 1939.

*Elsa Schiaparelli (wearing her shoe hat)—an Italian fashion designer
and Anna Banti (born Lucia Lopresti)—an Italian art historian
also inspired the story.*

Elsa Schiaparelli was an Italian fashion designer who worked in Paris during the 1930s. Before the war, she was outspoken in her criticism of both Hitler and Mussolini. As a result, she wasn't welcome in the city of her birth—Rome. Elsa started her Couture House in Paris in 1923. Between the two World Wars, she was more well-known than Coco Chanel and worked with surrealist artists Salvador Dalì, Man Ray, and Jean Cocteau. Elsa's fashion shows became a form of entertainment and were known as much for their artistic flair as for their fashions, set against a background of dramatic lighting, music, and fully-realized sets. She was a single mother who started a fashion empire and raised a child on her own. Among her clients was Katharine Hepburn. She also invented her signature color, shocking pink. Elsa is shown above wearing her famous shoe hat designed in collaboration with Salvador Dalì.

Anna Banti was a writer and art historian, and the first to write a novel about Artemisia Gentileschi. Banti was an art critic, born in Florence but who lived for many years in Rome, and along with her husband Roberto Longhi, they founded the art magazine *Paragone*. In the early 1900s, Roberto, fascinated by Caravaggio's work, first brought to light Orazio Gentileschi and his daughter, Artemisia. However, his assessment of Artemisia was dismissive, claiming she "was a first-rate painter technically", but he rated her intellectually inferior, even to her father. It was Anna who saw the true genius of Artemisia and decided to write a book about her to challenge her husband's assessment. But, when her first biography on Artemisia was destroyed when her home in Florence was bombed during the German evacuation in 1944, she began again, this time turning her manuscript into a semi-autobiographical novel. Banti wrote from 1938 until 1981, and throughout her work is the recurring theme of intelligent Italian women's low and lonely position resulting from societal pressures, oppression by family, personal relationships, and their duties. She believed suffering was the common bond uniting the female gender.

Acknowledgements

Heartfelt thanks to the women who inspired this story: Artemisia Gentileschi, Elsa Schiaparelli and Anna Banti.

Elizabeth O'Brien Bosch: Story editor, my Abra. I am eternally grateful for your help, insights, and feedback. I so enjoy our collaboration—you are a rare gift. We make a great team—una bella squadra.

Robert Schirmer: Editor, first reader

Amber Richberger: Editor and final proof reader.

Edith Pray: My mother who always encouraged me in all my pursuits and made me believe there was nothing I couldn't do. She continues to be a role model and font of inspiration. She will always be with me in spirit.

My Family Circle—My three sons, husband, and father-in-law, thanks for supporting me, putting up with my late-night writing hours and for encouraging me to follow my passion and journey to Italy.

Ryan Muldoon: Consultant on quantum physics, entangled communication, futuristic space technologies, and lengthy conversations about space travel.

Silvia Celli & Sara Chierchini: Friends and Italian teachers in Montepulciano. Through their eyes, I discovered the beauty of this small Tuscan town.

Debora Bresciani: Special thanks to my "little" sister in Arezzo, for all her love and support, and for helping promote my projects and books.

Marta Guerrieri: To my dear friend in Lecce, for her love and support, whose bright smile eclipses even the sun in Puglia.

Laura Ghezzi: A vivacious spirit and talented artist and fresco painter in Arezzo—my *anima gemella* creative spirit.

Dorie Nelson: Special thanks to my wise and insightful friend who is an avid reader, for enthusiastically embracing my books.

Much love and gratitude to My Circle of Women: To all my female friends—you know who you are—who build me up, inspire me with their stories, and make me laugh. From you I draw support, and each one of you makes me stronger.

Melissa Muldoon is the author of three novels set in Italy: *"Dreaming Sophia," "Waking Isabella,"* and *"Eternally Artemisia."* All three books tell the stories of American women and their journeys of self-discovery to find love, uncover hidden truths, and follow their destinies to shape a better future in Italy.

Melissa is also the author of the *Studentessa Matta* website, where she promotes the study of Italian language and culture through her dual-language blog written in Italian and English (studentessamatta.com). *Studentessa Matta* means the "crazy linguist" and has grown to include a podcast, *Tutti Matti per l'Italiano* and the *Studentessa Matta* YouTube channel, Facebook page and Instagram feed. Melissa also created *Matta* Italian Language Immersion Programs, which she co-leads with Italian schools in Italy to learn Italian in Italy. Through her website, she also offers the opportunities to live and study in Italy through Homestay programs.

Melissa has a B.A. in fine arts, art history and European history from Knox College, a liberal arts college in Galesburg, Illinois, as well as a master's degree in art history from the University of Illinois at Champaign-Urbana. She has also studied painting and art history in Florence. She is an artist, designer, and illustrated the cover art for all three of her books. Melissa is also the managing director of Matta Press.

As a student, Melissa lived in Florence with an Italian family. She studied art history and painting and took beginner Italian classes. When she returned home, she threw away her Italian dictionary, assuming she'd never need it again, but after launching a successful design career and starting a family, she realized something was missing in her life. That "thing" was the connection she had made with Italy and the friends who live there. Living in Florence was indeed a life-changing event. Wanting to reconnect with Italy, she decided to start learning the language again from scratch. As if indeed possessed by an Italian muse, she bought a new Italian dictionary and began her journey to fluency—a path that has led her back to Italy many times and enriched her life in countless ways. Now, many dictionaries and grammar books later, she dedicates her time to promoting Italian language studies, further travels in Italy, and sharing her stories and insights about Italy with others.

Melissa designed and illustrated the cover art for *Eternally Artemisia, Waking Isabella,* and *Dreaming Sophia.* She also curates the *Dreaming Sophia* Art History blog site and Pinterest site: *The Art of Loving Italy,* where you will find companion pictures for all three books. Visit MelissaMuldoon.com for more information about immersion trips to learn the language with Melissa in Italy, as well as the Studentessa Matta blog for practice and tips to learn the Italian language.

MelissaMuldoon.com
DreamingSophiaBook.com
Pinterest.com/DreamingSophia

Dreaming Sophia

Because dreaming is an art.

Winner of the 2018 Reader Views Best Adult
Classic Fiction Novel Award—*First Place*

Dreaming Sophia is a magical look into Italy and art history as seen through the eyes of a young American artist. Sophia is the daughter of a beautiful free-spirited artist who studied in Italy in the 1960s during a time when the Mud Angels saved Florence. She is brought up in the Sonoma Valley in California, in a home full of love, laughter, art, and Italian dreams. When tragedy strikes, she finds herself alone in the world with only her Italian muses for company. Through dream-like encounters she meets Renaissance artists, Medici princes, sixteenth-century duchesses, Risorgimento generals, and Cinecitta movie stars, each giving her advice and a gift to help her put her life back together. *Dreaming Sophia* is the story of a young woman's love for Italy and how she turns her fantasies into reality as she follows her muses back to Florence.

Sheri Hoyte for Blog Critics: Author Melissa Muldoon presents spellbinding artistic expression in her delightful story, Dreaming Sophia. Not your typical Italian romantic adventure, Dreaming Sophia is a wonderful multifaceted story that pushes through several genres, with layers and layers of exquisite entertainment. The development of her characters is flawless and effortless, as is her ability to draw readers into her world.

Dianne Hales, author of La Bella Lingua: In Dreaming Sophia, Melissa Muldoon weaves many strands of Italian culture into a delightful blend of fantasy, romance, art, and history. With an artist's keen eye and deft touch, she brings to life the titans of Italian culture in a touching tale of a young woman reeling from loss who discovers that Italy is the answer. The many Italophiles who share her belief will revel in the adventures of this kindred spirit.